Rachel's Children

The Library of Alabama Classics,
reprint editions of works important
to the history, literature, and culture of
Alabama, is dedicated to the memory of

Rucker Agee

whose pioneering work in the fields
of Alabama history and historical geography
continues to be the standard of
scholarly achievement.

Rachel's Children

Harriet Hassell

With an Introduction by

Philip D. Beidler

The University of Alabama Press
Tuscaloosa and London

Library of Congress Cataloging-in-Publication Data

Hassell, Harriet, 1911–1970
Rachel's children / Harriet Hassell : with an introduction by
Philip D. Beidler.
p.   cm. — (The Library of Alabama classics)
ISBN 0-8173-0499-1 (alk. paper)
I. Title.   II. Series.
PS3515.A82858R34   1990
813'.52—dc20   90-32564
CIP

British Library Cataloguing-in-Publication Data available

For

Thérèse and Hudson Strode

No character in this book is intended to represent any living person.

Introduction

Philip D. Beidler

The World of *Rachel's Children*

One still gets to the Hassell farm in northern Tuscaloosa County by the directions encoded in *Rachel's Children.* Crossing the river bridge from the old downtown of Tuscaloosa into Northport, one follows Watermelon Road until at about the ten-mile point modern development and suburban clutter suddenly open out into gorgeous rolling farmland. And just there, where Sokol Park now stands on the site of the old Boys' Colony of the Partlow Training School (the part of the land Jahn finally sells, in the novel, to Marston's Hospital for the Insane), one knows already that the house itself is near. At a small grocery nearby, the storekeeper I asked knew exactly where it was, or rather where I could find what was left of it—a fire had destroyed it several years earlier—and gave me accordingly precise directions. At the gate to the home place (in the novel again, the smaller, original section of the land Jahn elects to keep), so did two younger men I encountered, bird hunters, know of it and something of its history—the "How-zel" farm both of them called it—including the memory of a ghost one said he saw there on a drizzly winter's afternoon when he was a boy.

Exactly because *Rachel's Children* is a ghostly fable, dark and fated with the great rhythms of tragedy, I was glad that I had chosen the time to seek out the Hassell place I did, a late October afternoon in all its warm Alabama splendor. For I had come to see the chief character in *Rachel's Children,* which is, of course, even upstaging the monumental titular heroine, the land itself; and accordingly I wanted to visit the land in the fullness of its glory. I was not disappointed. As I crossed the open fields, great machines harvested cotton—itself something of a rarity in Tuscaloosa County now—on the acreage to the northeast. As if on command, a red-tailed hawk rose up and began to circle. Instead of coming up an old lane across open ground, I found a shaded, quiet path in a woodline. I saw the tin roof of a cattle barn. Then, shortly beyond, rose the twin chimneys, all that was left of the old house. And finally, parting the dense weeds and second growth come to reclaim the ashes, I walked inside the foundation line to find the other charmed space I had been seeking. For I had also come to visit *her*, of course. The woman who had been born here, inside these lost walls. The woman who had lived most of her early life here with her parents and her family. The woman who wrote *Rachel's Children* here. The woman who, from all I could tell, had in some way as a consequence of that writing elected to leave here, to live and die apart from the land and family she loved with the tragic love of art. And so I found what I was looking for, found what I knew I would find, the reason why, like the land itself, neither she nor her book could ever disappoint me. I saw why the novel had to be the way it was, the wonder, the sadness, the pull, the ache. From the old front of the Hassell place, with the western sun of an Alabama afternoon in autumn falling gloriously on across the treelines and fields, the world of *Rachel's Children* stretched before me far and away. And I saw.

Harriet Hassell,
The Author of *Rachel's Children*

Because of the enormous celebrity attendant upon the first publication of *Rachel's Children*, one who knows where to look is also now still quite vividly able to see Harriet Hassell, the author of *Rachel's Children*, as well. In the portrait photograph distributed to the newspapers and review media at the time of the novel's publication, she is of a beauty almost breathtaking in its demure freshness. Yet it is a beauty that puts the august *New York Times* quite off the mark in describing her as "a girl of twenty-six." Rather, it is clearly the beauty of a proud young woman: at once serene and vulnerable, imperious yet somehow shyly reticent. A second, less widely circulated photograph, in fact, picturing her seated between her mentor Hudson Strode and his own, quite beautiful wife, Thérèse, somehow gets it more right in its precise, austere dignity. The face we see there is truly that of the author of *Rachel's Children*.

As a consequence of the publicity mentioned above, we know rather a good deal more about Harriet Hassell's life prior to the publication of *Rachel's Children* than afterward. (Indeed, as will be noted below, we know so much that it must only deepen our respect for the privacy she sought in the more obscure years that followed.) "I was born Sept. 27, 1911," she herself wrote to James Saxon Childers of the *Birmingham News*, "on my father's farm, in the house where I live now. Between that time and now I have lived briefly in two towns, Northport and Greensboro. I have gone to school. I have lived at home. I have cooked, sewed, raised chickens, and sat on the front doorstep contemplating the color of the fields." She then goes on to describe the riches of fictional resource she has found about her:

> One does not, on a farm, have much time; nor have even that if he sleeps normally. It was, I suppose, the contemplation of this fact of having time and of time as circling always in enormous, silent gyrations about little farms, that first showed me the possibilities for a tragic novel in the life around me.
>
> Time, I felt, is the great essence of tragedy; and great character the palpable stuff of it. Great character is for the novelist—he has that much of the painter in him—very nearly synonymous with great faces. I had great faces around me on the neighboring farms and in the small towns I visited.

Yet in the same moment, with a characteristic serenity and reticence, she downplays the great creative enormity of it all, enlists herself merely in the company of those remarkable souls, to apply the words of the master, Henry James, "on whom nothing is lost":

> It would be easy to say that it was for these reasons that I have written
> my stories and my novel about the people and the setting I know
> best. But the real reason is that these people and these farms and
> small towns are all I know, and that I have not had enough physical
> energy and enough mental curiosity to go looking for new things. I
> think that I shall never have much energy and curiosity. It is better
> to sit on the front doorstep and talk to Mrs. Caldwell, who knows
> why Tom Phillips believes that men are only a little lower than the
> angels and where Old Man Roberts went when he was supposed to
> be in Northport and why Deacon McDowell tried to hide the fact that
> he has been married twice. It is better still to watch the fields and to
> say nothing.

Of her own early intellectual development and education, she
writes in another place with the same combination of stunning
perspicacity and wise self-deprecation:

> I grew up, and learned not to tell lies, except when I'm startled, and
> went to high school. I read Dante, and was fascinated by old maids,
> and wrote essays on the necessity of slang in polite conversation and
> on the complete repulsiveness of Benjamin Franklin and his "Auto-
> biography." When I was 15, I came to the University of Alabama,
> and read Thomas Hardy and the Greek tragedies, and knew that I
> wanted to write. I left school, and spent the next seven years in what
> I have since learned was a Hawthorne-like seclusion, writing, and
> rewriting, and tearing up.

And then, she goes on, she braved the return, another attempt
at the University with the specific "purpose," she says, "of enrolling
in Hudson Strode's class in short story writing, known in the
catalogue as English 115." "At the end of my first interview with Mr.
Strode," she confesses, "I walked into the closet instead of out the
door. Such abject terror must have made him sorry for me." Such
may have been the case. The *Story* magazine prize she shortly
received, however, for her magnificent tale, "History of the South,"

could not have made him anything but proud. He and everyone else knew that the writing program had found its newest thoroughbred. And then, of course, in astonishingly quick succession came the other great prize as well. "I spent the Summer crocheting, looking at the green hills in my father's pasture, and finishing my novel," she concludes in the letter just cited, "quite confident that Mr. Strode would, in the Autumn, rescue the book from whatever deformities I had managed to paint upon its surface." *Rachel's Children* had been born.

The rest, as they say, is history. The book was published to immense critical acclaim. In fact the attention was so fulsome, and so relentlessly tied up with the mystique of the Strode-Alabama writing program, that such celebrity probably mitigated against the book's getting even better reviews than it did. Some reviewers made much of the author's age and obscurity and hedged their assessments with ideas of "promise." Others, as noted below, joined in the general acclaim while sniffing in quite Northern fashion at the idea of a young woman's writing an Alabama Queen Lear. But the general sentiment was unmistakable. The operative word brought forward on the floor of critical debate was "genius."

Then, as the celebrity receded, the author began to fade from sight. There had been talk at the time of the first great novel's appearance of another already far along in progress. It did not see publication. There had been talk of the novel's creation of certain bad feeling in the family. This rumor seemed to be confirmed eventually by marriage and removal to a new life elsewhere. To be sure, for anyone wishing to look, there could and still can be found things to know. In the annals of copyright law, for example, one may find a renewal for the novel *Rachel's Children*, dated April 5, 1966, in the name of Harriet Hassell Gross, 133 Luquer Road, Port Washington, Long Island, New York. There is also the obituary, dated October 20, 1970, in the *Tuscaloosa News*, announcing Mrs. Gross's death on the day previous and describing her briefly as "a writer of note" who "was one of the first students in a creative writing class at the University of Alabama to have a novel published." The most important thing to know, however, is that Harriet Hassell, the author of *Rachel's Children*, seems to have elected in the years after its publication mainly to wish for a simple privacy that was her human portion. It was, in keeping with all else we know of her, a characteristically decent and modest request.

The Achievement of *Rachel's Children*

The response of a reader now encountering the achievement of *Rachel's Children* for the first time must still at least begin in amazed recapitulation of that of contemporary reviewers: one simply finds it close to impossible to believe that a work of such enormous power and vision was a first novel. Moreover, on continuing encounter with the text, one is so moved by the completeness of quiet virtuosity at work there as to propose a quite serious and documentable case for the status of the book as a modernist classic. For in the depths and richnesses of its art, it is written at that level of authority.

Indeed, like comparable Southern works of the era already listed in the high modernist canon, such as *The Sound and the Fury* or *Look Homeward, Angel*, it makes its meanings of an originality seemingly entire unto itself and in the same moment born of deeply assimilated appropriations of other major traditions and texts. As the title shows, of course, and as both the symbolic and dramatic structures reveal throughout, underwriting everything in this chronicle of Rachel Ibsell and her children is the Biblical drama of Rachel and, as in the massive tetralogy being produced in the 1930s by Thomas Mann, of Joseph and his brothers. In more explicit literary relation, Hassell claimed that Dostoevsky was her favorite novelist. *The Brothers Karamazov*, accordingly, is clearly here. She also, as noted above, mentions Hardy as an early passion, and similarly one senses throughout the latter's sense of naturalistic fatedness. And so present as well, as suggested initially, are more immediate modernist and Southern counterparts such as Faulkner and Wolfe.

[*xii*]

Likewise, in her spare and powerful dramatic construction, as well as in particular thematic concerns—her feminism, for instance, and the thread of insanity that runs through the novel as the family "ghost"—she suggests much of Ibsen, whom one suspects she read, in an interesting Alabama connection with her greatly talented contemporary Sara Haardt, by way of H. L. Mencken's 1935 Modern Library edition of the major plays. (At first, for instance, one thinks that "Ibsell" is probably just a turn on "Isbell," a fairly familiar Alabama name. Then one finds the cold, hard, intellectual son named Henric. Then further is revealed the genealogy of that second elderly husband, Larson Ibsell, and father of most of the children, a silent, shadowy Scandinavian.)

In an equally explicit dramatic connection, Hassell also reveals an acknowledged indebtedness to the great Greek tragedies and also to those, of course—she was writing under the tutelage of Hudson Strode, after all—of Shakespeare. And in fact, at the time of the novel's publication, amidst general praise, there was a certain bit of sneering by New York reviewers at the idea of Rachel Ibsell and her story as a kind of "Queen Lear in Alabama." Now one suspects that sneering may have had as much to do with the Alabama connection as the Shakespeare. For indeed, on one's re-reading, the inscription of the classic text seems deeply and powerfully vindicated. And truly the resultant novel is probably best described, and in the richest possible construction of the idea, *as* an Alabama Queen Lear, complete upon the kingdom that is the land: the one good child, Jahn Ibsell, fallible yet faithful, ultimately misunderstood and hated; the two wolfish offspring, James Forrest by the first husband, lost to war in Cuba, and Henric Ibsell by the second; the third Ibsell son, Zack, the harrowed mad fool, speaking the family curse. The old faithful family counselor, the lawyer Bard Lipscomb, heard but unheeded. Yet at the same time, as I have already suggested, the work could equally be called an Alabama *Karamazov;* an Alabama *Sound and the Fury;* an Alabama *Joseph and His Brothers;* an Alabama *Ghosts.*

And all of this, one should add, is mainly to set in relief the truly unique achievement of the book, which is embodied in the creation of its titular heroine. For in Rachel Ibsell, Hassell creates an original surely on the order of Faulkner's Thomas Sutpen, a modernist builder and survivor of true existential resonance and power. We witness her godlike rages and her petty, childlike machinations. We feel her stern pride in the land and her ferocious and ultimately devouring love of her offspring. We wince at the cold correctness of her associations with her daughter and stepdaughter and draw back from the meticulous cruelty of the calculated insults and affronts whereby she sabotages the relationships of her sons with the other women whom they would take as contenders for their own loyalty and affection. We feel the full horror, under the strain of love and prolonged conflict, of her psychological disintegration. We witness finally her dying, a gibbering, scripture-haunted ghost, in a bare room of the state asylum where she has been committed by the cruel sons whose legal machinations she can no longer bring herself to abet. Around her bed the assembled relatives shamefully squabble and blame to the last. Above rise the keening cries of the madwomen of the locked ward in the garret. This woman's version of a modern tragedy is complete.

It is also this latter point of woman's perspective that leads to a second and related assertion of classic status; and that is, if we may now claim *Rachel's Children* beyond local and regional concerns as a modernist classic, we may also claim it so as a feminist classic as well. Again, in one of her many interviews around the time of the novel's publication, Hassell herself provides a clue, claiming as her favorite book *Kristin Lavransdatter* by Sigrid Undset. This was so, she said, because it was "the only book by a woman I've read which you couldn't tell a woman wrote." The matter, of course, is a great deal more complicated that this, but it is a beginning. For the point simply cannot be overlooked that this book is, after all, the stunning work of a young woman of immense authorial presence, assimilating a literary body of essentially male tradition in an act of quite original creation. (Indeed, contemporary reviewers' remarks on the writer's youth virtually all carry the subtext of gender as well).

Similarly, like Ellen Glasgow's *Barren Ground*, a roughly contemporary Southern feminist classic of which it frequently reminds us, it is also *about* a woman of immense psychological and spiritual presence attempting to work her way amidst structures of power, property, authority, and genealogy in a world of laws and of other regulation essentially created, interpreted, and administered by men. It is about the particular problems of women as surviving parents, of widowhood, of solitary ownership and distribution of property, of testamentary intention, of standards of mental competency, of statutory definition and standing in courts of law. It is also, simply enough, about a particular woman's being lonely, growing old, and facing death. Finally, it is quite explicitly as well (in ways that are touched on only much more indirectly, for instance, by Faulkner or Wolfe) about the power, in a patriarchy, of matriarchy, the love of mothers for their sons and daughters in ways often at once creative and destructive. For all this, however, it is not a "women's" book. Rather, it is about women and men in their relation to issues of power and law in a context where the figure of woman is deeply asserted as a presence upon the Southern landscape.

Finally, there is the claim for this book's importance that also should be made exactly on the grounds of local appeal—for it *is* ultimately just this utter human concretion and particularness, as Hassell herself seems quite clearly to have understood at the time, that is also the key to the book's human expanse and universality. It is clearly *about* Northport, Tuscaloosa, and Tuscaloosa County, Alabama; and, as in the texts of T. S. Stribling's North Alabama trilogy, which it often resembles, it is so in ways that still have and should continue to have considerable appeal as important additions to the literary record of life in the state during the early part of this century. It is really definitive on matters of agriculture, commerce, law, class and race relations, local manners and folkways. The main characters, as they achieve mythic status, are also of their world in all its dark, earthy vitality. Likewise, lesser figures often produce the same effect. Rachel Ibsell's brother, for instance, the pentecostal preacher Zie Gurney, is a venal hypocrite of uniquely vivid creation, as are the two vernacular figures Long Jim Chambers and Mose Thurston, who at times serve as local chorus on the major action. Also remarkably evocative of the world depicted are the merchant Joe Rosenbens, Henric's Cajun wife Chanson, the servant Black Joe, and the alienist Dr. Stanhope. Finally, the litigation plot involving Jahn and his brothers over the disputed land at once recalls the all-consuming monstrosity of the law in Dickens' *Bleak House* and anticipates the use of the Southern courtroom in Harper Lee's *To Kill a Mockingbird* as a ground of intense social and psychological realism.

And this sense of local achievement, moreover, is a fit one on which to end in any appreciation. For it is exactly that testimony of deep relatedness, the capacity, as noted above, to ground the human and universal directly *in* the local and immediate that is the sign and index of this book's great, austere eloquence. *Rachel's Children* is an Alabama classic that thereby makes itself also a classic by a comprehensive standard of definition. As a writer in the *Tuscaloosa News* noted perceptively at the time of the book's publication, "It is merely 'the story of a consuming love which bred only evil' and it could have been laid almost anywhere. It as 'at once contemporary and timeless.' It merely happens that the woman who wrote the book lives among us, and she wrote of the people she knew best."

Rachel's Children

PART ONE

I

ON A NIGHT IN APRIL, TWO FIGURES CAME TO THE TOP OF ONE of the mounds in the Ibsell pasture, and stood there, looking northward to the white, square block of the house shrouded in low-hanging elms. The moonlight threw their shadows before them, down the slope of the mound, in waiting, motionless attitudes.

Rachel Ibsell gestured slowly, pointing out over the pasture and to the fields beyond. "And all that," she said in her strong, autumnal voice—"all that land there, you say you don't want and won't have?" Her tone edged with bitterness.

Without answering, Jahn Ibsell turned his head to follow the sweep of her gesture. His figure, of a muscular and powerful build, cut the gray moonlight around him as the sharp and final lines of granite cut the brilliance of sunshine in the day. Silhouetted so, against his natural background of farm and pasture land, his dark figure seemed to generate some power of omen together with a tingling and gentle sweetness. His features, at once sensitive and scornful, were more boldly carved than the woman's, the nose larger, very nearly aquiline, and the sockets of the eyes shallower, seeming in the moonlight merely another pallor like the broad, gleaming expanse of his neck above his open collar. He answered her abruptly and with amusement in his voice.

[1]

"You brought me here like the devil brought Christ to the mountain top, to show it all to me and tempt me, did you?" He laughed softly, and turned around to gaze off above his mother's head.

He saw there, behind him, ten miles off, the lights of Choctaw, and between him and them dark masses of woodland stretching turreted and blocked against the colorless night sky. Down below, at the edges of the woodland, rose a tangle of young thicket. The long furrows of the land ran out from the undergrowth and spread fanwise to the north and east as far as the eye could see in daylight. Beyond their wavering lines, the woodland rose again, encompassing the eight hundred acres of the farm on three sides as the sudden hills cut it off from the county road on the west. A single light glowed in a pin point of luminance through the trees on the top of the western hills.

"James' house," Rachel Ibsell observed in a falsely casual voice, as if she had abandoned the struggle between them.

"My brother James," Jahn said, gently, and with irony.

His mother moved and withdrew her hand from his wrist in a gesture of protest. "But you're right," she said then, "they treat you in an unbrotherly way . . . all but Zack."

"Henric," he said. He breathed the word lightly, yet the air around him was at once alive with scorn and with something like regret.

Rachel shivered. "Yes, Henric. . . . But you're part to blame," she added, presently. "You're too much what you are. I'm even afraid of you sometimes. And Henric always knew I loved you best."

"Henric," he said, "and James always knew I was not what they are." His deliberate voice, full of clear, clarion-like notes, changed suddenly. "They pinch around, sneaking, to know what I'm feeling, and then they come out in the open to tell me I'm ignorant and no credit to their good sense." He stopped as abruptly as he had begun, and pressed his wide, handsome lips together.

[2]

Rachel Ibsell touched his wrist, moved nearer to him, and was silent. After a moment, she pointed toward the other two mounds, rising in limpid green luminance from the floor of the pasture land. "It seems strange to think Indians buried their kin here," she said. "It's never like a graveyard to me. One night me and your father was out here walking, before you was born, Jahn, or even Henric. Your father showed it to me that night. If you stand over there to the roadside and look down this way, you'll see it in a way I bet you never thought of. The mounds there together and this one over here, it's like a woman; and there, where the persimmon trees and the haw bushes down under make a V shape, it's like her hair come down over her throat. . . . I never see it but I remember your father telling me."

He stood still, without answering, looking at her. After a moment she turned her face to meet his gaze.

"Yes, I think of James' father, too." She began to walk down the slope into the wide, flat hollow between the mounds. "But that's done for since James' father left me and went to Cuba to die," she said, and her voice sounded old.

Jahn looked at her again, slowly. Her arms were bare above the elbows, with the sleeves of her dark cotton bodice rolled back. Nothing of the texture of her skin could be seen, but the shape of her arms was full, strong, and middle-aged. She stood upright, her feet firmly planted, in an attitude of earth-bound dignity, her long, full skirts casting a shadow down the mound. Her profile was strong and regular, with a straight, narrow nose and full, firm chin accentuating the deep inward curve of her eye sockets over eyes whose fierce black light glowed out above the vague darkness in which the rest of her face was hidden. There was something so youthful and so fiery in her aspect that Jahn smiled, turning her hand palm upward where it rested on his wrist, and opened his mouth to speak.

But she went on wearily and half angrily: "It's a poor woman that'd go on remembering a man this long . . . and besides, I've give James his part of the land. The only thing

[3]

I'm sorry of is the way you and Martha hate him. He can't help he's a Forrest more'n you can help being Ibsells. . . . But that's done for," she said again, and turned to look behind her.

A sliver of sound, like the slide of a foot on wet grass, melted down the slope. "What's that?" she said, and then, "One of the cows, I guess." A slow, sardonic grin twitched her lips. "These mounds, Jahn, ain't like one of your modern girls. . . ." She said in a different voice, "All this belonged to your father. I put the rest onto it myself, eleven hundred acres onto two hundred in less than thirty years. The trash around here don't see how it was done. 'No money in farming,' they say. Whining, I call it! They don't know how, too lazy and extravagant to know."

"Red Valley," he said, "must have its ears burning right now," and glanced at her swiftly, with such a sharp, sweet mockery in his eyes that her heart turned over. She looked down at his wrist under her fingers and stroked for an instant the tawny hairs on his arm.

He walked beside her slowly, the cool wind blowing the open collar of his white shirt and lifting the dark hair off his forehead. A herd of milch cows sleeping against the curve of the far mound snuffled at their approach and moved their heavy, bunched bodies. The shadows of the trees, clumped together at the end of the valley between the two parallel mounds, covered them as they moved onward. The strange, indescribable smell of running water rose from the darkness in front of them.

He said, "I can remember Papa here; just being here with him. I was six or seven." He bent over to push the lower boughs out of his mother's path, and the darkly shining leaves of the young haw bushes brushed over his face, emitting a faint odor of lemon and magnolia as if they already had their blossoms on them.

"You'd not remember later than that; he died the next year," Rachel said. "That's when me and your half-sister,

[4]

Kate Ibsell, went to law over the two hundred acres your father left."

She had paused in the path under the trees and was looking down at the spring caught in a bowl of hewn rock at their feet. A single ray of moonlight split the water and lay like a quivering star on the white sand bottom. Momently, as the spring heaved in the sand, splinters of radiance rose from the prismatic edges of the light up through the water and washed out on the sides of the greenish rock cup. A small stream poured from the mouth of the rim through last winter's dead leaves. Farther on, under the pines, there was light again, and the flowing water dimpled in it. Rachel Ibsell put her hand on Jahn's wrist. "I wanted us to come here. I was down here the day before you were born."

He moved, incompletely, away from her, and then stood still, letting her touch him. "You think too much about me."

She looked at him in surprise, and was suddenly afraid, feeling his tensity and hearing the echoes of his voice, stifled and strange on the words. "Why not?" she said then, drily. "I'm your mother." She looked down at the spring. "It's pretty, but plowed land is better."

"A lot. This is the sort of thing Henric likes. Zack, too. They don't know it's the dirt that counts; this is just decoration."

She gave him a shrewd glance, her eyes veiled by the darkness. "You like decoration yourself. . . ." And then, coming back to it, "But why do I think too much about you?"

For an instant he was motionless, and then he turned slowly, and she with him, her hand still on his wrist. When they were out of the trees, he said, vaguely, but with warning in his voice, "I'm thirty-one."

"And I'm sixty-nine, though you say I don't look it." She gazed about her, knowing that the moonlight was in him, chafing her close, unromantic hold. "You're tired of it here at home with me." A slow bitterness roughed the words. "Well, I shouldn't have kept you!"

[5]

"That's not fair." He smiled at her sidewise, gently.

"Ah, you're a man to twist a woman any way!" she cried, impulsively, stopped herself, and began on a different note. "But you won't take the land now. You keep putting me off, something up your sleeve. A woman, maybe. You want land of your own. I know, and it's right you should, but this is here for you. I've told you a hundred times, and you keep talking about buying down on the river next to Choctaw. I like you living right up against Choctaw and the smell of the paper-mill floating down before you for breakfast! But I guess a girl would like it, so near town!"

He was standing full in front of her, with his face bent a little to hers and naked in the moonlight. A still impassivity sat on his high cheek bones and wide lips, held there, she knew, by a quietness in him, as of waiting and sounding his own being. He smiled again, suddenly. "What girl?" he said.

Her fingers relaxed on his wrist, and he turned around.

The rough, sweet cry of tree crickets rose abruptly and flooded the pasture as if every crevice of mound and little valley held myriads of the brown insects. The deep, murmurous thump of the ironworks in Choctaw sounded intermittently between the cry of the crickets. The mother moved nearer to her son. The call of the crickets rose pulsingly, and stopped suddenly as they do when an alien thing has moved among their trees. Somewhere near the spring, a shuffling of movement sounded on matted leaves. A twig broke on the ground. The two in the moonlight listened, their backs to the trees and the spring. The silence fused with the colorless landscape and sank slowly into the hollows between the mounds. After a moment, a valiant cricket cried again.

Jahn said: "Somebody . . . The corn's been going from that lower crib. . . ." He saw his mother's skirts shivering in the wind over her tensely held body. "You didn't give the keys to anybody, by chance, did you? I had three crib keys on my ring and one went on a Sunday afternoon."

Her shoulders jerked imperceptibly. "Who do you think

I'd give it to? Sunday afternoon. . . ." Her voice sank, and she did not look at him. "You know that's when Henric and James come . . . and Zack."

"You give them a lot. . . . James don't make any corn himself. . . ."

The anger died out of her, and the watchfulness. "I made Black Joe turn one of the sows to the pasture here this afternoon." She listened. "She'll be farrowing by morning. I expect she's moving about in her bed there."

After a moment he said, pleasantly, "I expect that's it." He laughed. "If it's anybody after the corn, we must be in his way."

"No doubt," she said, drily. "You're too suspicious. . . . But I can't blame you," she added.

She moved on, more swiftly now, through the dew-wet grass, and up to the roadbed. Over against the rail fencing a mass of foliage twined with the flat, wide flowers of white dogwood and the crimson-stalked tassels of buckeye, and moved in the cool wind with a soft, insidious rustle. Rachel Ibsell stepped across the road and took one of the buckeye tassels in her hand. The long, irregular throats of the flowers hung heavily downward and the ridged leaves gave off an odor of green sap. She broke the thick, wax-like stalk.

"You can have the dogwood, Jahn. But I always loved the round smooth eyes these things make in the fall."

"Dogwood is white and thick. It's pretty and it's stern-looking. Clean, somehow."

She came back to him, carrying the blossoms in her hand, and stood beside him, looking down the road, away from the unlighted house. "It must be near ten. Martha better show herself at home soon, or she'll hear from me. Out till all hours with that Billy Nelson!"

Jahn looked at the dogwood. "Nelson's all right."

She said, abruptly and with meaning, "I didn't like to see James marry." She twirled the stalk of buckeye in her fingers. "Nor Henric, either. . . . It's nights like this I get to seeing my life, and it bothers me. Things like when James come home from Pittsburgh in 'twenty-seven. It seems a long time now, and yet . . . I never did tell you how he set there in the living-room, looking all around like he couldn't get over my new green carpets and my brocaded window drapes . . . and glaring at pore Fanny 'n' his children if they dared open their mouths . . . And I give him the five hundred acres that afternoon. Well, what was he to do, come home like that and nothing to live on? I told him farming took brains; there's no union business to farming. But he sets over there on the hill, doing nothing but gloom and mistreat Fanny."

His anger blazed out suddenly, like a streak of white lightning. "Mistreats! He beats her ——!"

"Well, hush. No need for you to get mad about it. . . ." She sighed again. "Your uncle Zie had the face to blame it on me. He said nobody could say I hadn't set my mark on my boys, bringing 'em up according to the Scriptures to know a man was head of the house. I told him no man was ever head of my house. . . ." She stopped, drew in her breath, and twirled the flowers more rapidly. "No, Jahn, don't go calling James names in your mind; it won't help Fanny none . . . nor me none, either. I reckon Zie would blame me with Zack's spells of weak craziness," she went on, heavily. "if it wasn't he knows it comes from the Gurney side and he's a Gurney himself. The man side of the Gurneys was always crazy. . . . I hate my life on nights like this. First a Gurney and then a Forrest and then an Ibsell. A woman oughtn't to have three different names in one lifetime." She looked at the ground in front of her. "'Specially if she took one of 'em for a living. . ."

Jahn touched her forearm with the tip of one finger. "You're worrying yourself again. You've got that lawsuit with Kate on your mind. You ought not to think about it."

"Ah, but you'd think in my place! You think as it is. I ought not to have kept you here when I let the others go off to school. I ought to have educated you."

[8]

He said nothing, moving a little away from her, and she looked at him sidewise, at his clear, bold forehead and the sweep of his shoulder breadth. "You're such a man as don't happen often . . . and I ought not to have stuck you down here with me. But I needed you . . . and I loved you best even then. It looked like I couldn't stand to see you go off."

"The others were never further than Choctaw to go to school," he said, presently, and looked at her, swiftly and almost curiously. His mouth tightened. "You can't pay me now for what you let me lack then," he said. "The others won't stand for it."

"And what's it to them? They've got all they need and more than they deserve out of me. They got it out of you too as much as me; if you hadn't stuck by me there'd been nothing to give them."

He said, slowly: "I know . . . the land's mine in a way: I've earned it. But it's only on nights like this, when you get to thinking of Kate and what she said, that you're ready to turn it over to me."

The lights of a car showed dimly among the trees to the south, curving in and out and coming nearer. She said, "That'll be Martha and Billy Nelson," and began to walk swiftly back in the direction of the mounds. Behind her, he laughed. "Come on," she said. "I don't want to be bothered with Martha's talk now; she talks too much, anyway." Glancing backward, he saw the car pausing at the white picket fence and Martha getting out. Rachel Ibsell was already among the mounds, hidden from the road. A shadow moved in the moonlight in front of her; she stopped to look, and it disappeared. "Some cow moseying about," she said, yet she stood staring with tense eyeballs as if she expected some apparition to rise out of the Indian mounds.

When Jahn came up to her she touched his arm and said, abruptly, "Yes, I'm superstitious. Kate's curse worries me tonight." She stood below him where the valley sloped gently to the trees, and did not look at him.

"Maybe I had no business to go to law with her. But she was already married by that time and living in Choctaw with that widower she took up with. And I had James and your father's four little children to raise. . . ."

He said, "Mamma, you've told it a hundred times."

"I know, but there's times when I have to talk it out. If your father had left a will—but Larson Ibsell was not one to think of dying. I had to have something to raise you all on." She sighed, and for a moment her shoulders rested on his chest, taking comfort from him.

"So I went to law. And I won the land by right of my widow's dowry. Kate hated me then and I hated her, though we've made it up on the surface since. She told me that day coming out of court that I was cursed for stealing. She said I'd taken an old man to get what he had. Well, I can't blame her. Larson Ibsell was thirty years older than me and she knew how I still felt about James' father. She said I'd stolen Ibsell land, I'd stolen and I was cursed, me and my children and the land, all cursed. . . . I never will forget how she looked. . . ." She stopped and repeated slowly to herself, "Me and my children and the land cursed. . . ." She shook herself. "It gets on my nerves."

"You've got too much sense to believe a thing like that."

Her head moved slowly. "No . . . if you'd take the land——?"

Up the hill the car was moving, turning, and going back down the road. A door in the house slammed loudly. Jahn smiled. "Billy's gone; you can go back now without getting in the way of a love scene." He turned her around toward the house. "Don't think about it," he said again.

She walked slowly, leaning a little against him. Behind them, a shadow moved and grew long around the curve of one of the mounds. Her feet passed softly over the damp grass. At the edge of the road she stopped hesitantly, looked about her, and moved nearer to him, leaning more heavily on his arm. She opened her mouth, looked up at his face, and then away. She spoke in a soft, strained whisper.

"It's times like this with you make me know what the curse is . . . If you should ever leave me, Jahn . . .?"

For an instant his breath was held like hers. Then he moved gently, drawing her with him to the gate in the white picket fence and through it, onto the rock walk in the yard. The leaves on the roses along the walk moved softly in the little wind and their green glinted palely against the darkness under them. She stopped suddenly. Her dark gaze, hid in the shadows covering her face, rested vaguely, yet intently, on him. She said in a smothered voice, "I'll tell Martha to move that Talisman . . . too much shade here for it. . . ." The shape of his face moved above hers, came nearer, and he said, "You know ——"

He stopped, and she could see his eyes, pale and intense like a white light. He said, gently, "I promise I'll never leave you."

She stood without breathing, rooted to the spot by delight. Presently she put her hands up to his cheeks, gropingly, drew down his face, and kissed him on the forehead. She went swiftly up the walk then, barely pausing at the steps, and into the house. The door closed behind her without a sound.

After a moment he turned and faced the east and the land. It lay more darkly now, as if the moon had faded and the stars had not enough strength to raise it out of the shadows. The furrows seemed to rise and fall gently, imperceptibly, with a breath of their own, and to sigh out a faint music. He went nearer, to the edge of the yard fence, and stood holding to the white pickets and letting his eyes absorb the form and the body of the fields. The furrows reached for him with some passion of desire that had nothing to do with his flesh, yet it ached in his breast with the commingled pain of longing and the soft, unbearable sting of satisfaction. Suddenly, while he stood watching, the white mist of the dew rose over the dark earth. He shut his eyes briefly, as if they were too full of sight, and turned to the house.

A few seconds after the outer door had closed behind him, a short, bent figure emerged from among the three mounds in the pasture and looked toward the lighted windows of Rachel Ibsell's room. Then, stooping to lift a corn-sack over his shoulders, the man wheeled and began to run rapidly over the mounds. He avoided the east side where a group of Negro cabins, each sheltering a wakeful dog under the porch floor, huddled at the curve of the road. At the clump of trees near the spring he turned directly toward the west, and made for a thick tangle of undergrowth swathed in the endless, sinuous coils of old muscadine vines. Here, he turned again, searching about for a familiar, hidden opening, and then, hunching himself forward, he shot through the massed roots and vines and into impenetrable darkness.

Half an hour later he came out on the top of the hill, and paused to wipe his face. A few yards distant from him stood a tall, ramshackle house with one light shining through the kitchen windows. He glanced rapidly at it, listened to the silence, and then, assured that his wife and children were asleep, he bent over and began to take off his shoes. The moonlight, slanting through the pines above him, revealed for a second the sharp, avaricious bend of his nose, the gleam of teeth between the straggling ends of his walrus mustache, and the swollen veins on his forehead. He stood up finally, with his shoes in his hand, and gazed down the hill onto his mother's farm. His black, narrow eyes, set· lynxwise under his protruding forehead, glowed with a dull, malicious hate. "God damn the cheating bitch!" he whispered, suddenly, and then jerked around toward the house, with fear, as if he felt something listening to him.

II

Jahn Ibsell dozed in his chair on the lawn on a Sunday afternoon of the following summer, and awoke at four o'clock to find Henric and Zack and Henric's wife arrived from town for the weekly visit. Opening his eyes to see them standing over him, he was at first more inclined to take them for colored dolls than for living beings. He glanced at Henric's large, black car parked in the road and then to the house where Rachel Ibsell was still resting after the heavy midday meal and reading her Bible. Her voice rose and fell, intoning the familiar phrases in a slow, worshipful monotony that blended with the soft cluck-cluck of setting hens in the back yard. Near by, the vetch fields stretched like smooth carpets of green, rising gradually to the taller, checkered masses of cotton plantations. Far away, the tall cornstalks moved in the sunlight and glinted where their green leaves rustled. The high, Norwegian clock that had been Larson Ibsell's chimed four bell-like notes from the house, and Rachel's voice stopped.

Jahn's gaze went back to his brothers, but for a moment still they were blurs of white to him while he stared at the tall, lean grace of his Creole sister-in-law in her summer stripes and plaids. Her eyes were like cat's eyes, large and almost octagonally shaped, with points of a cruel and fascinating luminance informing their centers, so that she was not able to look at anything except as cats look, with desire and cleverness. Her unrouged smile disturbed him, and he stood up, coming awake to offer her a seat on the brown cushions of the lawn glider.

The two men sat down with her, and left him standing. He watched Henric cross his thin legs precisely, with great care for the knife-thin creases in his white serge trousers, and arrange the ends of his blue foulard tie on his shirt front. "You might wear a coat on Sunday afternoons at least, out of respect for Mother," Henric said to him, and that thin, perfectly enunciating voice went through him, first with angry pain, and then with a release of amusement. He lifted his skeptical eyebrows, sat down again, and said to Zack, "How's the loan business?"

Zack, less immaculate in his dress than Henric, but more cleanly built, with lovely small hands and feet, flushed out of embarrassment and pleasure. He lifted his wide, pale eyes to Jahn's face and then looked swiftly down again. "Henric runs it all. Ask him." His broad, pale face was neither intelligent nor foolish, but, rather, a blank for the marks of a queer, flitting fear.

Chanson, Henric's wife, was still regarding Jahn, brightly and attentively, with an evident mockery diluted a little by a wish to charm him, the female cat in her purring ever so slightly under the stroke of his male presence. "And this Martha?" she demanded. "She is gone out with Billy Nelson, eh? We never see Martha here on Sunday afternoons. One would say young girls no longer stay at home." She lifted her voice a little on the last words as if, Jahn thought, she wished Rachel Ibsell in the house to hear her voicing sentiments his mother would approve.

He nodded to her, and stared past Henric's flat, black eyes to the lane between the yard fence and the fields. Two fox-hound puppies lay asleep there on the clover, twitching their silky, reddish ears to the sunlight. "We'll have to try a hunt with them some night," he said to Zack.

Zack's eyes lighted. He turned to glance at the puppies. "I'd like that. It's been a year or so since we went fox-hunting together." His gaze came back to Jahn's face, shyly, as if to say, "It's so nice going through the woods at night." He asked, "How old are they?"

"Extremely foolish!" Henric commented. "To put on old leather jackets and torn trousers and ride bareback all night. Fox-hunting is, in reality, a social diversion. Pink coats, English squires. Quite senseless to treat it as rough-and-tumble."

Chanson laughed. "Ah, but this Jahn, he would treat any-thing as rough-and-tumble." A simpler woman might have spoken so and flattered him; Chanson's tone was a comment on boorishness. His cheeks flushed a little, and then he looked at her with a hard significance. "Always," he said.

[14]

She drooped her eyelids and raised her thick brows at the same time. "But a little gentility is always good, eh?"

"It depends on what you do with it."

Zack said, hurriedly, "What's keeping Mamma?" and Jahn laughed suddenly. "You're not up to Henric's refined standards, Zack; you still say mamma."

"You object, then, to 'mother'?" Henric fingered his tie and looked at his wife. "My dear, I suppose you had better start saying 'Mamma Ibsell.'"

Jahn had an instant of wanting to crush Henric and Chanson together in the trivial oil of their meanness. A peculiar, stiff smile appeared on his lips. "It might mean more if she did," he said, and immediately bit his lower lip in compunction. They always made him as small as themselves, as sharp and as foolish.

"You would not," Henric said, and seemed to examine Jahn, "like it if anybody appeared to care more for Mother than you do. It might come between you and the land."

Rachel Ibsell spoke suddenly from the porch steps. "Gurney enough in you for bickering, I see!" she said, bitterly. "Well, I'm coming out now, and you can stop it!"

She came down from the steps and out under the elms, walking swiftly in her black satin skirts. As he looked at her, a small image of a shadow moving and growing long on the mounds unrolled in Jahn's mind, and then, leaving no sense of meaning behind it, curled to nothingness. She went at once to Zack, and kissed him. "Well, boy?" she said, her tone and look made to give to a baby. He lifted his pale eyes, a little watery from emotion, to hers, and she backed off from him. "Well, sit down." She took the chair across from Jahn's.

Henric stared at the sharp points of his immaculate white oxfords. "How are you, Mother?" She raised her large, turkey-feathered fan and began to wave it back and forth before her face. "And how is your garden, Mother Ibsell?" Chanson began. Her firm, New Orleans' accent ran trippingly on the syllables, and Rachel turned with pleasure toward its strangeness.

"Well, Miss Chancie," she answered affectionately.

Jahn's eyes glowed like aquamarine between their short, thick lashes. "Let's have a look at the fields, Zack," he said, rising.

Zack's small feet in black oxfords set themselves neatly, in exactly parallel steps, on the wide path through the fields to the woodlot. The corn stood upright in the close summer heat, with its leaves veined out of the deep blackness rising from the earth into the feeding stalks.

Zack said, "James told Henric Mamma meant to give the land to you."

"James knows a lot." He did not look at Zack. "Maybe somebody was in the pasture that night, then." The fine, red dust in the path rose in little puffs under his shoes. "First the crib key went and then the corn." He chuckled faintly under his breath.

Zack's shoulders jerked. "James wouldn't do that. He told Henric about the land last spring."

"But he didn't tell why he was in the pasture? Or did he say where he was when he heard it? . . . I can't boast about James and Henric. I stayed here to let them go off to school, and all I've got out of it is Henric's nagging and James' pilfering. He was around here last night, getting money off Mamma."

"I'm just telling you, Jahn. I went off, too, and I like the farm as well as anybody, but they're talking about it down at Henric's. The worst thing," Zack said, and paused—"the worst thing is the way Mamma shows we're nothing to her against you."

"I stayed with her, didn't I, and I wasn't so old as Henric or you?"

"I guess you want the land a lot."

He looked sidewise at Zack, puzzled by the strange, accusing tone of his voice. "About as much as you do. . . . What does Henric say?"

They had passed through the corn-fields now, and over against the woodlot the green vetch-fields lay again. A few bees hovered over the little purple flowers that, for the most part, had given way to stringy sinews sticky with a sweet, leguminous moisture.

Zack said, "I don't want to tell you."

"Then I know. He means to have it himself."

He stared at the woodlot, shifting in all the shades of clumped and feathery green in his mind with a picture of a shadow moving on the mounds. He said, "So James was really there . . . and now they're rolling it around like a crumb in their minds and gathering all they can to it. . . ." The heat shimmered on the path ahead, and he felt sweat breaking on the back of his neck. "You, too, Zack . . . you're against me in this. . . ."

"No. No. . . ." Zack blinked his eyes nervously. "Let's walk on. I want to see if there're any ground cherries coming out yet. . . ."

Late in September, Martha brought Sue Hart home with her.

Henric and Chanson had gone that afternoon, and Jahn and his mother were sitting together on the front veranda, watching the Negroes come up from the cabins at the curve of the road and along the lane to the barn lot. They walked by twos and threes, the men in front, driving the cows up from the pasture, and the women behind, carrying the milk-pails for the men and with measuring-pans for grain under their aprons. Their loud, resonant voices lifted on the still air in spurts and runs of indistinguishable sound.

Three girls coming a little behind the others tossed their brown necks, flapping at their oiled, straightened hair with red bandannas. "You got gnats 'round heah, Ol' Miss," they called across the fence, and went off into shouts of slow, bending laughter. Rachel smiled vaguely, giving to them no more attention than she ever gave to Negroes except in moments of curiosity or emotion. One of the men began to slap on the ground his toeless shoes, bending his knees at right angles to his body, and walking forward a foot or two with each precisely rhythmic step.

"Sho got some full bolls down on 'at soufeast cotton. Wuz down 'eah 'is ev'nin'." The feet slapped softly. "How come yo' cotton so late, Boss?" Smats of blows on thighs darted through the crowd with a flurry of high, liquid giggles. "Boss, he know late cotton make the bes'!" They went out of sight around the corner of the house, still laughing and slapping their hands. "Hey, you Liz, you ain't feed 'em hens 'is ev'nin', I does 'at!" a woman's full voice floated back. The sounds grew faint, all in a minute, and blended with the afternoon stillness.

"Didn't see Black Fanny in that gang," Rachel said. "Late to get supper again. . . ." She rocked her chair gently. "I'm going to move that wistaria next spring. . . ."

He filled his pipe, pressed the tobacco down in the shallow bowl, and sat flicking at a match head with the end of his thumb nail. "Henric was sweet this evening, wasn't he?" he said. The flame flared up and he moved his thumb, and sucked in the thick smoke. "Chanson loves to get on your good side, too."

She rocked deliberately. "I always liked Chanson since the day she got rid of that nigger of hers to do her own housework. She's saving and industrious without the need to be either. What's a wonder to me, too, she's making a good Christian. I always heard Catholics kept hankering after their Masses and such, but she don't. She makes Henric a good wife."

He smiled slowly at the sparse autumn spills on the wistaria vine. "She suits him all right."

Billy Nelson's car was coming up the road, lifting puffs of red dust under the tires, and sifting it in faint streaks over the shining, blue fenders. "We need rain."

"Yes. . . . I'd get rid of that Fanny, but she owes me for old clothes."

Jahn laughed. "They always owe you."

"I get work out of 'em." She said, "There's three in the front seat. Martha keeps bringing these town sillies out here for me to bed and feed. Fashion! That's what she thinks it is."

"Let Martha alone; she's getting ready to be a good wife to Billy Nelson," he said, drily, and glanced at his mother, sidewise, with crinkled eyelids. She smiled unwillingly, and continued to watch the car, stopping now at the edge of the yard fence.

The three in the car sat still, and she could hear their voices, Martha's and Billy Nelson's, and a soft, whispery voice that was strange to her and immediately distasteful. Jahn knocked out his pipe against the railing, got up, and moved down the walk.

Two moonflowers, one in each of the large iron urns at the side of the veranda steps, floated on the deepening dusk like scalloped disks. She stared at them, and heard the car starting and the higher lift of Martha's voice. Jahn was standing outside the gate, between the two girls, looking down at them. They began to walk toward her.

"My mother, Sue."

In the first moment, Martha's laughter-flushed face and plump, compact body came between her and Sue Hart, and then the widow's peak of dark red hair impressed itself on the retina of her eyes, so that later in the darkness she could still see how that hair grew, in a soft feather of color, like the roached surface of a princess plume.

Martha came up onto the porch and threw herself into the swing. "We had a grand time. Sue, you'll have to do the talking now; I'm worn out. We went all over the place, Billy knows more things to do for fun." She panted slightly, exaggerating the autumn heat and her weariness.

Sue Hart moved past Rachel swiftly, so that she could not see how she walked, and sat in the swing with Martha.

Rachel's gaze turned to follow her. The especial delicacy of the little white forehead surprised her, and she grew aware that Jahn was still standing on the steps below them. She felt his eyes watching with hers the girl's forehead and the upward tilt of the golden eyes along the curved brows, and she thought, suddenly, "That mouth—geraniums!" She made herself turn around then, and look at Jahn.

He had not, she knew at once, moved since he reached the steps. He was leaning forward a little, with his head bent to look at Sue Hart, and his face still with an expression that had in it something of shock and something of delight. His eyes were wide and somber. He said, "I must have seen you somewhere before."

"I teach in the grammar school at Choctaw." The voice spaced each word and dropped it, breathlessly, so that it seemed to shimmer like a small globule of water. Rachel did not turn while it spoke, but remained staring at her son, something moving, searching, in her mind for a pretext to dislike. His face did not change. The girl's soft, shining voice hesitated a moment, and said, "I teach the fifth grade."

He raised his right foot and set it on the second level of the steps, moving unconsciously, without taking his eyes from Sue Hart's small, white face. "But you've always lived in Choctaw?"

"Yes-s." The gentle, dependent hesitation came again. "I've seen you in the curb market on Saturdays. Sometimes I go with Mrs. Thurber, my landlady. They have such lovely flowers, don't they?"

Martha moved the swing back and forth, briskly, with one foot on the floor and the other doubled under her. "Now you've got to remember her, Jahn."

His lips smiled faintly. "I do, but I don't know where."

The swing creaked from Martha's pushing foot.

"It seems awfully hot," Sue said. She got up to take off her white flannel coat, and Rachel turned her head. The girl seemed, in her high-heeled shoes, taller than she was, and more fragile. Her white flannel dress, belted in at the little waist, clung about her slender hips and divided between the high thrust of her small breasts. She looked, in the dusk, like a porcelain shepherdess clothed in a solid sheath of dogwood blossom.

A hot, righteous anger shot suddenly into Rachel Ibsell, like an incoherence of outrage. Her mind darted feverishly between the appeal of those unlaced breasts and the lacquering she had abruptly perceived on the girl's finger nails. She tried to look at Jahn again, and could not move her eyes around. Her lips felt hot and dry, opening on a protest. She got up brusquely.

"Jahn—! That Fanny's not coming. You better lay me a fire in the kitchen stove." She glanced at Sue, and made herself smile faintly. "We'll have supper after while, Miss Hart." She had moved to the screen door as she spoke, and now she looked at Jahn again. "Jahn—lay me a fire."

His face swung slowly away from Sue Hart's, and tilted toward his mother with a blank question that stared a moment and then swept under into comprehension. "Oh! Lay you a fire." He started, seemed about to come up onto the porch and through the house, hesitated, and looked at the girl again. "I'll have to go around for the kindling," he said. He turned abruptly, almost like one escaping, and brushed against the evergreens at the edge of the porch wall.

He heard the screen door slam behind his mother, and stopped against the wall, out of sight of the veranda, and stood looking down at the faint microscopics of fallen dew on the grass. He moved suddenly, and went toward the wood-shed by the back-yard fence. The red light from the lamp in the kitchen flared up and fell in an oblong shadow over his shoulders and over the woodpile. He turned the sticks of kindling, picked them up and put them down, and heard his mother opening the cutlery drawer in the cabinet and taking down the biscuit-tins from the high shelves behind the stove.

When he came into the kitchen, she was standing beside the

work table, a white apron tied over her silk skirts, rolling sausage patties between her hands. He let his gaze pass over her face. "Hurry up with the fire," she said. "You've been long enough already." He took the stove-lifter from the top of the warming-closet, raised the round lids in the top of the stove, and bunched the smaller splinters of litter in one hand. He tried to think of something to say. The flame from the match licked up over the red pine with a soft, flickering sound. He leaned over, laid the larger sticks crosswise on the grate inside the stove, and deposited the burning pieces on top of them. "Put down the damper," Rachel said behind him. "Looks like you'd remember."

The flesh on his shoulders itched a little, away from her annoyance. "Don't drop splinters on my clean linoleum," she said. He looked over his shoulder at her, and placed three sticks of stove wood on the burning mass in the grate. Lifting the iron lids into place again, he stepped back. "That's done," he said. He glanced at her, vaguely and obliquely, and remained a minute, watching the front of the stove where flecks of fire gleamed through the fretted door.

She came up beside him to set the biscuit-tins on the stove, reached back to the table for butter, and stood measuring squares of it into the pans. She said, "Butter biscuits tonight, inside and out," in a falsely equitable tone. The fork with which she spaced the butter on the bottom of the tins moved busily, and then jerked, as if her arm had jerked at the elbow. "Jahn, there's three kinds of women: females, feminine pieces, and women. I like women, and I can abide females—I can even like 'em; Chanson's one. But . . ." She stopped abruptly, moved the biscuit-tins from the stove to the side table, and turned to open the cabinet to the flour-bin.

He was aware of the shadows in the dark corners of the kitchen, and of her swift, vital figure moving before him, getting the supper backward, but he seemed to himself somewhere else. He said slowly, without thinking that he was answering her or making definite the reasons for his vagueness and her anger, "I thought she was nice . . . ladylike. . . ." After he had spoken, he heard the low echoes of his words and listened to them, still without any sense of all they meant.

She cried sharply, "You have to be a woman before you can be a lady!" and caught her breath, turning away from him to the biscuit-cradle.

He had some feeling then that he was too much a man to understand what she meant, or to split hairs with his being over it. Something moved, swift, up out of his consciousness and shone there a dazzling moment, vivid as a picture of himself possessing Sue Hart, and then dived under his mind in the streaked way of a fish diving under dark water. He said, "I don't know what you mean," and went out of the kitchen, through the dining-room, and back to Sue Hart on the front porch.

That remark and that act were like all he did that autumn, a refusal in two kinds, a darting of furtiveness through desire into the clear heart of his honesty in order that he might, at the same time, have what he wanted and keep his way with his mother truthful. He stood in the living-room windows on dark nights, looking out over the harvested fields and the pastures toward the lights of Choctaw. Sometimes, when Martha was there, she said, smartly, "Thinking of Sue, Jahn?" and his face flushed faintly. "Much good it'd do me if I was," he said, seeing how that small, soft girl retreated when he looked at her and came up to him when he turned his head away. He left the windows and sat down by his mother at the center table and watched her fingers turning her needle.

She told him, "I can't keep you here with me if you won't take the land; it wouldn't be right. . . . Henric's been asking about it. . . ." He said, "I don't want a fuss on my hands. Keep the farm awhile yet." He got up and walked around the living-room, and stood at the windows again, pushing back the heavy green draperies. His mother was silent behind him. He said, roughly, and always suddenly, "I think I'll go into town." Her bowed head nodded grimly, so that he noticed how white her hair was turning. "Suit yourself," she said.

Three times when he came home from Sue Hart, she was still up, with the door to her room open on the hall, sitting in her wicker sewing-chair as if she had not moved all night. She called him in to her. "I've been remembering Kate tonight and all she said." She rocked her chair, and he stood before her, silent, with his face turned aside half in pity for her and half in anger at himself. "You must take the land or you'll not stay by me."

He said, "I promised."

The second time, he said, "Not unless I pay them something." He looked at her then, and her eyes were frightened. "I don't owe it, I know that, but not unless . . . some way to keep them quiet." She was silent, and he turned to go. "Jahn . . ." He stopped, and she was staring at the fire on the hearth. She said again what she had said on the night they walked in the pasture. "I hated to see James and Henric marry. . . ." He was laughing suddenly, and he never knew why, except that he saw Sue Hart's golden eyes looking sorry for him when she told him the moon was called Cynthia. "What's marrying got to do with the land?" She turned her face up to him, and he thought for a moment that her eyes were blind.

She was hard and angry the third night. Something perilous and faintly smiling sat on the pink curves of her mouth. She began abruptly, and stood up as soon as she had spoken, facing him as if she meant to beat him down at last. "Either you take it, or I give it to James and Henric! You can choose. James has been asking, and Henric's been here saying he wanted it, he'd run it from town and keep you on as tenant; he couldn't be too hard on you." She smiled contemptuously. "So you can choose, sir!"

His shoulders bowed a little before her attack, and he tried to look out the window across the room, to find the fields. Then he threw back his head and looked at her. "I've not said a word to Sue Hart." Pallor spread over his face slowly, as if it were born out of the dragging accusation of his voice. "What have I got to offer her, anyway?"

"And you hate me for it!"

He waited a minute, looking at her with surprise, and then with tenderness. "No. . . . Did you think I could?"

She sat down, and raised her hands to stare vaguely at the finger nails. A sudden, shy smile hovered on her lips; she turned her head to hide it, and then looked back at him with moisture in her eyes. She said, "I've read my Bible for this. . . ." Her voice changed, "Jahn, the only feelings that count are family feelings. All the rest is nothing compared to what you feel for blood like yours and bone made from the same stuff as your bones. When you're old as me you'll know that."

After a moment he found himself smiling, palely. He put his hands up to the door frame on either side of his body. "You've not left me much way for knowing how I'll feel toward flesh and blood of my own when I'm your age," he said, and felt his tongue shaping the words delicately.

Color splatted across her cheek bones in a curious mottle of red and white. She put out one hand in front of her, pushing the air, and let it fall back helplessly. Her voice was dead. "I've loved you next to God. . . ." Her hands dropped onto her arms, the fingers nerveless where they touched the elbows. Her chest drooped over. She stared at the fire with eyes like burned coals.

The impulse of cruelty that had shaped his tongue fell in shame before her strange, defeated face. "Mamma. . . ."

He stopped, and came up to her, putting his hand gently on her shoulder. He looked out the window where the fields lay in a sleeping ecstasy of December moonlight. "I don't guess that matters," he said. "I'm not like Henric and Zack, to get what I want for looking at it."

"Don't." Her chest rose and fell swiftly, in a soft, agonized panting. "Don't—say I didn't educate you!"

He stared away from her, back to the window where the white loops of the bedroom curtains framed the still, moon-breathing furrows, and he was smiling then, and unable to tell whether or not he was lying. "It don't matter, does it?" he said. "You gave me something better. . . ."

He stopped and listened, wondering at himself, and his eyes became more brilliant than before, like blue flames in the heart of a fire.

He could feel her straightening, turning to look up at him with her eyes coming alive. He took his hand off her shoulder.

"I'll have to pay them something, though," he said. "Money ought to satisfy them. . . . I'll take the land," he added, suddenly, as if she had not been sure enough of what he meant.

She moved in the chair, and he thought she was going to get up, to kiss him, perhaps, as she had done before on the night when he promised not to leave her. He turned, roughly, and went out, unable to trust himself to look at her face. "God!" he thought. "God, what have I done!" and the moonlight struck across his eyeballs, lifting out of the still fields to drench his senses.

III

Rachel Ibsell sat at the head of the dinner table, with her four sons grouped on her right. Martha and Kate Ibsell were ranged beside each other near the vacant end of the board and across from them, on the left, Henric's wife and Fanny Forrest sat eating busily. The Christmas holly on the heavy brass chandelier above them quivered slowly, and paused an instant, and quivered again. Dusk had come on. The old-fashioned oil wicks winked a yellow dullness over the silver and china and spaced a fixed triangle of light on the disturbed slices of turkey meat. The room was queerly still, caught in silence under its human noises. The wind, going voiceless over the farm outside, seeped between the closed panes and the maroon-colored window curtains and pulsed soundlessly and continuously on the ear. Rachel Ibsell raised her head and listened tensely. Next her, on the left, sat Bard Lipscomb, the lawyer from Choctaw. She put her hand on his to make him listen with her.

"I hear it," he said, under his breath. His red, over-full lips grimaced, and his mad, black eyes peered at her under the white cap of his hair. "The farm's cracking in its ice sheath, Rachel!"

On her other side, James Forrest looked up. She met his eyes slowly, with the mixture of love and puzzled contempt with which she always regarded him, and let her gaze pass to the faces beyond his. Henric and Zack and Jahn were alike, she thought, looking at them, unable to perceive how her own harsh, arrogant blood showed itself in Henric to the exclusion of the Ibsell strain and how Jahn and Zack were really alike, even in their darkness, to her blonde Ibsell stepdaughter at the end of the table. Rachel's eyes moved on, over Martha's face without a glance, to Kate Ibsell.

Kate's clear, bitter-blue eyes met her black ones steadily and warily, with a distant, enigmatic gleam. Rachel's lips quirked in a sudden grim amusement. Behind her, the logs in the great stone fireplace glowed red and moveless, filling the air with a prickly, disagreeable heat. Kate's cheeks were unnaturally scarlet, and she twitched her shoulders inside her black velvet dress. "You're not hot?" Rachel said to her, still smiling. The wariness of Kate's gaze increased. "Not too hot," she answered. She raised her delicate handkerchief and slowly wiped the perspiration from her forehead, as slowly replaced the handkerchief in her lap, and arranged the waves of her thick, snow-white hair around her smooth temples.

Rachel frowned, and gave a vigorous, decisive push to the table, moving her heavy chair backward, and making what she always made, a sense of disturbance and abruptness. She stood up slowly, enjoying the start of tensity into the faces around her, and glanced for the first time at the faces of the women on her left. Fanny Forrest was dim and shaking; she gave a little cry of nervousness as Rachel's chair scraped over the floor.

Chanson gazed at her mother-in-law with soft, yellow eyes as patient as a cat's. A pleasant, cold malice touched Rachel for a second, and then she saw Kate staring at the walrus mustache and slit eyes of James Forrest. She felt a fleeting, finicking wish that James would shave his mustache, not be so country, and her cheeks flushed painfully. She stood up straighter, holding herself more formally above the heavy mahogany table with the rich, maroon-colored wall paper outlining the spacious curves of her body and the wide sweep of her black satin skirts.

"I didn't," she said, abruptly, "ask you all here to no purpose." She glanced out the window, past the black prongs of the fig tree there, toward the level sweep of her fields, smiled a little, and then peered vaguely toward Lawyer Lipscomb. He gave her a sudden, vivid, twisted smile. She swallowed deeply, her bosom rising on a renewed breath of resolution; yet before she spoke again her gaze went swiftly to gauge her sons' faces. An odd, fearful determination leaped into her black eyes, she gripped the back of her chair with both hands.

"I'm getting old," she said, suddenly, "and tired of worrying myself. And this is Christmas Day and Jahn's birthday." She did not look at any of them now. "Henric's been at me for a long time about my land, wanting me to come to some arrangement. But I guess you all know that. The point is, I've done it. I thought best to make a deed, to do it while I'm alive and can see how it'll come out."

In the pause, James laughed out stridently and nervously. "Come off!" he said. "You've not give it all to Henric. Part's mine!"

Her eyes flickered over him. "Part's always been yours, James, by fair means or foul. I've deeded the land to Jahn. I wanted you all here when I told you. It's his birthday, and I wanted you all to express thanks to him for what he's helped me to do." She saw Jahn's eyes, luminously blue and intent, fixed on her, and something pleading came into her voice.

"You all don't realize how much the boy's done for you and given up for us all." She sat down, looked at her plate, and repeated, "I want you all to express thanks to him on his birthday."

The room moved faintly in its stillness, as if the ice outside had cracked over the long, level furrows, allowing the exhalations of life room for sound. Henric rose impetuously.

"Thanks!" he cried, bitterly. "Thanks for keeping close to you and ousting me!" He sat down abruptly, limply, his eyes on Chanson's warning fingers curled tight on her napkin. James laughed again, snickeringly and senselessly, and Zack's pale eyes stared vaguely from one face to another.

Kate Ibsell pushed her chair back. "Rachel, I—" She glanced around for words, and suddenly reached across Martha to shake hands with Jahn. "I think our father would be glad of this day," she said, gravely.

None of them laughed. They sat, glancing furtively at one another's faces and trying to seem calm. In the middle of them, Lawyer Lipscomb speared a slice of white turkey meat, wrapped it in cranberry sauce and a sprig of celery leaf, and raised it to his mouth. Rachel looked at her plate.

"Well, I thank God!" Martha cried. Her large, dark-blue eyes shone with a vivid and almost practical beauty. "I've been so afraid she wouldn't do it! Isn't it wonderful? Isn't it grand!" she chattered. "I always said Jahn ought to have it all when he's been so good and—" Her laughter stopped all at once, as if their silence had struck her in the face.

Henric's wife spoke first. "It's nice," she said, "that Jahn is not educated and has never had a business for himself like Henric and Zack so that he'll stay here with you, Mother Ibsell. And it's nice, too, that he hasn't married, like James!" Her yellow eyes gleamed, taunting while she smiled.

Jahn looked at his hands on the tablecloth. The blunt, hard fingers wore the feel of the plowshare in their flesh. His large, subtly carved face was still, set, a humiliated red washing under the skin that would not move to show them his hurt.

James Forrest whispered to Zack and Henric, sibilance flowing around the bitten ends of his mustache and out over Chanson's speech.

Rachel Ibsell looked up slowly, sneering with anger. "Well, what ails you there!" she called, peremptorily. "Speak! Don't sit there mumbling! What can't be said aloud better be left unsaid."

"It's not fair, Mother. In effect, you disinherit us."

She stared at Henric scornfully, and knew what he was, prissy and cruel and lustful. But she knew, too, that she had made him what he was, created him with her early struggles, her scrimpings and savings, out of the fear that loved a dollar next to God. She forgave him for being what he was because he was hers and she had made him, but she spoke out harshly and strongly.

"Unfair! My soul, was it you labored here with me, working night and day when I hadn't but two hundred acres in the world and no man to turn to! Was it you stayed by me when the rest upt and went off to get educated and live it easy? Was it you sent the others money for schooling and did without himself? Ain't you got your business now, bought out of the cotton money from here, and ain't I give land to James . . .? Five hundred is different from eight hundred acres, I know," she said, more calmly. "But it wasn't James' father as left me with land rich enough to make itself into thirteen hundred acres in a few years and it wasn't James stayed here with me."

Jahn said, thickly, "Let it go; let it alone." He moved to get up, to have done with it, and sat motionless in a kind of sagging indecision. The blood that had been so hot in his face drained down to his heart, heavy there and sick. "Let it go," he said, faintly.

"No, not my father," James whispered, suddenly, with a kind of poisonous, pale brutality. "My father was white trash, but Larson Ibsell was a gentleman—!" He caught himself up, and made a shift at laughter with showing his sharp teeth between the straggling ends of mustaches.

Rachel Ibsell's eyes clouded. "Hush, James," she said. "You know well enough I loved your father. Larson Ibsell treated you right." She sat still a moment, avoiding Kate's eyes, and studying their rebellious faces. "I'll tell you," she said then, cajoling them with her sincerity now, "I know myself and I know you all. We take things too hard; it's like a disease with us. It come down to me from my father. But you, Henric, you and James, you know how to beat things down. You know, too, that you've had your just deserts from me in the business and the land and the education I give Henric and Zack. And Zack he knows how it'd be with him if he took what's not his.

"His conscience would work on him like it did when he was little, and he saw dwarfs riding along, haunting him and arguing out the right and wrong of what he'd done. He knows he don't want to go through that again, waking up in the night and screaming, or maybe seeing it in broad day. But Jahn, now. . . . I know how it'd be with him if I took his rights from him. He's been friend and boy and workman. And a comfort, like a husband near. And if I take his rights from him, it'll be like it was with my old daddy when the conference took his preaching. He lost his mind, died out at Marston's Asylum. I tell you, I know you all and I know your blood. There's things I've seen in my daddy and brothers, and already in you, I don't want to live to see come out strong in you. . . ."

Henric's voice was smooth, precise. "But, Mother, it's you we're thinking of, you and Martha."

"Ah, you're a fool!" she cried, bitterly, the Gurney passion flooding her temples. "Thinking of me to throw slurs on Jahn same as always and nigh tear my heart out to see the pain you cause him!" Her voice dragged for a minute, she turned her head wearily and stared at the thick, dark curtains shaking in the wind from outside. She jerked her head back and faced him. "Thinking of me, are you, sir! Well, let me tell you, I'm provided for. If I had to depend on you, I'd starve, for all you cared, and I know that well enough! I tried to give this land to Jahn without strings, except one I made in talking, but he wouldn't have it so."

"But, Mother ——"

She rushed on over him. "No, he's got to sign a paper to keep me till I die and Martha till she marries. Not provided for, eh, sir? He's signed the house site to come back to me if he dies first. That's what he thinks of your honor, Mister Henric! And he's signed to pay six thousand to you all, a promissory note secured by a mortgage and payable when I die!"

"Six thousand!" James said. "What's that?"

Zack looked at her, his eyes wide and sullen in his broad, weak face. "None of the land will ever come to us, Jahn'll outlive us all. . . . I wanted some of it," he said, slowly. His gaze went around the table. "I see now I was a fool to ever leave here, but Henric said to go, we had to be somebody, and Jahn was too hard to live with; he had you under his thumb even then."

The fire blazed up suddenly, with a hissing rain of sparks. Rachel Ibsell said, "If I was ever under anybody's thumb, it's news to me." She gazed at Kate Ibsell, blonde and serene at the far end of the table, and did not see her.

James Forrest's fists were hard on the table, his black, lynx eyes hard on his mother's face. "Mother, you surely don't think a scrap of paper ——!"

She grinned, with the sudden humor that came to her in moments of stress. "James, you sound like the Kaiser. 'A scrap of paper.'" She pushed her hand across her face. "It's my own land," she said, with weary stubbornness. "You, James, you know no more how to manage a farm this size than how to build a good corn-crib. Always going on about how pore your land is and you too lazy to rotate your crops— even plant 'em!"

She stopped suddenly, controlling herself, and looked at the lawyer. "Bard! Leave the sauce and turkey be; let Jahn have the deed." Her black eyes blazed all at once. "I'll do with my own now as ever!"

Bard Lipscomb laughed at her, twisting his lips with the fondness of long friendship. "Ah, darling, darling, and to think it's not my own boy getting your wonderful land!"

Rachel blushed faintly. "Well, you know why it's not! You a Catholic, and having your law books to pay for, too."

"You never looked at me, Rachel, you never even saw me."

He took the deed from his coat pocket, where he had kept it in readiness, and gazed at Jahn Ibsell out of glittering, speculative eyes. "Ah, Rachel, and I let old Larson have you, a Civil War veteran like that to have to put up with your jealousies and tempers! But I think the boy's eyes should be dark like mine, darling, if you want him to be a bachelor," he said, and winked at Jahn.

But Jahn Ibsell was staring at his brothers. His hands shook suddenly, and the blood washed back up over his face. His mouth opened to speak, and then closed. He took the deed in a white, creased silence, and twisted the paper in his fingers as if he were about to tear it. Then, abruptly, he glanced down at it, smiled, and put the deed in his pocket. He looked up strangely, seeing a lust visible in his brothers and feeling it in himself and knowing how, like all lusts, it bred a certain dishonor that the mind covered and excused.

IV

A sudden sound of wind broke on the corners of the house and shook the chandelier over Rachel Ibsell's head. She sat leaning her chin on her hands, alone at the dining-table, and hearing from the living-room the sounds of Henric's and Chanson's departure. She looked down at the table and began to make invisible tracery on the heavy linen cloth with her finger. The holly wreaths in the windows scratched faintly

[33]

on the glass as the wind crept under the sills and around the frames.

The front door banged shut. She heard the sound from far away, vaguely, and without trying to think who was leaving now. A girl's face formed with a slow glimmering on the linen cloth, weak and lovely and young, with the dark red hair curling over the strange curve of the brows and the golden eyes glowing between the delicately rouged cheeks. If she looked long, the small, virginal mouth would open and show the teeth in laughter, and already, even as she thought this, it seemed to her that she could hear in the air the vague, tenuous trill of the girl's mockery.

She turned around in the chair, away from the sound. Her lips moved uneasily. "But he promised me, he promised me!" She moved in her chair again, restlessly and angrily. The girl was nothing, a little, senseless orphan of no account but to teach in the public schools and think she knew it all. "Now, children, the sentence is a complete thought." Rachel Ibsell said it to herself, mocking the soft, hesitant voice, and then made a derisive sound. Jahn was no fool, and no cheat.

The front door banged again. Kate Ibsell spoke in the living-room and Fanny Forrest answered in a thin, coughing voice. Rachel got up swiftly, on a sudden eager to be away from the fear and loneliness of herself. She touched the bell on the sideboard behind her, at the same time calling out to the Negress in the kitchen, and left the table.

The window, she noticed as she turned away, was black now, with faintly discernible globules of dusk pressing on the panes. She went rapidly across the floor, and stopped on the dark threshold, confronted by James Forrest's small, bent figure. "Well?" she said, and stepped back. The hall behind him was unlighted, the door into the living-room closed. "I thought you'd come," she said, abruptly, and watched his face.

He was biting the ends of his grayed mustache, staring all around the room as if searching for something hidden in the corners, and fumbling his hands in and out of his shabby coat pockets. "Well, out with it!" she cried. "You're not content, I see, with the shame you put on me before Kate at dinner."

She walked back to the table. Black Fanny was taking up the plates. "Leave them," she said, and watched the woman walk out on high heels. "I give that nigger a good pair of high tops," she observed to James from a distance, "and she comes out in them things." He jerked his hands out of his pockets, raised his hunched shoulders, and stood over her suddenly.

"You poor fool!" he said. "You've damned well played it today, haven't you?" His thin, narrow mouth smiled steadily and contemptuously.

She stared back at him with a slight, unconcerned amusement, and then she looked down at her black shoes on the maroon-colored carpet. The circled patterns in the rug spread out in interlocking designs from her feet, rust on maroon and maroon on rust. She felt a vague impulse to lift her feet so as not to disturb the pattern.

After a minute, she said, "You talked different from this when you wanted my land." She heard the quiet sound of her voice flowing into the corners of the room. She said, "Why, you actually think you can call me a fool and have it all undone and the farm not give away!" She looked at him steadily. "You must be a little off, James."

His smile widened flickeringly. He put his hands into his pockets again. "You damned fool," he said, deliberately. "You've played yourself out. Don't you know he means to take the farm and leave you for that Hart wench? If you'd kept it, he'd not have left, he'd have hung around sponging on you the way you want. It's not rest you've got for yourself, but misery!"

A sudden wedge of terror blocked her throat, and then her anger spoke past it. "I give you your part and warning of what was to go with the rest of it." She paused, to let her scorn increase. "You said then that it was 'pious and kind' of me. 'Pious and kind'! But I knew you then. You're a cheat,

[35]

James, a cheat. Your part's not enough for you, you've got to have more and make your mother miserable if you can. You and Henric are in together on this." She raised her dark brows at him. "Henric ought to remember," she said, "how you used to burn his colored spools for the fun of hurting him."

His black eyes stared opaquely at her. "Not to hurt him, but because he belonged to that long slob, Larson Ibsell."

"You call your mother a fool, do you, James?"

His sudden, raucous laughter rushed out against her. "You're dam to more than me," he said.

She flushed hotly and stood up, her arm raised, threatening him. "If I lay with Larson Ibsell," she said, thickly, "it was to feed you." Her arm fell limply while his laughter grew soft. She stared helplessly at his gleaming teeth. She sat down suddenly, saying aloud in a dazed mutter, "I told your uncle Zie you was too smart."

She looked up at him presently. "God, he knows how he made us," she said slowly. "I meant this to be the happiest day of my life, and you've called me a fool and reminded me I'm dishonored in your eyes because I gave myself to feed you when you had nobody else to do it. If it hadn't been for you, I'd a married Bard Lipscomb; he was near my age, and I liked him, but I put up with Larson Ibsell's old, drooling ways for you, and now you— But you'll not turn me!" she cried. "Your father left me for a fool's idea, nobody cared about Spaniards in El Caney! And he never come back, not even his body come. My children have shamed me and been ashamed of me. None but Jahn has stayed by me!" She stood up suddenly and shouted straight into James' face, "Let him bring the Hart girl here, then. Will he leave for that?" She stepped back from him, and her mouth fell open in amazement and soundless denial.

v

The Easter morning sun shone through the green window drapes in the living-room and splotched pools of yellow light over the polished floor and the rugs. Out in the yard behind the house, Jahn whistled to his dogs. Rachel Ibsell spoke in the kitchen, her voice strong and deep against the Negro maid's clatter of copper pans and basting-forks. The scent of purple flags, bruised from the rain of yesterday, rose from among the lattice-work around the living-room floor. The high Easter wind swayed willow branches past the windows, sunlight glinting on the pale, delicate buds.

Martha patted the cushions on the brown, overstuffed divan. "Don't walk around, Sue. Sit down. You worry me standing up like that, as if you were really afraid of Mother." She laughed, confiding as always, but with a brittleness in her innocence.

Sue moved impatiently, smoothing the dark red hair on top of her small, oval-shaped skull, and frowned down at her white slippers as if they, and not Martha's incessant laughter, disturbed and bewildered her. She sat on the divan uneasily, with her pink-tipped fingers clasped tensely on the pale green froth of her skirt.

Martha touched Sue's painted nails. "I wish Mamma would let me do that." She was alive all over, her white teeth gleaming between red, unrouged lips, her eyes brightly blue, her hair gleaming purple black. She laughed again. "Do you know we're having an announcement dinner today? Paula Pollard and Zack—though Heaven knows when they'll be able to marry. Zack has his house to build yet." She glanced out the window, toward the drive. "I'm glad they've not come yet. I don't like Paula. Do you?"

Sue was listening past the dictatorial voice in the kitchen to the sharp, musical notes of Jahn's whistle. She gazed at Martha with wide soft eyes. "Not really?" she said.

"Really!" said Martha, mockingly. "Don't let Mamma see you hanging your ear out for Jahn like that." Her fingers touched Sue's hand again. "If you ask me, Paula Pollard is the last sister-in-law I want. Those big, stick-out eyes and that kinky black hair!" She sat back. "Chanson is bad enough.

Sometimes I wish the whole lot would go over the bridge into Sand Caves!"

Sue flushed vaguely. She was small, with delicate bones, and all her gestures seemed to flow out of a minute and precise limpidity. She never declared; she appealed. She was luscious, yet virginal; she seemed full of a lovely weakness, yet to strike her resolution was to hear the tiny and irritable tinkle of thin ice surrendering without submitting the change of its substance. Even the softness of her lips was prim. With her little mouth set in subtle disparagement and her faintly slanted eyes shuttering themselves, she said, "I thought your mother didn't want her sons to marry?"

Martha shrugged. "Oh, it's Jahn she cares about."

The gaze of the two girls slid warily apart. Sue turned the ashtray on the side table.

"But don't you care!" Martha said impulsively. She jumped on the divan. "She's just plain foolish, that's all; she'll get over it." She laughed briefly. "All she needs is a grandchild to bring her around. She's been awfully disappointed that way in Chanson."

Sue's face remained averted. "You're getting too far ahead," she replied in a low, thin voice. "Jahn and I are just friends."

Martha's laughter tinkled. "Friends, me eye! I know my own brother."

Jahn Ibsell came slowly around the corner of the house, past the chimney his own hands had built, and paused at the living-room window. He was gay this morning, vibrant enough to tremble at the audacity forming in him, arrogant enough for charm, and his flesh was knowledgeable flesh, well aware of what was inside the room, sitting on the divan and knowing he was outside looking in at it.

Martha laughed again, ripplingly. "Well, speak of the devil!"

Sue Hart's dark lashes were heavy and tipped with gold. She blushed, a clear, warm color that flooded her chin and crept upward to the curved, dark line of her eyebrows. He looked at her steadily, a little somberly.

"If you want, I'll show you the orchard. It's pretty this time of year."

His deep voice carried low notes that reëchoed clearly and strongly. His large, deftly sculptured face was shadowed around the stern, bright gleam of his eyes.

Sue hesitated, looking at Martha.

"Oh, go on. You'll be out of the way of Mother till the rest of them come, anyway."

He smiled. "I'll meet you at the front door."

The peach blossoms blew out straight against the sun, and the leaves turned themselves up to the wind. As soon as they came into the orchard they saw the little gray birds on the ground, twittering and swirling in their plumage. The birds came at their feet, a whole covey of them, and cried, and flew backward in fear, close to the soft crust of the earth, and hid in the winter-caked furrows. "Oh, the little free things!" Sue said, and ran after them. She went down on her knees in the furrow, with a foam of pale green skirts spreading around her, and called to them. Her skirt was like a clump of leaves to the birds, they smelled her and saw her, but she was so covered in green that they could not be afraid. Jahn stood where he was, behind her, with the high Easter wind blowing his brown hair, and the birds moved a little nearer to her, craning their necks in a long way. "Little free things," she whispered, and moved her fingers caressingly. Their bright eyes stared at her, steady and beady above their moving beaks.

Jahn leaned over her, with his hands on her shoulders. "You're not here to talk to birds," he said. The pigeons whispered all together in a soft, frightened sibilance, and swerved up in a dark block from the ground. She got up very swiftly, and shook down her skirts. "See, you've run them away," she said, pretending regret, and gave him a delicate, wistful glance out of her lovely pale face.

He smiled slowly. "You're an awful liar," he said, and took her arm and began to walk on deliberately. She held her face turned from him. "You're not a liar." Her voice was pale; she moved her lips and tried faintly to laugh. "Are you?" she said.

He walked slowly, looking down at her narrow feet. After a minute, he smiled again, but he still did not look at her face. "I was just thinking . . . I've never kissed you."

She stared at the black shadow of his beard under the fair, sun-darkened skin. She held her lips apart as if she were laughing. "Well, why are you so angry about it? You're not supposed to kiss me."

She saw his cheeks move a little and his lips twitch. He said, "You know all about it, don't you?" He stopped in the middle of the orchard, and stood there, leaning against a peach tree, not looking at anything, but standing and waiting with his fists in his pockets. He looked at her abruptly, with perplexity almost. "I feel like hell today. When I came up to the window back there, I thought I'd take you to walk and I'd—" He stopped. "I don't know what I thought. But now I feel like hell." His eyes gazed at her, bright and enigmatic.

The soft, pink petals swung in and out among the leaves, in and out, and above them billows of white clouds shifted in the stifling blue sky and rose and fell.

He said, "Sometimes, when I see you, I'm happy. I go to town sometimes just to pass you on the street when school is out and I know you'll be coming along." He looked away from her slow blush. "You blush like that when I pass and don't stop. That's why I don't stop."

"Because I blush?" she said, uncertainly.

"Oh, I don't know why. . . . If I stopped, I wouldn't know what to say. But when I go around to see you, it's easy to talk. . . ."

It seemed to her that he spoke in a dark way, that he smiled like a man toying with his pain in order to come nearer to the nervous area of his bliss. Something in her ran in fear; she moved, placing one foot in front of the other, and then she was standing still again.

He looked at her sidewise. "This is all senseless. You run from me and me from you. There's more than words. I keep holding back, and I don't know what I'm holding back or what for." Doubt and desire broke in his eyes, and then the stern blue iris was smooth again and secret. He picked a petal from the spray in front of his face, and turned it in his fingers, absently. "There's a thing Martha talks about—biology. Maybe it's just biology." He threw the petal down. "And loneliness. I've always been by myself."

The little birds were coming back by twos and threes, twittering shrill over the pink blossoms and down to the furrows. She saw, suddenly, rows of beehives under one of the trees with flecks of greenish-gold swarming like daisy buds over the wooden cones of the hives. "I didn't know there were bees," she said, automatically, and then she looked at him. "Your mother would hate me."

He gazed back at her without speech. He saw her face rapt in her red-gold hair, her face weak and vivid and patient, and the golden tips of her dark lashes frank against the deep curve of her brows. "I always think they brushed your lashes with pollen," he said. A glow burned faintly and sweetly under her skin, she shone for him as the peach blossoms and the sunlight shone, with strangeness and simplicity.

"If I kissed you—?" he said, more to himself than to her, and leaned over her, holding her shoulders and watching her eyes.

Half-turned from him, she shook her head. "No-o." While she waited, the dinner bell tinkled faintly from the house. The small, pealing summons sang through her, with its echoes somewhere far off, in a mist she could not see.

"Yes."

His lips came on hers slowly and not easily, so that she was dimly aware of something immutable in him and of something gentler than anything in herself. A fear grew on her with the warmth of his nearness, and because she hated the fear and it was delicious, she said, "I love you," saying it against his throat. When she heard herself, she jerked backward; yet, in the same instant, she was still to wait for his answer, she was even looking into his face.

His mouth was set and still, his eyes veiled. Without loosening their embrace, they stared at each other. "I wish you'd said it before now," he said.

With an effect of having begun long ago, the dinner bell rang again. Their arms moved, they stepped carefully backward from each other. "We're late," he muttered under his breath. She felt herself moving beside him, going in a haze of frustrate embarrassment. She said, "I'll have to ask Martha for something to clean my shoes."

He looked down at her slippers. Brown dust mottled the white suede tips and stained the high heels. "I'm sorry," he said, and after a moment, "I forgot the dust."

VI

"Another announcement dinner!" Chanson said. She stood by the fireplace with Rachel Ibsell, slowly stripping the black kid gloves from her long fingers. "I never think of this place without seeing masses of food." Rachel Ibsell was giving her hand to Paula Pollard, and Chanson smiled at the girl brilliantly.

Paula was short, like Zack, and plump, with exaggerated curves of calf and hip and breast. The thick smear of paint, curved to a cupid's bow on her narrow, full lips, annoyed Rachel. "I see," she said, "that you're like all the rest of the girls this day and time. You make yourself so much alike it's hard to see why a man 'u'd choose one of you above the other." She shook Paula's hand swiftly, with a masculine

[42]

firmness, and turned away from her to glance out the window toward the orchard.

Paula laughed and stepped backward. The large round brilliants which served for buttons down the front of her tight wine-colored taffeta dress caught the sunlight from the windows and threw swift circles of light onto the walls and ceiling as she turned. She had not spoken to Rachel Ibsell except with a nod and laugh. Now she grasped Zack's arm, languishing at him with her great brown eyes like full muscadines, and drew him off into the corner near the radio. After a minute she took Zack's guitar from the edge of the writing-desk and began to play softly, ignoring the rest of the room. Zack sat beside her, flushed and self-conscious.

Kate Ibsell glanced at them with sardonic eyes. She sat apart from the others, on the far side of the fireplace. "Love!" Kate said, to the room at large.

Chanson heard her, raised her eyebrows, and turned to Rachel. "Don't be looking out the window, Mother Ibsell. They'll be along in a minute." She moved slowly across the floor to the divan where Henric sat, facing James Forrest in the smoking-chair.

Rachel left the window and came back to the fireplace. Bard Lipscomb got up from the great leather sofa at the end of the room, leaving Martha and Fanny Forrest, and came to stand beside her. "Ah, Rachel," he said, teasing her as usual, "we're getting old. You'll be having other grandchildren than James' soon." She did not answer him, but stood smoothing the skirt of her deep purple gown. The thick green window hangings stirred faintly as the scent of freshly turned garden loam drifted in through the open windows. The small, spring fire crackled in the stone chimney, the willow logs burned down and shifted, rolling slowly on the brass andirons. Paula Pollard's fingers moved softly on the strings of the guitar.

Chanson Ibsell sat complacently beside Henric. There existed, Bard Lipscomb thought, a queer likeness between husband and wife, a likeness all the more apparent in that her eyes were amber and feline, while his were black and flat; in that her head sat so securely and confidently upon her small shoulders, his so loosely and rockingly along his neck. Bard Lipscomb, glittering with curiosity and a secret mirth, said to himself that they had walked, cheeping precisely and avariciously, from the same egg; and he included James Forrest in that harsh birth.

"For look, Rachel, there's no blood to tie Henric and Chanson and only your blood to tie James and Henric, but they're all the same." He paused to stare at them again, his red lip jutting against his false teeth. "It's quite apart from whatever matrimony or kinship may do. It's simply that without being one, they're the same. And what's in them to make them the same runs stronger in James than in Henric and Chanson."

From the back of the room, Martha laughed. "Maybe it's the devil!" she said.

Rachel walked to the window again, stood a moment looking out, and turned with a sigh of relief. "They're coming. Martha, you better tell Black Fanny to put the food on."

James Forrest said: "Well, well! So Jahn's out walking with his wench under his mammy's nose!"

Rachel gave him a fiery glance. "Yes, and James Forrest did the same afore now!" She stood close to Bard Lipscomb on the hearthstone.

"How strange it is!" Chanson mused, softly, looking down and smiling. "It's always seemed to me I could hear Mother Ibsell reading her Bible in these rooms; yet—all the quarreling, the card parties and the gatherings for fox-hunts. . . ." Her tone balanced nicely between sympathy and mockery.

Rachel laughed suddenly, giving her a glance of ironical appreciation, but immediately her eyes turned on the door, waiting for the steps in the hall. "Hurry up there!" she called. "Dinner's been waiting these many minutes." She gave Martha a look of displeasure. "Miss, I thought I told you to see to the table."

Martha got up slowly, just as Jahn came in. "Come in now and be a good son!" she said, gibing softly but loud enough for her mother to hear. She stopped on her way to the door. "Where's Sue?"

Then they all saw the girl outside in the hall, standing self-consciously, with stained slippers. Her little, pointed chin drooped under their concentrated gaze.

Jahn spoke hurriedly to Martha. "She wants to clean her shoes." He went up to Kate Ibsell and shook hands with her. He nodded vaguely to Paula Pollard and stood on the hearth with his mother and Bard Lipscomb. The old lawyer said, under his breath, "Has no one told you you're not supposed to have a heart?" Rachel turned around and looked at the fire, holding her hands out to the blaze as if she were cold.

The whorls of sunlight on the floor moved suddenly and deepened.

Chanson Ibsell rustled her skirts on the divan. "So you've been walking in the orchard this morning?" she said. She was intricate machinery polished to piercing brilliance, oiled with a slight, sexual vulgarity. The echo of her speech lingered in the tripped syllables, the whirring r's, the contagious beauty of New Orleans' accent. "It's a lovely morning, isn't it? The wind high and the white clouds swirling in the sky." Jahn thought, as always, that she talked like a book. She raised her heavy black eyebrows. "And I suppose you were simply exulting in the smell of the earth? It's odd, isn't it," she said, growing softer and more charming, "your love for the land when Henric and Zack hate it? Or do you really hate it, too?"

Zack spoke above the soft rhythm of Paula's music. "I don't hate it."

Jahn's eyebrows were brown, silky; slender carets above the shallow sockets of his eyes. "The blacksmith loves his forge," he said.

Martha stuck her head in from the hall where she was

standing listening and waiting for Sue. "Henric hates spoiling his pretty hands, that's what."

Rachel Ibsell stirred wearily. "We'll go in to dinner now. Miss Hart can join us in the dining-room." She led the way, turning her head angrily over her shoulder. "And this bickering can stop, too. Chanson, you started it. I've had all I'm going to have. Never a time do we meet here any more without it starting and you all saying the same things over and over again. I'm tired of it!" She plopped down in her chair at the head of the dining-table, and surveyed the food. "Sit where you want and eat what you like. I don't feel like being polite today."

Chanson slid smoothly into her seat, with Henric and James following suit. Jahn and Martha glanced at each other in dismay and uncertainty, and then Martha turned her head and called, "Sue? Sue, come on in to dinner. We're waiting for you, darling." Paula Pollard and Zack sat down now, smiling Fanny Forrest into imitating them. Kate remained standing, gravely, her hands on the back of her chair. Rachel looked up suddenly, flushed, and rose from the table.

Sue Hart stood uncertainly on the threshold, her white hands holding the ruffled flounces of her green skirt. Her golden eyes were proud and timid. James and Henric dropped their napkins and turned around to stare at her. Zack got up abruptly and pushed his chair back, as if to go forward and meet her. Yet, like Jahn, he paused an instant, between a step and no step at all, and in that instant of silence and embarrassment and indecision, they all perceived that she was alien to them. Her light and grace fell strangely on their heavy, passionate self-concentration, and they felt an awkwardness in themselves. Suddenly, Jahn went to her, took her hand, and led her to the chair beside Kate with an old-fashioned courtliness that reminded Rachel of his father. Just so Larson had led her before Kate on their wedding night. The girl looked down, smiling slightly with prim lips, and without looking at any of them, seated herself. They knew, dimly yet with certainty, that in that moment she had refused all of them except Jahn and Martha and Kate. Rachel took her chair again without a word.

"Yes," said James Forrest, returning to his grievance in the middle of the dinner, "there's a much of difference between five hundred acres of pore land and eight hundred good ones. Seven or eight times what my land would bring wouldn't buy this place. But, Mother, she can't see that . . . or won't. She's riding a whim to the destruction of us all, that's what."

Rachel Ibsell refused to look up from her plate. "Yes, and we've heard it all a hundred times before. You're fool enough and graceless enough to think you can bring this up before a stranger and change me. I've never changed yet for man alive, James Forrest, and you can take that and like it!"

Jahn raised his voice softly above his mother's, the whites of his eyes streaking with the hot Gurney blood. "I guess it was your father, James, fed and clothed you when you was young? If there's anything to be said about this, it'll be between me and Henric and Zack. They're on an equality with me, you're not."

Kate Ibsell was smiling, her eyes bluer than ever, her mouth perfect in its pink malice. She glanced at Sue Hart sitting upright on the edge of her chair, daintily using her salad fork. "Rachel, I've a crow to pick with you. You can judge its blackness by the public place I choose for the picking."

"Pretty public. All the family here to see we get it right and Lawyer Lipscomb to make sure we don't talk slander."

"Slander's not in my line," Kate returned, meaningfully, setting her head to one side in an attitude of suave defiance. "But Fanny Forrest here has been telling it around that Jahn's decided to remain a bachelor." Sue's fingers fumbled on the salad fork, and Kate's eyes grew warm and friendly. "Now, Rachel, it's none of my business, but we've all a friendly feeling for Jahn here. I have especially, I always say he's more like Papa than any other of your children, and I know what a young man goes through. So why don't you stop your foolishness, Rachel, and let the boy marry if he wants? You were always too tight for holding on, and you ought to know by this time that it loses you more than it gets."

She touched Jahn's hand across Sue, and laughed at him. "Be still now, son, and don't get so red in the face. This is between me and your mother. Well, Rachel?" she challenged. "What would you think of a young man that passed all the girls by to sit at home with an old woman?"

Chanson Ibsell whispered. Staring at his mother in embarrassment, Jahn felt the glow of a thin, dangerous anger.

"I mean friendliness to Jahn and you too, Rachel," Kate protested. She lifted her glass and drank calmly.

"Your friendliness is about like mine," Rachel broke out, in a voice dull with her effort at self-control. "We're both fools, Kate—fools enough to have married widowers, men worn out with one woman afore they got around to our beds, and we was both smart enough to lose 'em." She was shaking with a rough, desperate rage, so that she did not know what she was saying. "Jahn can marry if he likes, so he chooses a decent girl. But I've yet to see a decent one these days. Painted, red-fingered flippets!" Her eyes flicked hot hatred over Sue Hart's finger tips. "I've yet to see one I'd let come in my house to live!"

Bard Lipscomb spoke to his coffee-cup, easily and chafingly. "Better let a man marry," he said. He smiled toward Rachel. "And a woman had better marry. Ah, Lord, but I'm one to talk! Look at Rachel there and see the reason I'm lonely and crabbed today. I followed after her as after a strange woman, and she left me by. But I'm still senseless. I keep looking at Miss Martha here, and thinking a man could do worse."

The tension eased a little, and even Fanny Forrest dared to carry a bite to her mouth. Zack Ibsell began to smile diffidently, his lips timid, his beautiful fingers tight on his silver fork.

"Jahn ought to marry if he wants to," he said.

Chanson turned on him. "Oh-ho! That's your beautiful Paula speaking out in you. What does Paula think of all this giving of deeds and marrying?"

Paula shrugged her plump shoulders elaborately, the gesture of an adolescent enamored of sophistication. "I think it's lovely," she said. "Do you always quarrel like this?" Her eyes turned with a blue-white light to Zack's face and lingered there. "I do hope Zack's not quarrelsome. I won't let him quarrel with me." She pouted her painted lips.

"We're always in a row," Henric said, grimly. "Jahn's always been an example to the rest of us. Mother held his sanctity under our noses until we had to kick in self-defense."

Zack had waited patiently. He said again, "Jahn ought to marry if he likes."

"But surely—!" Chanson cried. "Surely not when he's promised Mother Ibsell to stay single! Zack, you can't possibly think it right for him to have everything? Henric has a feeling for this place as coming from his father. You can't possibly think it fair for every acre to be taken from you and him?"

Bard Lipscomb stared at Chanson. In his day women had attended to their own business, and if through misfortune they had a man's work to do, they did it simply and decently, they didn't curl their eyelashes back in a sweet squinch and bring up love-affairs against a man's sense. He said, suddenly, "Miss Chanson, I keep wondering what your interest in this is? A man might think Henric didn't feed you properly."

For an instant her cheeks flamed with anger; then she laughed. "Or didn't keep me properly in hand, eh?" She laughed again, softly, and crumpled her napkin between her long nervous fingers. "No. The truth is, I hate land. Dirt. Not for itself do I want this place. But I love money, power. I know too well what it is to pinch . . . to keep up appearances on nothing. I had to bow to a rich aunt for my clothes. Cast-off clothes. I know too much. And all because," she said, slowly, and lifted her eyes frankly—"all because my father was an honorable fool. He could have had what was needed if he'd been sensible. I intend that Henric shall be sensible even though there's no need for it. Besides," she caught herself up, "it's not right. Henric has a feeling for this land and a right to some of it."

Zack said, "It's not that Mother gave it all to Jahn. It's the way she did it. Telling us we were nothing to her because we hadn't stayed here when there was nothing here for us."

Rachel Ibsell stared at him somberly. "Yes," she said, "and I remember an evening when I went to your rooms at the university when you were boys. You and Henric had rugs on the floor and pictures on the wall and books. Your beds were polished and shiny. And me and Jahn had to ride home that night, ten miles in a jolting wagon, and sleep on corn-shuck mattresses. We had to do that so you'd have money for your books and pictures. I said then I'd make it up to Jahn some day. He didn't have what you all had. I don't guess he would have had it if it come, like yours did, at the price of leaving me to do without."

"He didn't want what we had at any price," Henric said, precisely.

"It's true," Jahn returned after a moment, slowly. He glanced at Sue Hart's still, pale face. "I wanted to stay on the place, in the dirt and the furrows. I liked that . . . that wet, clean smell and the feel of it." Sue Hart looked up at him suddenly, and he flushed a little and picked up his fork.

"But that was later. At first, when you went, I wanted to go, too. But somebody had to stay with her. You were old enough to make up your minds and go where you wanted— and smart enough," he said, with a slow bitterness, "to palaver her into letting you and paying your way. But I had to stay with her and pay my own way and yours, too. And then, later, when she could spare me, I was too old and too ignorant to be in school. I was ashamed, and I loved it here then and knew I loved it. The dirt, the thing that's first and makes all the rest. But I wanted schooling, too. It's no fun to a man when he gets old enough to know and it's too late. It's no fun to him to remember his father was a gentleman and learned, and to pick up his books and not be able to know what he knew. That's a shame to a man! I thought if I'd been able to have the chance you all had—but there's no use talking. Here I was plowing, going dirty, peddling in town like any no-account, going up to back doors when my father had set in the parlor. . . ."

Sue Hart's eyes were heavy with pity and love. Impulsively she touched his hand on the tablecloth beside her.

"What do you care?" she cried, speaking to him alone. "You're bigger than men that did go to school."

Rachel Ibsell's black eyes pounced hotly on that caress. "What's that?" she called down the length of the table to them. "What are you saying?"

The girl lifted her tender face. "I said he's bigger than men that did go to school." Her gaze faltered, she swallowed, and said, foolishly, "He . . . talks like a poet. . . ."

Rachel's eyes were still, the pupils pinched to narrow points of white-hot hatred. She did not speak for a long minute. "Poets, to my mind, miss, ain't much account to nobody." The harsh, strong voice moved hoarsely through the syllables.

Sue Hart rallied with whitening cheeks, and it was as if, suddenly, she had risen from the table and stood above Rachel Ibsell, beautifully and consciously superior. "Solomon and David were poets," she said, deliberately giving to her voice the cold primness of the teacher. "You think they were of some account."

"So they were." Rachel's mouth was thin and stiff. She laughed cruelly. "You put me in mind of your daddy, Miss Hart. He used to come around the stores in town after your mammy was dead and he'd left you in the orphan home to be raised, and he'd stand around the stores all day, quoting poetry. I guess he thought that was more than earning a living, and maybe it is." She saw the girl wince, and felt herself hot all over with mean triumph. "Maybe it is, maybe it is," she said over again, savoring the words.

Suddenly, a strange wind went over her, down her spine, and she saw Jahn looking at her, staring hard, his face blank and stunned, with contempt and hatred in his eyes where the iris flooded with a queer, veinous green. She stared at him, with her face sagging and her shoulders cringing. "Maybe it is," she repeated, slowly and without breath. She looked down at her plate then, and tried to make herself laugh. "You'll have to excuse me, Miss Hart," she heard herself. "I say what I don't mean; my tongue is sharper than I mean. . . ." She had no breath in her, no strength.

VII

June had come to Red Valley, bringing the annual joy of Decoration Day with all-day-singing and dinner-on-the-ground. Nazareth church-house rocked to music. The cemetery, cleared the day before of its brambles and sweet now with flowers and wreaths, sang with the buzz of living voices. There was a constant coming and going of cars, arrival, departure. Relatives of the buried had come from as far as Texas and Arkansas to stand a minute above the graves, to sing with the living, and to renew in some wise the half-lost memories of their childhood in Red Valley. Young couples strolled back and forth under the arching branches of the dark pines, and went down the steep hill to the rock spring. In the corner of the cemetery, next to the Ibsell fields, wagons stood filled with quilts and boxes of food. Horses and mules, tethered to the trees, switched their tails and lifted their hooves in a slow, patient laziness. Women flashed and men drolled. Summer was on the people and on the land and lifted the furrows richly.

Long Jim Chambers sat on his grandmother's tombstone, spitting judiciously from time to time through the split hairs of his waxed brown mustache, and watched Rachel Ibsell mount the steps to the church-house and disappear through the wide wooden doors. He fingered his round, dark chin, took snuff, and coughed fiercely. "I'd not hev it said," he told Mose Thurston, "as I spoke hit, but they do say as how Henric en James has quit speakin' to Jahn when they meet."

"I reckon!" Mose Thurston was wise with gossip. "They say as how Jahn told Henric he got the univ's'ty degree en the loan office out'n the land en' *he* got the third grade en the land itself. Joe Rosenbens he war a saying in his store Sat'dy night how it war all on account of Mis' Ibsell deedin' away her land like she done."

"Wel-l," said Long Jim, and nodded gravely, "hit could a been done a kinder way. She could a made hit seem like Jahn'd bought hit of her . . . or some 'at kind. I'm s'prised Mis' Ibsell ain't no smarter when hit come to family doings. She al'ays could beat ary man in the community when hit come to makin' en savin', but let hit be a matter of feelings, now, en she'll go wrong every single time! Hit do seem like she feels so hard herself, she ain't got mind left to see how another mought be feeling."

Mose Thurston rolled a quid of tobacco in one jaw with such freedom that small, livid lines of juiciness worked themselves among the harder, dryer lines of his chin. "If'n you ast me, she ain't no head fer her chil'ern atall. Thet James he's a born worrier en complainer, en Henric, he's so quick he shouldn't handle ary note of mine, not if'n my life depended on hit. Zack, he's well enough, but he ain't quite right, somehow. But James en Henric, them's too bad uns! They say James has got him a town womern over there on his place, a town bitch, falutin' her eround in front of his own pore wife without'n no more shame than a heathern nigger, en all the time he's a going to church en prayin' big sich times as he ain't kickin' pore Miss Fanny in the short ribs. I reckon Henric mought be some better'n thet, seein' his prissy ways, like some kind of morphodite or something, he's so girlish-nice, but I wouldn't trust him none, neither."

"Henric en his womern war up to see Mis' Ibsell," said Long Jim. "'Twar Friday. I seen 'em when I come up fum the bottom land whar me en Jahn'd been fixin' the bridge over Sand Caves. They war a sittin' on the front porch as grand as a buterler. I kain't see what ails Mis' Ibsell to be tuck in like that. I hearn her say hit myself, 'A crowin' hen en a whistlin' girl they come to no good end,' but thet Miss Chancie she strides eround town a-whistlin' big as ary man. Looks like Mis' Ibsell could see she ain't no good. . . ." He chewed slowly, with averted, brooding eyes. "Miss Martha she warn't there," he added, "en Jahn he went past out to the quarter where they're puttin' up them new nigger shacks."

"They're a right cuorious folk," Mose remarked, taking out his knife and going to sit beside some nameless wooden tombhead. "Jest like onto the rest of us, yet smarter in ways. Even Jahn he knows things. Fum his pappy's books like as not. Thet war a smart man, Jim, 'way head of his time. But Jahn he keeps hangin' back. No tractors, no 'lectric lights, no nothing! They say Mis' Ibsell had a fit when Miss Martha bought a radio, en I hearn it said Jahn told Joe Rosenbens he wouldn't hev the best car in the state fer his-self, not if'n you give it to him. Thet's the old lady's teaching now, but hit do seem funny. Don't look like she'd feel thet way, hardly."

Long Jim spat hugely. "Oh, I reckon hit's kinder like a religion with 'em. They're awful pious folk in their way, though not good. Like Abraham en sich. Gentile-Jew like, furren they seem to me. And then, why, they're the same as us, only different. . . ."

"Ast me, they're crazy!" Mose Thurston spaced his words, grunting out a phrase with a slice of grave-marker. "Look how Mis' Ibsell takes on erbout Jahn en thet Hart girl. Like some sin, hit is, en yet she's a good womern—I never knew a better."

Long Jim said, "Yander they go, Jahn en thet girl, off there in the grove." He grunted. "Reckon they're going down to the spring, but they do seem old fer thet foolishness."

Mose jerked his head up and stared with dazzled eyes. "Oh, Miss Hart she ain't more'n a kid, though Jahn he's pushing thirty en a good bit." He grinned between his mustaches sentimentally. "Ain't she a little thing over agin him? His shoulders, they look big as a barn door, don't they?"

Long Jim raised himself gravely, and spat with a faint disgust. "Sound like a yearlin' boy, Mose. . . . Come on, reckon we better go in if'n we want a seat. Things is perty full up today."

Mose followed him meekly. On the church-house steps they paused, solemnly spitting out snuff and tobacco cud.

"Mis' Ibsell she went in alone," Long Jim said. "Fust time I ever seen her without'n Jahn at public meeting."

"Oh, she's a unhappy womern, I'm shore!" Mose cried, and went eagerly ahead of his friend through the doors.

VIII

Rachel Ibsell sat alone in her pew, the blank stretch of board empty on either side. Neighbor women paused to speak to her, making as if to sit down, but her black eyes passed rudely and angrily over their faces. They faltered, licked their humble lips, and moved on to sit elsewhere. "Mis' Ibsell she's worriting herself," they told one another, and glanced back at her dark face. "Jahn he's got the Hart girl with 'im today," they said.

She sat bolt upright, as if she did not hear them, with her hands folded on her black-satin lap. Yet, with every step in the aisle behind her, she felt an almost irrisistible impulse to turn around and see with her own eyes the entrance of Sue Hart with her son. "I must not look back," she kept saying to herself. Every eye in the building, she thought, was upon her, greedily and gleefully. She looked straight ahead, with her strained gaze fastened upon her brother, Zackeriah Gurney, where he sat praying in the pulpit, with the choir behind him. She heard a woman in the pew in front of her tell another: "The young ones, 'specially them fum town, they wanted to put in an organ fer today. Pity folks kain't know Sacred Harp singin' don't go with no organ." The other woman said: "Yeah, en kain't know we ain't never had no organ here en never will long's Brother Gurney's here to preach gospel to us." The words passed strangely over Rachel's head; she heard them, yet seemed not to hear them.

The singing-master rose from the front row of the choir and came forward to speak to Zie Gurney. A young boy in new overalls and a white shirt front went up and down the middle aisle, handing out the Sacred Harp hymnals. She looked at him, and her mind had another picture in it, seeing Jahn as he had been years ago when he was this boy's age. He used to sit with her at night after the work was done; she would put little Martha to bed and Jahn would sit with her by the fire. She would read from the Bible and his face would be quiet and listening. He would say, "I guess old Zukey must be going to calve tonight, I put her down some extra hay to lie on." He was company for her; she was not alone then; she could forget the husband that died in Cuba and the life that had failed her. The overalled boy sat down in the back of the church, out of her sight. She watched the singing-master leaf his hymnal, still talking to Elder Gurney in a low voice.

Martha, with Billy Nelson's long legs coming behind her, passed Rachel and sat down two pews ahead. Rachel saw the faces turn to stare at Martha, and heard a buzz of renewed conversation rise from the slit Saxon mouths. "Mis' Ibsell's girl en her beau fum town," they said. "A likely couple, hain't they?" She saw the light filtering through the high windows in long shadowy streams. Billy Nelson, with his face turned so that Rachel could see, was laughing without sound, with an immense, crinkle-eyed relish. Rachel looked at him bitterly, thinking that he was here, but none of her sons. Her sons were all somewhere else with their women, too fashionable and too smart for Nazareth church. Henric and James were sitting together on the left side of the church, but she thought, "My sons are out there, walking around the churchyard, making a scandal by not coming in." She closed her eyes suddenly, and bent forward as Zackeriah Gurney rose to read the lines of the first hymn.

His voice cried above her head, strong and vibrant, nasal with the sing-song power of his great nostrils:

> "What wondrous love is this,
> O my soul! O my soul!
> What wondrous love is this
> O my soul!
> What wondrous love is this
> That caused the Lord of bliss
> To bear the dreadful curse
> For my soul, for my soul,
> To bear the dreadful curse
> For my soul!"

The singing-master shouted aloud, "All at once, brethern!" and the choir rose together, swiftly and boundingly. The busy fans in the women's fingers grew still and motionless. A man left the building, going on tiptoe down the aisle, frowning above the wide mouth of his screaming baby. A long, slow silence stretched itself over the waiting pews. The mouths of the choir hung open, in readiness, awaiting the first sweep of the singing-master's lifted hand.

In the silence, Rachel Ibsell could hear her heart beating. She leaned her head over between her hands and rested on the back of the bench in front of her. Her lips moved without sound, without words, even, praying helplessly until they were stilled by the slow wailing cry of the choir singing the major scale in soft, plangent minors:

"Mi . . . fa . . . sol . . . la . . . fa . . . sol . . . la. . . ."

[57]

The singing-master brought his arm down to his side. The choir waited, without moving, their hands quiet on the opened pages of the hymnals. The professor's hand swept up again. Lean and saddle-dark, he poised before them. His cheeks, folded precisely in the center, moved and the sorrowful mustache covering his lips swept upward as his mouth opened. The song burst from the choir's lips and over the congregation, shivering sweetly and dreadfully on Rachel Ibsell's ears:

> "What wondrous love is this,
> O my soul! O my soul!
> What wondrous love is this . . . "

A man's voice rearing up in abrupt, riotous strength from the crowd on the hard pews strengthened the bass notes. "O my soul! O my soul!" they sang, and to Rachel Ibsell the strong, hot cry, dull with Christian sorrow and quick with the lilt of angelic joy, resounded above and over itself. A man and a woman sitting together mingled their notes to form a bastard tenor. A lone woman lifted a sweet, plaintive treble. The volume of the song swelled, the singing-master beat time. Rachel Ibsell heard the voices march with a precise and lovely melody, shouting the poetry of God's love. Her closed eyes watched Jehovah recede in His wrath and His righteousness and fade like unreality itself before the tender face of His Son. She saw that pale, longing face bend over them all, she felt His hands touch her heart, and she bent lower and lower before Him, sparing herself nothing in the wonder of His pity, her bosom straining with desire to bow more humbly yet and to suffer her own annihilation for His sake.

But, slowly, around her the voices moved into silence, the last, lonesome notes of treble calling thinly, weirdly from the land her heart had entered. She sat up slowly and looked vaguely about. Henric and James sat across from her, leaning their foreheads on their arms, and Martha bent close to Billy Nelson. The choir sat down. Fans began to move under the chins of the women. Rachel Ibsell looked at them without care or feeling. Her face was smooth. The finger of the music had touched her muscles to quiet. Between the spaces of her times, the moment to come and the moment gone, she sat without anxiety or plot, alone without loneliness in a somber peace.

Zackeriah Gurney rose again.

> "Why should the saints be filled with dread,
>   Or yield their joys to slavish fear?
> Heaven can't be filled, which holds the Head,
>   Till every member's present there."

Rachel got up swiftly and went down the aisle and out of the church. On the steps she met Bard Lipscomb going in. "Well, Rachel, and I see you're happy now," he said quietly.

He stood beside her for a moment, with his eyes on her face. "You remind me," he said, "of a thing I read somewhere: 'Over them, time and experience will pass, blowing as a wind from the garments of the Lord, and though their hair should wave in that wind, their cheeks feel its sting, and the rafters of their houses shake under its impact, they will ask no single question nor open their mouths to the taste of its wisdom because of the fable that whispers in their breasts. . . . '" He smiled suddenly, and lifted his hands in a deprecative gesture.

She said, without knowing why she spoke at all, "God has been good to me today and me unworthy as I am." She did not look at him, nor was she speaking aloud except to herself.

From the church, the mournful, questing music lifted slowly and swept in mighty chords through the open windows and out into the churchyard where the young men and women were gathered in listening quiet, and on through the surrounding pine woods to Black River's cliffs, half a mile distant, where the rocks caught and flung back an echo at once feeble and spirited.

Rachel went down the steps without looking for Jahn, and

on through the crowds about the door. Behind her, the song dwindled. She went home across the fields alone.

IX

Her son saw her go and could not rest in the echoes of music. The mournful and the questing irked in him. He leaned more heavily against the rough trunk of the water oak behind him, and touched Sue Hart's hair for a furtive second. "It's queer," he said, vaguely, "how one music passes into another kind."

She looked up at him swiftly, her face quick and vivid in response and wonder. She smiled. "Sometimes I think I'll never know you."

But he was staring at the grave of his grandfather, a grave that was empty, for Aslak the sailor lay beneath an apple tree near Albemarle Sound; and from the grave he glanced across the churchyard beyond the pine grove to the dark figure dwindling in the fields. He remade a scene in his mind, seeing his mother, tall and dark in the moonlight, her feet passing swiftly over the pasture grass, hearing her voice, "All I own, the land, if you'll never leave me. . . ."

When he looked at his sweetheart again, sunlight sifting through the branches of the trees made a shadow over her face. He knew how it would be if he leaned against her, his breast hard on the softness of hers and his mouth on her mouth and the scent of her hair spreading over his nostrils. "I'm like a fool," he said, "caught between the here and the then."

He looked at his grandfather's grave and gestured slowly. "I think of that old man a lot of times. He married when he was old, a young woman that got him into debt. So he took my father and all he had and left his country in a ship of his own. And just when he got off the coast of the Carolinas his ship went down and he was drowned. He was different from

[60]

me; he spoke a different language. Kate told me when I was little he came from a 'far, northern country.' I got a kick out of hearing it, and when I said what country, Kate told me, 'Norway.' She showed it to me in the geography so I'd believe there was such a place. . . . But I never have believed in it," he said, softly, and laughed a little to himself.

"A far, northern country don't have a name. . . . I think how different my grandfather was from me, and how strange and sad his life must have been. And I'd like," he said, with his voice coming out stronger, "I'd like to carry on his life for him. Kate hasn't any children, nor Henric, either. I'm the only one to come after him, that's how it seems to me."

Sue Hart was not looking at him now; her eyes watched the women coming from the church-house with great boxes of food in their arms. "What do you mean?" she said. "You're not the only one."

He said, roughly and suddenly: "What are we waiting for? Fooling our time away!"

"It's not me you love. You wouldn't love me if you thought your mother would live forever."

The clear, sweet sound of hammers striking on nails rang from the pine grove where three boys had begun to raise the trestles to spread the day's dinner on. A smell of hot pine in the sunlight flooded against Jahn's nostrils. He waited, counting the strokes of the hammers.

"It'd be the same if she could live forever," he said then. "She'll always hate me."

One of the trestles was up now and fixed in its place with short boards laid crosswise on it. A tall woman with a brown, splotched face whipped a white tablecloth over it.

"It's not you she hates; it's an idea she's got in her mind." He stopped, and told her after a minute, "It'll be all right when she sees I won't forget her." He was close to her, bending to watch the pale, greenish shadows waver across her eyelids. He whispered, "I won't ever stop loving you."

She frowned, and smiled, and frowned again, lost in a dream that stopped her thinking, reluctant and half-frightened, yet glad, too.

"I can't go to live in her house."

He drew back. She said immediately, in a low, swift voice of timidity, "You could build another house—there, close to hers?"

"You'll get along when you know each other."

She looked at him. "Jahn—she'll never like me."

"She'd like you less if I left her to live in another house with you."

His face was turned away now, and his mouth hard with pain and denial. She gazed at him helplessly. She was, she knew, like a picture in his mind that he couldn't forget—a bright, swift thing that he must touch and call his own and use to serve his blood. But his mother was real to him, his heart was sunk in her. Only his eyes and his flesh wanted Sue Hart. A slow, wincing anger went through her with the wish to hurt Rachel Ibsell. "Very well," she said. suddenly. "I'll go there, then." Her lips pressed together in a prim and almost vengeful astringency.

He looked at her wonderingly, and she thought that a shadow crossed his eyes, of disbelief and fear.

"You're surprised. Maybe you didn't want me to say I would."

He moved away from the tree and stood up straight, with his feet apart, and his hands in his pockets. His eyes brooded on hers. "Yes," he said, "I wanted you to say you would."

She continued, recklessly, "But now you're afraid."

He smiled suddenly. "Maybe. She'll be hurt . . . but it's best for her in the long run."

She said, "You love her in a way you'll never love me."

He continued to smile. "It's different," he said, and touched her hand, drawing her toward the food-covered trestles in the grove.

Rachel Ibsell sat in her own room with the Bible on her lap, and heard around her the small, living sounds of a farm-yard, the soft, throaty call of hens scratching in new clover, and from further off the thick bawl of young calves and the high neigh of mules being turned from their stalls to the water. The sunlight moved on the grass outside her window, and went beyond the high marigolds at the yard fence and out into the land, a still coolness coming in its place and following after it. She watched and listened without thought.

All the angers and terrors of the past months were out of her, and she remembered them distantly, as one remembers the acts of a stranger. No face nor word nor gesture passed through her mind. She was like one whose awareness is behind him; there, yet not impinging; close, yet not real. The presence of her God had come on her in the way that it comes on old peasant women, with peace and forgetfulness; and going, it had left a mindless sensuousness like a still jelly on which such things as sunlight and sound of animals made a sweet impression. She did not move all afternoon except to stroke the rich leather binding of her Bible with slow, pleasurable fingers.

Yet, at evening, when she heard the lowing of the bull in the pasture and the swift, ringing thump of the horses' hooves passing up the dark lane, she got up, with fear shivering through her on the instant of her moving. She stood bemused and lost in the shadows of the room, gazing hard at the great darkness of her bed in one corner. "What is it?" she thought. "What is it?" Her voice was sharp in her skull. She listened a moment to it, thinking the sound was in the room; and then, turning, she laid the Bible on the window ledge. She laid it down carefully, watching to see that it did not fall off onto the floor. When she turned around again the room seemed darker.

She moved across it slowly, feeling the coarse grain of the gray matting through the thin soles of her Sunday shoes, and waited at the mantel with a match in her hand, ready to strike a light to the lamp. She still did not think anything; her mind was like ectoplasm forming its own shapes, willy-nilly, without meaning or derivation. She felt her breath coming out gray and formless in front of her face. Her finger nail pushed weakly at the red sulphur end of the match.

Then, while her breath was still flowing out of her mouth like vapor, she heard Jahn in the hall. Her thumb nail came down swiftly on the match head, the little light sprang up, and she turned to the lamp behind her. When she took the chimney off, she counted, without knowing she did it, the small blue flowers raised on the white glass.

His head appeared at the door, and she saw it thick and congested and bodiless, as if he could not show her anything but his face. The night wind came in at the door behind him and blew the flame of the lamp up and down, up and down. She said, "You're early."

His head nodded slowly; moving, she thought, the darkness behind it.

She put her hands in back of her, and moved up, standing with her heels straight against the dog-headed andiron on one side of the fireplace. Her hands were cold, and she moved them in front of her, suddenly, rubbing the fingers together. A hot pulse of excitement beat in the middle of her stomach, but the rest of her body was cold and quiet.

She swallowed slowly. "I know it. You're going to marry." She heard her voice, still, a little faint, and listened to its echoes. "You're going to marry." She said, "You told me you'd not do that."

He came into the room now, all of him. His cheeks were mottled crimson and his mouth strangely hard. "I never promised you that." His voice was firm, settled, the thing done for in his own mind. "I promised I'd not leave you."

She did not feel anything; her hands were cold.

"Yet you knew what I meant when you promised. And now—now you know how it'll be. I've never been able to get on with another woman or stand one in my house. It was that way when I married your father. Kate's ways were not mine. And I know," she added, humbly, "that I'm quick to anger and wicked in my angers, but to be so is the way of my people. . . ." She wet her lips. "The girl," she said, with difficulty, "has a right to her own home, free from me." She waited a moment, seeing how beautiful and dear he was. And then her voice hardened. "I'll tell you fair: I dislike the girl; she's not my sort."

Stubbornly he repeated, "I promised I'd not leave you and I won't."

It was his conscience speaking, she knew, and in her love for him she found a way to make him come right with his conscience, and a way to tempt him. She said, "Give me back my land, then, and go with her."

The words were bitter, her tone was bitter, but she had not meant it so. When he looked at her as if she were wild, and cried, "My God! am I a fool, then? I had a right to the land and I've got a right to Sue!" she bowed her head. "Yes," she whispered. "A right." She went to her chair, picked up the Bible, and sat down.

She knew how it was. You were born onto the earth, and it fed you and clothed you and gave you joy; and somehow as the years went along, you saw that it was God in His strength and His pleasure, and you gave your soul to possess Him. She sat staring at the darkened window panes, and on her lap the Bible lay open at Jeremiah's great, raving book:

For who hath stood in the counsel of the Lord, and hath perceived and heard his word? who hath marked his word and heard it?

PART TWO

I

IN THESE DAYS, A YEAR AFTER JAHN'S MARRIAGE, RACHEL Ibsell was a woman living on hatred and consumed by it as iron is eaten away by rust. She rose in the morning and dressed herself to the silent, hideous rhythm of hate, she walked with jealous despair all day, and at night she lay awake in a bed of bitterness. Minute by minute, she asked herself, "What can I do? What can I do?" and then she cried, "O Lord, show me a way, show me what to do!" And day by day she read in her Bible, searching for a sign, listening for a secret word from the Lord God of Israel.

Behold a whirlwind of the Lord is gone forth in fury, even a grievous whirlwind: it shall fall grievously upon the heads of the wicked.

Alone in her room, Sue Ibsell listened, lowering the paperbound novel to her lap, shifting her heavy body to a more comfortable position, forming the words silently with her lips. The sounds echoed in her brain: "upon the heads of the wicked. . . ."

She turned her face to the window through which she could see a square of green grass, dusty and hot in the late June sun, and the flaming red of a flowering pomegranate tree. The child in her womb stirred, sending electrical shivers of pain up her spine. The brown wires of the window screen moved before her eyes, ridged and tilted backward, and for a moment she was conscious of nothing except the desperate tension of her leg muscles pushing her feet against the floor. She relaxed suddenly, and moved her body again, almost as if its clumsy greatness was a thing apart from herself and had to be handled carefully because it was strange.

She was, she felt, standing away to look at herself, and a tinge of hysteria crept across her awareness of the feeling. If she kept her eyes open, if she looked straight ahead at one place, she would presently see that young girl with slim, virginal hips watching this ugly, swollen woman in the chair. She would see her own eyes looking at what she was now, she would feel the thin feet in high-heeled slippers comparing themselves with the thick ankles in the soleless easy shoes. . . . And even the hair, she thought suddenly, even the bright, shining hair would notice the dull, dry hair on this woman, herself—but not herself. . . . She turned her eyes swiftly, fearfully, from the window, and fixed them on the door. "Not myself," something in her said softly and vehemently.

Rachel Ibsell's voice had hushed; there was no sound from the next room. What could that old woman be up to now, what was she turning over and over in her mind? The empty house spread out around Sue, waiting. Jahn was gone to town, Martha was with Zack in Choctaw and would not be home until the next day, nobody was here except herself and Rachel Ibsell. Tense, as she had learned to hold herself during her mother-in-law's silences, Sue picked up the novel and pretended to read; and not aware that Rachel had slipped on noiseless feet to the back door and stood looking down at her bent head, she remained, eyes on the printed page, ears listening for sounds from the next room.

Standing there in the doorway, Rachel Ibsell cried to herself, "God, God, must I bear this? what have I done to have this pasty-faced thing in my house, under my nose, laughing while she steals my son further and further from me? God,

[67]

must I see him forget me?" Mad with jealous pain, she answered herself; "No, no! I'll not have it, I'll not bear it!" She started forward on stumbling feet, her eyes blind with hatred. "Ah, God, I'll keep silent no longer. I'll drag her in the dust, trample on her!" She heard her voice, hoarse and choked with rage. "Sue Hart!" She saw Sue's startled face jerk quickly to her. "Get up from here. You hear me! Work to be done and you sit stuffing your brain with trash. Never did I think to see the day Jahn 'u'd insult me with a thing that sat reading immoral messes and let the work go undone!"

"But—!" Sue attempted to compose her fear. "Black Callie's doing the mending, Mother Ibsell, I'm just resting a minute."

"Resting! Aye, resting while a nigger wench earns your bread for you, that's it!"

"Mother—" Abruptly Sue's voice shrilled and jerked, her eyes suffused. "Mrs. Ibsell. . . ." The child turned in her womb, stirring as if it felt its mother's pain. She shivered, and with a sudden flowing in of whimpering anguish, closed her eyes, crying to herself in a lassitude of weariness, "Oh, she hates me, hates me! And I'm tired, so tired and heavy. . . ." Resting a moment longer in this dreadful languor, and weeping softly without sound, she said, "You know how I feel now. . . ."

"Ah, and I know, do I? Pitying yourself! I know I carried five children and I've yet to whine and complain of the load. But I was a poor woman and had to work or starve, while you've feathered your nest, Miss, and can sit in idleness with your sins for an excuse!"

Sue sat up suddenly, anger beginning to sting in her. "I wasn't so careful when I feathered my nest as I should have been—!" she cried bitterly, and then shut her lips firmly.

"Or you'd 'a' waited till the nest was empty! I knew it. You wouldn't have looked at Jahn while he was a poor boy, helping his mammy, but once the land was his, you took him quick enough! And set yourself to have a nasty, sniveling brat so you'll be in line for a slice of it! I know! I should have kept my land and my son to myself; that's where I was a fool!"

After a moment Sue said, in a hard, tight voice, "You dare to talk to me like that, Rachel Ibsell! About your own grandchild! You'll pay for this, even *your* God ——"

"Dare!" She stepped forward, and stood over Sue, her features working convulsively. "You and your pretty harlot's ways talking to me about God Almighty! You and your Armenian sect! The Harts never saw the Light in their lives, and you sit there ——"

"Oh God, have mercy!" Sue strangled the cry with clenched teeth, pulling herself from the chair, and walking backward, her gaze fixed on that old woman who followed her, steadily, ominously, triumphantly. Her shoulders struck the screen door; she pushed it open, and began to run, screaming over her shoulder, "You sinful old woman!" She ran on and on, pressing her arms tight beneath the jolting weight of her swollen belly, sobbing aloud shrilly and hoarsely. Then, at once, she found herself in the barn lot, her body pushing mechanically through the door of an empty cow stall where the hay was clean and sweet.

She stood a moment, listening, frightened at what might be coming after her, more frightened by the streak of lightning-like pain that shot from her groin to her heart. She sank down onto the hay, crying bitterly and shaking with terror, a terror that rose out of her pain and increased itself as it rose. "Jahn! Jahn!" she cried without sound, and felt, on the instant, a tearing, pushing sweetness pervade her flesh while a livid burning came and went rapidly in her mind.

Bluebottles buzzed about the stall, swarms of black gnats wavered about her tumbled hair. Outside, the shadows lengthened, the heat lessened. The Negro men on the place drove the cows into the lot and milked them there, away from the sticky closeness of the stalls. She lay without sound now, terrified of them, ashamed of all she was and of all that had happened to her. The sound of milk streaming against the sides of tin pails grew loud and confused in her ears, rings of heat passed across her staring eyeballs. The Negroes left the lot and took the milk to the separator in the lane shed. For a long time she heard them there, then there was no more noise around her except the slow, whining buzz of the gnats. She lay upon her side, her head twisted awry beneath one upflung arm, the other pressed in a fist into her groin; and momentarily, she shuddered, her legs tensed rigidly and tossed until the hovering gnats rose in startled swarms.

II

Within the house, Rachel Ibsell took up the darning-basket, sewed for a minute and pricked her finger, knocking the basket and the scissors from her lap. Muttering, she bent to gather the scattered socks and stockings. Her hands groped on the floor, she stared blindly at the pattern in the carpet, she forgot what she was doing. Presently, leaving the basket upturned, she rose and began to walk up and down, up and down, with her head bent and her hands clasped behind across her buttocks. She talked to herself as she went to and fro, muttering in time to the rise and fall of her feet: "I but spoke the truth. The nicey-nice fool no more cares for him than I do for Black Fanny. Not so much, for Fanny's been with me a long time. Fool that I was to think I'd keep him by me! And now she gets herself with child. I know these town women, too fine for bearing. . . ."

Her eyes turned to the window as she passed it, and she saw that the sun was nearly down. "He'll be in from Choctaw afore long," she said uneasily, lowering the sash a trifle and beginning again her restless pacing. "It's none of my fault if the fool wants to let him find her out'n the house. I never asked her here in the first place; she's no concern of mine!" she said, loudly and defiantly. "Can I make her come in? Calling me a wicked old woman! We'll see who's wicked. . . ."

She went to the window again. The west was livid with purple, the air cool and misty with dusk. "He'll be here in a few minutes," she muttered again, fearfully, listening for the sound of the horses' hooves. "Henric told me how it'd be, him gone all day and her doing as she pleases, scorning me day and night. Her taking my house, trading on my love for Jahn, thinking I'll hold off on his account. All without a word, just the look and the air! Words 'u'd be easier to answer. . . . Miss Chancie she told me; she knows how it'd be to have your boy took from you without a by-your-leave. . . ."

Abruptly she hushed and stood listening, holding her breath. "Is that him?" she said. "Is that him talking to the horses out there?" The creak of the windlass on the well answered her. "Where is Sue?" she thought in swift panic. "The fool, staying out till all hours!" She heard Jahn step up on the back porch, and she went toward him swiftly, muttering as she went, "I'll tell him: 'sinful old woman'!"

The kitchen door opened, shrieking dully on its hinges and banged shut. "Why's the lamp not lit?" Jahn called. He stumbled in the darkness, dropped his bundles on the work-table, and moved across the room in search of a lamp.

"It's behind you," his mother said. "On the shelf."

He turned, fumbling in his pockets for matches, and peered through the gloom at her tall figure. "Where's Sue?" he asked, suddenly.

"I don't know and I don't care!" she answered, loudly. "Calling me sinful and wicked!"

Jahn's hand, groping for the lamp, was arrested in midair. He was silent, and Rachel cried out, striving against him.

"I'm sick and tired of being nothing in my own house! I told you not to bring her here. I said give me back my land and go with her, but you wouldn't, you had to take the land and then put that woman over me; you had to have your woman even if you did cheat your mammy out of her home. You didn't care, so you had your way! Her making my days a torment to me! I'm done, I tell you; I'll not have any more of it!"

"What else did you say to her?" he asked, with a dreadful quietness.

"I told her what she is, lazy, good-for-nothing, whimpering around to get the land for herself, that's what I told her!"

Jahn had not moved, but she stepped back suddenly, full of a feeling that he might strike her. "It's every word true," she said, dully, mechanically.

Still he said nothing, and she gathered courage. "I tell you it's true. But you're such a fool you won't believe your own mother!"

"No," he said, and his voice was strange, half-pleading, half-stiff, like the voice of a man whose unbending anger hurts him. "I know Henric's lies and James' lies even when you repeat 'em, I know their lies and Chanson's nasty little tales. You know why they've got so much to say, yet you listen to them like a fool. Between their jealousy and greed and your jealousy—" He stopped himself. "I want no more of it, bickering and toting tales," he said, angrily.

"You want no more of anybody that tries to do you good. I'd better have kept my land to myself and set you adrift like the rest!"

"Set 'em adrift!" he cried with sudden passion. "You sent 'em to school, you set 'em up in business! It's more than you ever did for me, and I turned over the best years of my life to you. You could see that once, but now you turn on me like — What do you think you're going to do, live forever? When I try to have a home for myself against the day when you'll be gone—!" He caught his breath, and spoke in a quieter tone. "I reckon you are afraid I'll get something out of life besides one eternal grind of sweat and dirt!"

The mother persisted jealously. "She's never done one thing to earn her salt since you brought her here. Sitting and reading!" Her eyes narrowed suddenly. "She never married you for nothing except to get what I give you."

"That's a lie," he said, shortly. "And if it was true, you're not the one to talk. You say yourself you married my daddy for nothing but a home for James Forrest."

She stood still in the darkness, staring without sight at the vague blur of his face, cut to the heart by this accusation which was so true and which her conscience had so often made against itself.

"Where is she?" he cried at her, suddenly. "What have you done?"

She started, and looked at him, as from a long way off. "James told me what I married your father for, too," she said, and it was as if she had not heard him.

He pushed past her, into the dark dining-room, and she heard his hurrying steps going through the house. She heard him call, "Sue! Sue!" She heard him coming back. She turned around and took the one step upward from the level of the kitchen to the dining-room, and saw the white expanse of his shirt running toward her from the bedroom door. She spoke slowly, without haste and without interest. "She went toward the lot."

"The lot!"

He ran past her, through the outer door onto the porch and was gone. Without moving, she waited in the darkness, listening, with a queer, soft pity for him coming to work in her breast. She was very tired, she stood limply, feeling the vague coolness of the unlighted room wash over her. When, after a minute, she moved, she walked slowly, without straightening herself, toward her own room. She shut the door behind her and sat in the center of the room in the darkness. Her mind was tired; she thought with detachment of matters unconcerned with all that had just happened.

III

There were two cold, small stars hanging in the mauve-colored sky. He kept calling her, "Sue, Sue darling!" His heart was thumping against his ribs, cold sweat trickled down his neck and chest. The odor of honeysuckle blew against his nostrils. He went stumbling over gravel in the lane, calling again. "It's James and Henric and their greedy lies," he said, suddenly, out loud. His right side crashed into the garden fence; he hung there for a moment, hearing the rustling of hay in the lot under the cows' feet. He began to run again, crying, "Sue! Where are you?" His feet slid in the wet grass.

The ridges of the cows' backs were faintly dun-colored in the starlight. He thought, "The niggers have milked," hearing his thought speak above his frantic searching, and feeling, too, a faint anger that they had forgotten again to turn the cows into the night pasture. He went over the lot gate and landed on the scattered hay. The cows turned, imperturbably chewing, and even at that moment, he saw something funny, distant, and unreal in their moving jaws.

"Sue! Sue!" His voice came back at him, and then, behind the echoes, faint and strange, he heard her answering him. He ran on stiff, uncoordinated legs. She was a small black shadow on the gray-yellow straw. He bent down and had his arm under her head, cradling her, and he was still calling, "Sue! Sue!" Crying, she said, "I hurt so!"

He stood up with her and came out of the stable into the lot. The moonlight was new; it slanted across her face against his shoulder, and he stopped to look at her. "Where is it?" he said. "What hurts?" Her face was old and drawn and her body was stiff with pain, so that he was afraid of the weight of his arms on her. "Where is it?"

She said: "They came and milked. . . . I was scared. . . . Those Negro men and there wasn't anybody anywhere. . . ." She began to quiver against him, sobbing now. "She says I'm bad, don't take me back there, that house!"

He put his face down on her hair and fumbled the lot gate open. "Don't cry," he said. "Don't cry." He was walking toward the house with his cheek laid against her hair.

She said: "I won't go in that house. . . . Jahn!"

[74]

He felt the edge of a plank under his toe, stopped, and stepped carefully over it. The dew glimmered on the grass. He cried suddenly, "I've got to get the doctor!" and began to run with her, running and sucking in his breath through dry lungs.

The child was born that night, two months before its time. The doctor went and the nurse came. Jahn walked up and down near the bed, trembling and happy over the extraordinary existence of the blue-faced mite on the pillow. Sue wept with her face turned to the wall because the child was a girl. And Rachel Ibsell stood outside in the corridor, working her mouth to make her countenance belie the ridiculous, unreasonable pleasure she felt in her granddaughter.

"I was always a dauncy fool when it come to babies," she said to herself.

IV

Carefully, Henric set the telephone down. "Well!" he said to himself. "Well!" He stood staring through the hall door into the summer night with intent, thoughtful gaze. The light behind him fell fanwise over his veranda and out over the gladioli and nasturtiums in the yard, melting into the stronger radiance of the street lamps.

Henric had bought his house the year before his marriage, in the first flush of love and the first triumphant affluence of the brokerage business he owned with Zack. The house was like him, as Rachel Ibsell's house of good plain timber richly stuffed with hot-colored curtains and rugs, was like her. The finicking cupolas and the mock bay windows of 1890 ornamented the chocolate-brown surface of the outer walls. Inside, there was a long hall, one side of which was half-filled by a twisted staircase with angels carved on the balusters and covered over with gilded plaster.

He stepped out onto the porch, glanced up at the colored

panes in the fanlight over the door, and then looked again at the street lamps. Beyond them, over housetops built in the same period with his, the low domes and blunted spires of the university massed themselves on the moonlit sky, with, behind them, the English turrets of Marston's, the state insane asylum. A restless, intermittent murmur of traffic came indistinctly to his ears from the far-off main streets of town. He turned, gazed blankly at the red and green letters winking above the roof of Choctaw's First National Bank; and then, abruptly jerking his tie into place and straightening the cord of his dressing-gown, he hurried through the hall into Chanson's bedroom.

He went softly, full of an impulse to furtiveness, and sitting down on the bed beside her, he looked up at the reading-lamp over her head and put out his hand to touch the gold fringes of her negligée. She smiled vaguely, and went on reading. Clearing his throat, he announced in a loud voice, "Jahn has a baby, a girl." His head rocked on his long, thin neck.

Chanson dropped her magazine and gazed at him silently. "So!" she said then. "A little girl, eh?"

He crossed his legs and stared at his feet.

"Who called?"

"Mother. She says they'll name it Jahnet Rachel."

Chanson raised her eyebrows. Her coarse, thick hair gleamed purple under the reading-lamp. "So?" she said again. And presently, "Henric, is it that you want a child yourself?" She smiled. "You are that sort of blood—nice peasants, you know, rich with purpose and desire. . . ."

Henric frowned. "As long as Mother has that brat to make over ———"

The thin white curtains swayed in the window behind him and were still again.

Chanson began to laugh. "But, Henric, must we poison the baby?" Then, seeing the sullen expression that spread over his face, she put her hand on his arm. "Listen. We'll ask your mother to visit us . . . she'll stay, once she's here. . . ."

He glanced up eagerly. "Do you think she'll come?"

"Oh, most assuredly! She hates Sue Hart—and she likes me. She points to me as a model of matronly virtue. And all because I keep the dust cleaned from my shelves. It's true that Sue Hart is lazy. . . . She is strange, your mother, but fine. I admit that, fine. She understands me to a great extent." She was silent for a moment. "And then we'll all be old some day," she said, slowly.

"She's a stubborn old fool!"

"No." Her fingers pressed his arm and her yellow cat's eyes gleamed disturbingly. "No. It's not true, and if it were it's better not to say some things."

Henric stood up, stripping off his dressing-gown. Vaguely he glanced at the silver toilet articles on her dressing-table and then at the lamp above her head. "Are you ready to turn that off?"

Moving over in the bed, making room for him, she nodded. The light snapped off and the bed creaked under his weight. Settling beneath the thin sheet, he coughed angrily.

"Zack and his sweetheart," she began. "This little Paula Pollard ——"

"Zack's a fool! One day he abominates Jahn, the next day he isn't sure. Maybe Mother knew what she was doing."

Chanson shrugged in the darkness. "You can wind him around your little finger," she said, serenely. "And Martha, too. Soon she'll marry this Billy Nelson, and then she'll forget her precious Jahn. I know these lively ones. When they're married they can think of nothing but what happened last night and will happen again tonight." It might have been old Rachel except for the accent and the laugh with which she concluded. Henric stirred uncomfortably.

"Ah, Henric, it's strange the way human beings blind themselves, the way they talk of beauty and honesty and virtue, and all the time they're mocking such fine-sounding words with the breath it takes to say them. There's not much goodness in the world," she said, turning to him, "and we're not better than the rest."

He said, suddenly: "James was in the office today. He's sold his little cotton at the wrong time again. He was fairly wild. His cotton, his corn, the weather, Mother—everything I could mention. He can't forget what Jahn said, 'You're not on an equality with me.' He won't forget that soon. He's always hated all the Ibsells, but this is more than hate. He's been to see Peebles—you know, the one that made such a stir in the Brighton case last year?—and he says Peebles is confident of a case against Jahn if Mother will consent. Lipscomb's the man to make her do that, though."

Chanson sucked in her breath. "So the little Forrest would steal from the man whose father fed him when his own father was dead. . . . I wonder what Kate Ibsell will say to that? She'll tell another tale of cursed blood, my Henric!"

He smiled drily and cruelly. "James is not fooling me. He wants it all for himself. He thinks he'll manage to get us all together to fight Jahn and then he'll take the farm from us. He thinks I don't see through him, the fool!"

"And will he get any of it, any of it at all?" Chanson asked, dreamily.

He did not answer directly. He said, "Jahn can talk about us doing what we liked while he stayed out there, but talk is cheap. I've sat staring at my books often and longing for a sight of the hill to the left of the house and the hollow and thicket that's honeycombed with cold springs. . . ." The bed creaked with his angry impatience. "It's mine, mine through my father. I'm oldest, and it's only right I should have the management of it all!"

v

Chanson Ibsell was not a woman to sleep much. Her mind was too energetic, too much alive, to grant itself a long oblivion. She lay with closed eyes, twisting possibilities to make the future. Very minute and practical were her calculations. Jahn Ibsell's eight hundred acres would rent for twenty or thirty dollars an acre; say a hundred and fifty acres, mostly woodland, were not cultivatable and, therefore, not rentable; then counting at the lowest figure—six hundred and fifty acres at twenty dollars. Thirteen thousand dollars each year. Divided among Henric, James, and Zack, that would not be much. But if one of them, if Henric alone, could control the land and the income from it. . . . Thirteen thousand dollars each year . . . not counting the profits from sale of the timber on the woodlots. Or Henric might cut the land into small plots for selling—but no, better to have a smaller sum coming in over a long period.

She smiled slowly, her eyes luxurious under the quivering lids. Zack and James were fools for trusting to Henric; but what happened to fools, she thought, was not the affair of people who had to live and get ahead. Henric must have all the land, James and Zack nothing. Once the case went through the courts, old Rachel could be induced to give Henric power of attorney. The rest, the tricking and hoodwinking of James and Zack, would be easy. She could do it herself. She never doubted that, nor the ultimate decision. Old Judge Whitten of Chancery owed money to Henric, she knew.

She smiled again. Traditions of power, appearances to keep up, gracious acceptance of the crumbs of rich relatives, these were what she had known until she married, and even now she could not disguise from herself the fact that there were Foys and Vaguers in Louisiana to say that in marrying a Protestant and a peasant she had married beneath herself. Money, she thought, makes nobility and power. It soothes all things, even the tongues of religious-minded, blood-proud relatives, and it justifies love.

It was not as if she schemed from jealousy and hatred. She did not dislike Jahn Ibsell or wish him ill except as ill was bound to come to him if good came to her. She lay on her back, and now she opened her eyes and gazed at the darkness around her. Henric hated his brother; he was jealous and greedy, and that jealousy was strange, for certainly he did not love old Rachel. Zack loved her and loved the land. Though, of course, Henric also loved the land, but differently. And James? she asked herself, suddenly, and shuddered, inclined for a moment to return to the superstitions of religion. James was the child of original sin. There was no rational explanation of him.

Her mind turned back on itself, swiftly, relinquishing James. Rachel Ibsell was the important one. All their plans turned on her; or rather, she was the lever and Jahn the pivot on which she turned, and by her turning made their lives one thing or another. Jahn, Chanson felt very distinctly, had his ways, his stubbornness, his charm, but in the last analysis he was little more than a vast awareness, a peculiar and nervous sensitivity. They were, these Ibsells, all oddly like catgut, taut and quivering and able to produce any sound you desired; but Jahn was more exaggerated in the family characteristics than the others. Perhaps he was finer, less calloused by sophistication, or perhaps he had more completely inherited that nervous disease of which Rachel had spoken on the day she gave the deed. However . . . Rachel was the important one.

Chanson sat up in bed suddenly, looked around her at the amorphous shadows in the room, and became aware that Henric was asleep. She leaned her elbows on her raised knees and pressed the palms of her hands against her cheeks. A thought, a fear, moved dimly in her skull and would not define itself. Yet, without knowing it, she knew that Jahn Ibsell was too much like his father, that wonderful and gentle old man, and too much like his mother to be unimportant. She repeated to herself, puzzled, "What he is doesn't matter"; yet, lying down, she had a fleeting realization of how a man may be honorable in dishonesty and tender in remorselessness. She frowned, considering the thought, and then she sat up again, remained arrested for a moment by the sound of Henric's breathing, and got out of bed to stand by the window and look out at the pallid starlight. When at last she went back to bed she still had not perceived that the foundations of her possibilities lay in Jahn Ibsell's character.

VI

Swiftly, shouldering his way, Jahn came down the walk from Saint Mark's Episcopal Church and joined Martha and Billy Nelson at the edge of the December lawn. Bridesmaids and ushers clung to them in a whirl of confetti and rice. They looked stiff and new in their wedding finery, wearing the flushed, amazed look of the newly married. Nelson's car waited at the curb, mechanically eager for the honeymoon. Martha turned and kissed Jahn, and her dark hair brushed his shoulder for a moment in a kind of trembling reassurance. He was smiling at Billy Nelson, a secret puckishness dancing for an instant in his usually stern eyes.

"Where's Sue?" Martha demanded. "Did she let Mamma scare her away, after all? I wish she'd come. Everybody's saying I joined Billy's church just to be fashionable!" She plucked at the cuffs of her wine-colored wedding dress, straightening them under her coat sleeves, and gazing self-consciously at the crowds still thrusting through the church door and moving across the walk. The stained-glass windows above the steps let a red and blue saint lean far outward above the brown grasses of the lawn. "If I'd wanted to be chic," she said, "I'd have married in white satin, I guess. Why didn't Sue come?"

He evaded her. "Little Jahnet's sick. Not much, but Sue didn't feel well herself and didn't want to leave her."

Martha laughed. "If you'd call that baby Rachel, Mamma would like it." Without stopping to catch her breath, in a near-frenzy of bride's fear she rushed on. "I wish I'd stayed at home last night, but Mamma would have me with her, and Chanson gave me fits—" She stopped suddenly, blushed bright scarlet, and made a little dash toward two bridesmaids in sealskin coats, kissed them fervently, whispered in their ears, and whirled around to Jahn and her husband again. "Well, I suppose you and Sue will be alone for a while now?"

His eyebrows curved briefly. "If Mamma stays with Henric . . ." The wedding attendants moved around him, pressing, talking. He shook hands with Nelson, and stood back, watching the car leap from the curb and slide down in the street. Other cars followed it. From the church lawn the people began to disappear, straggling, dividing, moving apart. By the steps, Henric and Chanson remained with Kate Ibsell, the Rosenbens family, and his mother. Two ushers in a red roadster swerved from the curb behind Zack's car, tooting their horn at a passing boy on a bicycle.

Dried brown leaves scattered on the sidewalk, riding the cold air with the last wisps of confetti. Jahn put his foot out, the leaves crushed into powdery particles. His mother came up to him, touching his arm lightly, and then stood silent, her eyes on the group on the church steps.

"Yes," she began all at once, with energy, as if he had asked her a question. "I didn't see her off, her and her Episcopal doings, getting confirmed and all. Not that she cares." She tossed her head. "You never saw such a girl for knowing it all. In my day," she said, "we knew, but we let on we didn't and the pretense gave us a sort of flavor. But Martha's the sort of female fool to tell a man things he never heard of . . . not that there's much any of them ever heard of."

"What kept you?" asked Jahn, without much interest. James and his wife, Fanny, had come out of the church, and were talking to Zack near the edge of the lawn. James' walrus mustache protruded belligerently above his narrow mouth.

"Oh, Henric and Miss Chancie kept holding back, talking to some woman that wanted to know how come I didn't give Martha away. I told her it was you raised her in a manner of speaking, and if your standing up with her was a breach of etiquette, why, I had my own ideas and they served me well enough."

[82]

She had changed, he reflected. Her sourness had turned flippant with the flippancy of bitter pain. His brows contracted. "I guess I better be going. The niggers are hog-killing at home."

"Suit yourself," she said in an offhand tone. "But look here, do you reckon Billy 'ull be pouting about me not seeing him and Martha off?" She was talking to keep him. "His father was always touchy. I remember once when you was little and I was peddling here in town, I went to old Jake's store, and there he was behind the counter with a book propped so high in front of him he couldn't see the customers. I always did hate a sluggard, you know, though I overlook it in James. . . ." Her lips compressed. "Well—I told him he shouldn't be lazying away working-hours. It got him; he turned red as a turkey gobbler. . . ." Her voice trailed off. "How's the baby?" she said then.

"Fine. Cutting a tooth." He smiled. "You're not wanting to go home, are you?"

She grinned almost painfully, with an effort of will. "You think that baby's got me, don't you?" She watched his flush, and added, airily, "Oh, I'm right comfortable at Henric's. They talk too much, but— Yes," she interrupted herself as his eyes darkened, shining with a light she found uncomfortable, "you think they're talking against you, and I'll tell you fair, they are. But they don't say much that ain't true." She paused a second. "This is the thing, Jahn. Your promise was to stay with me, and I took that word, thinking you understood."

It was almost a cry, almost a plea. Oh, tell me you didn't understand, tell me so I can think I wasn't betrayed!

He looked at her and looked away. The Episcopal rector appeared on the church steps in his white embroidered vestments, and moved slowly across the grass toward the rectory next door. Watching him, Jahn had something in his mind to the effect that a man must always betray some woman, his mother or another, to be true to himself. The priest closed the door of his house softly behind himself.

"I did understand." Jahn met his mother's eyes briefly. "Yes, I knew. . . . But who did you think you were dealing with, a child?" He swallowed painfully, flushing. "Not that I meant. . . . Maybe I said more to Sue than I meant to say."

Her breast lifted suddenly. "Jahn, you've a hard row before you. I wish I didn't hate that woman so!"

"You've no cause to hate her," he said, with assumed indifference.

Chanson's group began to move toward the remaining cars. A brown-and-yellow-spotted dog raced around the corner of the church, sniffed at the tan stones, and stood wagging his tail.

"That's not it. It's simpler than that, and harder," she told him, hesitantly. "You're mine. I had many a long year with you when the rest was off at school, and you . . . you got inside me in a queer way. I can't," she said, "say just how it is, but I know."

He stared at her helplessly. "I swear I couldn't help it!" he burst out, at last.

"I know," she said. She didn't look at him. "But that don't make it any easier for me." She paused. "But what I can't stand," she went on, grimly, "is for that woman to be in my house, living on my place. I want you to have it, but not her, now or ever."

For a second he let himself understand, and then a coldness, as of scorn and judgment, went through him. "That's an unfeeling thing to say."

She glanced up at him. "No. It's a thing with too much feeling behind it. But now—Jahn, if you'd let me change the deed. . . . Oh, I know you won't, but if you would! If I could fix it so the land would go to Zack. . . . Just to Zack, Jahn. You know Zack's not like Henric and James, you and him could always get on. . . ."

"And leave little Jahnet with nothing?" he queried, with a

slow wonder more unbearable than scorn. "That's not law; it wouldn't hold."

"No. . . . I don't know how, but some way, Jahn . . ."

He didn't answer her. And abruptly she found herself full of anger, shaking with frustrate love and baffled hatred, and without another word she went off to Henric and Chanson, leaving him alone there, rubbing his shoe back and forth over the brittle leaves.

VII

The walls of Henric's library in the rococo house on Melchior Street were lined with great, leather-bound volumes from the shelves of the dead Larson, but the musty and dreaming odor of old books was not in the room. Instead, there was the smell of furniture polish and of cleanliness. The thrifty, cool fire proper to late February burned in the small grate beneath the mantelpiece. Above it, the polished relics of Larson Ibsell's Civil War days glittered.

"It was a hacking sword," said Lawyer Lipscomb, gazing upward. His narrow black eyes shone with the light of his seditious fanaticism. "Ah, Lord!" he sighed. "If all those fine souls hadn't fought and died in vain ——!"

Henric nodded impatiently, and glanced around the long library table at the strained, expectant faces assembled there. Then, staring down at the papers in front of him, he saw their countenances again, reflected in the polished depths of the table like morbid flowers blooming in a wide, dank pool. He continued to stare at those strange faces, examining them separately and with a queer, trembling eagerness: James Forrest's keen, rattish features, twisted and angry, his upper lip drawing back from the grayed mustache; Zack's white face, turgid with conflicting emotions; Chanson's glowing cat eyes, large and fiery with anticipated triumph; and lastly, his mother's harshly folded lips and fiery, determined brow.

[85]

She spoke suddenly, bringing the words out with wincing breath. "Well, get on with it, boys! Bard . . ."

From the corner of her eyes, she caught Chanson's reassuring smile; and then, brisk and terrible, she heard the rapping of Henric's pencil on the table, and saw him leaning forward, his downcast eyes studying his white, scholar's hand. He cleared his throat gutturally.

"We all know how Mother feels, that she made a terrible mistake when she trusted her property to Jahn." Leaning back, he faced the lawyer. "Very naturally she wishes to rectify this mistake while still living and able to reapportion her property as she sees fit. In other words, she wishes to revoke the deed. Peaceably if possible, you understand. . . ."

Chanson's dramatic gesture completed the inference.

James Forrest said, swiftly, greedily: "What about it, eh, Lipscomb? Papers, proof, and so on? I saw Peebles a way back—" He paused and essayed a suave cackle. "Couldn't afford you then, Lipscomb, couldn't now if I had to go it alone. . . . But Peebles said we had a case. A chance, eh?"

The lawyer glanced at him, a mere flicker of inscrutable eyes. Bard Lipscomb told himself that he could see it all, he'd known it all long ago when the deed went from his hand to Jahn's. He'd seen how it would go, the boy marrying and Rachel jealous and angry and leaving her own house to live with suggestions and insinuations. . . . Anger moved stealthily beneath the white mask of his face as he stared at Rachel and listened to the covert impatience of James Forrest's breathing.

"Why, I doubt you have a chance," he said then, with a show of ironical reluctance in his voice, and waited, watching while they averted their eyes and moved in their chairs.

"But Peebles—!" James began angrily, and hushed.

Chanson leaned forward. "Have you considered everything, Mr. Lipscomb? Surely you know that Jahn promised to stay with his mother, promised to stay single?"

The lawyer sighed. "Ah, well, the aged are always at the mercy of the young," he said. "But that's fair enough, considering that the child is always at the mercy of the middle-aged." He shrugged. "No one, Miss Chanson, respects your intentions more than I do. Such daughters-in-law are rare indeed. . . . However," he went on, abruptly harsh, "a promise constitutes no obstacle at law except it be written and recorded." He turned to Rachel. "Was that done, my dear?"

She smiled faintly, astonishing them all. "You know well enough it wasn't. . . . I'd been ashamed to put it down in writing. And, anyway . . . I knew it wouldn't hold, such a promise as that. A man judge would feel for him, not for me."

"Has Jahn failed to provide for you?" he said, his voice tender, his eyes gentle on her bowed head.

"It depends," she said, slowly. "He broke his promise, he brought that woman there." Her face contracted spasmodically, and was still again. "He's dishonest. I won't leave my land with him!"

"Oh, Rachel, Rachel!" He stared at her, seeing her hair white and her face lined, while he remembered the beauty and torment of her youth. "Rachel!" he said, softly, under his breath. And then, "This is not a thing I can reason with you about. Nobody could ever reason with you. But let us consider: Jahn has hurt you, but isn't it true that you had no shadow of right to prevent his marriage? Sue's not your sort, but she's a good, gentle girl. . . ." He looked at her darkening face. "Bitterness, bitterness!" he cried, suddenly, scornfully, twisting his mobile lower lip. "And you an old woman!"

A kind of agony showed in her black eyes, her mouth trembled. "I know one thing, he tricked me, he got all I had, he won't give it back, my house, my land. I'm his mother and he cheated me. I tried, God knows I tried! He brought that woman there, and I tried to bear it, I let her have her finicking, superior, looking-down-on-me way . . . till I couldn't stand it and I broke out. He couldn't see, he wouldn't see. He took what I had, lying, and now I've got no place to go, no home."

[87]

"He earned it, Rachel. He's right to keep it. And Sue didn't mean to act superior to you."

"Something, my house, is due me, a mother and tricked," she answered out of her stubborn pain. "I'll not be cheated again in my old age."

Lipscomb stood silent, his lower lip pushing thoughtfully against the upper one. He shook himself. "You, Zack and Henric, what have you done to persuade your mother against this? No, you've fostered it! I know how you've pushed it along! Jahn's your brother. Are you shameless?" He looked at them with hard, hot eyes.

Henric shrugged. "I agree perfectly with Mother. She's been tricked. Most certainly," he added, coldly, "most certainly I don't believe Jahn ever earned eight hundred acres. Some of it is mine . . . and, of course, the others' too."

"Rachel, it'll get away from you," the lawyer warned. "You'll let them make you start it, and then first thing you know it'll be out of your hands. A lawsuit's like life, like a conversation, it starts with one thing and ends with another that has little or nothing to do with the beginning. You'll lose yourself, Rachel, your importance, your identity, even. It'll be Henric and James here against Jahn; they'll get the farm, and not you—unless Jahn holds it, and I think he will. . . ."

No one spoke for a moment. Rachel Ibsell had descended into a dark void of despair, and there, in that formless cylinder of pain, she sat tensing the muscles of her jaws as a sort of reflex to the tensing of her will; watching, as if from a distance, her agony spin wilder and wilder until she was dizzy with the sight and desperate to keep from screaming. Gasping, she attempted to rise. "I think . . . I'll . . . go to my room. . . ." Urging herself upward, she swayed, and held on to the arm of her chair.

"You're sick, Mamma!" Zack rushed to catch her.

"Why, Mother Ibsell—!" Chanson stood up, cool and smiling, at the end of the library table. "You were never like this, Mother!"

"You see!" Bard Lipscomb turned to Zack. "This is what will happen to her. If you love your mother, help her now. Keep her out of this. It's the bickering of lust over a greedy dream. She doesn't belong in it; it's not what she means."

Rachel, clinging to Zack's arm, heard, and a sudden flowing in of deadly anger stiffened her. "Shut up, Bard Lipscomb! I never thought you'd take up for trickery like this!" Her hands brushed Zack away. "Get back from me; leave me alone."

She stared at all of them with fierce, bitter eyes. "Jahn's a better one than you all put together!" she said, suddenly, out of something in herself that still clung to the truth her passions obscured. "A better one than you all!"

For a moment they stood regarding her with amazement, while she turned to the door, pushed the draperies aside, and went out into the hall. Her old feet in soft shoes fell with a whispering sound on Chanson's heavy rugs.

"She's sick!" Zack cried again, suddenly returning to himself like a distraught child, and went after her.

"Zack." Chanson's hand touched his arm. She stood smiling at him with charming, cool grace. "Your mother wants to be alone now."

He gazed at her doubtfully, became suddenly aware of the other eyes watching him, flushed, and went back to his place at the table.

Behind him, Chanson sighed with relief, and told herself that it would be well to keep Zack away from his mother in the future. Slightly lifting the curtains, she saw Rachel Ibsell walking stiffly down the hall, past the gilded angels on the staircase, and into her room.

VIII

The electric lights over the bed burned garishly, throwing sharp shadows onto the green rug and over the white chimney of the kerosene-lamp which she insisted should be kept in her room on the dresser. "Waste, waste!" she muttered, feverishly, fumbling in the pin-tray for a match. Finding it, she lit the lamp and stalked across the floor to extinguish the electric lights. "Fools, wasting what they've got when kerosene's good enough for anybody!" She searched in the closet for her woolen wrapper, and tearing off her heavy satin dress, she put herself into the more comfortable garment. Then, when she had found her spectacles, she sat down in the low, rush-bottomed chair near the lamp, and took up her Bible.

My soul is weary of my life: I will let go my speech against myself, I will speak in the bitterness of my soul.

Presently, letting the book fall onto her knees, she leaned back with closed eyes and clasped hands. The pale, soft glow from the lamp wavered on her tired features. Her lips moved. "O God, my God, Thou knowest . . . all I bear. . . ." She sat up, and opened her eyes. The familiar room whirled in a gray miasma; she fell forward across the dresser, displacing the toilet articles scattered on the shelf and dropping the Bible from her lap. Her shoulders shook, her teeth bit into the lower lip to keep soundless the cry that rushed outward: "Jahn, Jahn . . . my dearest, my littlest. . . .!"

IX

In the library there was a thin sound beating against the frustrate silence of Rachel's children, a sound tinkling and derisive that might have been the ghost of old Larson's laughter. They started and glanced covertly around at the leather-bound volumes, at the crossed sword and bayonet glittering above the mantel. Bard Lipscomb stirred in the corner by the fireplace, and let the laughter fade from his lips.

"I must condole with you," he said, lightly, "as one son with another. Our efforts to lead the old are doomed to inevitable defeat. They take our advice, but they take it amiss, and they hate us for it. We can only wait and hope, trusting that in heaven the Lord God will see to it that our mothers are grateful for what we tried to do for them."

"Really!" said Henric, and froze, staring at Lipscomb, who let his breath out in a slow, chiming laugh.

"Don't," Zack begged. "Don't. It's bad enough without . . ." He broke off helplessly, tapping the table with agitated fingers.

"Without what?" the old lawyer inquired, looking at Chanson, whose cheeks were scarlet with anger. The lawyer's strange, white face was madder, whiter than any of them had ever seen it. He caressed the back of the chair where Rachel's head had rested, as if he caressed that old woman herself, as if his pity loved her now as his heart had loved her when they were young and he was too poor to marry and she too intent on a living for her orphaned James to see him. He sent his gaze from one to the other of her children. "What, Zack?" he said again, gently.

Zack stared at him with pale, frightened eyes. "What's right?" he said, his voice low, ashamed. "Didn't he choose to stay there with Mamma? Why must he have it all for doing what he wanted to do and the rest of us be put off with money and the business? All that land, acres and acres of brown, rolling plain, hollow and swale and woodland. . . ." Ashamed, he broke off; and then, driven, he cried again, "Why should he have it all and the rest of us nothing?" His pale face contorted. "What's right, that's what I'm asking, what's the right thing!"

James snickered coarsely. "Zack's dwarf must be after him again!" He half-turned in his chair, muttering angrily, "The damned white-livered ——!"

Lipscomb spoke swiftly above James' muttered imprecation. "Zack, I can look into your mind and see your doubts, your hesitations, your shiftings and fears. But I can't, with a word, take them away and give you peace. I think," he said gently, "that you'll never know peace and assurance. For you'll always . . . desire. In you, as in Henric and James, this is more than greed, it's a lust. . . ." He took up his hat and stood turning it between his fingers, "Yet, Zack . . . will you come with me?"

Chanson's silks made a sibilant sound. She stood up and said, in a low, rough voice, "Will you get out of my house, Bard Lipscomb!"

The lawyer smiled. "You're smart, Miss Chanson, but you forgot yourself then. Daughters-in-law like you always forget themselves at some moment or another." He turned to Zack again. "Are you coming?"

Up the hall, through the purple draperies, came Rachel Ibsell's tired voice:

"Are Thy days as the days of man, and are Thy years as the times of man: that Thou shouldst inquire after my iniquity and search after my sin . . ."

James swallowed emotionally. "That's plain Predestination preaching for you! Mother's belief all her life, too! All's according to the will of God, and his elected are excused. . . ."

Lipscomb smiled again. "Zack?"

The pale face refused to look at him. "No. . . ."

"No? At last, Zack, I believe your mother. Your father should have lived . . . to save his sons from Predestination." He bowed, shielding his eyes, and went slowly to the door and put out his hands to push aside the draperies.

". . . there is no man can deliver out of Thy hand. . . ."

With his back to them, he said, softly, "Have you ever been to a Burial Mass, Zack? But of course not. . . . 'There is no man can deliver out of Thy hand. . . .'" The draperies fell behind him with a sinuous, lapping motion.

X

There was moonlight, Bard Lipscomb noticed, such cold, blue moonlight as he had not seen since the night he walked home from Gansaret church with Rachel Gurney and was allowed to hold her hand across the footlog at Pierson's Creek. Smoke curled from the chimneys and moved darkly against the glittering sky, embroidering it with great, furry dragons and tufted snakes; and in the air there was a smell that reminded him of underground cellars, damp and cool and full of cider-casks.

At the corner he met Martha and Billy Nelson. They were walking slowly, hugged together against the cold wind. Martha's clear features rose, gleaming like a cameo, from her black fur collar, and she was gay with a strange, steel-like gaiety that was, nevertheless, tender and profound. She stopped immediately in front of Bard Lipscomb and stood resting against her husband's shoulder.

"So Mamma's old beau has been to see her?" she said in her light, clear voice, laughing.

The lawyer frowned, and glanced at Nelson, who was smiling quietly with a shrewd, self-satisfaction. Lipscomb jerked his head in the direction of Henric's house, where the lights in the library and the lamp in Rachel Ibsell's room still burned. "Trouble."

"At Henric's?" Martha stared at the lights, tightening her hand on Nelson's arm. "What's happened?" she asked, finally.

"She wants to revoke the deed."

"It's James!" Martha cried, sharply. "James and that Chanson! Her smooth tongue! If it hadn't been for her, Mamma never would have hated Sue so. . . ."

"They'll go to court with it."

Martha's mouth opened in consternation. "No!" she whispered. "No!" And then, "Not that disgrace!"

Nelson said, in his easy voice, "Now Martha maybe it's not so bad as you think."

Lipscomb smiled, pushing his cheek up against his right eye to close it. "Why don't you see Jahn right away?" he suggested. "The boy ought to know what's going on. . . ."

He walked the three blocks to his hotel alone. The lobby

and the corridors were deserted, silent with that duskiness of
quiet which is unpleasant to the flesh and oppresses the heart.
Idly watching his shadow as it marched beside him up the
hall, he wondered vaguely at life, at living, at the mystery of
human existence; and finding himself before his door, he
kicked it angrily and sadly.

He stumbled a little in the darkness before he found the
electric button on the wall. Then objects sprang up with the
light, and he stared at them dully, marking the slender tables
and the dull curtains; and closing his eyes he thought of
Rachel Ibsell, seeing her as she had stood before him tonight,
angry and reasonless, and it seemed to him that there was
no word to describe any part of her long and sorrowful life.
Nor could he imagine any redress in heaven or earth for the
soul destroyed by the body or for that body destroyed by the
soul. With a shudder, he brushed his hands over his eyes and
went across the room to his desk, where he began to write
aimlessly, making notes that had to do with Jahn and with
the Red Valley farm.

As he wrote, he saw them all. Rachel with her head bowed
in shame and bitterness. Henric and Chanson starched with a
peculiar and subversive air of righteousness. James Forrest
crouching and waiting for slander and hatred to give him all
he could never deserve. Zack with his conscience hacking at
his flesh. And Jahn, Jahn lost to a word, buried between the
eyes of two women. . . .

XI

Two weeks later, at nine o'clock of a Monday morning,
Martha whipped her roadster over the Red Valley road in
such a fervor of excitement that, on rounding the last curve to
the farm house, she was trembling with anger and fear. The
tires slipped insistently on the damp red clay, the hot blood
flew under her skin. All at once, she leaned forward, staring
straight ahead at the weather-beaten touring-car parked

[94]

before the white yard fence. A deep sigh lifted her breast and let it fall back. She had come too late, Zack had not told her in time.

Rapidly, her high heels beating the gravel, she went up the walk and onto the veranda. From within the house came sounds of a hammer striking on wood and the rending, splintering screech of boards being prized from their nails. She paused a second, listening, and then she stepped into the narrow hall. The door of the living-room was standing ajar, and through the crack Martha saw James Forrest stooping over a packing case, his hands careful on a bundle of vases wrapped in woolen rags. He raised his bullet head, ridging his forehead, and peered at her, his mouth hanging open. The ugly wen on his neck glowed red. Behind him, Rachel Ibsell turned from the window and stared, with the draperies in one hand and a hammer and poker clenched tightly in the other.

Martha's heart thudded sickeningly in her throat. She cried, "You—vandals!" She rushed at her mother. "Leave those things alone; they're not yours!" Then, falling back, "How can you? How can you? Zack told me, but I couldn't believe it . . . Mamma, how can you? Where's Jahn, what makes him let you do it!"

The mother and son looked at each other with tightening lips. Then, snickering, James said, "He's out in the back somewhere, if that's what you want."

"If that's what I want! What do you think I want, you little Forrest, you!" To the name Forrest her tone gave a hissing scorn, her tongue repudiated it. "You're running us all crazy. Zack's half-crazy. You came in my father's house and lived off him, and now you think you can do this to us!" Voiceless with impotent rage, she stopped and stared at him, gasping. She whirled on her mother, standing motionless with the draperies fallen over the floor. "Mamma . . . it's not Sue you're hurting, Sue doesn't want this stuff, you can take all the chairs and rugs and everything and she won't care.

[95]

It's Jahn you're hurting. Mamma, Jahn bought this, he worked for us all . . . Mamma . . ."

The old woman's eyes were dim and fixed. She stood like a woman in a cold trance with her eyes fixed on one corner of the room and her ears numb to sound.

"Mamma. . . ." Suddenly, Martha heard her voice, high and broken, and that old woman's silence and stillness mocking it. She spun on her heel, and then, indecisively, turned back again. James Forrest grinned, wiping his mustache with a slow hand, as if to reveal by the gesture the hatefulness it seemed to wish to hide. From that, Martha ran, abruptly and fearfully, coming hard up against the half-open door, and then past it, out into the hall where the furniture from the rooms was crowded, and through the rest of the house.

Sue was sitting hunched on the smokehouse steps, one hand in the pocket of her green sweater. An overturned lardcan lay on the ground in front of her, and she kicked at it, without sense, listlessly. When Martha rushed from the house onto the back porch, she stopped what she was doing and sat still, staring at her. "Was there something you wanted, too?" she inquired, strangely.

In a breaking voice Martha demanded, "Where is he?"

Sue put both hands inside her sweater. "Up at the barn." Martha came down the steps, and Sue said, slowly, with no expression in her voice or on her face, "I wouldn't bother him."

"Oh!" Martha stopped. She began to recover her natural lively sensibility to practical event. "Where's the baby?"

"Behind you."

Turning, Martha saw Jahnet behind her on the porch, asleep in Rachel Ibsell's rocking-chair. The little girl's flannel-covered chest rose and fell with her gentle breathing and her cheeks were faintly flushed like two delicate, transparent roses. "Well. . . ." Martha's voice trailed off. She walked down from the porch, and sat on the smokehouse steps beside Sue.

For a long time, they said nothing. The winter sun was warm on their backs, a drowsy wind blew against them at intervals. Then, Martha demanded, "When did they come? I knew. . . . This morning Zack came to tell me, half-crazy. . . . What did they say? What did he say?"

Sue's back stiffened, and she spoke with a cold monotony of sound. "Your mother said they'd come for her things. I thought she meant the clothes she left here when she went to stay with Henric. I started to the closet to get them, when James Forrest said, No, she meant the furniture. She said she ought to take the house, too; it was hers, but she still had some feeling for Jahn if he was a liar and sneak thief."

"Did Jahn hear her?"

"He told her he hated to see her act the fool that way, and then James Forrest squared up and said he didn't want anybody talking like that to his mother."

"Oh, Sue . . . James Forrest!"

She took her hand from her sweater and looked at it curiously. "I oughtn't to have married him," she said, with a strange indifference of tone.

Martha got up briskly and moved the lard-can. "What did Jahn say to James?"

"Nothing. He just left. I think he was afraid to say anything then." Abruptly her face worked and she cried in a thin terrible voice, "Oh, I was never so sorry, never so sorry for anybody!" She stopped herself and gazed at Martha's miserably working throat.

"Then?" said Martha after a while. "What happened then?"

"They moved the things out of the kitchen and out of my room, so I came out here. They said Henric would send the trucks at ten."

Martha went to the kitchen door and glanced in. "They left the fire, anyway," she said, dryly. "We'd better take Jahnet in; she'll catch cold out here." She picked the child up and held her in the crook of one arm, dragging and pushing

[97]

the light rocking-chair into the kitchen with the other hand. Sue followed, and stood helplessly by the fire, staring into it, while Martha went out into the yard again and brought in the empty lard-can and a small, old chicken-coop.

"Here, sit on this," she ordered, turning the lard-can up on end and dropping down onto the chicken-coop. She laughed abruptly and briefly, and then fell silent.

"But why?" Sue burst out, suddenly. "If she hates me, if they want the land and think the deed's not fair . . . but to hurt Jahn like this! I thought she loved him, I thought she hated me because she loved him so!"

Martha moved restlessly. "She's not thinking now; she never did when she was angry. And, oh, it's James and Chanson! When I think of James, that lousy, low-down Forrest, daring to put his mouth into this and thinking he can have anything that came from my father . . . Oh, I can't see! She raised us to be decent and honorable; she taught us that ——!"

"They're tired of their raising, then," Sue said, with a prim bitterness, and added in a low tone, "and she's tired, too."

"You never did like her," Martha said suddenly, and stopped.

They glanced at each other, then, out of careful eyes, abruptly aware of the difference of their blood. After a moment, Martha observed, pleasantly: "Jahnet is certainly sleeping. She's so fair, like they say Papa was."

"Oh," said Sue, "I think her eyes are like my people's."

"Perhaps. But it seems to me they're like Jahn's, and she has . . . she has Mamma's mouth."

"I don't think so. Though her eyes may be like Jahn's. They're the same color."

Martha laughed suddenly. "At any rate, he can't say she's not his." She glanced at her watch. "It's nearly ten. Do you think they'll load the furniture without saying a word?"

Sue shook her head wordlessly. Then, soon, there came the rumble of trucks over the damp road, the crash of heavy beds swaying from side to side, and finally the creak and jangle of trace chains lashed around the beds.

Martha and Sue rose up and pressed out onto the porch. The trucks were in the yard, going around the corner of the house to the front veranda, the wheels cutting and marring the green turf, breaking the small shrubbery. Martha turned, with an expression of speechless dismay, her eyeballs shining and hard, and ran into the yard. A thin cry rang between her lips; she waved her arms and cried, furiously, like a child determined to create a scene: "Get off my roses! I planted those bushes! Get off them. You hear!"

"Here, what's this?" With James behind her, Rachel burst out onto the veranda. "What in tarnation ails you, Martha?"

"Make them get off my roses!" Martha cried, in a thick, sullen voice. "I planted them and tended them. I bought the furniture in this house, too, and Jahn's money paid for it! Make them get off my roses, leave things alone here. They're not yours. You had nothing to do with it. You'd have got along with home-made bedsteads if it hadn't been for me and Jahn!"

The old woman looked over her shoulder at James Forrest. "Just listen to that, will you?" she said, confidentially. "All that palaver for a sneaking thief and his no-good woman!"

Then, on the ground behind her, Sue heard Jahn's steps. She turned to him, and remained staring and speechless, seeing his gray face through a mist of fear, seeing his eyes, mesmerized by his look of ordered fury, perverted, intense, and fiendish because it was perversely ordered and not chaotic. She fell back before him, against the wistaria trellis. He was marching on her, coming, pacing as if he measured his steps, glancing neither to right nor left, but gazing straight ahead out of terrible, glittering eyes. She put out her hand. "Jahn!"

The whisper scarcely moved her throat; she heard it hanging in the air between him and her, small and terrified against his marching steps. "Jahn!" She touched his shirt sleeve then, and her fingers clung desperately. He stopped, but without knowing what had stopped him or why, and stood, not looking at her or at anything, his eyes blind. "Jahn . . ." She kept trying to hold him, to get her fingers caught some way in his clothes to hold him, to draw herself against him and around him so that he could not move. A spill of tears burst suddenly behind her terrified eyeballs and down over her face. "Don't . . . don't . . . don't," she kept whispering, afraid of her tongue, and then with a voiceless rush, "Don't, don't kill them. . . ."

His muscles trembled suddenly, like the muscles of a whipped horse. "Kill?" he said, vaguely.

Her terror rushed out of her, chattering, spilling over the bright sunlit yard. "I'll leave, I'll go, I'll give you up, I'll go away. . . ." She heard her gibbering voice, she even saw the grass green and still on the lawn, and Martha standing without a movement, her face white and staring. Her voice ran on, spoiling the sunshine and the day, and she could not stop it. "I'll go. I'm the one, I made the trouble. I knew when I came, I meant to hurt her. . . . But I had to come, I had to come, but I'll go now and you'll be all right; everything will be the same again; it will be all right." In her transport she began to speak softly, to soothe him, touching his hair and his face. Her eyes smiled widely and feverishly. "It will be all right then; she'll come back and you'll be all right. . . ."

The strange tremble ran again over his muscles. He raised his hands to her shoulders, moving unconsciously, and smiled. "You'll go?" he said in a soft, almost musing, voice. "Where?"

She heard the echoes of his tone running between her mouth and his, lying still and sinister on the bright winter air. She saw, suddenly, Rachel Ibsell's dark figure looming against the corner of the veranda. Like shivered ice, breaking only to reform, her character reasserted itself. She stepped back from him and stared, wildly pleading with the voice she could not find for denial, for speech to say she would not leave, she could not. "I can't, I won't, I'm your wife." She couldn't say it; her mouth remained a small, round cipher opening on darkness.

He smiled a little more fully, with intelligence coming back into his eyes. "What are you talking about?" he said, lightly, scoffingly. "What would you do with Jahnet?" He looked at Martha.

"Take her," she said. He waited until Martha had reached them and had her arms around Sue, who was sobbing now with the quiet tempestuousness of utter relief. Then, "Don't be a fool!" he said, with sudden roughness, while his eyes glowed gently, as if with a deep pleasure. He turned away.

"Where are you going?" Martha cried after him. Sue continued to weep with her head on Martha's shoulder. "To help Mamma," he said, and laughed.

James Forrest crowded back before him, giving ground as he came up the veranda steps. His mother was still, upright, her face raised to his and expressionless. Without looking at her, he turned around and ran his gaze over the nervous, uncomfortable Negoes in the trucks. A sudden perception of what they must have felt in the presence of the scene just passed twitched his mouth. "You, boys," he said, gently, "back your trucks, further . . . Just so . . . right up against the porch." He waited, not moving, and smiling all the time, until they had backed and turned, bringing the rear end of the truck beds against the edge of the veranda floor. "Now," he said, "one man in each truck and the others in the house. Get going, boys!" The Negroes swarmed over the high beds and into the house.

He turned slowly then, looking at his mother and James Forrest. James moved, sideling backward cautiously, afraid of the queer amusement in his half-brother's eyes. Rachel Ibsell still did not move or take her eyes from Jahn's face. Suddenly he felt an impulse to crazy, hysterical laughter, his abdomen heaved, and he saw them, standing like gawdy cardboard puppets, mouthing and plotting for nothing. He smothered a burst of laughter.

"Get out, James," he ordered. "Get off my land. Take your car out in the road and wait there." The heaving in his abdomen was suddenly rage, the blood rushed up hot under his forehead. "Get—you self-made bastard!"

"Jahn!"

He flicked his glance at his mother and said again, "Get out, James!"

James Forrest passed down the steps and out into the lane. He climbed awkwardly into his car, he fumbled with the starter and drove precariously into the road, where he stopped.

Rachel Ibsell shook her head a little. "He'll hate you now, sure enough," she said, under her breath. "You were always hurting his self-respect." She put her hand on his arm. "But you're the same as me . . . and now I've lost you. I always knew it'd come to this some day; that's why I held on so hard, I guess. The things you love . . ." She shook her head again, swallowing harshly.

He released his arm by spreading her fingers between his own. "Is there anything you've not packed?" he asked, flatly.

From the yard Martha said, "Jahnet's in her chair." She pressed Sue's face against her shoulder and stared furiously at her mother.

"In my chair . . ." Rachel said. She looked about her, bewildered, then her gaze fastened on Jahn's face again. "The things you love," she repeated, helplessly and without knowing what she said.

He dropped her hand. "Go on back," he told her. "Go back to Chanson and Henric. James is waiting. I'll load the things and send them after you." He smiled palely. "I'll do that. . . . It pays you out, eh?"

Without looking at him again, she went slowly down the steps and across the yard to the place where James waited for her.

XII

On the morning following the raid on the house in Red Valley, the Greek, Nicodemus, answered the telephone, and then traveled the three blocks from his bookstore to Joe Rosenbens' department store in three seconds flat. Mose Thurston had brought news to town.

Standing before Nicodemus and Rosenbens in Rosenbens' office, he unraveled the tale in twisted, fumbling strands. "I seen 'em when they passed with the trucks, goin' up thar," he said, "en I went out to the road en arsked 'em what war up. They took everything, hide en hair, all 'cept one ol' wicker rocker Mis' Ibsell war crazy to hev, en they couldn't git thet on account of the baby war a-lyin' in hit, en Miss Sue, she wouldn't let Jahn move the baby, though he wanted to, hevin' promised Mis' Ibsell he'd send everything arter her. But Miss Sue, she wouldn't hev it atall. She got fiery mad arter t'war all over en she'd offered to leave him . . . but she wouldn't hev when she thought about hit," he added, philosophically, spitting into the spittoon behind Rosenbens' desk.

"Miss Martha she tuck 'em in last night. Not hide ner hair left ner a stick to sleep on, so they come to town last night. I arsked the niggers on the trucks," he repeated, suddenly, with spirit, "en thet's how I come to know hit all."

"My God!" cried Rosenbens, falling back against his desk. "What miserable behavior! Nick," he said, solemnly, "this never would have happened in a Jewish family!"

"Nor among good Greeks. But think what pain to the young Jahn!"

"And to Miss Sue. Nick, I've visited in their home."

"Ah," sighed Nick, remembering words from the most advanced quarterly in his store, "these mercenary Yankees!"

"Well, now, I don't know erbout Yankees," demurred Thurston, fingering his mustache and taking snuff.

"Mr. Thurston is right," said Rosenbens, smiling faintly. "The Ibsells are Southerners. The South is captive to Wash-

ington as Judea was to Rome. Southerners always in everything as you are Greek always in everything, Nick."

"Ah, Greece!" murmured Nicodemus, closing his eyes and
then abruptly opening them as if startled. "One of your
poets," he said to Thurston, "speaks of the glory that was
Greece ———"

"Well, I don't know erbout poets now," interrupted
Thurston. "Thar war a preacher come with the Holy Rollers
a proselytin' eround Red Valley, en' he said as how Soloman
war a poet en wicked. But these here Ibsells, now, they
ain't poets ner Greeks ner Yankees ner yet Jews," he concluded, rising to forcible emphasis on the last word. "They're
stiff-necked en rebellious enough to be, but they ain't. They're
too proud fer living en too nicey-nice fer dying. Howsome-
ever, they air Southerners, bein' old Larson, who war a
Norwegian, fit in the Civil War alongside of Jackson. Least-
ways, I think hit war Jackson. Anyways, he fought, en thet
thar Henric he's got a document a-tellin' erbout hit. He's
always a printin' of hit in the papers. . . . En now, I reckon,"
he went on slowly and thoughtfully, "I reckon he'll print
some more in the papers sayin' how Jahn ain't his blood
brother, but thet thar James Forrest is, er something of the
kind."

Smiling, the Jew and the Greek looked at each other.

Nicodemus said, "Maybe he's at Garner's now. He'll need
new furniture."

Rosenbens reached for his hat. "I just remember a word I
want with Mr. Garner."

"I'll wait here, then," said Nicodemus, seating himself
behind the desk. "One of your poets . . ." he began again to
Thurston.

XIII

Jahn Ibsell still traded in Choctaw's Old Town. Bob
Garner's store was vast, rambling, one of those dark,

romantic warehouses of furniture in which the floors are uneven and creaky, the walls high and of wide, crooked boards, and the furniture everywhere. Bob Garner's wares were massive, like himself, a little crude and ornate, like his humor. Chairs and tables lay piled one on the other in the front of the store, the legs of the chairs interlocking from their position and the tables mounting in graduated size to the ceiling. The beds were, properly enough, in the back of the store, so that a customer need not feel that every loiterer in town had looked upon his mattress and springs from the sidewalk. Three counters sat in the middle of the store, placed end to end and forming a triangular inclosure toward the front.

In this, Garner read the papers and worked with his clerks on account ledgers. His customers stood outside, their heels backed up against a pile of rugs rolled inside out, and talked to him, staring over his head at the springs and mattresses ranged unevenly and curiously against a row of large and small refrigerators. Ice refrigerators were Bob Garner's one concession to modernity.

He wrinkled his pursy, yellow face at Joe Rosenbens in an unctuous grin. "We were just wondering when you'd be in, Joe."

The Jew glanced at him, nodded, and shook hands with Bard Lipscomb.

"I reckon you've heard the news?" Garner went on. "Never had such a trade in my life. People in and out all morning."

The Jew turned an opaque glance on Lipscomb. "You've seen him?"

"Not yet. I didn't hear about it until a few minutes ago. I met Kate. Martha had called her. The news up in my office this morning was about James." He stopped suddenly and pressed his vivid red lips together.

Garner stretched his puffy mouth. "He'll be in soon, all right!"

Lipscomb cocked an ironic eyebrow, and Rosenbens answered with a quick, sidewise glance. They turned and walked together the length of the building, past the busy clerks at the side counters, and stood in the doorway. The sunlight glinted on the rough cobblestones of Old Town's unpaved alleys and the red and white of the new garage across the street from the bakery. Lipscomb sighed.

"We're getting old, Joe, and the world's not getting better."

"Yes. It's what I remember my father saying."

Lipscomb leaned against the plate-glass window. He squinted in the sunlight, folding his lips together in a bitter grimace.

Three small children were playing with great iron hoops, the rims of truck wheels, in the center of the street. The hoops rang on the cobblestones, the sound running like a musical accompaniment under the high, piercing laughter of the little boys. A dray wagon hurtled past. The young Negro standing poised in the wagon bed held his mouth pursed to whistle while he seesawed the reins.

Lipscomb said: "You haven't heard about James? He whipped his wife in front of a bunch of nigger scalawags this morning."

Rosenbens looked at the lawyer. "Hadn't done enough yesterday, I suppose!"

"It was about a horse. One her father gave her. . . . God knows, who can say what ailed James this morning? Isn't he always angry? Maybe he's like the rest of us, got a conscience, and it worries him like ours does, to make him do worse than he's already done so as to drown his remorse. . . . The horse was old, but Fanny wanted to keep it. James had it shot and then whipped her for crying. Crying and not getting his breakfast, he said. . . . Long Jim Chambers was in to tell me."

In the back of the store, Garner moved and stood up and

walked from the angle of one counter-joining to the angle of another. The old floor boards creaked under his weight.

Rosenbens said, "There's Jahn."

Erect on his great sorrel stallion, Jahn Ibsell rode in the center of the street, handling his reins delicately, with extreme care. Behind him two wagons came on rapidly, carrying three-decker beds in which a number of Negroes lolled and stared.

Rosenbens laughed mirthlessly. "Eight hundred acres he has, and wagons instead of trucks, mule plows instead of tractors!"

The procession halted in front of Garner's store, and Jahn stepped down from the saddle. Simultaneously, the two old men in the door moved across the sidewalk. Their hands met his gravely, with strong grasps. They avoided his eyes. "Is there anything we can do?" they said.

He looked at them gratefully, but without speaking. Then they fell back into their former positions, leaning against the showcase, and he passed inside among the heaped furniture.

Directly across the street, a group of farmers from Red Valley, with Mose Thurston in the center of them, stood craning their heads, trying to see into the store, and talking in low voices. Jahn's Negroes stood in the wagons and surveyed the streets, the stores, the white trash with dark, scornful visages full of the fine insolence of Negroes who are the property of well-to-do folk. The wiry little Greek hastened up the sidewalk, his coat tails flapping behind him, and joined the two men in the door. "I saw him coming," he said, softly. He backed against the show-window beside Rosenbens and gazed steadily and silently at the crimson rosettes on the bridle of Jahn's stallion.

Presently Martha and Sue turned the corner from Barnold Street. They moved their heads inside their dark fur collars and looked at everything and everybody and saw nothing. Sue's pale face was set in an intense, painful smile. She listened without change of expression to Martha's embarrassed, determined chatter, or bent over the baby carriage to pat Jahnet's satin blankets into place. They turned into the cave-like façade in which Garner's door was set, and smiled at the men gathered there. Martha spoke gallantly. "Good morning, gentlemen!" and Nicodemus, his accent heightened by embarrassment, said, "Good morning, ladies!" The ladies bowed and smiled again, and Jahnet twisted her small neck around for a wistful glance at the wonderful men with smelly coats and tickly chins.

"Dad-da?" she asked, stumbling over the consonants, kicking her boots against the footboard of the carriage. The men laughed. "She wants her daddy, she does!" Her little face smiled as she disappeared into the store, rolling easily before her mother.

Lipscomb drummed his fingers on the wall behind him. "Well . . ." he sighed. "Did you know James took the furniture over to Milletson yesterday and sold it? He and Henric divided the money between them. Zack thinks the stuff's in your warehouse."

Rosenbens glanced sidewise at the lawyer. "And he'll never know the difference unless I tell him, eh?"

Lipscomb nodded. Turning to peer through the door, he saw Jahn pacing slowly the length of the building. "Miss Sue and Miss Martha must be buying the furniture," he said. "Well, I doubt if Jahn would know how to pick it; it's a woman's job." Jahn advanced slowly. In the dim, rich light of the overcrowded store, his light, bold eyes glowed with the strange, honest ferocity seen in the eyes of children and courageous animals.

Sue came up the aisle behind him, holding Jahnet in one arm. "Keep her, will you? She gets in the way." She turned back, smiling that set, painful smile.

"James—" Lipscomb began to Jahn, and stopped with a sudden, sibilant drawing in of his breath. Zack was coming down the street toward them, walking rapidly and shrinkingly. Lipscomb said, "I saw Kate this morning. She wants to see you before you leave town." He stopped. Rosenbens was speaking to Zack, and Zack was stopping, his pale, watery eyes uneasy on Jahn, who looked back at him coldly.

Suddenly Zack took a step forward and stood, his hands hanging limply, his eyes sick and pleading. His mouth worked soundlessly.

"Your mother's furniture, Zack, is not in my warehouse," Rosenbens said then, speaking gently, as if to himself.

Lipscomb touched Jahn's arm. "Jahn, Zack came to Martha to warn her before it happened. He was not in on it."

The silence ran over them in small, cold circles. Jahn's eyes were hard pieces of brilliance. He turned abruptly and sat the baby on a high desk just inside the door, and began to play with her, unlacing her boots. His back was stiff and cold. Another silence, stealthier, somehow despairing, settled over them.

"I told Martha . . ." Zack began in a thin, pleading voice. He stopped, trembling. "I didn't want it to happen. . . ." He batted his eyelids rapidly and fearfully, and then, suddenly, without waiting for an answer, he pushed past them all and hurried down the street. Jahn did not glance up.

A little cold wind went sweeping down the street, turning a pile of damp, brown leaves over and over. They whirled dizzily in the air and sank again to the ground.

"Spring," Lipscomb said. "Spring and plowing. . . ." He closed the heavy glass doors gently.

XIV

All that spring and summer Rachel Ibsell sat on Henric's veranda, staring out into the hard brilliance of Melchior Street. The Bible lay open on her lap, with the purple satin marker pressed between the pages of the Song of Solomon.

The voice of my beloved! behold he standeth behind our wall, he looketh forth at the windows, shewing himself through the lattice.

My beloved spake, and said unto me, Rise up, my love . . . and come away. For lo, the winter is past, the rain is over and gone. . . .

The words sounded in her mind, they sung there the song of her desire and her pain, she listened to them with her breath held for a new cadence, for a sign. "Oh, my dove, that art in the clefts of the rock . . . let me see thy countenance, let me hear thy voice. . . ." Her love spoke in her, softly, whimperingly, under the voice of this holy love, crying out and asking itself, "Shall I die, shall I suffer death, shall I be utterly done, my bright wings decayed and my beautiful eyes given over to corruption? Will no voice answer me and no hand lift me up?" The mournful whisper of her hatred answered her. "Never again, O never again will you walk beside your love, your feet passing softly over the dew-wet grass and your eyes looking up at the bright moon. O never, O lost, O lonely and unforgotten, O cheated, ravaged, despoiled by a stranger's hand!"

She saw the first buttercups gleam, she marked the rich beauty of their blossoms, and she smelled in this city street the divine and ineffable odor of newly plowed ground. She said, "O when will I go home again?" and hatred and jealousy answered her with anguish, "You have no home, no land. A strange woman rules back there." She got up, she walked in the yard through the dense masses of Chanson's shrubbery, among the Eastern colors of the nasturtium beds, and she saw a dim, sweet woodland, a spring that boiled clear and pure beneath a canopy of young pine needles.

"Forget, Oh forget the unforgotten, the never to be forgotten!" she cried in her soul, and her fingers went reaching, fumbling for a veil to hide the well-remembered, and finding no veil, no covering to her mind, no water and no tears to erase the indelible prints of her heart. For minute by minute, day by day, she called to her son, and he neither came nor answered. The heart and the flesh of a young golden-eyed woman pushed him away. For this there was no help and no surcease.

She went again to sit on the porch. A little wind rustled the morning-glory vine on the edge of the veranda, and she remembered the wind in elm trees, the glimmering haze of a long-ago morning. Oh, gone forever, Oh sun that never rose again!

Chanson came to sit near her, to talk, to pour an endless stream of words like sharp, jagged pebbles upon the soft, bruised tissues of her brain. She said, politely, "I'm tired, Miss Chancie; let's not talk of it now." And Chanson smiled and left her; but soon Henric came, and James. And day followed day, tomorrow and tomorrow and tomorrow, and all the time their words remarked, maliciously and calculatingly, the bleeding of her wounds. She could forget nothing, she must remember always, day by day, second by second.

Martha came to her crying: "You're ruining us, you're killing him, you're killing yourself!" She could not answer. She drew in her breath and let it out, and she knew that she ached with a profound and ineradicable sorrow for the love lost somewhere, somehow . . . because of that other love lost on El Caney's bloody hills. . . .

The days passed, the weeks, and then he was there, Jahn. She saw him coming up the walk, between the violets and the green blades of the tulip plants. This was he, this was her love, her son. Slowly, like the sun over a black world, a smile came to her face. She let it come, she held to the arms of her chair with both hands, she thought the glory of joy in her would burst her ribs: she saw him coming, her son, beauty walking toward her. . . .

They tasted salt on each other's lips, and drawing back, smiling tremulously, each saw the tears in the other's eyes. Smiles came and went and came again. He was down on his knees with his head in her lap, his shoulders shaking against her. She felt a graciousness of pity tear her breast: this is he,

[111]

this is my little one, my love. She put her hands on his dark curls, smoothing them gently.

But what could she say . . . what could she say . . .? There was anguish, there was jealousy and hatred for a woman who nestled in his bosom. Feeling a bitterness rise in her mouth, under her tongue, she cried, "Why did you do it, son? Cheat me, lie to me, fool me for that good-for-nothing woman . . .!"

She knew then, with a strange surprise, that he had risen and was looking down at her as if he had never seen her before . . . nor ever wanted to see her again. . . .

The veranda moved under her after he was gone, the walls tilted and the floor came slowly upward against her tilting face. Yet she still sat in her chair, the sun was still shining on the hot grass in the yard, on the violets and on the tulips, and time was passing over her head, easy and soundless and dreadful. The shadows of dusk moved toward her with deliberate wheelings of great wings. My beloved spake, and said unto me, Rise up, my fair one, my love, and come away.

Henric moved precisely up the walk, returning from his office, stepped up onto the veranda, and spoke to her. "Good evening, Henric," she said.

A chill moved in the marrow of her spine, her flesh circled with the cold air of evening. From far away she heard the stroke of the town clock above the City Hall. At three, she thought, Peter betrayed his Lord. "Thou, Christ, art the Son of the living God!" he cried out, and when the cock crew, he betrayed Him. She got up slowly, and went into the house. She walked on steady feet toward the library.

"Who was that man James saw, that lawyer?"

Chanson and Henric looked around at her, and got up, standing and waiting.

"Peebles."

"Call him, then," she said. "I must do something. I'll do it, I'll do anything. . . . The Lord is slow in answering. . . ."

PART THREE

I

THE LONG ENVELOPE LAY IN THE MIDDLE OF THE ROAD IN front of Jahn Ibsell's house. There was no wind; the white paper, with the flap wide and gaping where he had torn it, did not move, but lay motionless, gleaming against the hard, dark roadbed. From the window of the living-room, Jahn Ibsell glanced at it once, and then stared at his fields lying monstrous in the dusk. Brown and dun and orange and deep scarlet, freshly turned earth, acrid and sweet, and black-birds flying overhead. The bill of complaint crackled in his pocket.

Behind him, in the shadows of the room, Sue moved softly, and struck a match to the lamp wick. He watched his Negroes and mules in the fields, the little dark figures moving over the deep rich billows of his land, coming nearer and nearer with the slow patience of plowmen curving the last furrows of an autumn day. Smoke from the fire under the lye-vat in the back yard swirled slow on the corners of the house and in front of the window. He sniffed the burning oak, and stood seeing the fragments of dissolving smoke and the long, ominous smell of his land darkening before him; at the same time see-ing how he had gone all that day, talking with his friends in town, riding home in the early afternoon, and coming on the mail-box at the junction of the Red Valley road with the county road. The mail-box was a glare in the changing sun, like the glare from Sand Caves; he got down from the horse and opened it, seeing the letter there on the downward turn of the hinged top of the box.

"I put it in my pocket," he thought, "and came on to the fields and took one of the plows from the Negroes." The brown crusted earth had parted gently above the probing steel point of the plow, and had fallen back in great scallops of solid luxury, the subsoil red with the sheen of Greenville loam. The smell of burning grass and dried cornstalks had come across the long acres from Mose Thurston's field to settle in the furrows. "Smell that?" he had said. "Folks so lazy they burn their cornstalks to keep from plowing them under to rot for fertilizer. . . . Folks like that burn sedge grass in the spring," he had said to his Negroes, and the bill of complaint was in his pocket, rustling there as he stooped after the plow.

He had felt it, and had left the fields, but still with no diminution of pleasure. Rather, with vagueness and a perception of the shifting gray particles of falling dusk, he had come across the pasture and into the road before the house, where some automaton of prescience jumping suddenly in his skull had sent his hand to find the envelope and open it.

He could not, now, from where he stood, with his wife moving softly in the room behind him and his land in front melting richly to the dark cup of the sky, remember the words on the paper in the envelope. Nothing was inside his skull except the fierce spurt of terror, rising hard and dry among the uncertain gyrations of doubt and counterdoubt. "That's all," he thought of himself, "that's all. . . ." He turned suddenly, with a sort of blundering haste, and shoved the paper at Sue.

"Here it is; it's come." His voice was stiff in his throat.

She moved away from the lamp and came toward him, easily smiling, and he felt amazement that she could smile at such a time. "It's come!" he repeated, impatiently, explaining, and suddenly found words from the bill rushing on his tongue. *"Jahn Ibsell versus Mrs. Rachel Ibsell."* The words had a curiously sardonic sound as he spoke them. He stared at the paper in Sue's hand and at her whitening face and said, "Mother versus son. . . ." He laughed. "No, that's wrong, it's son versus mother."

Her hands were spreading the sheet of paper, smoothing it open, but her eyes were on his face in a pitying concern so wide that they seemed, for an instant, gray. He looked off from her, took back the paper, and read from it slowly, with an unused clumsiness.

> "Jahn Ibsell, et als.,
> Appellees
> Vs.
> Mrs. Rachel Ibsell, Appellant . . ."

" 'Et als.'?" he said. "What's that?" He pushed the bill of complaint back to Sue. She shook her head and abruptly stopped looking at him. She held down her face and seemed to hide the paper against her side. "I don't know," she said.

He heard Jahnet laughing in the kitchen, running on her soft baby shoes from the work-table under Black Fanny's nose back to the high step between the kitchen and the dining-room. He smiled automatically. "She's sliding off the kitchen step," he said, and was amazed to hear the light, abstracted sound of his voice. He sat down suddenly on the new black divan against the wall. He said, "I've hated this house since she took the furniture."

> Son, et als.,
> Vs.
> Mother, Appellant.

She was appellant and he was appellee, she accuser and he defender. He looked at Sue, still standing before him with her head bent down in an attitude of guilt and the bill hidden against the folds of her green jersey dress. He said, loudly,

"It's not true, it didn't happen . . .!" and in a lower, stunned voice: "It can't happen! My God!"

He got up and walked blindly toward the door, with his flesh full of impulse of his bruised heart, searching for some place to hide himself and pillow his head in darkness. He stopped, looking back at Sue, and returned to her, pausing an instant beside her, and then sat down on the sofa again.

The iris of his eyes enfolded and received without awareness the unfamiliar tan tuft of the carpet. Across the far end of the room, shadows from the lamp on the table lay in a formless pattern of reflected table legs and chair arms. His mind, relieved now of its first spurt of shock and terror, circled softly on its own grayness, and awoke slowly to hear an eerie echo: "Behold a whirlwind of the Lord is gone forth in fury . . . it shall fall grievously upon the heads of the wicked. . . ." His nerves coiled, sprang out from tensity, and his eyes turned swiftly on Sue. She looked up suddenly, meeting his gaze as if she feared to look at him, yet forced herself to meet an accusation; and then, moving forward a few steps, she sat down in the chair facing him.

"On the heads of the wicked," the echo repeated, softly, insistently.

He turned his hands over, and then over again, feeling in them a curious weakness, wanting, immediately he felt their weakness, to let them fall to his knees and never move again. His breath began to come and go heavily, bringing a ponderous ache, a pain like that from a wrenched muscle in his breast bones. He said: "She's at Martha's now . . . they let her go there to get rid of her; they won't want to be bothered with her now they've got their way. . . ." He said, "She don't want to see me. . . ."

Sue moved uneasily in her chair. "Jahn . . ." She closed her mouth, looked away from him, and back again suddenly. "It's not your mother," she said, tonelessly and steadily. "It's the others. Everybody knows that. She . . . she's old and they've led her into this. . . ." She stopped abruptly and

immediately looked away from him. He stared at his hands.
. . . "Why don't you . . . If you'd go to see her . . .?" A pale,
sick flush ran swiftly over her face. "Jahn, if you'd go to see
her again, maybe you could stop it before . . . too late. . . ."

His chest labored suddenly. "I can't," he said. And under
his breath, "She accuses me, her eyes accuse me. . . ." He
straightened up with a sudden anger and cried, "Why are you
telling me—defending her? I go, and she talks against you.
Quit defending her!"

She moved back in her chair, away from his anger, and was
motionless, with her eyes cast down and the little flush still on
her cheeks. The bill of complaint rustled between her side and
the arms of the chair.

The black onyx clock ticked on the mantel. He listened to
it dully, remembering that it had been Henric's wedding present to Sue, and then his thoughts fell away from it without
irony or emotion.

Sue spoke abruptly. "But, Jahn, what does it mean, 'et
als.'?"

He shook his head without looking at her. "'Appellees,'"
he said. "It calls me appellees as if I were more than one.
. . ." His voice died impatiently; he got up. "I'll call Lipscomb." He moved toward the telephone in the hall.

Behind him, Sue sat with her gaze cast down, vaguely following the slow movement of his feet across the hall. When
she heard him speaking to the operator, she turned her head
back toward the window where the dark pressed now, heavy
and motionless. The Negroes were at the well in the side
yard, drawing water for Jahn's sorrel, who had not been
turned into the pasture with the mules. She was aware, suddenly, of the click of the receiver coming to rest on the hall
table, and of Jahn's steps moving back across the corridor.
His face loomed strangely before her startled eyes, and then
the door swung to, shutting her off from his face and from
the sound of his voice when he spoke. She stared at the sep-

arating door, too amazed to realize her own breathless constriction.

Jahnet toddled in from the hall through her mother's bedroom, and sat on the sofa in front of her. Her stern blue eyes stared solemnly. "Supper's weady," she said, lisping, her two-year-old mouth striving to repeat exactly what Black Fanny had taught her to say. Sue got up and went into the dining-room, going through her own room and avoiding the hall. Jahnet followed her, steering carefully between the furniture, and waited by her high chair until Black Fanny appeared and lifted her up. "Black Fanny's little lam'," the Negress said.

Jahn came in, smiling with a strange, gleaming look of anger and triumph in his eyes. He pushed back his chair loudly.

"Well. . . . Lipscomb's for me, anyway," he said. His voice rang strongly, and he stood with his legs wide apart, his shoulders thrown back in determined challenge. "Know what they've done. . . . 'Fraud and coercion.' Lipscomb says she had to bring them in as parties defendant to make the bill legal. That's it, there they are stuck in with me as parties defendant!" He laughed briefly. His shoulders sagged suddenly, he sat down, and fumbled his napkin onto his knees. "But that's legal fiction; everybody knows better. They'll give testimony for her. . . ."

Sue moved the coffee-cups in front of her plate. "But, Jahn . . . how can they? They're named on your side?"

He moved impatiently. "It's legal fiction. . . . That's how it goes, work for them like a dog, and they get it all. Henric's got the books and the sword and the bayonet, everything of my father's. . . . I ought to have known what was going on a long time ago. I was a fool!"

Black Fanny brought a plate of hot biscuits, pushed the steak into the center of the table, and glanced at Jahn slyly. Her black eyes circled in swimming points of light under her wrinkled yellowish eyelids.

"You ain't findin' out nuthin', Mis' Jahn. We done all

know hit when we seed Ol' Miss handin' out them little bits of yo' money to Mis' Henric en James way back."

She stalked into the kitchen, her knees stiff, her high turned-over heels heavy on the floor. Jahnet giggled softly, looking at her father out of sly blue eyes.

He roused. "Well, one thing's certain: this is not the first family that's disgraced itself in court."

Sue moved the coffee-cups again. "Jahn, don't you remember telling me about Long Jim Chambers and his father? He took care of his father, and then when the old man died ———"

"Long Jim Chambers!" He looked at her, curling his lip. "Who cares what the Chambers did!"

He flushed faintly, ashamed, and was suddenly aware of her beauty sitting in the bud of his meanness, forming it. He burst out, "How could I walk around and look people in the face if I didn't know it was all a lie? I didn't cheat her. . . . I . . ." But it wasn't a lie, he thought. It wasn't all a lie; he hadn't meant to, but he had cheated her. . . . He stared at Sue, seeing his mother as she would be on this night, alone in her room at Martha's, gazing into the darkness and hating him she had loved.

II

That long autumn before the trial began moved in Zack and his mother with a slow, twisting torture. He sat in the office with Henric, waiting for the time, the day to come, the fragments of all his life flitting communally with the family on the screen of his conscience. His face turned from Henric, in aversion and fascination; his soul spoke to Henric demandingly, crying, "What is it, why is it, what are we doing?" and he was not able to speak at all. He had, in his patience of waiting, a sense of time indivisable by the phenomena of day and night; yet it was by day and night that he counted, setting these spaces before him to be interrupted by his meals, by visits to his sweetheart, Paula Pollard, and by disconnected and unreal hours at Martha's house with his mother.

Henric told him, "We begin tomorrow." He was going out of the office, and he turned around. "Tomorrow. . . ." He repeated it tonelessly, and without being able to raise his pale Ibsell eyes to Henric's black gaze. He went out of the office and there was no place for him to go. He stumbled in the early December darkness, in the teeth of the small, sharp wind, and the hours were going; the morning, the day, were coming. He found himself on the sidewalk before Hooper Pollard's house. A dead vine rustled on the white trellis at one end of the wide veranda. Electric light proceeding in long pale streams from the living-room window fell over the vine, which showed a spotted color, slick like the backs of certain snakes. He stepped into the yard; dried grasses crackled and hissed under his feet.

Inside the house, Paula's throaty voice answered her father. "It's already nine. . . ." Hooper Pollard jeered pleasantly. "Your beau's not coming, girl!" She began to sing, strumming lightly her guitar:

> The sky was blue
> > and high above
> The moon was new
> > and so was love!

And then an old song, sorrowful and sweet.

> London Tower is fallen down
> An' I maun fa' so swiftly. . . .
> O girls, remember me!

Far up the hill, stumbling on cold feet, Zack heard her voice, "O girls, remember me." The town clock struck, booming hollowly across the shrill whistle of the wind. A streak of light, peculiar, purplish, the filament of his own imagination, crossed his path. Behind it, clinging to the air, rode the dwarf he knew from his childhood. The yellow, peering face worked like cheese. He saw the sinister dissolving of the face and the flash of sharp, slender tusks. Turning his head this way and that in furtiveness of terror, he saw that the town was dark, all the lights out in the houses, the street lamps glimmering wanly. He moved his hands; the dwarf's face crackled putrescently under his fingers. He drew his fingers together, held them stiff, and then, jerking his hands to his face, he began to weep with his eyes wide open.

A whistle, eerie and full of a wailing sorrow, sounded somewhere behind the dark hills above Choctaw. The whistle cried again and yet again, and now, behind its wail, came the soft, pervading sibilance of far-away wheels turning on steel tracks. A flaring white light spangled the sky, grew, focused, wheeled in vast arcs above Lecker Street where Billy Nelson's house stood among the sprawled houses on the shoulder of the hill, and shot downward into the dark bowl where Choctaw lay.

Raising his head, Zack fastened his eyes on the darkness of Lecker Street. He stood up, all madness cleansed from his brain, and went slowly across the hill, moving like a man in a dream in which there is no drama but the drama of a strange and abrupt detachment from self.

He came with steady feet to Billy Nelson's house, where the moonlight shot itself over the tall, old-fashioned veranda columns, and went across the porch, into the hall, and up the stairs to his mother's room. The door knob yielded without sound to his turning fingers, and he came like a ghost across the threshold into a space glimmering with pale light from the open windows, and found her sitting there, in her chair in the middle of the room, like another ghost. She did not move, except with the startled reflex of her shoulders and the slow steadying of her eyes to recognize his face.

He said, "It's tomorrow." A sudden, chill terror came out of her and over him, lifting faintly the roots of his hair. Her voice answered him, strange and crackling with a dry helplessness of assent. "Yes, tomorrow, Zack. . . ."

She rocked her chair, back and forth once, and nothing

seemed stranger to him than that slow, mourning motion abstracted from itself. He stood waiting, watching the turn of the light from the window with the shadows of the room. She got up suddenly, and held to the back of her chair, looking downward at the floor. She said, "I've been waiting . . . and God He knows for what." She turned her face toward his, and it was dark and formless with nothing but her eyes shining in it with the fevered shine of unshed tears. "What made you come tonight?"

It was not his own voice that answered. "I saw the dwarf. . . ." He waited a minute, and then he said, "You . . . we have to do something. . . ."

She turned again, coming closer to him, and touched his shoulder. He put his arms around her and held her and stared above her head at the fluctuations of darkness past the window. Outside, in the hall, he heard Martha's slippered feet stirring and coming toward them. He and his mother moved together to the opening of the door and the click of the light bulb.

"Zack saw the dwarf tonight," Rachel said. "I guess that was what I was waiting for." Martha's countenance glimmered before her, and the vivid blue eyes swept over Zack, lightening with comprehension. She held to the door knob in silence, waiting for them to know what they wanted. She said, "I'll get Billy's car keys for you."

Rachel stepped backward against the dressing-table. She gazed above Martha's head, blindly staring at the door where all her life seemed to meet and fuse in this moment of acceptance. "Yes," she said, "bring the car keys and let's go to stop this. . . ." Her old, dry mouth worked suddenly, and then queerly smiled at Martha's hastily retreating back. "I guess I was waiting for an excuse. . . . Zack, I think I must ask you to forgive me for bringing you into the world. I made you out of the sickness my father handed down to me, and that's how it is. . . . I have an excuse tonight to go to a woman I hate and lower myself to her. . . ." Her hand groped for his, and her eyes filmed as they turned to hide themselves. "Zack, was it very bad, the dwarf . . .?"

The leaves of all her winters, swept on the roadsides of a hundred nights, floated in her mind when they came finally into the Ibsell road and stopped before the house Jahn had built for her. She got down from Billy Nelson's car immediately, and stood beside it a moment, gazing at the gray rock chimneys, and waiting while Zack turned the ignition and set the hand brake. The moonlight was unreal to her, gray and sick with the streak of dark wind-blown clouds careening above the browned floor of the pasture lands where once she had walked with Jahn and tied his life to hers in words that stuck in her throat and never meant more than the torture she had made for herself out of her blood. While she looked, she saw a light come on in the house. Sue's small, slender body passed the window in a blue satin negligée.

"I never," she said to Zack, "had silk and lace to wear. . . ." The words crumbled on the air in front of her like dried leaves into powdery evanishments of dust. She bent her head shamefully, and sucked in her full lower lip. "And that's me," she said. "I'm so little I can hate her for being what I could never be . . . and that's why," she added, walking forward, "she can have what I never had . . . silk and lace. . . ."

She moved apart from Zack when they were through the yard fence, and went halfway up the walk alone, but there, suddenly, she stumbled on the flagstones, and found him behind her, steadying her with his arm. Raising her eyes, she saw Sue standing in the doorway, waiting, with the hall lamp swinging from the ceiling above her head. She grasped Zack's hand swiftly, and knew then, as from outside herself, that he was leading her up the steps, drawing her after him into the house.

The girl's white, frightened face fell back before her against the neat, impersonal arrangement of the new furniture in the living-room, and she thought, "This is some other place, this

is not—mine." Her body drooped to the sorrow of her strangeness here, she knew nothing but the defeat of her shame in
alienation. Zack's voice came to her, loud in his embarrassment, bursting through the mists clouding her awareness, and
she straightened herself and listened tensely. Her eyes wandered on the tan surface of the new rug.

"Jahn—where is Jahn?" Zack said.

Sue's small, rose-tipped fingers held together the folds of
her negligée at her throat. Rachel saw suddenly the swift,
startled twitching of her upper lip.

"I don't know. He hasn't been here all night." The breath
fluttered in her throat, and caught, so that she said abruptly,
with accusation, "When he's worried he goes off by himself.
. . ." She looked away from them; her hands moved in little
jerks at her neck.

"I know," Rachel said. "He goes to the barn. He's always
done that." She stopped, and listened to herself, feeling some
calmness come over her shame and abasement, and some
warmth building in her to the realization that they were both,
she and Sue alike, women. She said, in parenthesis and without stemming more than momentarily the reawakening flow
of her purpose, "He'll have seen the car lights; he'll come in
a moment. . . ."

Her voice deepened, the warmth grew in her, but with
loneliness now and even with pleasure in its strength as
separate from the shame she had. "I'm here to ask you how
we can stop it. I guess I'm even here to beg your pardon and
say I'm wrong." She stopped and looked at the girl, and repeated, "I'm here to say I want to stop it. . . . It all come out
of my hating you, and that was wrong, too, but I did it. . . .
I did it because we were different and I wanted to keep him.
He had," she said, with difficulty, "a right to leave me for you.
And I can't say more than that. . . ."

She moved backward in sudden exhaustion, seeking a place
to sit down in the strange room, and saying, dully, "But I
wouldn't have done it even then if they'd left me alone." She

found the unfamiliar divan, and sat on it uneasily, and heard her voice continuing to speak out of her.

"I blame them now, and that's wrong, too, because I made them. I tried to live, to keep on having my life. . . ." She broke off, and said, "God knows there's nothing worse than trying to live." She looked up at Sue strangely, without seeing anything of her except the great, golden eyes watching her with the expression of pity that had always been like contempt, and said on the last ebb of her strength, "I think God hates life. . . ."

The sudden stillness of the room washed over her, and she knew that that creeping, distrustful quiet came out of her son's wife, standing upright against the center table, astringently withdrawn. She watched the small, pale face and the twitch of the small mouth and flinched before it opened. "I did nothing to you," Sue said. "You hurt me and my child; you wanted us to die."

"No, no!" Zack cried, hastily. He backed out from the window and into the room. "She didn't mean . . ."

His confusion crossed them weakly and fell flat against their intent and unlistening ears.

"If I wanted that," Rachel said, "I'm sorry. There's never been any way for me to say what I wanted except my son. You love him, too, and you can forgive me for that."

Sue looked at her steadily. "You wanted the land. You told him to give back your land and go with me."

There was, abruptly, an amusement in Rachel, growing out of an old, self-wrought scorn for the financial economy of marital love in women. Her lips moved, and then grinned ironically. The malice in her spoke clearly to her own ears, "I knew you'd not have had him without anything!" But then she bit her lip, she made her face grave, and said, "I wanted something of my own to keep . . . you understand that."

The girl did not answer her, she stood drawn back against the table, with her face pale and closed, waiting still and unforgiving. Her breast was motionless under the cream-colored lace crossing her bosom. She said, "You waited a long time to come."

"I know, and you're hard on me, but it's not me and you, it's him. He's my son and your husband. He's a man and he's got to live and do all that it falls on men to do. About us it don't matter. We're got nothing to do but take what he gives." She lowered her gaze from Sue's face and looked at the spread fingers on her lap. "That's it," she said. "That's what I didn't know at first, I'd done a man's work for so long. But I can see it now, and I know we don't matter. We've got to give up for him."

The girl stiffened abruptly, and a frightened, angry eagerness struck out of her against Rachel's lowered face. "What is it you want me to do? Go away, leave him to you? I offered to do that once, and you heard him; he kept me ——"

"And let me go," Rachel interrupted. She watched the flush in the girl's cheeks. "I know," she said, and got up, hearing while she rose a noise on the back veranda and in the kitchen. "He's coming now, and we've got to get it over with before he gets here. You and I have always been too quick with our tongues . . . or maybe I've been the one, and not you. But it don't matter now ——"

She stopped suddenly, the uprush of her defeated love throwing against her face, like a merciless blow, the force of her own acknowledgment: He let me go. . . . She stood staring, her hands coming up to hold her breast against that bruise, laboring with it, her lips moving thickly and ineptly to cry out, "Why did you say it? . . . He let me go! Oh, to run your triumph over me like this now, to say it. . . . I was right to hate you!" She turned half-around, bent over on herself with her angry grief, and then she knew that he was in the doorway, that he had come in and found her without victory. She straightened, she pretended he was not there, she raised her face to look at Sue, and said, "But that don't matter. I must stop it, and whatever he says or you say, it's

ended. . . ." She faltered and looked at him. "It's stopped.
. . ."

He filled the doorway with his height and the breadth of
his shoulders. A sudden terror rushed over Rachel from his
size, so that she could not see him except as bone that was
like rock bound with implacable muscle, his face white and
carved by lines of accumulated resentment and shining with
a sweat of anger and grief that no human being could ever
reach past again. His great, farmer's hands swung at his sides,
restrained, convulsive, jerked by the animal heaving of his
chest. The imminence of danger rushed from him over the
room, and then, distinctly, they saw him catch himself up,
and hold with his nerves what residues of sanity, grief and the
unendurable sense of betrayal had left to him. A slow blackness, the measure of his control, pouched under his eyes.

"You're here hectoring her again!" They saw him stop
and catch the sides of the door frame with his hands turned
outward. A sudden exhaustion passed over his face, steadying
it. "I thought there was enough for you to do in court tomorrow without coming tonight to work out your meanness on
her."

"You didn't hear it all," Zack began, stammering, after a
minute. "It was me, she came for me. . . ." Some nervous
timidity kept him from mentioning his dwarf again. "She . . .
we wants to stop it now." His voice wavered helplessly, he
looked to his mother and Sue, and edged back again into the
obscurity of the window.

"You can't stop it," Jahn said. "It's done."

Rachel Ibsell looked at him, and then at Sue, leaning motionless against the table, with her eyes lowered and an expression of wary triumph setting her prim, sweet lips. Rachel
felt suddenly the truth of what he had said. It was done; it
could not be ended. Her mind circled helplessly, so that she
was for an instant aware only of how they looked, standing
so, separate each from the others and bound indissolubly by
that separation, and she thought, "He's thin . . . the collar of

his shirt needs turning." She thought, "I am still his mother, but he doesn't know it. . . . My shoulders ache. . . ." Then, again, she knew that her errand was purposeless, she could undo nothing and end nothing; life turned out beyond the extent of her reach. "But I started it," she said, abruptly, out loud, and looked from one to the other of them. "I started it . . . ?" Her voice rose and broke.

"You did start it," Jahn said. "You are my mother and you've brought me to a shame I can't live with or ever live down." He looked beyond her, his eyes fixed on space with the black pouches under them standing out startlingly. Sue moved in front of him, and opened her mouth halfway to speak, and then closed it firmly while two spots of hectic red began to burn on her cheek bones.

"That's what I have to live with all my life, that I came from your wickedness, and I never can get away from it. I have to know that, and remember how I clung to you and was here with you, loving you and letting you make me what you wanted, a ninny and an ignorant clod that shamed my brothers till they learned to hate me.

"I have to know that," he repeated in the rapt, even voice of a man reciting a litany, "and remember I gave up all my life to you because you had to rule somebody and I was your son and you didn't care what you did to your son if he couldn't stop you. The only thing I can thank you for is the drop of my father in me that made me choose Sue and go against you for once—the only thing I can thank you for is for hating me for having that much of my father in me and wanting more than your selfish rule. No, you can't stop it. You don't want to. That's not what you came for. You came to browbeat my wife—" His voice dwindled suddenly, and he stood in the doorway, clasping it with his hands to hold himself up, and gazing beyond his mother as if the hatred in him dared not look at his love.

The thin, piercing cry of a child awakened in the middle of the night in a lighted room rang faintly in the abrupt silence.

He moved, answeringly, and brought his gaze down so that, for a second, inescapably, he saw her face, dead and floating in a mist of stunned oblivion; and then, for an instant, he saw Sue's eyes, terrified, half-remorseful, yet shining with a covert triumph. A sickness shuddered through all his flesh, he hung in the door, holding himself up before them, while the child's thin cry rang monotonously and fretfully, and then, somehow, he turned and was in the hall, escaping.

Behind him no one moved. The light shone steadfastly and coldly on the women's pale faces. In the next room the child hushed. The cessation of sound floated over them, and they shivered, unable to bear their closeness in silence.

"Jahn's happiness means more to me than to you," Sue said, defensively.

Their eyes turned, they glanced at one another, and then away. The lamp sang on its fallen wick.

"We must go, Mamma." Zack came out from the window and stood beside his mother.

Sue stood away from the table. She carried her hands folded across her diaphragm like a woman appearing before an audience, and said, "I said nothing because that would have made him worse. . . ." She looked carefully away from Rachel, and stood aside to let them pass. She knew that she could not have spoken, and that now she never would.

"Yes," Rachel said. She stared at the strange new furniture. "Rachel Ibsell must go home." She walked steadily, and without feeling, out of the house.

III

In the far corner of the courtroom, the radiator made a hissing sound, loud in the silence. They sat, all of them, in a motionless suspense, subduing the informality of Chancery court to the unbreathing shame of their beings. Standing above them, beside the judge's bench, Bard Lipscomb was not able to separate even himself from that silence. James waited in the witness-chair, straightening his tie, smoothing his gray mustache, but whatever was to be said, the lawyer felt, was not in James and not in this room.

He looked suddenly for Sue, and finding her not there, a curious, streaked irony livened his mind for an instant, as if her absence here, at the events her existence had made possible and even necessary, proved them with some unforeseen amusement.

Across from him, on the respondent's side, Jahn moved and set his feet together. The brown splotches on the wall at the far end of the courtroom wavered above Rachel Ibsell's head, and she looked up. Those two pairs of eyes, so alike, so different, charged equally with the fate of their common blood, met and fell apart, but not before it had seemed to Bard Lipscomb that Jahn was here in his mother's bosom as the embryo of his future had lain in her womb. But the faces of the others pressed over that intuition, and erased it as the hiss of the radiator suddenly erased the silence. The lawyer glanced down, moved the papers on his table, and turned to the witness in the chair.

"Now, Mr. James Forrest, will you give us your opinion of Jahn Ibsell's agricultural ability?"

The witness glanced at his mother's dark dress and folded hands. In the front row, Henric and Chanson sat up stealthily, keeping their heads turned from Martha across the aisle. A small, thwarted sound burst from Zack's throat; he swallowed, and kept down his face. The witness looked away from him, out the window at the top of Joe Rosenbens' store, brought his eyes back to question those of Mr. Peebles, attorney for the complainant, received his reassuring nod, and then gazed boldly at Joe Rosenbens and Kate Ibsell. Behind him, Judge Whitten stirred restlessly, settling the tails of his brown sack coat over his plump stomach. The witness smoothed his mustache again.

"Jahn Ibsell is fair, I reckon. But I don't know much about it." He straightened his shoulders proudly. "I was in Pittsburgh most of the years he farmed for Mother. But I heard from Henric Ibsell that Jahn was taking Mother's orders and doing as he was told."

"Jahn Ibsell was an obedient son, then?"

The complainant leaned forward, raised her head, and stared at the witness. Her dark eyes glowed with a light deep and strange, like the blue-pearl light that bursts from the center of black opals. She looked steadily at James, resisting the pull of her thoughts to Jahn's face, lifted blindly beside the platform on which Lipscomb stood.

The witness flushed. "Well . . . obedient in that."

"You went to Pittsburgh immediately after the death of your stepfather, Larson Ibsell, and stayed there until about six years ago?"

"I was . . . I was . . ." The witness floundered, sensing an accusation.

"You were what?"

"Nothing."

"Ah! Like God Mr. James Forrest was—but what, deponent sayeth not!"

"Your Honor, I object to the hectoring of this witness!" Mr. Peebles smoothed fiery red hair with pale, nervous hands.

Judge Whitten leaned on his elbows, chin in palm. The money he owed to Henric formed and dissolved before his eyes, buying and selling him with its power on the instant. The triangular points of his eyelids lowered over his full staring pupils. "Witness must answer fully in order that the court may be informed," he said. His eyes closed on the flush of disconcerted blood into Henric's face.

"I was in Pittsburgh," said the witness, with super-distinct and pious enunciation, "and I didn't know what all was going on back here. If I had, I'd a taken steps to protect my mother's interests!"

Jahn Ibsell's hands moved on his knees. He glanced at them, slowly, as if with amazement to find that he had still a body. The tips of his fingers trembled slightly, with a rhythm more evident to his feelings than to his eyes, and the hard tips of the nails seemed faintly blue. He sat staring at them, all his faculties concentrated on their shape and color, and then, abruptly, all that was in the room swung like a flood of water over him and he felt himself plunging under, curved in a long arc of flesh, swept by the chill tides of an immutable and unseeing atmosphere. He came back, not easily and not immediately, but with a sense of swiftness, to his chair, wondering when he found himself there; and then that too passed out of him, pierced by the high, caroling sound of Lipscomb's mockery.

"I suppose, Mr. Forrest, that you were regularly sending a sum of money to your mother, your share toward her support? Will you name the sum?"

The witness bit his mustache. "I was not able—I had my way to make without help and I was married ——"

"Were Mr. Henric Ibsell and Mr. Zack Ibsell contributing to the support of their mother?"

"They were in school here in Choctaw."

"Who paid their board and tuition?"

"Mother."

Rachel Ibsell's lips moved. "Jahn," she said, but under her breath, so that no one heard her but Kate Ibsell.

Bard Lipscomb smiled at Chanson. He glanced at the stenographers, busy with pencils and notebooks. "Is Jahn Ibsell a good farmer?"

"Fair."

"Above the average?"

The witness fidgeted. "I reckon."

"Now, Mr. Forrest, what would you do with the lands in question if you ——?"

"Objection!" cried Peebles, wildly. "Objection!"

"Objection sustained," said Judge Whitten.

"Now, Mr. Forrest, can you tell the court if any of your mother's children suffer from any physical or mental disability that would prevent them doing farm work or contributing in some way to her support? The court would be glad of a reason why Jahn Ibsell was the only child who worked for her and why the others received help from her."

"Object!" said Peebles, more mildly this time. "The question is irrelevant; honorable opponent is seeking to influence the court."

"Witness may answer," sighed Judge Whitten, observing the top of the bench with sly, amused eyes.

The witness licked dry lips. "Jahn Ibsell never had any desire or ambition to make a way for himself."

"He was solely devoted to his mother, then?"

"No. That is, he wanted to stay on the farm to get round her."

"Is it true that your mother deeded some land to you when you returned from Pittsburgh? Just as she deeded land to Jahn Ibsell later?"

"Yes. Five hundred acres. My land was not so good ———"

"The court will please have Mr. Forrest's property evaluated, also please compare present evaluation with that made at the time the land was granted him. . . . Mr. Forrest, when did you first hear your mother say she wanted Jahn to have the lands involved in this suit?"

"I can't say; I don't know as I ever heard her say it."

"Figure back, and see what year it was."

"I really can't say without figuring back."

Martha laughed shortly and trillingly.

The witness flushed, looked stony, and said, "I really rather not say . . . answer the question except as I have answered it."

"Witness released," murmured Lawyer Lipscomb.

The stenographers looked up, pencils poised. Judge Whitten shifted his position. Chanson smiled at Henric and Martha at Jahn. Zack moved unhappily. James Forrest came down from the witness-stand and sat on the row of seats behind Henric.

Rachel Ibsell's steady, strained eyes turned slowly in their sockets, paused, and did not look at Jahn. The bare, brown walls of the courtroom closed on her, receded, and closed again, telescoping all her years to this quintessence of brown walls and bitter breath. She said to herself, "I am an old woman, an old woman." All her life had come to this, that she was old and repudiated by her son, and her flesh and blood warred in a dingy little room three stories above the earth. Noises of traffic came up from the streets below. She shivered, hearing iron wheels on stone. Who was it told her queens went to their deaths to the accompaniment of that rumbling? Larson . . . Larson had told her. But it didn't matter, it didn't make sense. She was old and there was no more to say. When you were old you were a foolishness rotting in plain sight of people. . . .

Bard Lipscomb was reading a paper into the evidence. "'I, Jahn Ibsell, promise to pay. . . . Given under my hand this twenty-seventh day of December. . . .'" The stenographers moved their hands across the notebooks. December? December? It was December when he promised, and this was December again. . . . Henric was in the witness-chair, leaning back, looking down at his boots, smoothing his trousers leg with long, white hands.

"You have heard the conveyance read into the evidence," said Mr. Peebles. "Was this mortgage and promissory note given willingly or was it exacted by Mrs. Rachel Ibsell as a measure of protection to her children not favored by gifts of land?"

Henric raised his flat, black eyes to the ceiling. "I'm not perfectly certain. That is, we knew nothing of the matter until Mother presented the deed to Jahn Ibsell at the Christmas dinner of which you have heard."

Mr. Peebles smirked at Lawyer Lipscomb.

"Then you were not aware of Mrs. Ibsell's alleged purpose to convey the lands described in the bill of complaint to Jahn Ibsell?"

"We knew nothing of it."

He glanced downward at his mother as he spoke, and her dark face was turned full on him, waiting and tense, with the muscles of her scorn moving rigidly under the jawbone. One instant of fear went through him, like the sound of her voice denouncing his lie, and then he knew that she was still silent, acquiescing, and he jumped in his chair, loosening his gaze from hers. "She did not tell us," he said, his hands tight on the arms of the chair.

Lipscomb's strange, vivid face gleamed at him, smiling under the cap of white hair with the familiar push of his lower lip against the upper one.

"To the best of your knowledge, what was Jahn Ibsell's attitude toward staying on the farm with his mother?"

"Objection!" murmured Bard Lipscomb. "Witness cannot testify concerning respondent's state of mind."

"Witness must answer."

"Jahn Ibsell was not willing to stay there. He complained that Zack and I were in school. He seemed to feel envious, to have a feeling of what might be called rough inferiority in our presence, and to think that we were mistreating him. He behaved with some unpleasantness. The matter was painful," said Henric, "to Mother especially."

"Then," said Peebles, pressing the point with some eagerness, "you never heard Mrs. Ibsell express a purpose to deed and release her land to Jahn Ibsell?"

Henric hesitated, and dared not look at his mother where her black eyes burned in hatred of a lie. A long time ago, not in this dingy courtroom, but elsewhere, she had said to him, "I mean Jahn to have the farm . . ." He put his hands together, and shifted his feet.

"Witness must answer," said Judge Whitten.

"Well . . . she mentioned the matter to Zack and myself, but she seemed to have no fixed purpose about it. She couldn't make up her mind. She was always . . . angry and troubled when she spoke of it."

"Then you never really imagined that she had any intention of disinheriting you in favor of Jahn Ibsell?"

"I fear the vague phraseology of my opponent misleads the witness," said Lipscomb, ironically.

"Rephrase the question, Mr. Peebles."

"Then—you never believed that your mother would deed the property to Jahn Ibsell?"

"Never. Not unless she had been cajoled or threatened."

"Your witness," said Mr. Peebles, happily.

The drawn thread of Rachel's attention fell away from the shifting of the stenographers at the long desk beyond the platform and the judge's bench, and traveled backward across the room into herself. She sat listening inwardly, as if to hear within her breast the snuffle of Jahn's choked breath and the swell of his arteries to the gall she had bequeathed him. She thought, "He doesn't breathe," thinking it clearly for one moment, and then looked at him sidewise to see how pride stiffened him in repudiation of his mother. The carved loneliness of his face was queerly like innocence. "His lies," she thought, suddenly, "were never like theirs," and then she knew that he had not hated her last night except with his pain.

Her gaze moved slowly away from him and onto her lap, with presently some reserves of unused cunning thrusting in her to shape the lines of her face to a passive demureness in the face of Henric's lies.

Bard Lipscomb rose to cross-examine.

"Mr. Ibsell, prior to the conveyance of this deed you had not heard your mother speak of her desire to give the property in question to her dear son Jahn?"

"She had mentioned it, yes." Henric licked his lips, watching warily. "But not as a fully formed intention."

"Can you recall the words she used in speaking of her intentions?"

"Not exactly. . . . She said once that she meant him to have

[136]

the farm. But that was before she bought the other land, when the farm meant the two hundred acres left by my father."

She was looking at him now, the scorn in her eyes drawing him on to half-truths, the set softness of the lines about her mouth befuddling him with an uneasy reassurance. "She mentioned it to Zack and me . . . but hesitantly, as if she were sounding her own thoughts concerning the matter. . . ."

He saw her smile, and knew, at the same time, how Lipscomb was rolling a pencil between his long, tapering fingers, twirling it swiftly three times and then, once, dragging it between his thumb and forefinger.

"That was when you suggested it might not be amiss if you yourself had the property, eh?"

"Object!" cried Peebles, rising, stretching his thin, colorless mouth. "Your Honor, the witness cannot make his way among opponent's suggestions!"

Henric's muscles, already gathered in the instinctive movement of escape, crawled on his shoulders. He flushed, and held his breath, his stare tense on his mother.

"Witness must answer," prompted Judge Whitten slowly, after a moment.

Henric said in a low, secretive voice, "I never suggested that . . ."

On the instant, then, before his breath could leave his throat, he knew that she had fooled him, purposely and maliciously. She was standing up, dark and vague against the spotted wall, and her voice was coming out over all of them.

"Henric has forgot. He told me years ago he wanted the land, he wanted to rent it out and keep Jahn on as tenant. . . ."

She sat down at once, without waiting to see what was on their faces.

Some one stirred, far off from her, and a chair creaked

through the steady hiss of the radiator. She stared down at the oiled floor, pulses of excitement beating in her ears, her neck stiff and turned away from her desire to see Jahn's face. A foolish glimmer moved in her mind, a glimmer as of his face changing, glowing all at once with a bright and wonderful love and forgiveness. But she could not turn to see, the tendons in her neck held stiff and averted. A dirty shade, rolled high in the windows above Zack's head flapped once and then lay idle. She watched it with a childlike absorption of timidity and hope. A whisper that she knew was Henric at the judge's bench spun a string of sibilance over the room and was broken by Lipscomb's loud voice.

"Your Honor, the complainant has, by her remarks, repudiated the grounds of her case against respondent. Respondent begs a discontinuance. . . ."

She looked up then, but not toward Jahn. Martha, she saw, was standing, and James and Chanson, all standing apart, yet together in eagerness and fear; and past them, his chin leaning on his hand, Judge Whitten's round, red face gazing solemnly at her. The bent eyelids moved over the unblinking pupils, and she closed her own eyes against their still, withheld light.

"Complainant's case is not impaired in law by an irregularity in the memory of the witness named in the bill with respondent. . . . Court recesses. . . ."

They moved past her out into the echoing corridors. Martha's hand was at her elbow, her arm at her back. She stood up again, and at last, timidly and with fear, she dared to look at Jahn. He talked with Lawyer Lipscomb, he did not glance at her. The two men, her son and her old friend, held their heads turned self-consciously away from her direction. She did not wait then. She was old, and they would come back here many times, over a long period, at the court's pleasure. . . . The sound of her footsteps on the dirty corridors struck back at her with the muffled throb of a clock that catches on its gilt hours, and ticks, and will not ring its own release.

IV

The March wind, Zie Gurney thought, turning the corner of Broad Street beside Rosenbens' store, was nigh to lift the breath out of a man's throat. He caught himself upright with one hand against the rough brick building, and stood adjusting the folds of his black muffler under the tight brim of his tall black hat. Passers-by brushed hurriedly against him, knocking his arm down, and he jerked the muffler off, staring resentfully at their warm overcoated backs.

James Forrest and Long Jim Chambers emerged from Rosenbens' door. He lifted his voice at them. "Aye, but I'll be fit fer preaching with cold in me like this, Brother Chambers!"

"You'll do us out to Nazareth Church in airy case, Elder Gurney," Long Jim said, offering his hand. "I reckon as how yer're in to see yore sister Rachel today?"

Zie's small black eyes avoided Long Jim's and glanced slyly over James Forrest. "Aye, pore Rachel. God be with her! I'm called fer witness when the case comes up ag'in in August." He shook hands gravely and portentously with his nephew. "How's yore mother, James? I come in to learn her wishes fer my testimony."

"Perty early fer thet, seems to me," Long Jim remarked.

James shook his head from side to side. "Porely, Uncle Zie, porely. . . ." He retained Zie's hand in both of his, pressing it affectionately. "Going downhill fast under the strain."

Zie released his hand, wrinkled his nostrils again, and stared at Long Jim's short leather coat. "I'm bound ye're warm in that, Brother Chambers," he said. He looked at James again. "Not sick, is she? Not in bed, eh?"

"What beats me," Long Jim observed, leaning against the building beside James and biting a plug of tobacco neatly with his long, yellowed teeth, "is the way hit drags on. You all, you ain't met with Jedge Whitten but once, hev you? I'd say as how I'd not stand fer sech delays. You arsk me, Jedge

Whitten's a-cheatin' on Mis' Ibsell, somehow." He spat with grave, dark dignity.

"It drags," Zie murmured; "it drags. Pore Rachel, a woman that saw well to the ways of her household, better than rubies and diamonds, and this her reward—rebellion frum her son! But I knowed when she married Larson Ibsell, these many years ago, there'd be trouble to pay. Jahn's got the Ibsell biggitiness. Ol' Larson, he'd look at ye in a way to lower ye to nothing, and no more religion to him than to a horse. . . ."

Long Jim spat again, suddenly and vigorously. "Well," he said, "there's bound to be two ways o' thinkin' to everything. I'm fer Jahn myself, en I jist told James here so."

James, looking reverently at his uncle Zie, ignored Long Jim. "I can't see," he said, "how Jahn can stand out so against Mother. Why, if it was me, I'd be up there on the hill to Marthy's right now, tryin' to comfort my mother and begging her pardon!"

"No doubt ye would, James." Zie Gurney nodded affectionately. "But ye've got no stubborn Ibsell blood in ye to make ye cantankerous and mean. . . . Not that I want to talk ag'in Henric," he added. "Henric's a good boy." He stared solemnly at Long Jim's cynical grin, turned about, and gazed up and down the wind-swept streets. "Where's yore Ford, James?"

"Down the street a bit. I was going to Henric's, and I don't take that rattle-trap in front of Miss Chancie's door. Ask me, that woman's due a takin' down." He guffawed senselessly.

Zie frowned. "I wanted 'specially to see Henric afore I went to Rachel."

Long Jim stirred, taking the hint, and thrust out his hand to the preacher again. "I reckon yore cold 'ull be better, Elder," he said, and paused. He continued to shake hands slowly, with an ostentatious reverence in which there might have been discerned anger and a sly imitation of James' manner with his uncle. "I reckon as how hit'll shore be O. K. when Lawyer Lipscomb arsks you in court if you ain't 'ware Jedge Whitten is owin' money to Henric," he said, and felt in his fingers the sudden contraction of Zie Gurney's hand. "So James' wife is telling it erbout," he added, smiling slightly and chewing as he moved back into Rosenben's door.

For an instant Zie Gurney was motionless; then, observing the sudden swelling of the veins on James' forehead, he beetled his thick, gray brows and focused his pupils on James' eyes in a stern radiance of small, dark light. "Trickery, eh, James!"

The veins on James' forehead continued to swell thick and purplish, standing out like the roots of a small vine on his mottled skin. "By God! I'll beat Fanny's life out'n her!" he cried. Suddenly he lowered his head, brushing his arm over his face, half-smiling with peculiar, anticipatory relish while he did so.

"Aye, son," old Zie said. "Yore wife's been talking too much and ye been showing off afore her." He paused, and the significance of that stern ray from his eyes revealed itself for a second. "Ye'll let all that's in it 'fer ye get away with yore boastin'. . . . Ye needn't think ye're baitin' Fanny's religious feelings when ye tell her how clever Henric is!"

James glanced up, still smiling. The red wen on his neck glowed a fiery scarlet. "Maybe we better go see Judge Whitten?" he suggested, sullenly.

"Fer what? The honor of the family at stake, and ye go wantin' we should walk right up to Whitten's office in plain view of the town! Maybe ye want witnesses there to say we asked him leading questions, eh?" He stood a moment, watching the slow blowing of the limp ends of James' mustache in the wind. He sneezed suddenly. "I got to git in out'n this cold. Reckon we can walk over to Henric's if Miss Chancie's too good to hev yore car around. . . . Aye, son, she's a mite above herself. Maybe she'll not like us comin' in around dinner time, eh?"

James grinned. "She'll feed you if she thinks there's anything in it for her."

"Might be," old Zie said.

They walked slowly, breasting the wind, their thin coat tails streaming out behind them. Zie sneezed again, and looked sidewise at James. "Trouble is," he said, "we ain't neither of us got an overcoat nor money to buy one. It's a shame how some has and some don't hev. . . ." He shook his head with pious resignation. "But to them that hath it shall be given and frum them that hath not it shall all be taken. . . ." They stood a minute on the street corner, waiting for the light to change.

James said: "I ain't got a lick of work done this year. How's a man to work? Besides, with Jahn managing things out to the farm, I ain't had Mother to go to like I used to. If I had the niggers Jahn's got ———"

The green light glowed dully and they moved forward, across the street.

"Preachin' don't pay," Zie continued the conversation. "I go about like the pilgrims of old, with nought but sandals and script. I ought to hev something laid up fer myself. . . ."

James nodded. "Mother ought to have give you something."

"I'll hev to miss Annual Conference this summer to testify fer her," old Zie said, and did not look at James. "Only money in preachin' is in the collections took at Conference." He sighed heavily. "Speakin' of your mother . . . women don't spend money right. Got no business sense. I reckon sometimes my advice to her has been worth a lot to yore mother."

"Women don't thank you," James said. "She ought to a turned the timber lands over to you."

"Aye. . . ." Zie nodded. "Them pines 'u'd cut a good length fer the paper-mill. . . ."

The cobblestones of Old Town played out in a narrow strip of sand. They stepped across it and were on the pavement again, half a block from Henric's house. Old Zie began to walk rapidly, holding his shoulders high. "Aye," he said, and laughed. "I jist got to thinking, 'twas Jahn's side that subpœnaed me . . ." He laughed again.

James turned into the shrubbery-bordered walk before Henric's veranda. "You ought to a had the wood lands," he repeated, with emphasis. "If I've got any say-so, I'd say they're yores, anyhow. Mother 'ull change things considerable when she gits the land back in her hands."

"The thing's the family honor," Zie returned, gravely. "That's what we've got to think about with this talk going around about Henric hevin' the judge in his pocket. . . . Seems like you could recollect yore mother wasn't quite right when she give that deed to Jahn," he said, complainingly, and stepped up on the veranda. He laid his finger on the door bell. "Why, she come to my house the fall before and she was queer . . . jist downright queer, James. . . ."

v

On this same afternoon, Rachel Ibsell, alone in her room at Martha's, laid aside her Bible, and sat staring at the blue covering on the dressing-table bench and listening to the sound of the wind. She was thinner than she had been in December, and her large, handsome bones seemed to glow starkly under her skin and through it, giving to her face a tragic luminance. Her hair, no longer rich and smooth and merely flecked with gray, appeared to lie on her head, fluffy and unalive with the peculiar, dead beauty of cotton locks. Under it, her eyes shone with a gleam more red than black. When she turned them up as she did now, and sat listening, the light from them bleared with a gradual sinking dullness, so that they passed through all the stages of expression from the quick, startled gleam of laboring fear to the unblinking emptiness of depressed sorrow.

The March wind fell on her ears in a series of muffled tears and jerks, coming out of Red Valley, she thought, swooping up from the furrows there in whirlwinds of red dust, raving over the woods between, and scooping the surface of the river in stiff, cold curls of water. She made with her fingers a motion for each beat of the wind, swooping, tearing, lifting like it, doing it all gently and dreamily, and listening until she felt the soft, malleable stuff of her brain rise and curve in rhythm with it.

When suddenly she got up, dusk was in the room. "Zie ought to come; Billy said at lunch he was in town," she thought, opening the door and beginning to pace up and down the long hall. The thick red carpets appeared to run backward, and her feet, it seemed to her, fell silently, like two black crows alighting on red earth. The white paneled walls wavered, fleeing past her dark figure. In the mirrors of the hall trees she saw her white head passing and repassing.

She stopped. "What did Billy's mother want with all these hall trees?" she asked, aloud, as if she had just thought of the oddity of four such articles in one corridor. She stared at them, noticing for the first time that they were all alike, shaped like a chair with a high back in which a mirror had been set and with dog claws carved on the arms. Glancing up, she saw her figure in profile in one of the mirrors, bent a little from the waist, the shoulders still straight, and the hands clasped behind across the buttocks. She jerked her hands from behind her and frowned at the reflection. "What a fool I am!" she said, angrily, and went down the stairs to the door of the sewing-room, turned the knob, and went in.

Martha sat at the machine, upright, with her lips compressed, pedaling furiously against the yelp and swoop of the wind. She turned around, still sewing.

"I called you to come down and sit with me three hours ago." Her feet slowed on the treadle, she spun the wheel and lowered her head again, guiding the cloth under the needle. "Billy will be in from the store in an hour now," she added. The small electric lamp fastened above the steel arm holding the needle shook from the force of her pedaling.

Rachel stood by the door. "Zie ought to come," she said. "I've been looking for him all afternoon." Something querulous and old touched her tone for a second. Frowning, she walked across the room, stood behind Martha, and bent over the whirling wheel. "What are you sewing there? You're going too fast. That's no way to sew, girl!"

She noticed suddenly the material, white flannel, the shape of it and the small size. "Oh-h" she said, without glancing at Martha. "Well, Miss?" She walked away to the window, and looked out over the winter-swept lawn. Behind her, Martha sewed less rapidly.

"So you're going to have a baby?" she said then.

The machine stopped, and she felt Martha looking at her back. She turned around.

"No, not me," Martha said. She began to pleat the flannel with her fingers. "No . . . it's Sue. Sometime toward the end of the summer." Martha glanced up sidewise and smiled. "A boy this time, perhaps."

She watched Martha's fingers pleating the flannel, letting it go and then catching up new pleats. "Sue . . .?" she said. "I couldn't tell it when I was out there in December. . . ."

Martha looked up at her. "Mamma! Of course you couldn't tell, it'd just started then. . . . Anyway, she carries her babies high. You couldn't tell before till she was far gone, you know."

"No . . . you couldn't." She stood gazing down at the pale straw matting on the floor, and heard Martha raising the steel foot on the machine, placing the flannel back under the needle. "I reckon I ought to be glad for her," she said then, steadily and drearily. "I was always happy to carry a child. I felt strong and I knew my part and what I was made for. . . . But my time for that is long gone," she added, suddenly, and sighed.

The whirring of the machine rose again, loud and senseless. Above it she heard the long, hollow roar of the wind. Listening a moment, she continued slowly, with a rising inflection.

"But it's bad blood coming to the child. . . . The day of death is better than the day of birth. . . ." She said, loudly, "'The fathers have eaten sour grapes and the children's teeth are on edge.'"

She heard her own voice as if it had no connection with herself. "The day of death is better . . ." She began to walk up and down the room, her lips moving soundlessly, her eyes on the floor. "You're sewing too fast, girl!" she said, and did not realize that Martha had stopped sewing and was watching her.

"Mamma ——"

"Yes, I know. I know, girl." She walked more rapidly, bending from the waist wearily. "You're trying to tell me this puts him farther than ever from me; you're trying to say it was for this he left me—for children. A man's got to know his seed are in him to some purpose. It was for that he left me. . . ." She smiled mockingly. "A man's got to go and fight, too; he's got to prove he's a man. Women know what they are, but men— Women know it's all foolishness. Nobody here cared two cents what happened in Cuba, nobody cared, but he had to go and prove he was a man."

Martha stood up, holding an edge of the flannel tight in one hand. "Mamma! What are you saying! Sit down."

Something of the low excitement in Martha's voice reached her. She stopped and stood looking at her. "Don't worry, child. They shan't bother me." She walked up and down, up and down again. She laughed suddenly. "Henric and Miss Chancie and James—bah!" She heard herself, she hushed on the draw of her breath, and stared at Martha with dilated eyes. "What am I saying . . . ?"

The door bell rang harshly through the house. She saw Martha turn her face. "Why, child!" she said. "Did I scare you? It was nothing; you just told me too quick and I got excited, I got to thinking of all my troubles at once. . . . It was nothing." Martha's hand was pulling the flannel, making little frayed threads start out on the cut edges of the soft fabric. "You're ruining my grandson's little clothes," she said, and smiled.

"Oh!" Martha turned around, lifted the needle, and rolled the flannel up. "I guess that's Uncle Zie at the door."

"It's just that I get excited," Rachel said. "I'll go let Zie in." She knew that Martha was staring at her back as she walked from the room. "I'm getting so I've no self-control," she thought, and opened the front door to Zie.

He embraced her, both arms curved, she thought, distastefully, like long black talons while his great nose pecked at her hair. She released herself at once, and straightened her lace collar. "There's no need to be so affectionate, Zie. I know you're my brother without that. . . . But sit down," she continued, watching him settle his hat over the arm of one of the chairs. "Sit in Billy's smoking-chair and be comfortable till he comes in. I always noticed you Gurney men had to sit soon's you saw a chair. . . . You must a been to Henric's?" she asked then, seating herself in front of the door. "I expected you earlier."

"Aye, Rachel," he said, taking out a large handkerchief and wiping his thinly dripping nose. "If I ain't caught my death today, out in this wind without an overcoat. James was in the same fix. . . ." He shook his grizzled head from side to side, and pressed flat the reddened tips of his ears. "Well, Rachel, I'm called for witness this summer."

"And proud of it, I see ! . . . Get back my money from Henric," she said, suddenly, "and you and James can have an overcoat out of it."

He looked up, scowling and alert. "Henric has got yore money? How come?"

"You ask him. First, I loaned him what I had left when I went to his house, a thousand dollars and some odd change. And then my checks from Jahn every month, Miss Chancie said she had to have some for my board. I turned it all over for them to pay Peebles, and they ain't paid him, that's what."

"But ye've got checks frum Jahn since ye come here to Marthy's, ain't ye?" he asked.

"Not for you to get an overcoat out of, Zie. You get that back from Henric and you can have some of it."

He shook his head slowly and folded up his handkerchief. "Aye, it's turr'ble, Rachel, turr'ble! When I think of what the family's come to," he said, and leaned forward, lifting his voice to preaching tones. "It's turr'ble, I tell ye! To think of a child rising ag'in its parents, its lawful guardeens, like yores has done. But that's what's wrong with the world, rebellion and uprising ever'where. The wives thinking they're better than their men, the way Fanny Forrest's a-doing, going around talking in the community ag'in' James. Rebellion and uprising! I've seen it coming these many year, and I've preached ag'in it. But Armenian doctrine's got the world in thrall. Why, ye've got to have an eddication to preach now!" he cried, suddenly. "Ye've got to go to school now, the Call ain't good enough fer 'em!"

Rachel regarded him with dark, glistening eyes. "You're a good preacher, Zie, but there's no need to be preaching outside the pulpit. You put me in mind of Papa in his last years."

He sat back, striking his head against the coral-colored shade of the reading-lamp beside his chair. "Aye, and luxury, too!" he muttered, giving the lamp a resentful look. He turned to Rachel again. "Why, sister, it was you I meant to ask about Papa's last years. Seems like I've forgot 'em 'most. I was thinking the other day and I couldn't recollect. 'I'll ask Rachel,' I said to myself."

"Looks like you'd remember he died in the insane asylum north of town here!" she said, tartly, and looked at him with the scorn she always felt for a liar.

"Aye, and so he did! 'Twas jest that at last preachin' somebody asked me, and I was so tuck up with church business, I couldn't recollect to save my life." He paused and looked at the lamp again. "I saw Billy across the street this

[148]

morning. All duded up like a circus tout. I can't see how a girl raised like Marthy can put up with it! Silk handkerchiefs in his coat pocket and silk socks. Make no doubt Jahn's gone into silk, too, since he got rid of his mammy!" he said, loudly.

"Looks like you'd control your tongue!" she said, hotly. "S'pose Martha was to hear you? Me and Billy don't jib none too good, anyhow, without you making trouble." She stopped, and cried with sudden, wrathful pain: "I wish I had my own house back. I wish I'd not started this. I wish I'd never signed a single paper!"

"Eh?" The old man stared cunningly at her. "That's what I say, ye'd never a done it if he hadn't tricked ye with promises and threats of leaving ye!"

She shook her head impatiently. "You know that's not what I mean. . . ." She leaned back and closed her eyes, listening a moment to the wind. "Zie," she said, suddenly and softly, "do you forget, too? I get jumbled sometimes, so much together to think about, and then when I want to talk, half of it's gone. . . ."

"Aye, sister Rachel." He leaned forward and watched her with brooding eyes. "Air ye jist now finding it out? I been noticing it a long time in ye . . . and in myself, too," he added, hastily. "It comes early in our family." He lifted his glance and fixed it on the white paneled ceiling. "You and me's in seventy, and I been noticing it since we was fifty, little things we'd forget," he said in a whining tone.

She began to rock her chair softly, leaning forward with crossed arms on her knees, and gazing past him. "I remember my first man more than ever now," she said, drearily. "It's so strong seems like I see him and hear him talking, saying things he said way back before we married. And it's all so mixed, so jumbled I get his name and James' confused. And I know none of my troubles would ever have come on me if he hadn't gone to Cuba and been killed there . . . I'd a been a different woman if that'd not happened."

"Aye, Rachel, we always knowed it. They was saying out to Henric's today ye wasn't yourself when ye give the deed."

At first she seemed not to have heard him. Then she stopped rocking and sat motionless, as if she were listening. "What?" she said, sharply. "What is that?" Her face changed, flashing with anger, and with a kind of sardonic shrewdness as she looked full at him. "Did they send you here to put words in my mouth, Zackeriah Gurney!"

He put on a smile. "Come, Rachel, we'll not fight; there's trouble enough in the family already. I can't make ye out tonight; ye're not yoreself; but I reckon it's the weather and yore age," he went on with a high, sing-song inflection that moved her strangely. "Trust in the Lord, Rachel. Trust Him. For He has appointed us. By His fore-knowledge, He has elected us. Not a shadow, not a jot rests on our titles, Rachel. Rejoice in the God of Israel and trust in His goodness."

She bowed her head, murmuring; but then, abruptly, she looked up again with suspicion. "You say they're talking it that I wasn't myself when I give the deed to Jahn . . .?"

"Now, Rachel, ye can't blame them. They're good children, and they love ye and want to do yore will. They can't understand yore attitude, sister, nor why ye wanted to give Henric the lie in court. Ye hurt the boy bad there, Rachel. Seems there's no way to explain it but with yore age and forgetfulness."

She was silent a moment, watching him with eyes in which a pent terror began to circle. "You're putting words in my mouth for them!" she cried again, and suddenly could not see his face except as a gaunt, red shadow before her.

He drew himself up, appeared about to relax and smile, and then swiftly and decisively he rose. "Put words in yore mouth! I take shame to hear ye talk. Ye're accusing yore betters when ye accuse me!"

"My betters!" His loud voice roared in her ears. She stared at him, bewildered, uncertain, and suddenly grasped the arms of her chair with both hands, letting the Gurney anger pour through her. "You start too, will you! Not one of the family can ever be with another without a fuss starting. And you a preacher! How are you better—I'd like to know how you're better than me!"

A dull glassiness flowed over her eyes as she spoke the last words. She saw him vaguely and incompletely, knowing that he was snatching up his hat and cramming it onto his head. "If ye don't know, talking won't help ye none!" he shouted, contemptuously. She raised her eyes a little; he was standing over her and she cowered back. "Ye're crazy! Crazy! Ye been crazy for ten year, and anybody can tell it on ye now, ye fool!"

She thought she was trying to get up to stop his loud voice. Her hands pressed down on the chair, she raised one foot slightly to balance herself. "Go on," she said, "go on. . . ."

She could not breathe until she heard the front door slam behind him. Then, slowly, feeling the wind on her, and knowing that the door had opened again to let Billy Nelson in, she began to tremble. "Martha!" she said. "Martha!" Billy stood staring at her, and Martha was running up the hall. "Martha . . . I don't forget. . . ."

She heard her weak voice begging Martha, pleading childishly and half-crying. "Why, how foolish this is!" she said, suddenly. She drew herself up from the chair and stood erect. "I mustn't forget again," she thought, "or they'll use it to beat him. . . ." She locked her hands behind her back, as if with that gesture she contained her failing faculties and hid them forever.

VI

Zackeriah Gurney walked toward Melchior Street, going rapidly and looking down at the pavement. "Never in my life!" he thought incoherently, with a mixture of anger and glee. "Never in my life, and my own sister, too!" His long legs cast shadows before him down the hill, the street lamps glowed dully like rheum-sick eyes staring wide and sightless in the face of the wind. "Accusing me like that . . . accusing me, a servant of God and her own brother!" His throat swelled, and he could hear in his skull the sound of his righteous thoughts. "Playing the smart one with me, trying to trap me. . . ."

"So I'll tell it at Henric's!" he decided, suddenly. "'Aye, Henric,' I'll say, 'she's swearing ye've stole money frum her' . . . and James will be setting there, listening. . . . I'll say, 'She's accusing ye of fraud, that's why she give ye the lie in court.'" A thick, stiff grin appeared on his cold lips; he lifted his hands and rubbed them together, raspingly. "'Aye, Henric, the fever in ye's evil. . . . Ye must do the Lord's will with me, Henric.'" He slowed his pace, glancing up like one facing an audience, acting his rôle.

He stood, he saw, in the middle of Melchior Street with the unfamiliar houses rising around him and a single street lamp burning at the corner. "Aye, but I've come fast!" he thought gleefully, and then, turning to the left, he moved up the side street and into Henric's yard. "I'll tell 'em!" he muttered. "'Why, Zack's crazy—I jist passed 'im on the street— crazy as a bedbug. Ye can't depend on him. Not and the whole town and country saying ye're trying the dirty with Judge Whitten. Ye must depend on the testimony I'll give. . . . Where's the money?' I'll say." He rubbed his hands together again, the pride of conspiracy hot in him. "'Where's the money?' . . ."

Henric was waiting for him just inside the front door. He switched the lights briefly to let his uncle's feet find the height of the steps, and then switched them off. He came out onto the veranda and shut the door behind him. "Well . . .?"

"Aye, pore Rachel, she ——"

Henric interrupted, anxiously. "James and Chanson are in there, waiting. Peebles is here, too. Chanson doesn't like it. She sat there without saying a word all afternoon, and now she decides she can't have us doing that to Mother. I don't know what she means!" Exasperation sharpened his voice; he shivered in the cold. "Zack's not here, either; he's never here any more!"

Zie moved past him and opened the door. "Couldn't wait, could ye?" he gibed. "Zack, he's out in town, running around with one of his fits on him, I reckon!" He laughed. "I'll hev to git a-holt of Zack and preach some Gospel to him." He began to talk loudly as Henric led the way along the hall to the library.

"It's got ye, Henric. Ye're like a gambler, wild with hope, hanging on the turn of chance. But trust God. The fever in ye's evil!" He pushed aside the draperies, reaching in front of Henric, and continued triumphantly and arrogantly, "Ye'll be a changed man when ye've turned over the money yore mother give ye!"

James, arrested in a movement toward the papers lying around Peebles' briefcase on the table, sat motionless, staring at him. "You fool!" James said, low, and bit his mustache. The lawyer's sallow face was still and watchful; his gray eyes slid along the length of Zie's tall frame, and the old man knew suddenly that he had been a fool; pride and glee had betrayed him. Chanson's yellow eyes gleamed at him in one fierce glance, and then changed, glowing with a sly amusement as they sought Henric's face over his shoulder.

"Well—!" Zie let his breath out with explosive humility and moved his red hands deprecatively. "Maybe I've spoke out of turn, eh? Maybe Rachel's wrong. She's got so she imagines things; she hears her first man a-talking to her. . . ."

Chanson's gaze moved again, from Henric's face, and rested on his. "Why, Rachel's mixed turr'ble, she is!" he cried, still humble and placative. "Why, she don't know James here frum her first man! She's in a' awful fix. Pore thing, I hated to look at her ——!"

He saw Peebles pursing his thin, flat mouth, and hushed in

[153]

spite of himself. The lawyer looked at Henric slowly. "About that money, Mr. Ibsell . . .?" The iris of his narrow, gray eyes seemed to ridge back on themselves like glass crinkling above a thin point of heat. "Do I understand Mrs. Ibsell intrusted a sum of money to you for—ah, legal purposes?"

Chanson interrupted smoothly. "My dear Mr. Peebles . . . not for legal expenses, no. Mother Ibsell is right now entirely too distrustful of Henric for that. No, she was trying to tell Mr. Gurney that she wishes Henric to give him some money. Is that not so?" She smiled at Zie.

The old man nodded, reddening faintly. "Aye, Miss Chancie, that was it. Rachel she's in the habit of loaning me fertilizer money in the spring, Mr. Peebles. I'm one of them preachers has to live some other way than preaching. Like the pilgrims of old ——"

"Exactly," Henric said. "Well, Uncle Zie, we'll let you have the money in Mother's stead. I don't suppose she felt up to writing you a check herself tonight."

"I see," Peebles said. "Then her own money is in the bank?" He looked carefully at Henric, rose, and began to stuff his papers into the black briefcase. "I see. Then, I think . . . I've heard Mr. Gurney's opinion. I hope we may consider Mr. Gurney a witness?" His thin lips parted clammily. "I'll have you subpœnaed in the morning, Mr. Gurney. Surprise to Lipscomb? . . . But I suggest, Mr. Ibsell, that we call in an alienist, possibly Dr. Stanhope from the asylum . . .?"

"No," Chanson said. "No, Henric will not permit that. Mr. Gurney can say that his sister is forgetful, if that is what is needed to win the case. He can say she is old and forgetful. But Henric will not permit that other. He does not try to prove his mother is crazy. No," she repeated, and looked at the lawyer.

Mr. Peebles nodded cautiously. "I see," he said again, and parted the draperies with the hand holding the briefcase. "Well, good-night. . . ."

[154]

"I'll just see him out."

James rose hastily, pushed behind Chanson's chair, and followed the lawyer from the library. There was an interval of silence, during which the sound of their feet on the rugs in the hall did not return to Chanson and Henric. Then the front door opened.

"James," old Zie began, half whispering, "he's been on to Rachel to discredit yore testimony, Henric, and approve his. . . . I don't see what he's up to." He watched a mottled red stain Henric's cheeks. "I guessed you knowed it already," he said. The door closed in the hall. "Rachel she's old now, old and sickly," Zie said, loudly. "She stayed young a long time, but she's come to the partin' of the ways now. . . ." He paused as James appeared again between the draperies.

Chanson said, "You'll have to deposit Mother Ibsell's money in the morning early," and looked steadily at Henric.

"By God! if you didn't play it, Uncle Zie!" James thrust into the room and dropped into a chair at the table. "Now that skinflint Peebles 'll be nosing around the bank all the time!"

"Well, I done my best," Zie returned, loudly, in an injured whine. "If I made a mistake, such is the way of man. . . . Anyway, they'll see it warn't all ye having Whitten in yore pocket, Henric. Fer nigh onto seventy year I've had the favor of my God, and while I live I'll not stand by and see one of my sister's children cheat the others!"

Chanson moved suddenly and almost waspishly. "But if he did succeed in cheating us, it would be God's will, eh, Elder Gurney?" she said, smiling thinly.

He intoned humbly, yet with an arrogant relish, "'Good and evil alike proceedth out of his mouth.' But ye can't be said to understand these things, Miss Chancie. Ye was raised a vile Papist, given over to idolatry with the Scarlet Woman of Rome."

"So!" said Chanson. "But I'm a heretic now, Elder Gurney. I should be gaining in light and knowledge every day!"

[155]

"Oh, to hell with it!" James cried, suddenly. "This ain't getting us nowhere!"

"Imputing a stain to your own blood will get you nowhere," Chanson said, softly, after a moment, and smiled with a strange, almost oily blandness.

"A stain! What stain!" James demanded, belligerently. "What I want to know is what we're going to do about Zack?" He looked pointedly away from Chanson. "He's got no guts, damn him, the white-livered fool! First one side and then the other, that's him. Tooting his damned conscience!"

Chanson said, with the same blandness: "He is at Paula Pollard's tonight. You are not gallant, Mr. Forrest; you do not understand love." She got up before he could speak and moved into the hall.

"You better take yore woman down a notch!" James muttered to Henric. "Damn' women, putting in their mouths! She's getting a conscience too, I reckon."

Henric looked at him coldly, his head beginning to shake on his long neck. "I think I can manage without your aid, James."

He stood up. After a moment, James and old Zie rose too, and stood facing him, but without looking into his countenance. "That money Rachel wanted me to hev . . ." old Zie began. Henric turned to the door and held the draperies aside. "I suppose you'll go out with James tonight, Uncle Zie?" he said.

"Aye, with James . . ." the old man repeated vaguely, and found himself walking up the hall, with Henric following behind. At the door he said again, "That money . . ."

"Next week, Uncle Zie." Henric held the door. "Goodnight," he said.

"That money!" old Zie shouted from outside. "I better git that money next week, Henric!"

Henric bent and locked the door, and then waited a minute, listening to James' and Zie Gurney's footsteps

[156]

crunching on the pavement. Behind him, in the house, he heard Chanson moving. The light in her bedroom switched off, and the bed creaked under her as she sat down. He turned swiftly and went toward her, pausing at the bedroom entrance to switch on the light again. She was sitting on the edge of the bed, her elbows on her knees and her eyes covered by her hands. He looked at her and moved across the room to run his hand along her bare arm. "Tired?" he said, gently. "Or worried?"

She uncovered her face and smiled faintly. "No," she said, abruptly, "not tired, nor worried, exactly." And then, with an obscure reluctance, turning her face from his, "Henric . . . I like your mother."

He stared at her, frowning. "Like her? What has that got to do with it?"

At first, she was not sure she had heard him rightly; and then suddenly she sighed. She stared back at him, thoughts of no form wavering in her mind. She shrugged and said, obliquely, "Zie Gurney is a wicked old fool."

Henric smiled. "You're illogical, Chanson."

"No." Her face hardened. She stared at the dressing-table, wondering at herself.

"Just because he disparages Roman Catholics ———"

"No." She stood up and began to loosen her hair. "You are like a gambler, as he said. Once you listened to me, but now you are wild on this case. You will do anything . . ." Her hair fell on her shoulders, purplish, coarse, and gleaming. "Some things one does not do. One does not say, 'My blood is tainted; I have seeds of insanity in me.' One does not do that; no, Henric."

He smiled at her with faintly derisive eyes. "James says you're getting a conscience, like Zack."

"Yes." She turned away, toward the dressing-table. "Like whose wife? The pillar of salt? I'm looking back." She sighed almost imperceptibly, and stared at him in the mirror.

His face was still and grim, his eyes shuttered. "This

clinches the case, though!" he said, suddenly, and looked up, his eyes brilliant with an odd, gloating rapture. "God, Chanson . . . we've got it . . .!"

She turned and felt a shiver running deeply in her muscles. "No . . . no, Henric. . . . You are indecent!" she said, slowly, with her voice heavy and cold.

Arrested by that sound, he stared at her. Her mouth was faintly twisted, as if, having discovered at last the extent of her own willingness in guilt, she had learned a chill, warped disgust with any righteousness which stopped short of hers. Her mouth twisted again.

"You've bought yourself a fool in Zie Gurney," she said. "He'll suck you dry. You've not won; you've lost today."

VII

Jahnet Ibsell lay on the sand pile her father had built for her beside the front veranda, and squinted between her lashes at a square of July sky showing between the leaves of the elm trees. She was a month more than three years old now, and she could remember her last birthday. "I had candles and a big doll and a little set of dishes," she said, suddenly, looking at Black Fanny. "And you made me a big cake and a man out of dough." Her mother's voice on the veranda stopped, and then said, politely, "How can I read, Jahnet, if you're going to talk?" Jahnet kicked her legs out from under the white pleats in her skirt, and her mother's voice went on: "'And then the knight rode out of the woods on his great, white horse and faced the wicked giant. "Where have you hidden the lady Emily?" he demanded, loudly. . . .'"

Jahnet squinted at Black Fanny's face. The sand crawled under her bare shoulders to the place where her shoulder straps lay, and itched under them. She sat up and gazed at the young corn, waist-high in the fields, and began to scoop sand into her blue pail with the little shovel Aunt Martha had given her. She packed each shovelful down with her fist until the sand was flat in the pail and faintly yellowish, not white like it was on the pile. "'The Lady Emily sprang up from the forest floor and ran to meet her knight,'" her mother's voice read. She lay down on her stomach, with her legs across Black Fanny's white apron, and studied the planks her father had set in the square shape of a box around the sand pile.

Lying like that, touching with her fingers the roughness of the planks, she smelled the roses along the walk. She sat up, and drew her legs across Fanny's apron so that she was sitting in her lap, and began to push her fingers lightly into the deep, folded wrinkles around the Negress' mouth. She said, "Did you know my uncle Zack got married this morning and my daddy didn't go?" She patted Black Fanny's cheeks softly.

"Jahnet!" Her mother had stopped reading again, and was angry now. "Jahnet, stop worrying Fanny."

"She don' worry me none, Miss Sue." Black Fanny's yellowish eyelids batted slowly at Jahnet, slowly and comically. "Jes' a little lam', that's all, jes' a little lam', Miss Sue. . . ." Her starched, blue-striped arms enfolded Jahnet's head, pressing it against her deep bosom.

Sue said, "She's a bad little girl, that's what," and Jahnet's head came back out of Black Fanny's arms and lifted to regard her mother. She shook her short yellow curls. "My daddy rides a big horse, too," she said, defensively.

Black Fanny's throaty, crooning chuckle rode over her mother's laughter. Jahnet lay back with her head in the sand, lower than her fat torso, and blinked at the sky again. The elm leaves moved a little, through her eyelashes, and the sky showed crisscrossed with black lines as if she were looking at it through the mosquito netting her mother put on her bed every night. She heard Black Fanny say, "'Twuz Miss Marthy called up 'bout Mis' Zack's weddin' this mawnin', wuzn't it, Miss Sue?" and she thought, "I didn't get my little set of dishes in a store; I found them under the house. I went under the house and dug by the chimbley, and I found my little dishes with pink flowers on them, and I brought them in and my daddy said, 'Where did you find your little set of dishes?' . . ."

Her mother was saying, ". . . he broke the engagement twice, Fanny. People saw him running about the streets at night, talking to himself. He'd go to her house and leave without speaking. She put up with it, and people thought . . . She's so pretty. . . . He'd got a notion he'd built his house for his mother. He kept telling her, 'You can't live with Paula, you can't live with any more strange women. . . .'" Sue's voice broke off to exclaim: "Now isn't that just like them? 'Strange women!'"

"Yas'm, fum the Bible. Ol' Miss wuz pow'ful strong on Scriptuah. They all got it fum her."

"Every time he'd break the engagement, she'd cry and take on ——"

"Miss Paula, mam?"

"Yes, she'd cry and go running to Miss Chanson and say she'd die if he kept on like that. But it wasn't really Mr. Zack, Fanny; she just wanted to get married."

"I figuhed that. Womens don't bother 'bout mens soft as Mis' Zack." She chuckled slyly. "No'm, that they don't, not 'bout the mens theyself. It's jes' hankerin' atah marriage does it. Mis' Jahn, now, he's diff'unt."

Jahnet sat up and saw a bright flush fading on her mother's oval cheeks. Sue turned her face a little to one side and continued swiftly: "So he gave in like everybody knew he would, and she said that his mother could live with them as soon as they got back from the honeymoon." She glanced down, lowering the golden tips of her eyelashes, and pulled the flaps of her white maternity dress closer together. "So I suppose she'll leave Miss Martha's right away now."

"Yas'm I spect so." Black Fanny's eyes flashed ironically. "I spect Mis' Zack gonna fin' out 'fo' this day ovah he ain't got no lovin' daughtah fo' Ol' Miss. Womens, they'll do anything to git the mens." She raised her voice at Jahnet suddenly. "You git outn that spot o' sun, chile. Ain't you learn you don't tan, you jes' blistahs?"

"Yes, Jahnet . . . I see your daddy coming." Sue spoke to Fanny in a hushed tone, while Jahnet, watching her father come up out of the pasture, felt everything around her grow brighter and quicker, a swift, delicious silveriness swirling through the air to her vision of him. "You'd think he'd be used to it now (hold that child, Fanny, and clean her skirts); you'd think he'd be so he'd not mind it, but I believe this marriage has hurt him as bad as anything yet. I do wish Miss Martha could learn not to tell him everything."

"Stan' still, chile, le' me dust yo' skirts fo' you runs to meet him." Her yellow, white-lined palms flipped smartly against Jahnet's dancing knees. "No wondah, mam. Mis' Zack wuz al'ays his best love 'mong the boys. . . . Now you kain run, lil' missy. . . ."

Jahnet's white sandals flew over the grass; she swung her arms to keep her balance, and her chest muscles labored toward him while she laughed and panted. Three steps from the gate, when she saw his hands reaching down to pick her up by the shoulders, her breath drew in, sharp and sweet, and held like that, in a cold frosted ecstasy as if icy lemonade poured down her throat. He lifted her up, and all the cold thawed softly in the warm comfort of touching her daddy. He swung her onto his shoulders so that she could clasp him around the neck with one arm. "Daddy's beautiful doll," he said, laughing a little, and opened the gate. She rode triumphantly to the veranda, looking down with pity on Mamma and Black Fanny, who could not sit on Daddy's shoulder.

He tumbled her off onto the steps, so that she was flat on her back, kicking at him with flying legs, and punched her stomach with his finger. She could see now that his face was a little red, flushed, as it always was when he was unhappy, and that he had purplish shadows scurrying behind the clear blue of his eyes. He stopped playing with her suddenly, glanced at her mother, and sat down on the steps. "I thought maybe Martha'd come out this afternoon and tell us all about the wedding," he said, his voice faintly ironical.

Black Fanny got up from the sand pile, dusted her skirts, and grinned at Jahnet. "Reckon us'd bettah git 'round to the back, lil' missy, ain't we?" she said. Jahnet moved closer to her father on the steps, and Black Fanny went off by herself, carrying Jahnet's pail in one hand as if to make her come after her.

Sue said, gently; "Jahn, there's absolutely no sense in you feeling like this about it. Zack's all right. You wouldn't have wanted to be there even if they'd asked you."

"They didn't ask me." He looked back at her again. "How are you feeling?"

"All right. But I'm worrying about you. You just must stop caring about it. Goodness! you didn't expect it to be like nothing had ever happened, did you?"

He clasped his hands between his knees and looked down at his field boots. He said, "Poor Zack. . . ." He was silent for a long moment, and then he sighed slowly and heavily, almost convulsively.

"Jahn . . ." Sue stopped, and then said, "The way Zack talked about making a home for your mother is no reflection on you. It was his own conscience." She paused again, and said, softly, "You could make it up with Zack. . . ."

He sat still, as if he hadn't heard. His hands, clasped between his knees, looked heavy and ponderous there, as if they hung without a resting-place, and waited, without knowing what to do. Jahnet got up and stood on the step between his knees, touching his fingers and rubbing her hands over the backs of his palms. He smiled at her vaguely and picked her up and sat her down beside him again. He said, "I suppose Chanson was running things. . . . Has anybody brought the mail? The paper might have something in it about it. . . .

Chanson'll be glad enough for Mamma to go to live with Zack. Martha won't be around to talk against them."

Sue said, "Why don't you go to Zack ——?"

"I told you a long time ago: it's done now, and nothing can ever change it or bring back what used to be."

He spoke with his head down, staring at the grass below the steps. He did not glance up when Sue rose heavily and went into the house. Jahnet sat still beside him, gazing at his thick, black eyelashes and wanting to touch them. After a moment, she got up, pushed herself between his knees, and patted his cheeks. He raised his head and looked at her, distantly and almost sternly, as if he did not see her at all. She put her fingers softly against his lower lashes, and jerked them away when he flinched slightly. His eyes shone at her, blue and alive and beautiful, like little pieces of blue shining between the elm leaves. Her finger tips itched to touch them. She drew back, and tried to pull herself up on one of his knees. "What do you want?" he said, and smiled suddenly. "You want to sit in your ol' daddy's lap?" He lifted her up.

"Daddy . . .?" She tried to remember what Black Fanny had said. "Daddy, was my uncle Zack your best love 'mong the boys?" She thought his eyes closed swiftly, so swiftly that she wasn't sure, and then he was looking at her sadly. "I guess so, baby."

She pulled at his fingers and stroked them slowly.

"Daddy . . . I can read, too, I can read jes' like Mamma. . . . I found my little dishes under the house. . . ." He wasn't listening to her. "Daddy," she said, "what's a brother?"

He turned his head toward the corn-fields and the corners of his lips quirked a little. "You might have a brother," he promised. "Sometime soon."

Her blue eyes stared back into his. "Can I play with it?" she asked, finally.

He moved sidewise and rested his shoulder against the porch post beside the steps, leaning back. "I guess so." He ran one of his fingers up inside her soft, short curls. "I played with your uncle Zack . . . and your uncle Henric. . . ."

She got up and straddled his lap, and stared at him solemnly with her hands pushed against his diaphragm. "What did you play, Daddy?"

"Nothing much. Little games. I was younger than they were." He took his fingers out of her curls and smoothed them gently. He smiled faintly, with his eyes cast down. "Sometimes we were bad little boys. Once, when your grandma was gone to town, we got in her sugar and carried it out in the yard. Your uncle Zack spilled it on the ground, around there by the kitchen chimney, Jahnet, and we poured water over it so she couldn't tell we'd had it out here. We used to get into the hands' tobacco, too, and build bonfires down under the hill so she wouldn't see the smoke from our cigarettes. . . .

"Once," he said, "your daddy had a little cat, and somebody put it up in a tree. It was too little to climb down and your daddy was too little to climb up. He stood down under the tree, crying just like the cat and telling it, 'Little cat, I told you not to go up there. . . .' And your uncle Zack climbed the tree and got it down for your daddy. . . . Once," he said, and looked at her slowly, with eyes she couldn't understand, "we played like that together. We were little together . . . like you. . . ."

VIII

The town clock, in a tower on top of the City Hall, struck twice, its dull, slow strokes booming through the heavy August silence, tolling over the roofs of Choctaw. Judge Whitten came through the door at the back of the courtroom, pushing his round belly before him, and sat down behind the judge's oak bench. Martha shifted her white slippers on the floor and glanced once at Jahn, and then away. As if he had felt the look, he turned his head and fixed his eyes on the back of the empty chair in front of him. His forearms were sweating slightly where his shirt sleeves rolled back, the sweat glistening in little drops like dew on the bronze hairs. Judge Whitten's fingers ruffled a sheet of paper, he stared at the stenographers gathered around a table near the open window, and sighed. "All right, let's get on with it." He frowned, glancing furtively about the room, and moved his plump thumb to turn on the electric fan beside him. Zack stuck his face in at the door from the hall, withdrew it, and they heard his steps going clumsily down the stairs. Rachel Ibsell gazed at the judge from the seat between Chanson and Henric on the front row.

Mr. Peebles glanced at Lipscomb, and then rose, pushing his blazing red hair back from his yellow forehead. "Mr. Zackeriah Gurney!"

Lipscomb seemed to sit asleep, his mocking, black eyes lightly closed.

The preacher stood up in the back of the room, taking his time, letting everybody see how his six feet of lean bone carved his flesh to a pious angularity. He walked forward, down the aisle between the two rows of benches, stepped up onto the witness-stand, and took his seat in the swivel chair. His voice rose monotonously, intoning the oath. "Amen!" he said, and leaned back, setting his face in dark, religious lines.

"Mr. Gurney ———"

Bard Lipscomb rose, interrupting Mr. Peebles. "Your Honor, I must protest the introduction of this witness by complainant. Respondent had subpoenaed Mr. Gurney. . . ."

Judge Whitten leaned his face on his hands. "You should have spoken before the witness was sworn in, Mr. Lipscomb."

"Nevertheless ———"

"Witness is complainant's, Mr. Lipscomb."

Bard Lipscomb sat down.

Peebles smoothed his red hair again. "Mr. Gurney, you have been visiting your sister, keeping in close touch with her, and receiving her in your home?"

"Aye. Rachel comes to me for the Light and I do my best for her."

Rachel Ibsell bowed her head. Her lips moved a little.

"She visited in your home something like a year ago, on the occasion of a church meeting at Nazareth Church?"

"Aye."

"Will you relate any details of that visit which may have a bearing on Mrs. Rachel Ibsell's confusion of mind?"

"Confus—!" Rachel Ibsell raised her head, gazed at Zie, and suddenly looked down again. Bard Lipscomb stared at her, pushing his lower lip against his teeth and holding his breath. Beside him, Jahn sat motionless, like a figure graven in stone, huge and still and vaguely ominous.

"Well, Rachel, she come with ——"

Lipscomb stood up. "Your Honor, I protest again. Witness is respondent's. If complainant insists on retaining him, I move an adjournment in order to call Mrs. James Forrest, who will swear that Mr. Gurney's testimony involves a gift from complainant's son, Henric ——"

"Your Honor!" Peebles shouted. "I strongly protest this slander of my client and my witness!"

Bard Lipscomb's mouth curved briefly. "Honorable opponent will please to remember that Henric Ibsell is named in the bill with Jahn Ibsell, the respondent. Witness is also respondent's."

Judge Whitten's eyes turned and rested on Jahn Ibsell's motionless face. They turned again, and met Bard Lipscomb's gaze, and were shining unpleasantly. "Mr. Lipscomb, your unrestrained rhetoric is not helping respondent's case. The court wishes to hear the testimony of the witness. Court refuses an adjournment . . ." Bard Lipscomb sat down swiftly. "Continue, Mr. Gurney."

"Well, Rachel, she come with James Forrest out frum town. We was settin' at table when they got there. We et, and then we all set on the porch, talking Scripture till bedtime. She asked where her room was to be and was told. Well, she went off down the hall, and in a minute or so we heard her bust her head ag'in a door way off frum where her room was. She called out she'd lost her sense of direction and her memory."

He paused, cleared his throat, and looked down at his sister's bent head and murmuring lips. "Her mind's been gittin' bad for some year now."

Jahn Ibsell's hands moved and fastened on the back of the chair in front of him. He looked up, straight ahead, his eyes blue and blind as if a white film had covered them.

Peebles glanced at him furtively.

"You've observed other things in Mrs. Ibsell's behavior that would imply impairment of her mental faculties?"

She glanced up now at her brother, and her eyes were strange and sick. She rose suddenly, and moved from between Henric and Chanson, across the aisle, and sat by Martha. Without looking at her, Martha took her hand and held it lightly, as one holds a child's hand to comfort it.

"Aye. She's mixed turr'ble, Rachel is," Zie Gurney said. "Down to Marthy's this spring she told me she got to thinking she was young again. She said she was mixed, she often thought she was young again. She said she'd got so she couldn't tell James Forrest here frum his father who's been dead since the Spanish-American War. She said, 'I tell ye, Zie, I'd never a signed a single paper if Jahn hadn't threatened me into it.'"

Jahn Ibsell's hands moved again, queerly, as if the fingers struggled, and grasped the chair more firmly and were still.

"Your witness," invited Peebles, smiling.

"Your Honor ——"

Lipscomb stood a moment, watching Rachel, and then turned swiftly away—"Your Honor," he repeated with a definite, sneering emphasis, "I have been patient, I have endured in this courtroom a—" He stopped himself. "At risk of again impairing respondent's case in the court's most generous mind, I must protest again the introduction of this irrelevant testimony. I beg to remark that the condition of complainant's mind last spring has no bearing on the validity of the deed in question. I beg to remind the court that this case is four years old in essence and that the deed was given five and a half years ago."

Judge Whitten said, wearily: "Court considers the testimony relevant. Testimony is already on the records."

"I move that the testimony be stricken from the records!"

"Court considers the testimony relevant, Mr. Lipscomb."

"Exception."

Without moving, Lipscomb said, "Now, Mr. Gurney, have you told the truth, the whole truth, and nothing but the truth?"

Peebles leaped to his feet. "Objection!"

"Sustained."

Zackeriah Gurney was staring at the lawyer from small, black eyes, his head lowered. "I've said what I hold to be true," he announced, heavily and swiftly, "and my holding is as good as any Armenian lawyer's! All that man does is a stinking rag and a filthy nostril in the sight of the Lord God, and so is my truth, but I ain't set myself up fer better than his Book!"

Lipscomb waved his hand, smiling with his cheeks flushed under the white cap of his hair. "Is it true that your sister had not been in your house at any time during the two years preceeding that visit which you have recounted with such charming verisimilitude?"

Zie Gurney stared. "I don't know what ye mean!"

"Ah!—Mr. Gurney, was the hall dark on that night when Mrs. Ibsell started for the room assigned to her?"

Zie Gurney lowered his chin still further. "The hall was a mite dark, yes!"

"Your Honor, opponent's questions are leading!"

"Sustained."

"Exception. . . . Mr. Gurney, is it true that your sister told you she thought she was young again?"

"I have said!"

"Does not this confession convey to your mind the idea that she is well aware of her forgetfulness and so can not be insane?"

"She's crazy as she can be!"

Rachel Ibsell cried under her breath, "Zie, Zie!"

"Did she say, 'I think I'm young again'?"

"She said, 'I often feel like I'm young ag'in.'"

"She used those exact words in that exact order?"

Zie Gurney flushed angrily. "She used words similar."

Lawyer Lipscomb pursed his red lips. "I see. Then she didn't say, 'I'm young again,' but she used words whose meaning would prove that she is well aware of her peculiar feelings and, therefore, cannot be insane?"

"I hold no truck with yore foolishness!" Zie Gurney sat up straight. "Nary one but a educated fool 'u'd think to ask such, and nary one but a educated fool 'u'd answer. That's what's wrong with the world, fools settin' themselves up in wisdom, quarreling with the wisdom of Almighty God!"

"You, Mr. Gurney, are not Almighty God. You suffer from mania grandiosa."

"Your Honor, I beg protection for my witness!"

"The witness, your Honor, is mine."

"Restrain yourself, Mr. Lipscomb, if you please."

"Mr. Gurney, are you quite sure that your sister is confused as to the identity of her son James Forrest?"

Loudly Zie Gurney replied, "She said that sometimes it seemed to her like she confused them. Now you make it not so!"

Lipscomb rocked on his toes, gently and reflectively. "Your Honor, respondent begs to introduce a witness in rebuttal."

The judge blew out his pink cheeks. "It's irregular. . . . Who is your witness?"

"Complainant's daughter, Mrs. William Nelson."

Judge Whitten's cheeks deflated slowly. He put out his

thumb and turned off the electric fan while his bright, round eyes under their triangular lids studied Martha's face. A slow curiosity moved his small, pink lips. He turned his eyes away and switched on the fan again. "You've not finished with Mr. Gurney?"

"No, Your Honor."

He sighed and pillowed his chin in his palms once more, leaning forward. "It's most irregular. . . . Very well. Mrs. Nelson can testify from her seat." He watched her fingers tighten on her mother's hand, and glanced up at Rachel Ibsell's dark face. She held her lower lip tight under her teeth, and her features seemed to work around it, slipping from that shamed control to the exercise of their grief. "All right, Mr. Lipscomb."

"Now, Miss Martha, tell the court whether or not you've heard your mother say anything to indicate she confused James Forrest with her first husband."

Martha saw Jahn's face moving, turning toward her, and suddenly it seemed to her that he had no expression, his countenance was like the countenance of an old man stricken with paralysis, lying and waiting for death. Her lips parted slowly.

"No. I never have."

He looked away from her, at his mother, and his eyes filled with light and then with dark, veinous shadows, and turned carefully away.

"Has she ever shown confusion of mind in your presence?"

"No, sir."

"Mr. Zack Ibsell invited her to leave your house and live with him, did he not?"

"Yes, sir."

"Why has she not gone?"

"She knows Jahn would never go to Zack's. He might come to my house and she could see him."

"You never heard her say she felt she was young again?"

"No. She's always dignified and self-contained except when she's angry, and even then she's in command of herself."

"What is her present attitude toward this suit?"

"Objection!"

"Mrs. Nelson may answer the question."

Martha's eyes flashed. "She said she wouldn't have filed suit if Chanson and James and Henric had left her alone. . . . On the night before the trial began," Martha said, slowly, "she went to Jahn to try to find some way to stop it. . . . But he didn't understand what she had come for. . . ."

She sat back slowly, watching Jahn's eyes, seeing how his features changed and seemed to float white and still on the wash of cold air that tingled up the nerves of her arms.

"You hear the testimony, Elder Gurney!" Lipscomb's voice rose in a sudden, rough burst of oratory, drawing the gaze of the courtroom away from Jahn Ibsell's marble-carved face. "You hear the testimony? Mrs. Ibsell's only daughter swears that her mother's mind is not impaired. She swears that her mother said, 'They forced me into this.' Is this honest and reliable testimony consonant with yours, Elder Gurney? What is your reply to it, Elder Gurney?"

Old Zie moved, heaving himself out of the witness-chair, and stood glowering, his heavy, wrinkled jaw pushed out. "I say Marthy lies, that's what I say!"

There was a tangle of chairs, a swirling of overturned benches, a sound that reverberated sharply. Jahn Ibsell had slapped the witness in the mouth with his open hand. The witness spat blood and licked his cut lip. Rachel Ibsell stood up, stumbling, her hands out, crying, "Jahn, Jahn. . . .!" A vacuum of greedy, excited silence fell on the courtroom. She stared all around her, slowly, like a woman who has just awakened from a nightmare in a strange place. Below, in the street, somebody whistled merrily. Jahn Ibsell moved a step toward his mother, and stopped; arrested, Martha thought, by a line, a thread, a marking invisible to the rest of them. Rachel sat down, hiding her face in her hands.

Judge Whitten said, coldly: "You are under arrest for assault, Mr. Ibsell. In addition, you are fined fifty dollars for contempt of court. . . . The court recesses. . . ."

Jahn Ibsell's throat moved. "Fraud and coercion!" he whispered.

The judge glanced sharply at him, and he was standing motionless, his eyes intense and blue, balls of unearthly light fixed on his mother.

IX

Chanson Ibsell sat on the bed and laced her riding-boots. The house was quiet, with no sound in it except the dim, far-off monotony of James' and Henric's voices murmuring in the library. She turned her head and glanced over her shoulder at the closed door of the bedroom, and listened a minute, expectantly, for the ring of the door bell which would announce the arrival of Mr. Peebles with Dr. Stanhope from Marston's, the insane asylum north of town. They would not, she thought with a certain dreary pleasure, see her when they came. The voices rose and fell in the library like the buzzing of flies, unreal, nagging, so that for an instant she half-felt that her nerves imagined the noise.

She looked back at her riding-boots, stretched her legs, and bent over to examine their glittering polish. Staring down, she could see her face swimming in the bright glow of the leather, the planes and angles of her face wavering, floating to and fro like yellowish seaweed. She sat still and watched, half-amused, half-frightened. Then, wrenching her gaze away, she looked out the window where the September marigolds were beginning to bud. "It's only the boots," she told herself, "that make me seem so." But she thought, "I'm changed—a little. . . ."

The buzzing of those flies in the library went on, and the door bell had still not rung. She rose and put on her brown gabardine coat. Standing in front of the dressing-table, she

[172]

straightened the collar of her plain linen blouse and set her hat carefully on her head, tilted over one straight, thick eyebrow. Now, looking at herself again, an obscure amusement, the irony of the subconscious, began to move in her, and she laughed, oddly and without sound. Her face, sallow and handsome, framed the fascination of her catlike eyes. Beside it, and suddenly, yet she had known it would be there, she saw Jahn Ibsell's carved nose and handsome mouth and stern, brilliant glance. The amusement in her spread out, startled, and she heard her husband's voice lifted briefly on three words . . . "kill her if. . . ." The rest sank under in a muttering noise and the mutter went on like a single bass note thrumming over and over on itself.

She stood without moving, all her muscles suddenly caught in stillness. An abrupt noise sounded from the hall, like a foot lumbering on the uncarpeted edges of the corridor. She turned swiftly and went to the door. The knob moved, she thought, with difficulty in her cautious fingers, but the hinges made no sound louder than her breathing. Across from her, a little way up the hall, the purple draperies at the library entrance rippled softly.

Her gaze traveled past them. The front door stood open, as if a wind had blown it back against the veranda wall. Through the opening she saw her rented mare standing with bent neck at the curb, the reins fastened in the iron lattices of the gate where she had laced them when she came in to dress. She glanced back around the hall, past the gilded angels on the staircase, and let go the door knob in her hand. Again, over the quick energy of her movement, and flowing out of those murmurs in the library, came that sudden stillness of the muscles.

She rose on tiptoe, her boots careful on the rugs, and stole across the corridor, and leaned against the wall, back a little from the draperies so that their rippling edges should not reveal her boots. She balanced herself with one hand, the fingers bunched lightly on the high woodwork. She listened.

"Let it kill her, then," James Forrest said in the tone of a man who has been arguing that it won't kill her. "Let it! She'll be out of the way and we can prove what we want without her giving us the lie."

"Yes, James, yes. I suppose we can carry on the suit in her name! Don't be an utter fool! We'd have to begin all over again, and it's been long enough as it is. Five years. . . . God!"

He drew in his breath and there was silence. Staring up the hall, through the open door, Chanson saw her mare move and the sunlight glint on the black flanks.

In there, James chuckled softly. "You know, Henric, I keep thinking—!" He stopped, and his soft, whispering chuckle came again, floating through the draperies like the fouled strands of a black cobweb. Chanson drew her face back and brushed her hand across it. A chair scraped on the library floor. James' voice, changed now and concealing something, exclaimed, "Why don't that damned Peebles come on! We wait ourselves blue in the face!"

"Be still!" Henric said. "I hear something!" The brief instant of his silence bent Chanson's knee to move, to get away, and then he spoke again and she knew that he had not heard anything. "You jump too much, up and down, always jerking. Can't you be still? If you'd kept your mouth shut and let Uncle Zie alone, all this would be unnecessary. Whitten was all right, but you had to let an insignificant fool like Long Jim Chambers frighten you."

"You mean yore woman's scared and you're jittering around yoreself, scared of her!"

"She's sense enough to know we're making fools of ourselves!"

Chanson's fingers, bearing her weight against the wall, cramped and she moved them and stood slowly upright. A car was nosing past her horse at the curb. Staring at it, listening, she saw vaguely the two figures in the front seat, and knew that Peebles and Dr. Stanhope had come.

"If you're so tired o' waiting," James said, his voice soft

and smiling again, "I can help you out maybe." He began to laugh between his words. "That spot in the road, Henric, just before you turn off for Jahn's place, that spot where the underground sand shifts and eats out across the road, Sand Caves. . . . Hah, Henric, what are you jumping for?" He laughed out loud suddenly. "Jahn fixed it up again this spring, he put a bridge under and covered it over with dirt. The sand's going to eat under the foundations again some day, Henric. . . . I keep seeing it . . . Jahn coming on it some night, and the foundations loosed so as not to hold, eh? Eh, Henric, wouldn't you do it like that? He'd go over slow, the horse first, and then him. The road jest caved out, Henric, that's all, the road jest caved!"

Afterward, Chanson Ibsell could never tell whether Henric cried out first or whether she flung the draperies back before he spoke. "Hush . . . hush!" he cried, and she saw his face strained and fixed, and his fingers bone white around the inkwell on the table. Suddenly, his hand came up and the inkwell pitched across the table past James' face that stared at her without fear or distrust . . . merely stared, with the black, lynx eyes still and coldly hot.

Whatever she had had to say when she flung back the draperies went out of her before the fixed menace of that animal stare. She heard the inkwell rolling on the floor and jolting against the wall in the corner of the room. Outside, the soles of men's shoes moved on the paved walk, coming toward the house, making a flat, rasping sound. She stood without moving, the picture of Jahn Ibsell's horse rolling over and over in her mind, and that picture framed in darkness with, somewhere on the edge of it, Henric's hand blood-covered. Suddenly, the thought of her family, those Foys and Vacquers in Louisiana, darted into her mind like her own voice ironically commenting how she had urged Henric to greed in order to justify her marriage before them—"And murder, murder, I get murder!" she cried, and laughed.

She heard Peebles and Dr. Stanhope at the front door

then, and her voice was sounding more clearly in her mind than in the air before her. James' eyes remained unmoved, and Henric was leaning over, white-faced, staring at James with fascinated hatred. Perhaps she had not spoken at all, she thought. She let the draperies fall a little, half-covering herself in them, and glanced over her shoulder. The lawyer and the superintendent of Marston's stood on the veranda, looking in at her. Peebles raised his hand and rapped his knuckles on the door-facing. She looked back at Henric and James.

"Hadn't you heard?" she said. "Jahn Ibsell has heirs, his wife and two children. The son is three weeks old; he came home today from the hospital with his mother."

A strange laughter froze out of her, like icicles forming on her lips. She jerked the draperies across the entrance, and went up the corridor toward the two men at the door.

"Ah, Mrs. Ibsell, going riding?" Peebles smiled thinly, his lips seeming like a shark's to her. "Mrs. Ibsell, Dr. Stanhope."

She stood still, her glance passing contemptuously over Peebles and fastening on the solid gray eyebrows and the cold gray eyes of the doctor. His gaze fell on her with an almost ponderous gravity and seemed to sink into her eyes, behind them.

"Dr. Stanhope," she said, automatically.

His mouth curled a little, smiling faintly in its Saxon leanness. "Mrs. Ibsell."

"Going out, are you?" Peebles suggested again. She looked at him sidewise, seeing that he was afraid of her new reluctance in conspiracy and wished her gone.

She walked past them, out onto the veranda, and paused to stare a moment longer at Dr. Stanhope's chiseled inscrutability of countenance.

"Yes," she said, suddenly and waspishly, "I am going out. I am not common trash, Peebles. Not for money do I make my blood rotten or murder an old woman or—a young man!" Something moved, flickering across Stanhope's eyes, and she started and smiled suddenly with joy. "You will find in the library two crazy men, Doctor!"

She went down the steps and out to her waiting mare. She looked back. Dr. Stanhope's eyes were following her. Smiling again, she loosed the reins and turned the mare's head toward Red Valley.

X

To Rachel Ibsell this afternoon seemed like no other she could remember. Martha had called her down at three to sit in the living-room. "Come listen to the radio, Mamma," Martha said. "You ought not to sit off by yourself, brooding." She walked down the stairs to the sound of voices filtered through the octagonal-shaped mesh of the radio cabinet. She sat listening with her senses alert and intent, her mind rapt away from her so that she understood nothing of what the voices said and sung, but heard clearly and with pleasure the dropped recurrence of piano notes sprinkling like rain behind the rush of a dusty contralto. Martha lay on the long chintz-covered divan, crocheting, with her feet crossed in red house slippers. Rachel's eyes kept moving again and again to that shiny patent-leather red as if, in the color marked against the light chintz and the white walls, there lay some secret to explain the strangeness of the afternoon.

She got up presently and began to pace the floor, looking out the windows as she passed them. A great cool shade lay all across the green lawn. The round, crisped leaves of the magnolia tree by the sidewalk floated down slowly, one by one, and swirled, cups of brown-yellow, on the grass, or scampered lightly like kittens off down the paved hill and dropped with it, sheer, over the flat tile-and-stone roofs of the business district.

These roofs, Rachel felt, wore this afternoon a frail bright radiance, the glint of the lowered sun on raised coping, a patience that smothered inertly, yet lively, in the lucid, watchful air. Far off, in the great pines behind the house, on the furthest summits of the surrounding hills, the lost, sad thunder of the autumn wind rang like muffled gongs, intermittently. All this, sight and sound and feeling, converged upon her senses, making in her its interpretation; and she looked at the world with delight, pressing her heart against it, and with aching pain and surrender, as if knowing somehow that she would never see it again; her eyes were filled with the gaze of the dying, who look now, and then no more. "And yet," she said aloud, uncertainly, "I'm in good health . . . considering."

Martha looked up from the pink fragment dropping over her fingers. "You ought to sit down. You're thinner than ever."

Rachel laughed briefly, without mirth. "I'm skin and bone. I always noticed how old people shrink in size, like old monkeys, and I saw this morning I'm getting the look. . . . But I can't rest, child, I never knew how to rest."

"None of us do," Martha said. "Except James."

"James don't rest, either. He keeps thinking out a way to kill his old mother. . . ." She drew in her breath sharply. "Martha, do you reckon there'll be any more—?" Her voice, dry with pain and fear, dropped suddenly into the silence in her that covered, and forbade her to speak of, their efforts to prove she was insane.

"No . . . there won't be any more."

She stood a moment, listening to her daughter's voice comforting her with the tone of a mother to a child, and then she turned back to the window. "I know there'll be something. . . . Something is in the air, pressing down on me to look and wait and telling me to be ready. . . ."

She saw the car while she spoke and did not notice it except as a passing, unimportant vehicle. "I've not loved you enough, Martha," she said; and now, while she hushed and watched the magnolia leaves turn brightly in the air, the car stopped under the tree. For one second, before the terror skirled in her, she saw its black paint glittering dark on all the lawn and town and air. She felt herself turn rotten inside, seeing the men start up the walk toward her, and she heard the striking, sweet gongs of the wind, so muffled, so far off, the sound hers while she could hold it against those advancing figures, and then hers no longer.

She turned around calmly. "It's Henric and James," she said. "And two others. Go out and keep them off if you can." She sat down in Billy's smoking-chair, with Martha's swift gasp flowing sharp in her ears. The afternoon lay dead around her.

After a moment the voices coming through the radio turned brittle against those other voices from the veranda. She heard Martha say; "No, you can't bring that man in here or do that to her. She's under my care." The room was dark around her; she thought, "I am alone, alone." James cried, "We'll have you know she's our mother, too, our right's equal to yores!" Henric's voice murmured, its indistinguishable suavity falling like a hideous balm over James' loud anger. She thought, "I am alone, alone. . . ." And now, as once before, some power entered her to the knowledge and the fact of that loneliness. The dark in the room shifted and glimmered like the shift and glimmer of purpose in her skull. Her heart contracted on a hard, aching malice. She rose; but now, standing, her inwards turned rotten again, she wavered to and fro, frantically trying to think what meaning she had had for one instant and lost. But suddenly a new voice spoke out there, rumbling in to her like intelligent thunder, like and not like a voice she knew. "Mrs. Nelson. . . ." A joy grew softly and unreasonably in her; she could hear nothing more of what the voice said. She began to walk from the room, striding forward like a young woman, with her long, full skirts rippling about her and her eyes fixed in the blind, malicious glee of fighting terror.

Her greeting rang out in the hall.

"Good evening, Henric, James!" She held her head thrust forward, her chin bitter and determined. "Good evening, Peebles!" She reached the door. "What's the fuss out here about? Come on in. I want to talk to you. I've made up my mind at last. . . . This business is a disgrace, and I mean to stop it now once and for all. I'll have no more tiddley-doing, I'm calling a final halt. . . ." She stopped herself, and stared at Dr. Stanhope as if she had not noticed him before. "But who is this gentleman? I don't think we've met before."

Henric cleared his throat and she observed, maliciously, the shaking of his head on his long, thin neck. "My mother . . . Dr. Stanhope."

"Why, what ails you, Henric? You're shaking like a leaf, I declare anybody'd think you had some nervous trouble!" She glanced at Dr. Stanhope's thick gray hair. "Somebody in your office, I reckon, Peebles? Well, you need somebody! But come in, come in to the living-room where we can talk!"

She grinned suddenly, and winked at Martha's astonished expression, winking ostentatiously, full in their uneasy faces. "Lead the way, Martha. It's your house!" She walked energetically down the hall, forgetting her weakness and the old, weary bend of her waist from her hips. She was full of the great, hot glee of acting; she turned dramatically at the living-room door, bowing to them. "Be seated, gentlemen, and let me tell you what I want to do. . . ."

She sat down and watched Peebles twist the dials on the radio to turn it off. "Pass Billy's tobacco, Martha, and let this strange gentleman make himself comfortable. . . ." She stared at him suddenly, studying his huge, granite-blond solidity almost with love. Something wakened in her, an emotion thinly like the response of dark, quick, and passionate women to the still humor that lives, enigmatically and comfortably, in the persons of fair men whose huge bones and unmoving flesh give out nothing but the sense of their strength. She stared at him, and forgot that her sons were sitting there, uneasy and treacherous, waiting for her to betray herself. She said, "You're in some way like my son Jahn. . . ."

She moved, and touched her tongue against her dry lips. "In some way like him," she repeated, and went on, oblivious and forgetful; "It does me good to see you so, for I've spent many a day and night longing for him, and I've learned that hunger of that sort moves in the bowels as much as any other hunger. . . . I've learned David's cry to his son Absolom. . . . But you're older than Jahn," she said, abruptly, and still gazed at him.

Dr. Stanhope sat without moving, his gray eyes fixed on her. His thin mouth curled a little, gently. "I am sixty, Mrs. Ibsell, not much less than your age."

"And have you children?" she asked, leaning forward a little and clasping her hands loosely over her knees. "Have you children to know how the evil of them in your womb and the pain that brings them out is nothing against the evil of their black hearts and their cold eyes on you when you've raised them to grownness and they learn to hate you? Do your sons hate you, Dr. Stanhope?"

Henric said: "Mother, I'm ashamed of you! Don't listen to her, Doctor, her mind is wandering."

"Yes, listen to her!" Martha cried, suddenly. "Listen to her, Doctor!" She started up and sank back again, breathing swiftly, with something like triumph on her face.

Dr. Stanhope turned his huge head for an instant. "I am listening, Mrs. Nelson."

"Do your sons hate you?" Rachel said, and bent closer to him across the room. Her eyes, set a moment before in hard, fighting pain, were soft now and humid, with great, splendid lights raying from them; she leaned forward, humbly and wearily, in the posture of old peasant women tired with life and learned in its pain. "I was good to my sons, Doctor. When they were little, after their father was gone, I took them out of my own father's house, where they weren't wanted, and took them to Larson, and Larson was good to them till he died. When they were little, Doctor, and I hadn't enough for myself and them too, I let them have it all, I wore old skirts out of washed, clean tow sacks for my work dresses, and they had pictures in their rooms at school. . . .

"All but Jahn, all but Jahn!" she said, and began to rock back and forth gently. "All but Jahn, O my littlest and my love! I gave him stones for bread and left him naked but for his proud brothers' cast-off clothes, and I woke him in the morning when he should have slept. . . . Oh, he was little, Doctor, and rosy, and his eyes moved in my head day and night!" Her voice went low, crooning deeply, and she cried, "I see his eyes now, turned up to me, asking, and he goes little and bent under the wind, and I'm too far off to read what his eyes say. I see his eyes always . . . his eyes . . . !"

Martha's throat tore suddenly with an ugly, smothered sound. Dr. Stanhope's gaze turned to her, and moved, and saw James Forrest stealthily rising.

"Have your brothers betrayed you, Doctor?" Rachel said, and rocked back and forth, slowly, monotonously, rhythmically. "Has your brother come to you to trick you and then set in the courtroom and made you rotten, rotten, and old before all the world? Have your sons smeared you with that rottenness, and hated you, and have you heard the tumbril wheels turning on cobblestones? 'Queens go to their deaths so,' Larson said, and knew . . . he knew, long ago Larson knew. . . ."

"Hush, Mamma, hush! You're—you're letting them see —!" Martha leaped to her and bent over, holding her shoulders, and then knelt beside her with her head down, her hands caressing Rachel's old, twisted fingers. "Be still, Mamma. . . ." she said.

"Have you doubted your God, Doctor? Have you seen your God grow dim in your mind and doubted him because them that were meant to show His light to you were evil? God moves in a mysterious way . . . His light is smothered in the wind, and I have lost my God, lost my God. I go stumbling, Doctor . . . Doctor, I go stumbling and needing help, stumbling through that blood at El Caney, knowing men never come back to the heart that needs them, and women are lost and alone, and there is . . . no help," she said, looking up and gasping, "No help . . . and no end. . . . I am alone, alone," she said, "and too far off to read what his eyes say."

She saw, suddenly, with an abrupt perception of what was about her, the doctor's gaze fastened on something diagonally across the room from him, something close to her, something she felt over her. She looked that way slowly, like one looking through darkness. James' wild, lynx face shone brilliantly before her, hitting her gaze like a hard, shooting light, and she looked at it with wonder, without fear or surprise. His hand came swiftly on her shoulder.

"Why, Mother," he said, "why are you talking so? Have you forgot it's Jahn that hates you, while we others love you?"

He was smiling, he was kind, but his fingers pressed in the thin skin of her shoulder. Fear chilled the roots of her finger nails: she saw, for one lurid instant, that hand raised to strike her and his smile a devil's grin. She screamed suddenly in her throat and fell back over Martha's raised face. She screamed again, faintly, with exhaustion of terror as Henric and Peebles leaped to their feet.

"You fool!" Henric said. "Why couldn't you keep your hands off her. Why couldn't you keep your mouth shut? Couldn't you see she was—?" He stopped himself, his long neck vibrating from side to side.

Peebles crashed suddenly in between them, squalling crazily in white-faced rage. "Be still, will you? Be still, will you?" He pushed their faces apart with the flat of his hand. "Not for forty million . . . to be associated with you. . . . Be still!" He foamed inarticulately, and panted, and pushed their faces backward.

[183]

"Shut up, God damn you. You're the one that's giving it all away!" James cried. The lawyer was abruptly still.

"Hush, Mamma, hush. . . ." Martha said, and stroked her mother's hands. "Hush. He didn't hit you, Mama."

She sat up slowly. "He didn't hit me? He raised his hand . . ." She looked around the room with wonder again, and saw Dr. Stanhope sitting motionless, gazing at her. "He raised his hand?"

"No, Mamma, no. . . ."

A confusion of memory worked in her tired mind, she felt the whorls of her brain moving impatiently and fearfully over the rough stuff of her recollections. She said, "Child . . . I'm sorry, and you going to have a baby. . . . I'm sorry. . . ." She stared a long time at the doctor, unaware of Martha's swift movement of protest and denial.

"I'm all right again," she thought, out of the slowing beat of terror in her mind. She remembered how she had gone to the door, determined to behave before the doctor as if she knew nothing of their plot, determined to talk of how she wanted to end the lawsuit and of her reasons. "But he looked like Jahn, some way," she thought, "and I forgot that plan. . . ." She gazed obliquely at her sons, still standing in a frenzied knot in the middle of the room with the lawyer, and turned her eyes back to Dr. Stanhope's face.

"I'm not crazy," she said.

He nodded and rose. "Mrs. Ibsell"—he bent over her hand gently—"you're quite sane. . . ." His sudden, glittering smile, like Jahn's, she thought, met her own. She lowered her head swiftly and touched her lips against the backs of his fingers, and heard him go out. The front door closed softly behind him.

She thought that James was coming toward her again. "But you are crazy, Mother—!" Henric's hand caught his shoulder and turned him around, stopping his mouth and his gesture. She leaned her hand on Martha's head, where she still knelt beside her.

"This is bad for you in your condition, child."

"Mamma—! It was Sue. . . ."

Rachel looked at the lawyer. "Good afternoon, gentlemen.
. . ." She began to try to stand up, and Peebles' white face
stared at her for an instant. "Come on, get out of here!"
he said, frantically, pushing them toward the door. She
leaned back and closed her eyes. They were gone, she
thought, they were gone. . . . The wind in the crisp, autumn
leaves rang sadly like the cry of lost splendid victory: she
did not hear it. She said, "The curse is on me . . . my sons and
my land. . . ."

XI

Chanson heard Negro voices at Sand Caves while she was
still in the bend of the road, out of sight of them. In her a
peculiar wonder poised trance-like for a second, and then,
while she defined it as the culmination of the absorbed vagueness with which she had ridden nine miles, it departed and
left her feeling a little sleepy and uninterested. She reined in
her mare. On the left, where the road fell sharply off into
traced and ravaged gullies, she saw the beginnings of the
Caves. Far down, the white sand lay glittering poisonously in
the sunlight, the motes of its glitter seeming to shift and
change in a smiling mockery of Long Jim Chambers' sparse
fields where they rose, leftward, above it. The scent of
water and of wet, lichened earth seeped strongly in front of
her, on the ledge of hill that jutted from the wooded slope
of James Forrest's lands and curved the road.

She brought her mare up nearer to it, giving her her neck
so that she might drink from the spring falling out of the
brown, rusted rock. She watched while the soft nose slithered
over the wet fronds of wild maidenhair, and gazed at the
water with something turning in her mind on the difference
between the dark water-glitter and the livid, pulsing sand-
glitter. Heavy autumnal heat rushed up at her from the first

gulch of the Caves, and met across her with the cool, shadowed mist of the spring. The Negro voices ahead, behind the ledge of rock, ran on in a vague, tumbled music. She glanced up to the swift, downward rush of the hills on her right, at the dwarf sourwood holding its roots in the thin, loamy soil there as if to balance itself against the slide of the earth. Then she heard Jahn Ibsell speak above the rounded confusion of Negro tones, his speech sharp and clarion-like. She jerked her hand on the bridle, so that the black mare under her quivered an instant, and then turned out around the rock and went past it.

She was not, for a full half-minute then, aware of herself or of what she meant. The horse went on toward the lifted Negro faces, and set her hooves on the timbers of the bridge Jahn Ibsell had laid over the snuffling, devouring lip of the sand. She saw the black fists pulling back the shovels and the Negroes standing away from her, their backs to the glittering chasm. Jahn Ibsell's face looked at her from the other side and waited. The mare's hooves struck solid earth again, and she reined her in automatically, and sat gazing down at her brother-in-law's brown khaki breeches and field boots and at the small, white rim of sweat on his forehead.

She said, "Good afternoon," and smiled. "How deep are the Caves here under the bridge?"

She watched his eyes gazing back at her, clear yet opaque, giving no hint of what he thought; and saw him glance abruptly past her to the Negroes.

"Get on with the work, boys. It's late."

The shovels struck on the wood of the bridge, and dirt plopped softly downward.

"How deep is it?"

A dry amusement passed over his face. "A hundred and seventy-two feet from the floor of the bridge to the bottom."

She turned around in the saddle and looked. The white sand lay under there, drifted in shoals like water, soft and flaky on the top like quicksand, and glittered with a look of bubbles rising in the motes of its brilliance. "So you're un-covering the bridge today?" she said. "Looking for a slip in the foundations? Do you, too, have intuitions?"

He looked at her without speaking, waiting. She took off her hat and pushed back her coarse thick hair.

"Sue and the new child are home from the hospital, eh? What have you named the boy?"

Something ironic twitched faintly his silken, brown eye-brows. "Lars," he said, briefly, and added, "Kate came out this morning."

She fanned herself with the hat, holding its brim crumpled under her fingers. "So Kate is here, then?" She gazed past him, up the road through the woods, as if to see past the second curve in the road to the white farmhouse.

The soft fall of the dirt on the wooden bridge behind her hemned her in and made a ring for the certainty of her ab-stracted emotion. She did not feel his presence sharply or even actually; the sickness that lapped in her when she saw Hen-ric's desire and fear of murder was turning on its other side and questing outward toward Jahn Ibsell with the instinctive, childish search of women for a figure, vague, hard, looming, on which to leave the mark of their disillusion. Without look-ing at him, without allowing herself to remember the sharp, subtle radiance of his difference, she felt an intimacy with him grow in her thinking. Through it, she felt his waiting and a little something of his amusement.

She said, musingly, "Henric would like a child, I have al-ways thought."

His lips moved with laughter, grew swiftly still, and he said, gravely. "I'm sorry Henric has disappointed you."

She knew that the great burst of his laughter lay behind the words, smothered there with irony and waiting; yet she was still undisturbed. Her immense, female complacence turned about and preened itself. She gathered up the reins, causing the mare to fidget in the dust of the road. "The devil is no myth," she remarked, abruptly, to herself. "Supersti-

[187]

tions are never myths. Many men have seen the devil's horns and sold themselves for his pitchfork." Staring at the round, smooth eyes of the buckeye bush on the red mound of dust at the edge of the road, she repeated, vaguely, "Many men . . ."

Jahn's voice said, slowly, with meaning, "And some women."

She jerked her head in dissent and sudden annoyance. The patterned lines on the tan eyes of the buckeye shimmered, marked in a liquid red-brown like the color of sherry. She looked at him sharply, and said, "I am, unfortunately, not an introspective woman." Something of her usual scorn of him returned. "You understand that—'introspective'?" she asked.

He flushed slowly and palely, and she felt his humor withdrawing, turning cold and brittle. He said, "I understand you're Henric's wife and Henric hates me."

She began to smile sourly, gibing at him. "Why must you always think I hate you?"

He stared at her steadily. Behind her, the red, soft dirt plopped on the wooden bridge and the shovels scraped clinkingly and rasped and drew up to the Negroes' deep chest-grunt of exertion and energy. She smiled again, with amusement, and shrugged. "I come to warn you and you behave so —in your old way. You are laughing at me first and then hating me. Perhaps I had better go without telling you, eh?"

"Perhaps," he said. "You couldn't bring me a warning that wouldn't be a trap."

Her yellow eyes moved and fastened on him, with something like pain flaring the black pupils so that he saw them change shape and become like the triangular, warm-shimmering centers of a cat's eyes when it faces the light suddenly. She laid her hat over the horn of the saddle and smoothed its rough felt slowly.

"So?" she said. "And you do not want me to tell you. . . ." Her fingers crumpled the hat brim. "I do not know why I came. . . ." She sighed strangely, and looked down at him

[188]

with a puzzled frown. "I watch that Henric walk up and down the floor of that library, shaking with nervous wickedness—!" Her voice frayed angrily and paused. She looked away, back up the road through the woods. "Henric has disappointed me," she said, and heard her tones falling, dead tired, against his enemy flesh.

He said, softly, with the swift brilliance that rayed like lightning out of his sculptural inexpressiveness, "For a smart woman, you can act the fool!"

She looked at him slowly. "Yes," she said. She picked up the reins again. "I think I'm hunting Henric in you perhaps, eh?" She laughed. "And I always hated you for not being like him. . . ." She shook her head and turned her mare back onto the bridge.

The hooves struck the new heaped dirt, sinking softly into it, and jarring her to the ungiving impact of the wood underneath. She stared at the Negro faces as they moved back, drawing their shovels out of the way, and it seemed to her that she was passing between them for the first time: all that she had said to Jahn Ibsell on the other side of the bridge was unreal; she could not, now, hear it plainly in remembrance. She went over the bridge without looking down at the sand scooped and whorled in sinister brilliance below and onto the roadbed again. Behind her, the shovels moved and the red dirt plopped against the planks. She reined in her mare, turning half-around in the saddle.

A little, bent man writhed up from under the banisters close to the mare's hooves, and slung his hammer against the dirt heaped at the end of the bridge. "Foundation gonna slide ag'in some day." he said in a grumbling voice. "Foundation boun' to slide." His skin glistened with the greasy, sour smell of black sweat. He wiped his face with small, gnarled fingers and then rubbed his hands through the woolly, gray mat of his hair.

"Why have you uncovered the bridge today?" Chanson said to him, suddenly.

He looked around at her with eyes rimmed by lids lighter in color than his forehead and cheeks, so that his pupils had the round, cold stare of an opossum. "Yas'm. . . ." He saluted nimbly, spitting the tobacco in his mouth onto the palm of his hand. "Yas'm. . . . Bridge cave' in halfway las' night. . . ."

She thought, sharply, "He had already done it, he knew he had already failed—!" She said, "What's your name?" Behind her, she could hear Jahn Ibsell rub a match over the wooden banister. The fragrance of his tobacco floated past her nostrils.

"Oh, I'se Joe, Miss Chancie. You done forgot? Black Fanny's husban', mam."

She said: "Black Fanny's husband, eh? You've been a long time with Mr. Jahn, have you?" And then, slowly, "Tell your master he must watch the bridge. . . . Remember that, he must watch the bridge." She struck her mare suddenly with the flat of her gloved hand, sending her around the great, water-rilled rock in the curve of the road, and back toward Choctaw. She glanced up at the rock as she passed it, and at the leaning sourwood above. Something moved between the trees, a woman in a grayish cotton dress with a white square of apron over the skirt. She thought for an instant that it was Fanny Forrest, and then, glancing more sharply upward, she saw nothing.

XII

Martha turned the door knob again. "Unlock the door, Mamma; unlock the door and let me in." The knob clicked fruitlessly and slid back around in her tense fingers. "Mamma —!" No sound came out of Rachel Ibsell's room. Bent forward to listen, Martha stared at the blank white surface of the door. All the silence in the empty house seemed to rise around her with a ghostly creak. She wrenched at the knob desperately. "Take the key out of the lock, Mamma!" Her own voice fluted thinly, with the anger of fear in it. Then for a long minute her ears drummed to the grave-like stillness circling beyond the door.

Down below, on the near streets or perhaps in the town, there was a muffled movement like the distant passing of a car. She turned from the door abruptly, and walked the length of the hall aimlessly, with her hands crossed tight over her breast, looking intently and sightlessly down at the red carpet. At the head of the stairs she whirled loosely and went back to the door. She rapped on its thick, cold panels. "Mamma, if you don't let me in I'll call Billy." She waited, knowing that her mother would not believe her: Billy did not allow himself to be disturbed at the store. She said, "Mamma! I mean it, I'll call him!"

Abruptly it seemed to her that she could hear breathing, loud, suffering, in there on the bed or on the floor. Her mind flickered with vague, alarmed pictures of her mother ill, dying, perhaps. "What are you doing in there? Let me in!" Something moved, answeringly she thought, on the bedroom rug, and stopped and moved again. Suddenly there was no sound.

"Mamma!" She pulled hard against the knob, bracing her feet and leaning back. She let go abruptly, in exasperation with herself, and stood regaining her balance and listening again. A sharp crack of little hinges crawled out of the room. "She's at her trunk!" she thought, and grew still all over. Distinctly now she could hear a movement from the closet in the north corner of the room to the trunk. She counted the steps and the pauses, so many steps and then a pause, so many steps and then a pause, seeing at each intermission of sound how her mother must be taking garments from the hangers in the closet or, if she were on the other side of the room, folding and laying them in the trunk.

"What are you doing with your clothes?" she cried, fiercely. "Open this door!"

The footsteps stopped at once, furtively, and she could hear, on the other side of the door, Rachel's listening. She drew back from the wall, and glanced down the stairs with that queer, irrational expectance of some one entering which intersperses such moments of helpless exasperation and fear. She raised her fist and banged on the door, against the furtive listening in there. "Billy's coming. You open this door!" She wheeled, without waiting, and ran down the stairs, two steps at a time, hurrying for the telephone in the lower hall.

The dark figure frostily outlined against the glass in the front door stopped her at the bottom of the stairs. She made a single other step, caught at the newel-post, and stood still, looking over her shoulder at the shadow. It had been motionless, she saw, at the top of the front-door steps when she first caught a glimpse of it; now it was moving slowly toward the door, putting out its hand to ring. She leaped against the door, wrenched it open, and stood panting in James Forrest's face.

"What are you doing back here!"

He raised one hand slowly to the corner of his mustache. Behind him, at the curb, his battered Ford sat facing downhill. His foot moved, wedging in the crack of the screen door. At the same instant he opened the screen, and his foot moved over the threshold. His black eyes gazed at Martha, shining, and he curled his mustache.

"Billy at home?" he said, almost casually.

Anger frothed in her, under her tongue. Her cheeks burned a sudden, spotted red. "You know darned well he's not!" Her fingers itched to slap across his staring, smug eyes. "You get away from here!" She stopped, her tongue buckling with incoherent hatred of him.

"So Billy's not home?" he said, slowly. "Well, well! He's outa town, I guess, Marthy. I jest come by the store and they said he'd gone out in the country to see about a piece of land he's taking a mortgage on." His pious voice droned numbingly.

She said, fiercely, "He is in town, too!" and did not know why she said it.

"No, he's outa town, and Zack's not near by, either." He curled his mustache and smiled suddenly, with bawdiness waking behind the cold, shining film of his gaze. "I declare you're right perty, Marthy. . . . It's a pity you're my half-sister."

She slammed the wooden door against his foot; his fingers caught the edge of it. She jerked it back and slammed again frantically. His foot and his extended right arm held it firmly against her.

"Why, Marthy!" He stared, with an expression of shocked respectability and she knew, furiously, that her upper lip had snarled back over her teeth with harsh effort as she strained the door against him. "Why, Marthy, this is right 'bad for you in yore condition,' ain't it?" he said, quoting Rachel with sly mockery.

She let go the door suddenly and stood facing him while the shamed blood ran under her skin over her throat and face.

"That's right," he said, calmly, coming inside and leaning against the door frame. "Billy's outa town and Zack's outa the way, and Jahn's where you can't git him quick. So we jest thought we'd come and git Mother. She ain't doing so good here with you. . . . She don't like Billy," he said, and leered softly.

She stared at him. "You get out of this house! You hear me? You get out!" Her thick, incoherent voice, like an angry child's, confused her further. "You get out! You hear me ——?"

He crossed one foot over the other and took out his pocket knife and a small piece of dirty wood. He began to whittle.

"Why, Marthy, you won't deny me the right to come in and see my pore ol' mother . . . my crazy ol' mother?" he said. Slithers of wood curled thinly back from the stick in his hand; he turned the knife and the slithers fell off. "You ever see the scars on Fanny's arms?" he asked, casually.

She pushed him suddenly, blindly, and jumped back with

all her muscles jerking in terror. He grinned slowly, with a wet-mouthed relish.

"Why, Marthy, when you git mad you're 'most as perty as my woman out to my place." He laughed, a thin wild snicker.

She said, hoarsely, "You can't come in here."

"Can't, eh? Oh, you're the mistress here, I reckon, and I can't come in?" He snickered again and folded up his knife. "You'll be a perty mistress when I put my fist in that belly of yores, won't you?" he said, leaning forward, his mouth open and his eyes blank in a lust of cruelty. She gave back, he advanced, she moved again, and he followed her, almost to the foot of the stairs now.

"I guess you see," he said, softly. "If I put my fist in you, you'll be a fine Ibsell, won't you . . .? Eh?" he said, his fist lifted and jabbing the air near her, grazing her stomach.

She caught his arm frantically, for one instant, screaming, "You leave me alone! You leave me alone! I'll call Billy!" and then she let go, sick from touching him that little.

"Oh, she'll call Billy," he said, as if addressing a third person. "She thinks she'll call Billy." His arm swept out, knocking her lightly back from the stairs, and his face changed, reddening and swelling with arrogance. "I'm a-going up, Miss, and you can keep still or I'll gag you, damn it!" His soft black chuckle came again. "I'm a-going up to git my nice ol' mother, my sweet ol' mother, and take her out to the bughouse." The thick tip of his tongue swabbed convulsively at his wet lips. "They'll lay the lash on her out there if she gives 'em any fits like she did us today."

"My God! Hush! hush! you hush!" she cried, wildly.

He mounted the stairs swiftly, looking back down on her and snickering. Her eyeballs blared, following the turn of his head as a bird's eyes follow the lick of a snake's tongue. She thought she saw the door at the head of the stairs move. She screamed, "Mamma! don't let him in, Mamma!" and turned suddenly, with a convulsive motion of horror, and ran down the hall. "Don't let him in! Don't let him in!" she kept crying in her throat. She stumbled against the telephone stand, whirled, and grabbed the cord of the receiver, jerking it off.

XIII

An hour before this, immediately after Chanson turned her mare around the rock ledge and rode back toward Choctaw, Jahn Ibsell left the bridge above Sand Caves and walked swiftly through the woods and across the pasture to the house. Behind him, the slight figure of a woman skirted the bridge and the working Negroes, going around the shoulder of hill above them, and slipped into the pasture. She was not more than forty, but the extreme emaciation of her work-rounded shoulders and the weak, hip-dragging weariness of her gait stamped her figure with a look more pitiable than that of old age. Her small, bone-thin face carried upon it skin that folded and crossed into innumerable expressionless wrinkles, and her drab gray hair, pulled hastily back from her yellowed forehead, lay pinched in a coarse-stranded knot on the back of her head. As she followed Jahn Ibsell, stealthily darting behind the screen of the pasture mounds when he paused, her large, slate-blue eyes turned from side to side with a look which is seen only in the eyes of sick, over-worked mules or of women who exist without hope. Her thin hands, gnarled blue with labor, moved ceaselessly in her apron-front, rolling it over and over until it covered her hands and arms like a huge, white cocoon. Now and then she coughed wetly in her throat, turning her head and smothering the sound with her mouth pressed against her shoulder. Then she looked up again and went on.

Jahn crossed the top of the last mound, stopping there an instant to glance eastward toward the corn-fields. The yellowed stalks bent toward the ground, robbed now of their ears. Farther off in the fields, the blade of the reaper hummed with a high steel singing under the call of the Negro driver to his mules. Behind it, a little group of dark bodies moved, bending and binding the corn in sheaves for winter fodder. The reaper curved round in the corn, turning back, and Jahn stepped down from the grassy hillock, and walked forward, cutting diagonally across the north end of the pasture to the yard gate. The woman coughed again, gently, and stood waiting, half-hidden from the house.

The front door flew open, and Jahnet raced down the steps and across the walk, calling aloud. She clasped her father's legs and made a little jump, as if to be lifted up. Watching from behind the mound, Fanny Forrest saw Jahn turn the child around, take her hand, and lead her toward the porch. "Daddy, she says he's a black Ibsell, Aunt Kate says he's a black Ibsell," the child said, her voice high and urgent with the shrill bird-call of children. They went into the house. After a second, Fanny climbed over the mound and followed them. She coughed damply, rolled her hands tight in the apron, allowed it to unroll, and then pulled it back again.

"Daddy, he's a black Ibsell jes' like I'm a blonde one, Aunt Kate says," Jahnet repeated, loudly, on the threshold of her mother's room. Her father stopped and stood against the door frame, looking in at Sue on the bed and at Kate fanning herself by the window. "Don't you want me to move you out on the side porch?" he said to Sue, and watched her hand stroking the wispy black hairs on the head of his new-born son. Her hand moved gently, the slender fingers pliant and close together, smoothing softly and lovingly. She turned her head and looked at him in the doorway. "No. I'm all right in here. Kate may be hot, though."

Kate rustled her paper fan, stirring faintly the close, white waves of her immaculate hair. "I'm all right as long as I can fan." She glanced at the branches of the alphea tree spreading with wan, lilac flowers across the window screen. "There's a little breeze in this tree."

Black Fanny's heavy tread sounded in the kitchen; her iron thumped hard on the ironing-board. Jahn walked across the blue rug to the other end of the room to sit on top of Sue's cedar chest. Jahnet climbed up beside him and spread her tan Indian-head skirt just above the dimples in her knees. Kate watched them serenely, her head a little to one side, and fanned. Jahnet stared at the precise folds in the fan, noticing minutely and with possessive fascination the sharp, vertical cut of the brown figures on the white paper toward the celluloid handle.

Jahn said, softly, "Chanson's been out. . . ."

Sue turned sharply in the bed, pulling the mosquito net hanging on the foot rail awry, and Kate's hand paused in the air. The slow movement of dread crossed Sue's face and darkened her eyes. She stared at her husband without speaking.

"What for?" Kate said, suddenly and briskly.

The tension in the room relaxed. Jahn smiled. "To warn me," he said, his tones slightly ironical. "She told Black Joe I must watch the bridge."

"The bridge!" Sue exclaimed, faintly.

Jahn looked at the floor. "Well, it was half out when I came home last night. . . ." He glanced up and met Kate's still, bitter-blue eyes. "The foundations had been dug out too much; the sand didn't wait for my weight on it. . . ."

Sue sat up suddenly, and turned the baby over with fumbling, reasonless hands. His little, red face stared at them for a second with the blind eyes and half-comical, half-choked expression of very young infants. Then she laid him back on the small pillow beside her and pulled a corner of the mosquito netting over his head. She remained propped on one elbow, gazing at her husband with fear-darkened eyes.

Jahnet saw Kate's fan begin to move again, slowly, as if she only half-remembered its presence between her fingers.

Outside, on the front veranda, a dim, dragging step sounded.

"Chanson draws the line somewhere," Jahn said, and turned his head to listen. The screen door slid to with a faint, crisp noise of the long spring that held it. Sue's face turned sidewise toward the door and whitened tensely. Kate said, "Now, what can that be?" and got up. Jahn rose, too, while the steps were coming along the hall and stopping and coming on again.

Fanny Forrest stood in the doorway. For a full half-minute she stared at them with a blind glance curiously like that of the infant Sue had just lifted from the pillow. Then Kate advanced toward her with welcoming hands. "Why, Fanny! Come in. . . ." Fanny turned aside suddenly, smothering her cough, and they saw almost with terror her dull, hopeless eyes filling with uneasy tears. Kate took her hands from under the rolled apron and held them without speaking, while Fanny turned her face back and looked at them. Her features worked against the slipping tears, as if by the intense corrugation of her wrinkles she could hold them from sight. "Fanny! Come in," Kate said, gently, and led her to a chair by the empty fireplace.

She went limply and let Kate push her into the chair. She knew what they thought, that James had beaten her again. "James is been in town all day," she said. She looked up, saw Jahnet staring at her from the top of the chest, and wiped her cheeks. "I'm jes' give out," she said, quaveringly, and began to roll her arms in the apron again.

"Of course; it's a long walk," Sue said. "Jahn, tell Black Fanny to bring her a glass of that blackberry wine."

"No, no!" Fanny cried. "No, Sue, I don't want any, I must hurry." She cowered back against the cushion in the chair. "I'm . . . I must hurry."

"You must rest a minute," Jahn said, grimly, and went from the room to the kitchen for the wine himself. His going made a curious emptiness between them, so that Kate stood without moving and Sue leaned forward on her propped elbow, staring vaguely at the door through which Jahn had gone. On the cedar chest, Jahnet was still, her gaze resting on Fanny Forrest's face.

"James has been in town all day," Fanny repeated, weakly,

offering the remark out of a dull, hopeless pride, to prove to them that James had not beaten her today. She said, swiftly, "I wanted to see Jahn," and relapsed into a sad, nervous apathy, folding and unfolding her arms from the apron.

He came back, held the glass of wine to her, and she sat up and sipped a little. "It's good. . . ." She turned the glass nervously until Kate took it and set it on the mantelpiece. "I left a bucket hid in the woods," she said, "to fill with muscadines as I go back."

Sue pushed the mosquito netting aside from Lars and began to stroke the top of his small head. She glanced up at Jahn. "Fanny wants to see you."

Outside in the lane, Negro voices rose tumblingly, in a hushed, dark rhythm of sound. The hands were coming back from the bridge. Black Fanny's iron made a hot, sizzling plop against the ironing-board and they heard her go out onto the back porch. "Joe, you git me mah stove wood quick now!" She came back in, banging the screen door.

Fanny Forrest stared at the empty fireplace, her wrinkles moving spasmodically from the slight nervous tic in one cheek. They waited, looking at her. Jahnet saw her mother's face whitening slowly, and stared at it without comprehension, yet with the feeling of dread moving stealthily in the room. Kate turned abruptly and sat down again by the window.

"It's your mother . . ." Fanny said, and coughed. The swift movement of her mouth against her shoulder was somehow terrible. "Your mother, they . . ."

"Mamma—?" Jahn's eyes went swiftly to Sue's face and circled back concealingly. He sat down beside Fanny. "What is it?" he said, something at once helpless and swift in his lowered voice.

She burst into tears, her mouth working in a long, whimpering sound. They stared at her during a slow minute. Kate stood up again. "Give her the rest of the wine, Jahn." He rose and looked vaguely about. Then abruptly he bent over, grasping Fanny's shoulders and pulling her face up so that her tear-filled eyes met his. "What is it? What's happened!"

Sue moved on the bed, protestingly, and raised one hand as if she must stop something. Then she was still again.

Fanny tried to wipe her face, averting her eyes and saying, unsteadily, "They're going to put her in the asylum, in Marston's." She broke out loudly, now, and swiftly, "Oh, Jahn, they've got Dr. Stanhope to say she's crazy. James told me last night; he—laughed—!" she said, as if she had not lived long enough with James Forrest to believe in his laughter. "They're going to take her away from Martha's and keep her at Zack's till she's crazy, and then they'll put her in Marston's. James says they'll get the land then; the deed will be revoked because she's crazy. . . ." Her voice snapped.

Jahn Ibsell stood up from her. He moved with the slow, tortured gesture of a statue animated by a sculptor's sick dream, and then he was motionless, staring into space before him, so that his stillness carried a momentary wonder to Sue and Kate that flesh and bone could be more enduring and more implacable than the stone it resembled. His eyes stabbed out from his silence, across them and beyond. Suddenly a gray shadow swept over his countenance. It gleamed at them for a second, and was gone, and there, strangely, was his face growing weak and tired, as if, one by one, his features succumbed to an illness caught interiorly from the stoppage of sound in him.

He moved again, vaguely, and his eyes turned from space toward Sue's eyes and stopped there, asking something of her, pleading. The dark shadow of dread, growing all afternoon behind her golden iris, loomed at him. Her hand moved frantically, piteously, thrusting away fear, holding back from her his pleading. Her throat worked. "No . . . no! . . . I can't!" He turned from her jerkily, and looked at Fanny again, and then, dimly, about the room. He backed against the mantelpiece.

"Well, Fanny . . . I'm sorry," he said, and his voice seemed to come, smothered, from a long way off.

She folded her apron. "I thought you'd go after her?" she said, with puzzlement.

"No, Fanny!" Sue started up in bed suddenly. "I can't have her here. . . ." She began to cry. "Oh, Fanny, you know I can't, with the new baby!" She turned over and sobbed with her face down.

Jahn looked at her steadily, with a faint, sick contempt sitting on his lips. "We know it, Sue, you can't have her." At the sound of his voice she sobbed more loudly and childishly. "I can't!" she cried, lifting her head a moment and looking at him. "She made me miserable once, I won't have her!" She stopped crying.

He turned away from her as if he saw, terribly and hauntingly, the accusation of her tear-suffused eyes. The baby beside her awoke, cried feebly, and then hushed. Jahnet slid off the chest and stood by the bed, putting her hand under the mosquito netting to touch lightly her little brother's head. She stared wonderingly from her mother to her father and back again. Kate fanned herself. "You better drink the rest of that wine, Fanny," she said, imperturbably.

Sue sat up again and cried out with anger: "She left you! She treated me like a dog and left here, she accused you of everything she could think of! I think it's little enough for you to do for my sake to leave her alone now. She's where she wanted to be and she's got what she deserves!" She glanced fiercely at Kate for confirmation.

Jahn looked at her. "Be quiet, Sue!" His face whitened, and he walked aimlessly past the bed and back again to the fireplace. Fanny Forrest was staring up at him, puzzled and meek. "I thought you'd go after her?" she said again. He looked away from her.

"Thank you for coming, Fanny."

"I thought—" She stopped herself and got up slowly, standing there with thin, bent shoulders, her hands fumbling

her apron and her eyes gazing around at them humbly. "Well
. . . I must go. . . ." She seemed to wait still.

Kate said, suddenly: "There's nothing you could do, Jahn.
If you went, you'd get there too late."

He looked at Fanny. "I'll call Black Joe to drive you back
in Sue's car. You musn't walk that distance again." His voice
moved through the words without feeling.

"No," she said, quickly. "No. James would see the car
tracks and wonder where I'd been." She stopped, and looked
at him lamely. "I left a bucket in the woods, I'm going to
pick some muscadines before I go back." She went to the
door while she was speaking, and he moved after her, slowly
and almost gropingly.

"You ought not to walk up that hill," he told her again.

Jahnet left the bed and walked behind them, touching her
father's hand, up the hall to the front door. Fanny opened the
screen. "Well . . . I better hurry on now. . . ." She coughed
furtively.

"Thanks for coming, Fanny."

"Yes. . . ." She went quickly down the steps and across
the yard, hurrying and folding her arms in her apron. Jahnet
held her father's hand more firmly.

"She's a poor ol' woman, Daddy," she said, with her voice
coming out soft and spaced like her mother's. He grasped her
shoulder. "Jahnet—!" She looked up at him, confused and
frightened, seeing his face turn slowly red. He took his hand
off her shoulder. "Jahnet, don't sound self-satisfied. . . ." He
turned suddenly and led her back down the hall. He walked
heavily. She tugged at his fingers. "Daddy—" she said, and
saw her aunt Kate stop whispering and lean back from the
bed. Her mother looked at her father, bit her lip, and then
gazed at the alphea tree outside the window.

"It's better so, Jahn," Kate said, after a moment, briskly.

"Better—?" He moved, heavy-faced, to sit down. The telephone rang once, shrilly, jangling across his nerves so that he
started and flushed. He went out swiftly. Behind him, Sue sat

up in bed, stealthily listening, her face growing white and pinched with a determined anger.

His voice said, "Hello?"

They could hear Martha's tones crackling hysterically in the receiver. He moved his feet once, stumblingly, on the rasping surface of the hall matting. "No. . . ." he said. "No. . . ." An odd, convulsive sigh seemed to rise out of the monosyllable, through it, over it, and then to sink downward into the thick grief of his chest. "Sue has the new baby," he said in a dead voice. He moved his feet again, and then, after a second, the receiver clicked on the steel bracket.

Sue said, fiercely, "One minute of peace from her, one minute, that's all I ask and I can't have it!"

His feet came steadily to the door; he stood there, looking in at them with a still film of sickness covering the sight of his eyes.

After a minute Sue said, with a faint, placative remorse, "Don't you want to look at the new baby, Jahn? You haven't been near him all day."

He stared at her without sight.

She said, turning her face with a sudden flick of anger toward Kate; "Jahn is exactly like his mother—she loved her sons and he loves his daughter. His son doesn't interest him."

He shook his head vaguely, dully. "James is at Martha's, trying to get her to . . . She's locked in her room."

"And where is Billy?" Kate said, sharply.

He looked at her slowly. "Billy's not her son," he said.

XIV

When she heard the click of the receiver at the other end of the line, Martha's mouth opened in a cold bafflement. She held the telephone out from her breast and stared at it. The queer, clucking noise of a buzzing line came to her ears twice, and then the operator's voice, "Number, please," with James Forrest talking abovestairs in a tone she knew was meant to go through a closed door. She set the telephone down. She was, she felt, extremely calm, like a person who has seen the world slide from under her. A strange stillness of cold flesh covered the distant hum of her blood in her ears. In the upper hall, James Forrest spoke with a round, mealy pleasantness. "Now, Mother, you might as well come out. You promised to go to Zack's this afternoon." Martha walked unsteadily out from the telephone stand under the stairs, and stood by the newel-post, looking upward. She could see him dimly there, outside the door, bent over, his head turned to listen and his face wreathed in the false smile of his tones. He saw her, and they stared at each other, with hatred, over the length of the stairs.

He said, "You ought to have a key to this room, Marthy."

He turned his head swiftly, with a lithe, flickering motion, and said, "Ah, Mother, is that you moving about in there? I hear you packing yore trunk, gitting ready." His head turned back, and he grinned at Martha, his tongue swabbing his lips.

"You sure you ain't got a extra key to this room, Marthy?"

She held the newel-post tight with one hand, leaning on it, unable to speak or move.

"Why, thanks, Marthy!" he cried, suddenly, loudly. "I guess this key 'ull jest do the trick . . ." He made sounds of fumbling a key over a strange lock in half-darkness. Her throat opened to say that the key was in the lock on the other side, and then closed, and she stared steadily, with sickness in her, up the stairs at him. He continued to scratch his finger nail over the lock. "I declare, Marthy, seems like I can't git it in. Maybe you better try yoreself." He twisted the knob, making a loud noise that covered the low sounds she thought she heard in the room. Her throat opened again, in fear now, and she could not call out. She waited, her knuckles growing white where she held the post, pressing her will against the feeling of that old woman beyond the door there. "You come away from there!" she said, suddenly, in a voice so low and

[204]

constricted she could scarcely hear it herself. "You come away!" Her throat closed, and she could not call out to tell her mother that James had no key. "Yes, Marthy, you'll have to try yoreself," he said, and stepped back.

The door burst open, swinging wildly outward, and banged on its hinges, and then swung waveringly back for one instant before it settled against the wall. In the dark opening Martha could see nobody. She darted half up the stairs before she heard James' pleasant, "Why, Mother, don't be so violent!" She stopped, as if his voice were a net to hold her instantly rigid, and saw her mother standing furious on the threshold, her eyes burning on his smiling face.

"Can't you leave me alone?" The cry burst out strongly, like the thick, tortured protest of a man's rage. "All day . . . all day . . .!" she cried, and raised her arm swiftly, her fingers spatting hard across his nose. "All day long, worrying me!" She drew her fingers back, shaking them as if they tingled, and said in a high, shrill voice near to tears: "I wish I'd blinded you! Yes, I wish I'd put your eyes out to stop them looking at me with your father's look and your own sneaking treachery showing through!" She stumbled out from the threshold, toward him, lifted her arm again, and suddenly laid it over her face. "Oh, my God!" she said. "Oh, my God!" She swayed against her arm, pressing it before her face like a bar to hold her erect.

On the stairs, Martha stood without moving, holding her breath. James took out his handkerchief, wiped his nose, and then looked closely at the handkerchief, as if he expected to see blood there. It seemed to Martha that his gestures held, each of them, in a separate instant of time. He thrust the handkerchief back into his hip pocket, tucking the corners in with careful fingers. The red wen on his neck glowed like red coral, shining and seeming to pulse in its strange, unfleshly texture.

"You got yore things packed?" he asked his mother, and his voice was casual, pleasant.

Rachel remained holding her arm across her eyes, but gradually her tall, thin figure stopped wavering; she grew still, listening, it seemed, and then she took her arm down and looked vaguely about. "My things?" she said. "Yes, I knew I was going somewhere. I had to go, to get away—" She gazed at him, frowning, unable to remember clearly what had just happened. She did not see Martha on the stairs. "You say I promised to go to Zack's?"

Without moving, James seemed to dart in on her, to flatten her back against the wall with his quick, harsh voice. "Yore things, Madam! Hurry now. You're keeping me from my work!" She trembled at the loud bluster, stumbling backward and picking suddenly at her collar with limp fingers. Her eyes stared at him confusedly, not turning from his face when Martha cried upward, "Don't go with him. He's lying!"

He walked briskly toward her, caught her shoulder in his fingers, and peered an instant into the room. "Come on," he said, and turned her toward the stairs.

She did not cower back from him now; she seemed to have no fear that her body could express. Slowly, feeling for the steps with her soft, old-woman's shoes, she went down before him, guided by the pressure of his fingers on her shoulder. She went down, and Martha, in a fascination of helpless horror, counted the steps. Her eyes, queerly light now as if they had never gleamed black, rolled slowly from side to side in their deep, shrunken sockets, over the walls and over the empty space in front of her, seeing it empty as if Martha were not there. She bent forward from her waist, holding her hands shaped like a cradle in front of her stomach. The faint, withered smell of old women emanated softly from her black garments. Above her, pressing over her head, James Forrest's sharp teeth gleamed jaggedly under his gray mustache.

Martha stared at him, and suddenly touched her mother, stopping her. "Don't go. You never promised. You don't have to go with him. He can't—" She stopped suddenly, knowing that he could make her go; they were helpless, defeated, before him. She heard her voice coming swiftly, full of frightened breath, and felt herself staring at him, watching his teeth and his eyes. "Mamma, I'll take you to Jahn. . . . I'll take you to Jahn if you want to go!"

Rachel's arm moved slightly under Martha's fingers.

"Jahn?" She said the word as if she had heard it too long inwardly, repeating it with the savor of torture coming through her lips into the single vowel sound and sharpening on the consonants. Martha looked at her then abruptly, and saw her eyes gazing wide and still, with the brilliance of a hurt child's eyes. "I've no place," she said, "no place to go. . . . I must go somewhere, anywhere, away. . . ." Her arm moved slightly, restlessly.

Against her, just above her head, James' pious voice said, "Why, Mother is going to see Zack, Marthy. She knows Jahn's dead." His swift, flickering grin leered and was gone.

A dim choke of horror rose in Martha's thoughts; she drew back on the stairs, trembling. Suddenly, then, she felt herself grow still all over with cold.

James grinned again. "Why, he fell in Sand Caves last night, Marthy!"

The cold went out of her to make room for a circling hotness of fear. His insane chuckle bounced swiftly over her; he peered sidewise down into Rachel's motionless gray face, giggling and saying, "He's dead, dear Mother, Jahn's dead, dear Mother!"

Martha whispered, "You know it's a lie ——!"

Rachel's eyes moved slowly back and forth over the space in front of her where the stairs widened to the glass in the front door. "Jahn's not dead . . . not dead," she murmured, and smiled peculiarly.

James pressed his fingers hard in her shoulder. "Go on down, then!" he bawled. "I'm tired a waiting on you, you old fool. Go on, git down these steps!" He pushed her roughly, and she began to descend again, slowly, searching for the steps with her feet. Her black skirt dragged over the carpet behind her.

Martha turned around slowly. "I'll call the police, James!"

"You won't," he said. "She's going of her own free will, ain't she? Besides, you'd be ashamed."

Martha remained procrastinating with fear and resolve, thinking suddenly, "She wants to go, to go anywhere, to get away. . . ." The words beat through her mind: "To get away, anywhere, from herself." She cried: "Mamma, you wanted to go somewhere. I'll take you to Jahn. Mamma, don't leave like this . . . !" She could not move down the stairs after them.

She cried again, "The police—James—I'll call them!"

Rachel turned around. "I'm going to see my mother," she called, and smiled, turning eagerly back to face the door James opened for her. She stepped over the threshold, and James' arm reached past her to turn the knob again.

"Martha!" Her cry rose thinly. She whirled around and was leaning over that arm toward Martha, turning her face up in a desperate, wild agony. While Martha was still in a fearful knowledge that she had known all the time what was happening, a thin thread of patience seemed to stretch over that face and then to swathe it like a cloth, hiding the wildness and the terror. She straightened, looked again at her daughter with eyes in which there was no feeling but a frozen, sharp light of intelligence. She turned slowly away from the house.

"It's best, Martha, for me to go, and you not well."

Her voice came back full of a dreadful matter-of-factness.

"Mamma, Mamma!" Martha stumbled over the steps and caught herself on her knees at the bottom. "O God, Mamma, it wasn't me, it was Sue ——!"

The door closed like a dark thing, swift and soundless. She heard the footsteps on the porch, on the walk, and then the rattling roar of James' Ford at the curb. She got up slowly, saying over and over, "It wasn't me, it was Sue!" Her voice stopped suddenly, impotently.

XV

A slow, thin flange of light filtered through the windows in
Zack's new house on Barnold Street. Rachel Ibsell's closed
eyelids twitched faintly and were still, and then, while the
light grew, twitched again. In the next room Zack and his
bride of five months slept in twin beds set against opposite
walls, the distance between them evidence of Paula's feeling
for Zack since she discovered her pregnancy. The morning
light washed over her face, olive-tinted and faintly drawn
from its daytime cosmetics, and into her dream where an old
woman came walking, ghostly and querulous, walking nearer
with the sound of soft shoes on a carpeted floor.

Paula's relaxed body grew stiff, her hands drew slowly up
and clenched. Tap-tap! Tap! Down the hall, nearer and nearer.
Paula turned sidewise, murmuring fretfully. She sat half up
in bed and was staring at Zack's broad, white face turned
pastily up to the light. He slept stupidly, with a faint, sibilant
whispering of breath through the wide holes of his nostrils.
She flung herself back against the pillows and closed her eyes.
From far off, through the still, December air, came the clink-
ing of coal against frozen iron. Belfry, the man-cook, she
thought dimly, had come. She turned on her side, away from
Zack's bed, and slept again, hearing once more the sound of
soft shoes walking.

Rachel Ibsell opened her eyes to stare at the white ceiling,
sat up, and got slowly out of bed. Standing in her white
flannel nightgown, skeleton-thin and bent with weariness, she
performed the rite she had performed every morning since
she had come to Zack's house: she took her mind into her
hands, her events and memories like palpable things, and by
the effort of her will she lifted them one by one into that
compartment of her brain which would hold them most securely against the sly encroachment of her nerves. She raised
her hands, she made a gesture of meticulous placement; her
eyes closed a minute. She said, "I will not forget today or be

mixed. . . ." She opened her eyes again, feeling sanity strong in her by reason of her will. The pleated, beige curtains at the window across from her stood out in the still air. Her bare feet crunched on the floor with a sound like tender bones breaking as she walked to the closet and took her wine-silk dress from the hanger.

Today she must testify in court, she must sit on that raised square of polished wood and answer their questions. She dressed slowly, her face sleep-drenched, as if the night had laid a thin patina of radiance over her features. Gently, then, she sat down beside the window, taking a blanket from the bed to cover her shoulders, and put on her spectacles. She reached to the tumbler of water on the dressing-table, lifted out her teeth, and set them over her gums, at the same time picking up her Bible from the window sill. While she opened it, running her fingers lovingly over the thin paper, she gazed out the window at the soft mingling of midnight and dawn between her and the next house. The pages of the Bible were dim in the light; she raised the book toward the window, sidewise a little, so that she could see to read.

"Now Israel loved Joseph more than all his children . . . and he made him a coat of many colours.

"And when his brethren saw that their father loved him more than all his brethren, they hated him, and could not speak peaceably with him. . . .

"And it came to pass, when Joseph was come unto his brethren that they stript Joseph out of his coat, his coat of many colours that was on him. . . ."

Her whispering voice stopped; she pushed back her chair and got suddenly up. "They hated him and could not speak peaceably with him . . . they stript him out of his coat of many colours," something said to her, letting the words drip slowly through the channels of her brain. She stared at the creeping light on the winter sward of the lawn. "Rachel weeping in the wilderness for her children," that voice said stealthily. She listened. "No," she said. "Not like that. How does it go?" She picked up the Bible again to look for the passage, and then softly, the voice told her:

> In Ramah was there a voice heard, lamentation, and weeping, and great mourning, Rachel weeping for her children, and would not be comforted, because they were not. . . .

She laid the book down. "It's a type," she said aloud, "a figure of Israel's sorrow when Herod slew the children of Bethlehem."

But she did not see the mothers of that small, Oriental town kneeling with gnashed cheeks and torn hair; she saw a dim, dark figure searching a desert wilderness, she saw the hard-packed red earth, the lacing branches of cedar bent to harp back on the wind the loud cry of that woman's heart, and somewhere, somewhere, in the woman's mind or out on the red baked plain the black gaping mouth of the dry pit in which her son lay trussed while the merchants with spice and balm came on camels to hasten her betrayal.

Slowly she walked forward across the room, her eyes staring at that dark figure in the wilderness. Slowly she turned and paced back. Up and down, up and down, listening, hearing from the cedar branches the long, wild cry:

". . . never again, O never again. O hour that will never come, kiss that will never touch my cheek, O flesh that is mine and gone away, lost from the womb that conceived you. O blood that knows the walls and stops of my veins, and hair that my hands have touched, moving softly over your head, my fingers spread to the feel of your hair and my eyeballs alight with the dark glitter of your hair. O tissue from my tissue, muscle that grew in my womb, and eyes that saw my breasts first of all things on earth. . . . O lost! . . ."

She looked up suddenly, seeing the white walls of the room and hearing from far off the dwindling tremolo of that cry. "Joseph?" the voice said sharply. "Joseph?" as if another Rachel whispered it to the empty darkness.

But there was no darkness here. The day had come, the windows were alight. She heard on the street the whir of passing wheels. The morning paper plopped against the steps to the front porch. Belfry swabbed the linoleum on the kitchen floor with a wet gray mop. She walked up and down, up and down, slowly, looking at the pattern in the taupe rug.

The bed in the next room flounced under Paula's tossing body, and Paula cried, "For God's sake, Zack, can't you stop it? Walking, walking!" The voice rose in a throaty yell. Rachel Ibsell grinned suddenly, with a wry, flushed anger. Zack's feet stumbled sleepily on the floor, coming through the hall to her. His pale-striped pajamas hung in huge wrinkles about his short legs.

"You look about ten," she said.

He rubbed his matted lashes with his fist. "Mamma, oughtn't you to sit down till breakfast? You've got to go to court today."

She gazed at him with her tart scorn. "I declare, Zack, sometimes I think James does better with his wife than any of the rest of you!"

He sat down on the edge of her bed. In the kitchen, Belfry rattled the dishpan against the stove. She stopped grinning.

"All right. I owe you something for keeping James and Henric out this week." She sat down in the rocker across from him and folded her hands.

He looked up eagerly, his pale eyes watering with pleasure. "I have kept 'em away from you, haven't I?" A certain amazement sounded in his voice. He laced his beautiful hands over his knee and looked at her with the glance of a proud, timid child.

She nodded, lifting her hand to pleat her lip nervously. "But they'll get in when they want," she said, dully. "When they want money. . . ." She raised her hand to her mouth again, and let it fall.

"Zack! Zack!" Paula's fretful cry rose hysterically. "Zack,

can you come here one minute? Do I have to stay by myself all the time while you run after your mother?"

Zack's head turned slowly; he flushed and got up. "I guess she's sick," he muttered.

"I guess so," Rachel said, drily. "Sick with meanness. . . ." She rose and turned her back in bitterness. "Go on, boy. Jump when she calls. Women bear girl children to have 'em tear the heart out of some other woman. . . ." She heard him go out, shuffling his bedroom slippers on the floor, and suddenly, with that queer, hot malice that pervaded her relations with her daughters-in-law, she began to follow him, sliding softly along behind his back, up to the door of Paula's room.

The girl lay in a pink kimona on top of the covers, as if she had gotten up once and had fallen back with sickness at her stomach. She glared out of her dark, sour face, the great muscadine eyes full of a liquid poison, and her round mouth twitching with hatred. "Get out!" she said. "Get out!" She burst into hysterical sobs. "You've both ruined my life! Get out, old woman! I hate you!"

Rachel grinned slowly and mockingly.

"Why, there's no wind," Rachel said, going up the steps of the courthouse with Zack. "There's no wind. I hadn't noticed it, Paula's been so loud, but the wind hasn't blown in three days." She paused, her weight on his arm, and listened. "It's so still. . . ." she said.

His pale, harassed face frowned. "Come on, Mamma, we're late already." He led her up the stairs, past the brown walls, and onto the third landing. Ahead of them a door stood open, the sound of Jahn's voice coming through it.

"They've got him on the stand," she said. "It's twelve, we had no business fooling around so. Paula wasn't sick. . . ." She stopped and caught her breath, listening to that voice. Suddenly, she let go Zack's arm and walked forward, alone, to the open door.

For an instant the room swam before her eyes, the vague

outlines of their figures wavering in a gray, translucent mist; and then, slowly, the figures grew still and solid, and she saw Bard Lipscomb sitting in a chair down below the witness-stand, his lips pushed together in a vivid, red grimace, and across from him, standing in front of Henric's chair, Mr. Peebles. His mouth was open, angrily shouting: "You don't deny it, then? There was a secret understanding between yourself and Mrs. Rachel Ibsell at the time the deed was made?"

She took another step forward and stood, seeing Jahn's face, motionless and pale above the great bulk of his shoulders in the witness-chair. "No," she said. "There was no secret understanding."

His face lifted and looked at her, the blue eyes shining so that he seemed to her all light, casting from himself a marvelous and ineluctable gleam like that she had seen once from a piece of marble laced with bronze lettering. Behind him, Judge Whitten's round, rosy face leaned forward, and the pent brilliance of his eyeballs struck against her. "Order!" he said, coldly. "Come forward, Mrs. Ibsell, and sit down."

She looked at him, puzzled. "I said, there was no secret understanding." Judge Whitten leaned more heavily forward, the pink tips of his fat fingers coming to grasp the outer edges of the vast oak square in front of him. Martha rose and came down the aisle. "Sit down, Mamma." She spoke in a whisper, guiding Rachel into a row of chairs across the aisle. Rachel stared at them and sat down, and looked up slowly, in bewilderment. Zack was sliding into the chair next to her. She turned her face around and stared at him.

"Get on with the questioning, Mr. Peebles," Judge Whitten said.

Peebles' voice came out suave and sharp. "The witness has not answered the question concerning a secret understanding between himself and Mrs. Rachel Ibsell at the time the deed was given."

Jahn's gaze lifted from his mother's face and his eyes closed suddenly, briefly. Below him, Lipscomb sat motionless, chewing his lip and waiting.

"The understanding was not secret," Jahn said. "Everybody knew she expected me not to marry. I promised not to leave her."

His voice moved over Rachel like the tones of a clarinet, stronger than anything else in the room. Against it, the walls were like dust and those other human beings thin shapes of withered paper.

"You promised not to leave her," Peebles sneered. "By that she thought you intended not to marry?"

Lipscomb still waited, staring now at Henric and James.

Jahn's face turned slowly toward the window, and his profile shone against the light. He said: "I don't know. . . . I don't know what was in my mind or in hers. . . ."

Peebles grinned slowly, stretching his wan lips, and looked at Lipscomb. "Your witness again. . . ."

Lipscomb leaned from his chair toward a sheaf of papers on the table in front of him. The papers rustled in the waiting silence. Jahn Ibsell's head turned back again and watched Lipscomb. Rachel's glance fell away from him, toward Henric and James, seeing their darkness as cheap and villainous against the carved gleam of his bronze head. She noticed, suddenly, that Chanson was not there beside Henric. She sat up straight, and stared, searching for her dark, Creole face on the sides and in the back of the courtroom. Against her, Zack said, "She's not here; she wouldn't come. . . . She says she's through. . . ." Rachel sat back, with her heart beating loudly and painfully in her ears. "She wouldn't come," she said, aloud. Lipscomb's papers rustled, his chair scraped on the oiled floor, and he stood up, tall and bent. She thought, "She wouldn't come. Now there's hope. . . ."

"Your Honor, may it please you, we'll go through this rapidly. My client has been on the stand during four hours, and we have nothing to prove that has not already been amply proved by the evidence of complainant's witnesses."

Judge Whitten nodded wearily, his eyes half-closed and gazing at the back of Jahn's head.

"Now, Jahn, when did you first begin to make a full-time farm hand for your mother?"

Without moving, Jahn stared at him and said, slowly, "When I was thirteen."

"You went to school how long?"

He flushed suddenly, turned his face to the window again, and stared at the top of Joe Rosenbens' store. "Through the third grade."

"How old were you when you assumed complete control of the farm for your mother?"

"Seventeen."

Staring at him, hearing his voice say, "Seventeen," another voice said in Rachel Ibsell's mind: "They hated him and could not speak peaceably with him . . . they stript him out of his coat of many colours. . . ."

"All responsibility was on your shoulders?"

"Yes."

"You worked without remuneration?"

"For my board and clothes and some spending-money."

The voice said, "They stript him out of his coat of many colours. . . ." Behind it, another whispering formed and unformed, too far for her to hear except as an echo. She bent her head and stared at her hands crossed, trembling, on her black leather purse. The voice spread out around her, syllableless, and then cried, "The dream? What dream . . . ?"

"What would it have cost your mother per month to hire a hand to do your work?"

"At least thirty dollars a month and his board."

"That would be three hundred and sixty dollars annually?"

"Yes."

"That sum multiplied by the thirteen years in which you acted as overseer would amount to four thousand six hundred and eighty dollars?"

"Yes."

[216]

"Could your mother have hired an overseer for thirty dollars?"

She raised her head and looked at him, staring hard as if to see behind his set, gleaming features the countenance of the young Joseph . . . the young Joseph who had a dream and told it to his brothers. "And when his brethren saw that their father loved him more than all his brethren, they hated him. . . ." She thought slowly, "He was hard for them to get on with; he was a little opinionated—like me."

His voice came clearly. "An overseer would have cost her a good deal more."

"How much?"

"At least seventy dollars a month and board . . . his own house, probably."

"You acted as overseer from the age of seventeen until you were thirty-one, when she gave you the land in payment for your services?"

"Yes."

". . . Israel loved Joseph more than all his children. . . ." The whispering sounded in the back of her mind, trying to tell her, saying the Lord God of Israel had sent her a sign. She moved passionately, sitting forward, lifting her dark eyes to the stern gleam of his face. "A sign! A sign!" she thought. "The dream . . ." And could not remember.

"Now, Jahn, list in order the improvements you have made on the place since you were seventeen."

His eyes met hers, changing, she thought, growing dark with shadow. His shoulders moved faintly, he looked away from her, and said, "The first thing I did was to build a three-room Negro cabin. Then I built six log stables. After that, I cleared, one summer, two hundred acres of new ground. The next thing, I moved a barn, thirty-two by thirty-eight, if I remember the right size. . . . That winter, I cut timber off a new lot she had bought, one hundred and sixty acres. About that time, too, she bought the place James Forrest is living on, and I had the stumps drug out of it. . . ."

She saw him coming in from the west ridge beyond the hills in the evening, his shirt black with sweat and torn, his boots scraped by the drag of the trace-chains over them when he leaped back and the mules heaved the stumps out of the damp red clay. His eyes shone with laughter. "Sixty out today!" he said, and drank thirstily at the well, splashing the water over his face and shoulders. And then, she thought slowly, he went off to the barn, and it was nine o'clock before the feeding was done . . . and he was up at dawn the next day, Sunday, going with salt to the pasture for her cattle and currying her mules till he hadn't time to dress before Henric came out from town sniffing his nose. She saw them standing in the yard. . . . It was before the new house was built, she thought, painfully . . . standing together in the yard. . . .

From above her, Judge Whitten's languid voice said, "Court recesses for lunch."

She got up automatically, and stood watching him come down the aisle, hurrying with the same walk he'd had on Sunday morning when he must curry her mules because there'd been no time on Saturday. The voice said, loudly, with a peal of joy through its call: "And Joseph dreamed a dream. . . . For, behold, we were binding sheaves in the field, and, lo, my sheaf arose, and also stood upright; and, behold, your sheaves stood about, and made obeisance to my sheaf. . . ." Her breath sucked in her throat and burned a sharp, lightning pain of joy down her breast. Suddenly, leaning across Zack, she touched her son where he came past her, touched his arm and then his hand, and he stopped.

His face looked at her impassively, but with something moving behind the cloudy shadows over his blue iris. She stroked her finger down the length of his hand and could not speak. Her breast rose and fell joyously. "Your sheaf," she said, stumbling, choking, "your sheaf, Jahn . . . they bowed to it . . . !"

She could not see now what moved in his eyes, she was blind with wonder and delight. "The Lord sent me a sign.

Your sheaf. . . ." His mouth smiled slowly, faintly, with a reluctant pressure. He touched her arm gently, smiled again,
and drew off. She stared at his retreating back, saying over
and over: "and behold, your sheaves made obeisance to my
sheaf . . . !" There was no sound for her but that: in the silence
of the spent wind, their sheaves bent, yellow and sere, to the
strong green of his great, wheat-packed shock.

XVI

Rachel Ibsell heard, loud in the December stillness, the
town clock striking two. Mr. Peebles rose, lean and red, and
stood beneath the witness-stand. "Mrs. Rachel Ibsell!" She
leaned forward, between Zack and Martha, and began to
tremble, slowly, all over. For an instant, she could not get up,
but remained gazing at Judge Whitten's round face and the
hooded-hawk light in his eyes. A strange, sick shame circled
in the pit of her stomach. She thought, "I have sinned, I have
sinned against him," and she was looking at Jahn, knowing
somehow that her shame and her sin would lie, a division, a
line she could not cross, between her and him forever. "And
your sheaves made obeisance to my sheaf," the voice said to
her while the shame grew, making her sick.

Judge Whitten said, wearily, "Please come forward to the
witness-chair."

She flushed bitterly, and got tremblingly up, and began to
walk down the aisle. Her wine-colored silk skirts rustled with
a loud sibilance. Behind her, the radiator hissed weakly. She
passed Henric's and James' faces lifted to her like black
masks she could not read, and came nearer to Jahn and
Lipscomb. She bent over, touching Jahn's shoulder. He stood
up and helped her onto the stand. Sitting slowly down, with
his hand holding her arm, helping her, she lifted her head and
felt her face convulsed by a pang of terrible love and grief.
She looked away from him, out over the seats in the courtroom to the brown splotches on the back wall. He drew

away and sat down again. Somebody thrust a Bible under her face. She touched it, and murmured after somebody's voice. Peebles moved, and stood to one side of her.

"Mrs. Ibsell, you are the complainant in this case?"

She spoke carefully, slowly, choosing her words with painful exactitude. "My sons Henric and James are the complainants in this case. I filed suit, but that was because I was angry without reason."

She felt, rather than saw, Peebles bite his lip; her eyes were fixed on the back wall.

"You admit, then, that you insisted on calling a lawyer to discuss possibilities for beginning the suit?"

The word hurt her breast; she felt its sharp, irrevocable sound beginning in her and tearing outward: "Yes." She heard a noise on the street below, the turning of wheels on pavement. "But I never meant—" She stopped weakly, heard her voice trailing, and suddenly drew herself up. The voice that had spoken in her all day whispered there now, comforting her. "There is none like to the God of Jeshurun, who rideth upon the heavens in thy help and in his excellency on the sky."

"Jahn Ibsell first made the suggestion to you that you owed him the property in return for his services?"

The sly tones, trying to trap her with suavity, rippled through her, angering her. She waited and looked at Lipscomb, and he was sitting still, staring at her with soft, wild eyes. She grinned a little abruptly.

"I first made the suggestion to Jahn about taking a deed to the property." She made her voice formal and measured. "He declined then; he talked some about buying land for himself. He never asked me to give him a deed. I was the one . . . that tried to coerce. . . . I was guilty of fraud and coercion," she said in a suddenly loud voice, folding her hands tensely on her lap to stop their trembling. "I didn't say what I meant to him; I tried to trick him. . . ." Jahn moved, as though to speak; she lifted her arm in a gesture to him to be quiet, and said, "I tried to bribe him with my land, and he didn't know what was going on. He's a man; he couldn't know some things. . . ."

She sank back against the hard wood of the chair, feeling Judge Whitten's eyes on the back of her head and seeing hatred on James' face. She panted, with all the strength gone out of her.

Peebles' sly, sharp voice came swiftly, striking. "You left Jahn Ibsell's house and went to live with your son Henric a little more than a year after the deed was made. Why?"

"The eternal God is thy refuge, and underneath are the everlasting arms," she heard softly whispering. She looked up, and stared all about the courtroom. Chanson was not there, she noticed again . . . not there. " . . . and underneath are the everlasting arms. . . ."

"I was wicked," she said, softly, "and full of hate. His wife was a good, sweet girl, but I wouldn't let myself live with her."

"She was unkind, she tried to take over your house?"

Her face lifted, rapt and quiet above the crowded faces below the witness-stand, and gazed past them, shining with a peculiar and infrangible light. She smiled a little, faintly, with her old lips. "We were different, that's all," she said, dreamily, and began, with one hand, to caress the arm of her chair. "Women like her have always scared me and always beaten me. Kate was like that. I can't talk to them or fight with them. I can't work with them. They don't work; they just putter around, and smile all the time like they knew something nobody else knows. I guess they do." She heard her voice, but she was talking to herself; she was saying to herself something that there were no words for. "They're the sort of women men would make if they could . . . maybe they make them. I'm afraid of them; I can't talk to them . . . But they're all right," she said, suddenly. "They're good and kind . . . they're too kind; they beat you with their softness and their helplessness. I was different from her," she said, and caressed the arm of the chair. "That's all. No man ever needed to watch over me . . . except James," she whispered, suddenly. "James married me when I was sixteen. . . ."

She heard the silence in the room beating in upon her with the restrained, frightened breathing of her sons. Mr. Peebles flushed and bit his lip, and looked about him with impatient helplessness. Far beneath the sudden hurry of her breathing, she felt a slow, grinning malice move and dart to the surface of her mind. She grinned suddenly, mocking him with her eyes.

"James is your first husband?" he said swiftly, pouncing.

"Yes, James was," she said.

His mouth opened and shut again; he did not, she saw, know how to go on with his advantage. He turned around, facing the judge's bench. "Your Honor, we ask a recess with this witness in order to call medical testimony. . . ."

The silence beat in again, with somewhere, outside of it, the sound of horses' hooves trampling on pavement. She stared at the window, waiting, frightened.

"Very well. . . . Do you release the witness to Mr. Lipscomb while awaiting medical testimony?"

"Yes." Mr. Peebles sat down jerkily and frowned at her with hard gray eyes in which a shadow of puzzled fear moved.

She turned to Lipscomb, who was rising slowly, unbending his long figure from the low chair. For an instant they looked back at each other, their eyes alike in darkness and strength and wildness, and then slowly he smiled. She looked away from him, and blushed a little with remembrance.

He said, "Rachel, will you be good enough to point out to the court the identity of James Forrest?"

Automobile tires drawled on the street below. Her breath rose in her throat, too hot and full there, and she sat staring at her eldest son's face, seeing his purple-veined forehead, his mustache, and the red wen protruding from the side of his neck above his collar. Her eyes closed slowly.

"There were two," she said. "Now, there's only one. This one here is James' son . . . the other one married me when I was sixteen and left me and died in Cuba . . . and since then I've been cursed. . . ."

She opened her eyes, and stared dimly upon the darkness within herself.

Lipscomb said, as if the witness had been respondent's, "Respondent rests his case." He sat down slowly.

From the darkness into which she looked, she heard the whispering: ". . . the everlasting arms of God. . . ." Judge Whitten's voice buzzed faintly behind her, ". . . may release the witness, allowing her to go home now if she likes. . . ." She sat up, waiting for somebody to help her down from that square of polished wood. She could rest now, she could hide herself from the eyes of her soul, wrapping the woman that had been Rachel Ibsell in the soft, thick substance of a brain that was old and worn; she could wait until she felt underneath her shoulders again the strength of arms like those of one who had died at El Caney and never come home again. Her eyes dilated suddenly, knowing Jahn's hands on her, helping her down; she stood below the platform and looked at him, holding his arms against her.

She said slowly, "Why, son, your face is wet with sweat!" and lifted her handkerchief to wipe his forehead.

He leaned back, turning his head from her. He said, "Hadn't you better . . . better come home with me now?" and looked at her again. He smiled suddenly, with pain.

Her throat burned with the wonder of that smile. She knew again that she had sinned against him. "Yes," she said, and laid her head against his chest. "Yes . . . Jahn. . . ."

She felt him move, vaguely, and knew that they were all standing up in the courtroom, the others standing and crowding nearer to hear what she said. She looked up blindly, turning her face against them. Behind Jahn she saw Bard Lipscomb's dark eyes gleaming at her under the white thatch of his hair.

"No . . . !" she cried. "No!" She started back from Jahn. "No, I've sinned. . . . I'm guilty . . . !"

Jahn stepped away from her a little, still holding her hands. "You must come home with me," he said.

She gazed at Bard Lipscomb's red mouth. "No. . . . You don't beg me now. . . . You wait to see what Sue says. . . ." She closed her eyes. "I've sinned against you, Jahn. I must pay for that . . . to wait will be my atonement. . . ." She smiled. "When it happens, when you win, then I'll come home . . . when you know the land is yours and I meant it to be. . . ." She backed off from him slowly, and moved toward Bard Lipscomb. "Then I'll come," she said over her shoulder, her voice rising with a pealing note of certainty.

"Bard . . . help me out now. . . ."

She put her hand on Lipscomb's arm and moved down the aisle. At the door, Zack stood waiting for her, but she could not see him clearly. Sudden tears ran down her face and burned salt in the corners of her mouth. "I'll go home, Bard," she whispered. "I'll go home. . . ."

He lifted her hand from his arm, and laid it on Zack's. His face was turned away. "Dear Rachel," he said. "Dear Rachel. . . ."

PART FOUR

I

LATE IN THE DARK HALF OF THE FOLLOWING FEBRUARY A farm wagon, traveled in the night from Choctaw to Red Valley. A small, red lantern clamped to the front plank of the low wooden bed received the misting rain on its glowing surface and jumped now and then as the vehicle went up or down hill or bounced over one of those small hillocks of dirt which form on country roads. By the light, two reddish-colored rawhide boots could be seen clearly, set one on each side of the lantern. The dim shape of a third boot, protruding from a long shank covered by a woolen sock and the cuff of an overalled leg, appeared occasionally as the light jumped in the glass globe. A mittened hand, evidently belonging to the owner of the single boot, remained constantly in the light, holding fast to the edge of the wagon seat a pint bottle in which a yellow liquid gurgled and bubbled, throwing iridescent sparks past the lantern into the heavy, rolling blackness of the atmosphere.

The wagon appeared to move in stratiforms of sound, the lower noise being that of the iron-rimmed wheels cutting the scurf of frost and ice on the roadbed. This noise, withheld from the upper groans and lumberings of the wagon bed by the vacuum of air created by its passage, seemed to possess, as if from the property of aloofness, a complete separation from the long, sharp whistle of the wind about the boots on the front plank and from the slow thud of the mules' feet ahead. A fifth noise mingled with these manifestations of night travel, and passed through them, becoming so inextricably one in rhythm with their recurrence that its first dissonance came to the ears of the travelers in the wagon like a sound heard in memory: the swift, clean beat of a horse's hooves rang once between the slow rise and fall of the mules' shoes in the middle slush of the road.

One of the knees above the pair of boots hugging the lantern moved and bent so that it was evident its owner was trying to look backward without turning his body around. A gaunt shadow formed above the lantern, looming like a more solid projection of the darkness back of it, and a faint grunt passed out from the peaked top of the shadow. Then the knee straightened and the shadow fell back into the obscurity of the general blackness. An instant later the front half of the wagon dipped downward, the red light gleamed on muddy brown water, and the mules splashed heavily. The beat of hooves on the roadbed behind sounded again, clearly now and loudly, so that to the listeners in the wagon the sharp flinches of iron on pebbles appeared to pass through the breast of the hill behind them. The front end of the wagon tilted upward, and crawled lumberingly out into the roadbed. The hoofbeats behind were again indistinguishable in the common melee of sound.

The half-obscure boot on the front plank moved nearer to its opposite, unrelated fellow, and its owner spoke whiningly. "Why'd you come through Two Mile Creek, Jim? A fellow 'u'd think you'd go on the bridge above a night like this'n."

"You heered in the Creek, didn't you?" a voice answered from above the rawhide boots. A brief sound of scorn followed the words.

"Didn't hear nuthin' but horse's feet. Don't mean nuthin'. . . . Jahn Ibsell he ain't a-comin' on now. Hain't left town yet, belike."

"Kain't know yore neighbor's horse, Mose, you better go back to school." The shrill wind blew through the trace chains, curling like a sharp whistle in the steel links, and died suddenly as the wagon climbed the hill and started down, veering to the left.

The single boot moved back into the darkness and jumped slightly as if the leg attached to it had jumped on the wagon seat. "Oh, he's a most miserable man tonight, I do know! If'n I could a seen ahead to Jedge Whitten's doin's I'd never a gone down today to hear the decision give. No, I'd stayed home not to shame Jahn by my presence!"

"Keep a quiet tongue in yore head, then! He's a comin' on."

The hoofbeats rang out now, separating themselves from the soft thud of the mules' feet, their sound seeming raised a little from the earth as if the horse traveled at a height six or seven inches above that of the wagon.

"Oh, but I do know he wishes tonight he'd stayed a single man!" Mose cried again, leaping about on the seat but never moving his hand on the pint bottle.

"Talk like a fool, Mose. He's got his chillern, hain't he?"

The wagon drew further to the left, and stopped. In the sudden absence of clanking trace chains and lumbering bed, the noise of the following hooves spread together, running one into the other with a sucking sound like the pull of rounded sticks from frozen slush. Mose Thurston moved restlessly. "Ah, but many a man he's wisht he could drown his chillern out o' sight en mind!" he cried. He raised his voice in a faint, falsetto song:

> "Little Lonely, little Lonely,
> I'll tell ye my mind,
> My mind is ter drown yer
> En leave ye behind. . . ."

"Be still!" Long Jim muttered, fiercely. "Act like you're drunk en ain't had but two swallows!" He turned around on the spring seat, and sat facing backward, listening while the

[227]

horse came nearer, rising on his strained sight like a bundle of darkness looming out of the surrounding float of night. "Belike we should see 'im o'er Sand Caves tonight, eh, Mose?" he whispered, suddenly.

The hoofbeats stopped at the tail of the wagon. The heat from the horse's body flowed near, across the cold, misting rain, in a formless stream with the stench of wet hair cutting it acridly. A small sound like the wrench of leather moved faintly in the stillness. Then, abruptly, the horse moved again and came alongside, his head showing in the red glow from the lantern.

"Who's there?" a voice said.

Long Jim straightened and let out an explosive sigh, turning at the same instant to his reins and clucking the mules onward. "Thought it was you, Jahn," he said.

The wagon moved, and the horse kept beside it. No more was said. The noises of travel rose rubbingly now, as if the layer of silence which had separated the turn of the wheels from the lumbering of the wagon bed, and that from the wind and the sound of the mules' shoes, had disappeared. Only the click and suck of the horse's hooves sounded loudly and strangely, as if from an elevation above the wagon and a little way off. The rain misted more steadily, slanting obliquely downward and across the tin top of the lantern so that it seemed not to strike the hot glass globe.

"Who's that with you, Jim?" Jahn Ibsell's voice came suddenly. "Mose Thurston?"

Mose jumped responsively on the wagon seat. "Sure, it's me, settin' in silence but feelin' fer you. We'll see you across Sand Caves tonight!"

The sorrel-colored tips of Jahn's stallion's ears moved in the lantern-light, and then the horse drew back a little, and went downhill behind the wagon. From the bottom of the hill came the sibilant gurgle of rain-flooded ditches.

Jahn Ibsell's voice said, lightly, as if he had deliberately abstracted from his throat all awareness of emotion, "There's no need of that, Mose." He laughed once, briefly. "James 'ull let me live tonight; he's got it all now."

From somewhere above the men, a loose limb whipped the tree from which it hung. Long Jim Chambers cleared his throat, and let the wagon go on a foot or two before he spoke.

"Well, Jahn, you know best." His dark, grave voice moved uneasily through the channels of his thought. "But seems to me like with all this here other comin' up, the case tuck to the state S'preme Court en all . . . why, James, he kain't feel yet hit's all his'n."

"Oh, you've got 'em beat, Jahn! Me en Jim, we said hit today when Lawyer Lipscomb he got up soon's the Jedge stopped talking, en said 'We're a-carryin' hit to the state S'preme Court. Our briefs en evidence is ready; they go in the mail tonight.' We said you'd beat 'em yet, didn't we, Jim?"

Jahn's stallion moved close to the wagon bed again, and neighed suddenly and angrily, stretching his head toward the mules. Jahn's hands moved a little, forward into the lantern glow, and pulled up the reins. Above them, his face shone an instant with the rain slanting across its set, carved lineaments. While Long Jim and Mose stared, he drew back into the darkness. "Steady, boy," he said. "Steady." His voice was light and metallic. The deep, uneven wagon roll rose around it and over it.

Mose shifted his feet loudly on the front plank. "Seems like I kain't git that courtroom out'n my mind tonight!" he confessed, abruptly. "I kin jest see hit all now, thet jedge settin' there, sayin' you was proved by the evidence guilty o' unduly influencin' yore mammy. . . . If'n I'd a had it, I'd a jumped up en crammed Henric's money down his throat! He's shore a trickster if'n one ever lived. Why, thet man ort to be put in jail fer misguidin' his office, he ort!"

"Shet yore mouth, will you?" Long Jim's heavy voice moved against Jahn's light, brief laughter, and stopped.

Jahn said, "What's that you're holding on the wagon seat, Mose?" His head moved forward into the light again and bent over while he peered at the yellow liquid in the bottle. "Corn?" He laughed. "Well, I've never been a drinking man." The strange, twisting brilliance of his voice tonight rose higher on the words and fluted, as if with mockery of himself. "I'm proved a liar and a cheat against my mother in court, but I'm not a drinking man. I'm nearly as good as Henric!"

Long Jim moved uneasily. The wagon bed lurched slowly over wet rocks, standing sharp in the center of the road. "We're nigh on the curve before we turn off fer Sand Caves," he remarked, and added slowly, with his voice changing, "You're such a man as can take this, Jahn."

The horse's hooves sucked in the mud and clicked on the sharp rocks. "But can my wife and children stand it?" Jahn Ibsell's voice said, sharply. The horse and the wagon moved on, side by side again.

Mose Thurston's mittened hand lifted the pint bottle and shook it in the lantern-light. "Well . . . here's havin'!" he said, with incongruous cheerfulness, unscrewing the stopper and lifting the bottle to his lips. The liquid gurgled once and then fell downward, swiftly, lowering against the short neck of the flat bottle. He sighed abruptly and lustily, and took the neck away from his mouth. "Who's havin', too?"

Long Jim took the bottle and passed it over the horse's shoulders. "Drink," he said. "Life's short. . . ." He stared down at the lantern, waiting; and presently he received the whisky again and drank. "Mem'ry's short, too. . . ." he said, and fastened the stopper back into the glass flask. He tossed it behind him, and heard it rolling briefly on the wagon bed, jolt into a corner, and roll out again.

Jahn Ibsell spoke. "My little girl said the other day, 'I know brothers hate each other.'" In the pause of his voice, the wagon turned again with the heavy smell of the wet lichen on the rock near Sand Caves sweeping over it. His

[230]

stallion's feet grew light and quick on the sharp rocks in the road, picking their way with drawn, delicate muscles ready. His voice came again, slowly, "I guess that's true. . . ."

" 'Twas strange fer a child to say hit, though," Long Jim said, heavily and gravely.

"Ah, but there's nought a child won't say!" Mose cried. "Why, I've heered 'em pick the very lock o' life itself without knowin' on it!"

The wagon wheels rolled from the sharp, hard rocks of the roadbed, around the curve of the overhanging hills, and came onto the soft mud near the bridge. Above, in the darkness, the dwarf sourwood on James Forrest's hills bent, shapeless and unseen shadows, vivid in the imaginations of the three men. The wagon paused, with the horse beside it.

"Well, the world keeps spinnin', hate or no hate!" Mose said, and sat still, listening to his own voice. After a minute, Long Jim bent over the lantern and unclamped it from the foot rail. The lifted lantern, dangling from his hand, threw concentric circles of alternate light and shade over Jahn's face, showing the blue eyes still and motionless. He moved his head suddenly and looked at Long Jim. His lips smiled slowly, as if with a dim, self-appreciative amusement.

"You needn't look over the bridge, Jim. James has got it all tonight."

The lantern swung down from the wagon and spread a pool of red glow over the wet banisters of the bridge. "Jim 'uz al'ays a careful one!" Mose said, excitedly. "He'll look the thing o'er from beginnin' to end!" Chambers' long body moved shapelessly behind the lantern light, with a spread of brownish cloth showing abruptly on the point of his shoulder, and descended to the edge of the road where the white sand gleamed leprously under the angles made by the banisters with the floor. He went suddenly out of sight, dropping over the darkness of the roadbed, streaks of reddish rays swimming upward as he descended.

Mose cleared his throat and spat. "Hit do look scary, don't

hit?" he said in hushed tones. Across from him, Jahn's stallion lifted one foot and set it down, obliquely to the earth. Suddenly, the light drew upward with steady, climbing jerks, casting gules of light above it, and Long Jim's head appeared, mushroomed to vastness between the abutting points of glow and darkness.

He stamped his feet on the planks of the bridge, the lantern swinging backward and forward from his arm. "Hit'll do," he said. He stood waiting by the bridge, holding the lantern up now. "You go on, Jahn, we'll wait here till we hear you're through the woods." He lifted the lantern yet higher, as if to see Jahn Ibsell's face, and then set it on the banister behind him. A swift, stealthy darkness flowed over the bridge except for a circle of wet planks under his feet.

The stallion moved past the mules, stepping daintily again and nickering at them with vicious, deceptive softness. On the bridge, his hooves rang vauntingly, but with a hollow sound at the center. The men's voices rose all together, vague and blown by the slanted rain: "Good-night. . . ." The three different names seemed to fall back from one another in the loud jar of the stallion's hooves across the planks, and to sink, severally, into the soft thud of the ground. The faintly sour smell of rotten pine needles drifted back through the woodlands ahead.

Long Jim picked up the lantern and climbed into the wagon again. From far ahead, in the pine timberland, came the soft, wicked neigh of Jahn's sorrel, flung back to the mules in contemptuous challenge. They raised their heads, clanking the harness chains, and nickered patiently at the rain snuffling past their eyeballs.

"Well, he's a unhappy creature," Mose said, weakly, and shuffled his feet on the wagon bed.

"Listen!" Long Jim whispered. From the neck of the woodland, where the road curved the pasture, he thought he heard a voice, light and mocking, calling across the pasture mounds. "Father! . . . Father! . . ." he thought the voice said. He stirred uneasily, the hackles of his hair cold on the back of his neck, and whispered, "Is that Jahn?" The voice moved out on the shrill whistle of the wind, past his chilled ears. The mules shifted suddenly, turning sidewise in their harness. "Hush!" he said.

Mose said, "Why, it's nought, jest the wind a-comin' down o'er the pasture mounds the way hit do."

Long Jim gathered the reins in his tense hands, turning the mules back straight in their harness. The chill ran again on his neck, and he heard himself saying, "Lord! . . . Larson Ibsell's bones, they're white in the earth en uncarin'. . . ." Light from behind him shot over his shoulders and past his face, onto the bridge. He turned swiftly, with Mose's face showing strangely beside his own, and saw the car's black nose edging the rear of his wagon. The lights went slowly out, leaving a glow from the dashboard shining bluely over Zack Ibsell's white face and over a dark, unmoving shadow on the seat beside him.

II

Sitting in her room, with her trunk packed and her hat on, ready to go home with Jahn, Rachel Ibsell waited. Judge Whitten had said they were to be in the courtroom above stairs at two o'clock. He would not, she thought, take more than thirty minutes to give his decision. Then Zack would come for her and take her to Martha's to meet Jahn. She kept getting up to look in the mirror at her hat. She could hear Paula in the next room, smacking her mouth over an apple and wriggling on the bed. The dressing-table looked bare, the whole room was bare and empty-looking, waiting for her to go. She gazed at her hat in the mirror, and fumbled at the black satin pleats on the crown. Two spots of color glowed in her thin cheeks. She straightened the lace collar on her gray wool dress, and smiled, thinking suddenly of Bard Lipscomb. "You old fool!" she said to herself. She walked up and down the room until she heard Paula flinging magazines on the floor beside her bed, and went hastily to the chair by the window.

At two-thirty, Belfry went home: she heard the kitchen door slam behind him and knew that it was two-thirty. She sat forward a little in her chair, waiting, her pulses beginning to hammer in her wrists. Paula was eating another apple. Once she thought she heard Zack at the front door, coming in; and then she knew he was not there, and she sat back, holding her wrists tight with her fingers to stop the beating of her pulses.

She noticed when it began to rain at three o'clock. The rain misted on the window beside her and the drops, half-congealed by cold, clung a second and then fell down slowly, like the tears she had seen falling from some woman's face in a picture show Zack had taken her to see. She tried to remember the picture, but she could see nothing of it in her mind except the woman's face, thrown suddenly close to her own, large and grayish, and the tears shaped like liquid pears before a slow stream ran out from their smaller ends and fell down the immense gray cheeks. She stared at the window, with the slate-gray particles of cold and early dusk coloring it, and watched the raindrops run down one by one, silently. On her right side, out where the door of the room was, a light grew. She felt its glimmer, knowing it came from the reading-lamp above Paula's bed and that it lay in a pale circle on the hall floor. She sat between the phosphorescent gleam of the rain-wet window and the vague light in the hall, with darkness over her. She no longer moved or listened.

Sometime later, when the window had ceased to glow and she knew the rain was there only by its soft, sibilant dripping, she heard Zack in Paula's room. His voice said, "They've beaten him." She knew, somehow, that he stood at the foot of Paula's bed, looking down at her. He said, "O God! Paula, I didn't do enough, I didn't. . . . If I had realized before it started . . . !"

She listened to him, and his frightened, wordy gasping was like something which had mattered once and was no longer important. She tried to rouse herself; she made her thoughts say, "That is my son in there. I must care, I must be worried," but she could not feel.

She heard Paula scream: "Then she can go home! Take her out of my house, out of my sight!" A slight amazement at such passion stirred in her.

Zack said; "Jahn's at Rosenbens'. He didn't say anything. . . . I don't guess he expected her to go when he lost the case. . . ." His voice grew stronger. "It's raining too much for her to start tonight."

Paula shrieked: "Get her away. She was going. Take her on to him now! I've had enough, I've had all I'm going to stand!"

A long moment of silence passed stealthily. He said, "I'll call Henric. . . ." His voice trailed weakly.

"Call the whole dam' lot of 'em, but get her out of my house, get her away from me!" Paula said between her teeth: "I hate the very ground she walks on. I hate you!"

His steps went out of the room, up the hall, away from the circle of light on the floor. Rachel could not hear him at the telephone.

She stared at the black window. It was like a square of onyx in the dark shadows of the room now. Occasionally, from the outside, a twinkling bead of brilliant white gleamed evanescently. She tried to think whether or not Sue had ever said she should come home when the lawsuit ended. Something said to her, "She ought to have sent you a note . . ." Presently, she got up and turned on the lights and began to look in the top tray of her trunk. "A white sheet of paper," the voice said. The papers there lay in neat, string-tied bundles; she picked them up and put them down. Suddenly she noticed a white box. Her hands hovered over it and then took the lid off. She held the box against her breast, gazing down into it, and seeing, one by one, the folded yellow papers, the dried buds of roses tied with a pink ribbon, and the dried petals of white Cape jasmine bundled against a piece of yellowed fern. She went back to her chair, holding the box against her bosom, and sat down. She stared intently and almost somnambulistically at the flowers.

The voice said to her, "He never told her; he kept putting it off, thinking it would be all right when he won. . . ." She set the box on her knee and took out the yellowed papers. After a moment, during which she heard, "He's gone on home without you," she opened one of the papers and looked at it. The black letters at the top said Marriage Certificate. She opened the other paper, and stared at the same letters. Then, still holding the papers in one hand and hearing outside the drip of rain, she put her fingers inside the box, lifted out the flowers, and scattered them slowly, with a backward and forward motion, over the floor. She bent forward a little to see them better, and smiled strangely with her lips stiff. Slowly, without turning her eyes to see what her hands were doing, her fingers ripped through the paper of the marriage certificates. When the white strips fluttered to the floor past her knees, she knew that she was free of herself. She picked up the edges of her skirt, flirted them, and watched the box slide off her lap. . . .

The faces that pressed around her grew on her sight one by one, so that she marked with particularity the identity of each, its expression, and the position of the body under it. Her flowers and the strips of torn paper lay on the floor around her feet. She gazed at them, and then back at her sons and daughters-in-law, and heard them speaking, one of them saying, "It's the only way to impress public opinion, to get at the court. . . . Let her take possession tonight, show an eagerness to take possession again, as if the verdict brought relief to her." The voice was Henric's, coming from the middle of the room where he sat on the dressing-table bench with James standing beside him, pulling his mustache and gazing at her. She looked past them and saw Paula sitting on the edge of the bed in a pink kimono, a little dirty, and resting one hand possessively on Zack's bent shoulders. Rachel stared a moment at the side of Zack's face, noticing how his white hands covered his eyes and how he bent over in a picture of weak remorse. She glanced abruptly downward again, at the strewn flowers and strips of paper, felt her lips smiling slowly, and looked up to see Chanson leaning on the dressing-table in front of her and watching her with pitying abstraction. The rain fell softly across the black window beside her.

"This is all foolish," Chanson said. "Do you think the Supreme Court, those judges you don't know, will notice how or where she went tonight? They will read the records of the case, that is all."

"And I won't take her!" Zack cried. "I won't. Not on a night like this. Why she . . . she'll take cold!"

James snickered. "Pore Zack! He's afraid of meeting his dwarf on the road!"

"Somebody else can do it. I won't."

Paula's plump, olive-colored hand caressed his shoulder. "Zack, don't quarrel. . . . I do hate quarreling," she said prettily to Chanson.

"Do you?" Chanson looked at her once and then gazed at Rachel Ibsell again. "Mother, do you hear what they're saying?"

Rachel shook her head, smiling a little, and noticing minutely the sharp corners of Chanson's unrouged mouth.

"It's the only thing," Henric said again. "We could take her out to Marston's, but there's a doubt whether or not Stanhope would receive her. . . . So this— She must appear to take possession with relief, as if this were what she's been waiting for!"

Chanson stared at him wearily.

Zack raised his head. "Why don't you take her, James? You're the one that goes out that way; it's on your way home. Why don't you take her if you're so anxious for her to go tonight?"

James shrugged his shoulders. "I ain't after being killed," he said, and laughed shortly, biting his gray mustache.

"But suppose," Chanson said, softly—"suppose Sue won't have her?" She leaned back with her shoulders against the mirror of the dressing-table, and crossed her arms over her breast. "Do you want to go, Mother?" she asked, and did not look at Rachel.

"Go where?" She plucked at her gray wool skirt, trying to pull the gores straight. "I've been dressed all afternoon. . . ." She felt the hat still on her head. "Is Zack going to take me to Martha's to meet Jahn?"

Chanson said, "Jahn has already gone, Mother Ibsell. He left word with Martha that you were to come tomorrow." She looked at Henric again with steady, tired eyes. "Don't you want to come home with me, Mother?"

"I won't have her!" Henric said, angrily and precisely, and closed his lips, his head shaking on his neck. His flat black eyes gleamed dully. "Not tonight, Chanson," he said, with mock gentleness.

"Home?" Rachel said, suddenly, and stared at them. Her voice deepened in her throat. "These many years I've had no home, no place to call my own. I gave all I had to my children. . . ."

Henric said, smoothly: "You have your house in Red Valley. You have your land there, Mother."

She looked at him, shaking her head slowly. "No. No. . . . That's all Jahn's. I won't go there. I'll stay with Zack. . . ." She looked around at him and smiled, with a sickly pretense of assurance on her lips. "I'm strong, I'll stay with Zack. I'm able to look after the house for him while Paula is lying in bed and whining. . . . Zack is my baby," she said. Her voice, weak and pleading, lying to save herself, frightened her.

Zack did not look at her. He stared steadily at the floor and said: "I won't take her tonight. Some of the rest of you

[238]

can if you want to." His uncertain voice knocked at the fear in her breast.

She said: "Sue won't have me out there. I looked for a note. . . . She never asked me to come back. He just went on, thinking it would be all right. . . . He's afraid of her." Her mouth crumpled bitterly. "You're all afraid of your wives, ninnies that I raised!"

Chanson said: "Henric is not afraid, Mother Ibsell. James is not."

She looked at Chanson slowly, and saw something sick in the woman's cat eyes. She said, begging pardon for all that she had been and for all that her being had made of her sons; "I'm sorry, Miss Chancie. I always liked you."

"I know," Chanson said, drearily. And then, without moving her arms from across her breast, she turned both hands outward in a cynical, deprecative gesture. "We've come upon strange days, my mother-in-law, you and I."

Rachel looked at her sons again. "I'll stay with Henric," she said. "Henric will be glad to have me."

"No, Mother!" His angry voice swept shortly across her. "I can't keep you now. You must go to Jahn's until everything is settled."

Chanson looked at him steadily, without moving, her eyes shadowed. "So!" she said, under her breath.

The rain slid across the window and dripped somewhere outside . . . from the drain-pipe at the corner of the house, Rachel thought after a minute. Yes, from the drain-pipe. She tried to stand up. "Then I'll go to Martha's! Where's my coat; somebody give me my coat. . . ." They stared at her without moving. "Where is Martha? Why's she not here?" she cried, and heard in the echoes of her voice Billy Nelson's dislike. "But no," she thought, "I'm imagining things. . . ." She cried, "Let me go to Martha's. . . . Boys, I've been good to you all! I don't ask anything but this. Let me go to Martha's. Martha's waiting at her house for me; she expecting you all to bring me there, and Jahn to come after me!"

James came close to her and put his face down to hers. "Nonsense!" he said. "Martha thinks you're going tomorrow. Why should she be here? Quit acting the fool, will you? You've got to go back home and take over yore place. You might as well make up yore mind. Mother! D'ye hear? What ails you now? Henric told Martha you were going tomorrow!"

She drew her head back, away from him. "Your father—" she began, weeping. "Your father—" She saw on the floor the dried petals of flowers and the scattered strips of paper.

"Come!" James commanded. "Let Miss Chancie help you get ready. You might as well make up yore mind to it and go on tonight. The sooner you get there, the better it'll be for yore case in the Supreme Court's mind. Come on, Zack 'ull take you."

"I won't!" Zack said, but he stood up.

"Take her on; get her out of my house!" Paula suddenly screamed, and writhed over on the bed, wrenching her face as if with agony. "Oh, my back, my side! . . . Oh, I'm at the limit of my strength! . . . Take her on!" she moaned.

"I won't," he said. "James can take her." He looked at the floor, standing slackly before them all.

"In my Ford!" James said, and laughed. "Talk about colds and pneumonia, and then want me to take her in my Ford. Quit being a fool, damn you!" He leaped across the room and shook Zack's shoulder. "Come on, git ready now!"

Henric rose with dignity, his hands in his pockets, and tilted his head back with an air of satisfaction. "Yes, Zack, it's getting late. We must hurry on with this."

Rachel sank slowly into her chair. Her hands trembled on the wicker arms. Circles of a vague and shadowed crimson drew near to her staring eyes and fell back, growing as they turned to vast, soft blobs of darkness. She scarcely knew that they were there. She said weakly: "Where is Martha? Somebody call her and tell her!"

"Hush, hush!" Chanson touched her hand, and she saw the coat hanging from Chanson's arm. "It's my coat," she thought, surprisedly, and stared at Chanson to see what was in her face. The yellow eyes looked at her wearily, with pity, asking her to get up and have her coat put on. "There, it'll be all right. Perhaps it's even best so," Chanson's voice said. "Put on your coat now and wrap up warmly."

Henric said, "Don't take so much time." His tones changed. "You'll go right into the garage, Mother, without getting wet at all."

"Yes," she said. "Yes, the garage is built onto the house . . ." Her long, black coat hung heavily from her shoulders. Chanson reached up and tied the old-fashioned, scarf-like veil about her hat.

Zack cried: "This is not right! This is . . ." His voice broke and stopped, and she saw his wide, pale eyes staring at her. He went to the door and stood there, waiting for her.

She began to walk toward him, guided by Chanson, seeing all their faces recede from her. Paula lay on the bed, gazing up at her with brilliant, wicked eyes, her face still contorted as if with pain. Rachel felt the door frames sliding backward, moving like objects from a swift train, and she was in the hall, going across the solarium. Behind her, James and Henric walked. Their feet were heavy on the rug. Zack opened the doors into the dark well of the garage, and then the lights were on there, and she saw the car. She turned around and looked back at the room behind her. Henric's and James' faces were round blobs of shadow. She gazed past them and seemed to see on the floor of the room she had left particles of withered keepsakes. She said, "Good-by, good-by," calling out like a child. "Good-by. . . ." The rosebuds stirred on the floor, she heard the sound of the rain, and the crumpled tears of paper rose and floated softly up and down, up and down. . . .

III

When he came through the woodland, out where the road curved the pasture, Jahn Ibsell got down from his horse and walked. The bridle dangled from his hand and his boots slipped a little in the wet red mud. In the sky black clouds boiled one over the other and fell back down the edge of darkness, hiding the moon's face. Fog hung to his lashes, mingling with the white curl of his breath against the cold, lisping rain. He stopped in the road, knowing where he was, and held the bridle tightly, turning a little and raising one hand to the stallion's muzzle. Down below him, in a darkness through which he could not see, the pasture mounds lifted calmly to the laced sibilance of the rain. His throat opened on amusement. "James!" he said. "James, are you there now?" The stallion's sleek shoulder nudged against his wet back.

Presently, he wiped the rain from his face and went on again. At first there was no light in front of him; and then slowly he saw the lamp-glow from the windows of Sue's room. The horse's feet paced behind him, sucking up from the mud, sounding rhythmically in his mind. From far off, in the woods and beyond them, he heard Long Jim Chambers' wagon turning, backing slowly and lumberingly on the bridge. He turned around. A brief, dull jar, as of the rear axle coming hard against the banisters of the bridge, rose over the crunch of the wheels. Listening, he walked on, going swiftly now and seeing the lamp-glow reach out to the white pickets of the side yard just beyond Sue's windows. When he looked back again, a flood of light slanted upward through the woodland, coming on slowly, with the fringes of tree branches cutting the wavering brilliance. He thought: "They've stopped at the bridge; Long Jim is turning to let them pass," and he knew who was coming. He laced the stallion's bridle in the yard gate, stripped off his raincoat, and flung it over the horse's shoulders and went swiftly through the gate and up the walk onto the porch.

The door opened in front of him, across the hall light with a wedge of thin, black line, and Sue's body pressed against his own. "I know," she said. "Martha called me." She pressed the palms of her hands tight on his cheeks. "Your face is so wet. . . ."

He went with her into the hall, and stopped, blinking at the high lamp swinging from the ceiling. He shut the door, reaching backward to it, so that she could not see the car lights coming up. She was staring at his face. "Jahn! You look—*bruised* . . . !" She came close to him again, touching his shoulder. "Aren't you wet through?"

He drew his head back. The sound of the tires slipping on the roadbed was soft and low. He said, "We carried it to state Supreme Court."

"Of course, darling." She spoke softly, watching him. "You'll have honest judges there."

He stared past her shoulders at the open door of the bedroom, hearing inside there the soft, nuzzling sound of sleeping children. He thought, suddenly, that he had not requested his mother's blood, he owed nothing to her. A man must look out for his seed and pamper the blood he had made. He said, "Well . . . it's no worse now than it's been all along. I asked for this, I asked for all that's happened."

Her white hands touched him again, gently, and moved back. Her face was still. "You musn't talk like this; you don't mean it."

He said, "I'd like to quit fighting. . . ." He looked down at Sue's hands strangely. "I'd give them every inch of this land, every penny I've ever made, every year left to me . . . if I hadn't you and the children to think of. I guess I'd like to pamper myself to come to terms with them." His mouth curled faintly. "It'd be easy not to have to wait any more to know what's going to happen . . . and easy to say, 'I'm guilty, somehow.' But I can't be that good to myself," he said, "saving my feelings at the expense of the children. A man has to respect the world and respect his own reputation before it, or else his children will be ashamed of him."

She swallowed. "If you want to stop, Jahn—I—we can live somewhere else."

He looked at her slowly, hearing outside the wet slither of car wheels turning by the yard fence. "I can't quit. If I did, that would be admitting I was a cheat and guilty of fraud to her. I can't do that, I can't ask you to live under that—or live under it myself."

She tried suddenly to draw him through the door into the bedroom. "Jahn . . . come and sit down. You must take off those wet clothes."

He stayed where he was, smiling with his lips curled at one corner. "They've beat me," he said, oddly, as if he had just realized it. "I'm a liar, a sneak, a cheat . . . and they're clean, sweet angels. They've got the land, they've got everything. O justice, justice!" he cried, bitterly. He stopped himself and shut his mouth, bending over a little to grasp her shoulders. "And now they're bringing her back to me," he said, and waited.

Her wide eyes dilated yet further, sharp rings of a dark brown ridging suddenly the golden iris. In her slowly whitening face the delicate bones stood out taut and rigid. The tip of her tongue touched her lips and she spoke around it, whispering hastily, "What do you mean?"

Outside, the yard gate turned dully on its wet hinges. He felt her shoulders soft and thin under his great hands. A swift, blinding tenderness gazed at her from his eyes like a realization of how much he had paid for her. "Poor Sue!" he said, gently.

She struggled back from him. "They . . . Who are they bringing?" She cried, "They can't do this to us now!"

He held her shoulders, steadying her. "They've got the land, but they can't take it yet while it's still under litigation. That's why they're bringing her back now. . . . Wait," he said, and watched her growing still again, staring at him with her eyes dark and fearful. "I thought awhile ago I didn't owe anything to her for being my mother, but my feeling was against that thought."

Footsteps were coming up the walk over the flagstones.

They came slowly, with a pause between each sound of the shoe moving over the stones and then a shuffle before the foot set itself down again.

Sue's face turned a little, while her eyes remained on his face. She cried suddenly and irrelevantly: "Martha didn't know! She kept saying she wouldn't go around to Zack's tonight, she couldn't do her any good. . . ." Her voice sank to an accusing whisper. "They made her believe she was all right tonight. . . ."

The steps touched the veranda, rising slowly to the level of the floor, and he knew Zack's walk beside that other shuffling, strange one. He said: "You have to do this for me now. . . . Let her come in here and stay. You don't have to speak to her."

His hands relaxed on her shoulders, and at that swift releasing of her and her will, she stepped back, stared at him, and slowly drew herself up. A grave and astringent pity began to shine in her golden eyes. "I'll speak to her," she said, hardily, with color running back into her cheeks.

"I woked up with a light in my face." Jahnet stood sleepily on the threshold of the bedroom, holding up her white pajama legs and shaking back her hair. While they turned to her, the knob of the hall door shook and knuckles rapped timidly on the shutter. Jahnet moved her head and gazed at the black knob. "They's a car out there."

Sue said, automatically, "Jahnet, you ought to stay in bed when you wake up." The silence in Jahn stretched out then, like a sound. The knuckles rapped again, lightly and humbly. Jahnet stared at the door and at her father's face, and he was looking at her mother, seeming to wait for something. She said, "Open it, Jahn." His fingers grasped the knob, turned it, and the door came back against his side. He moved, and the door was fully open.

The darkness on the edge of the veranda was the only thing that moved. In it, their dark figures, standing side by side, remained motionless, seeming without life. The long, black folds of Rachel Ibsell's coat hung about her feet and her shoulders glistened damply. Zack's face grew out of the darkness slowly, raw and quivering with his voice.

"They made me bring her. I didn't want to. They said she had to come tonight and I must bring her."

Jahn opened the screen door. "Come in, Mamma." She stood without movement, staring past him into the hall. Her gaze traveled slowly over the face of the child in the foreground, looking at her without expression or acknowledgment, and met Sue's eyes. "Scorn!" she said then, and folded her lips bitterly, after the manner of old country women remarking the appearance of a stranger. Jahn put his fingers on her arm and pushed her gently across the threshold. She was motionless again, with her back to the door, and let her gaze fall down on her folded hands.

"Is that my Grandma?" Jahnet said. She held up her pajamas more tightly, stretching the cloth back across her thighs, and leaned toward the old woman.

Jahn looked at his brother. "So they're through with her now?" he said.

Zack's pale eyes watered. "Jahn"—he looked down and swallowed—"Jahn, I'm sorry. We used to be—used to be friends."

"They've taken all we had from her and me; they've made us hate each other; and now they're done with her and sent her back to me."

The hard, clear voice rose swiftly and stopped all at once, as if what it had said might not be true or might be more nearly true than he could bear. He reached toward the door and drew it slowly back against himself. "Good night, Zack." Some warp of tenderness threaded through his tone and frayed. In the instant before his arm drew the door slowly to, the brothers stared at each other. Zack did not move when the door closed in his face.

In a minute they heard his feet turn on the floor and go down the steps and along the walk. The car started.

"Who was that man?" Jahnet said. "Is this my Grandma?"

Her father grasped her shoulder. "Hush!" he said, almost angrily. He looked at Sue. "We better put her to sleep in my old room tonight," he said. "In the morning Black Fanny can look after her.

Sue nodded, her small, delicate face impenetrably grave. She turned and went before them into her own room, which had once been Rachel's. Jahn guided his mother through the door.

She came slowly, still ignoring the child beside her, looking up and staring. Across the black orbs of her dim eyes, the pale blue wallpaper struck coldly and strangely. She gazed from one article of furniture to the other and saw nothing clearly except the fire. Toward that she walked, passing abruptly around Jahnet, and paused on the hearth with her arms crossed behind her back. A little to one side of her stood a white crib with tall latticed sides and long white rockers resting on the small hearth rug. Her eyes passed over it without notice.

She said, "It's kind of you all to put me up for the night."

She did not look at any of them when she spoke. Through the front windows of the room she saw the car lights moving ahead of the dark engine down the road and spraying over the vast shapes of the woodland. "It's cold out," she said.

Sue picked up a pillow from the bed and paused, turning her body slightly around, while she looked at her mother-in-law. The white lace on the end of the pillowcase touched her chin. Jahn gazed at his mother from the doorway, touching lightly Jahnet's head where it rested against his thigh as she stood before him.

He said, almost timidly, "Take off your coat, Mamma."

She glanced at him swiftly, and then away, and looked back. While she stared, her eyes puzzled and hot in the thin, yellow gleam of her features, her hands rose automatically and struggled with her coat.

"She can't, by herself, Jahn," Sue said. She put the pillow

down and turned back the sheets on the bed. She heard Jahn move to the hearth and take off his mother's coat. "Did she bring any clothes?" She turned around, with the counterpane folded in her arms. "Jahn! He's gone off with her trunk!"

Rachel said: "I forgot it. I was in such a hurry, I didn't say a word."

She straightened her cuffs and collar, looking down at her coat on Jahn's arm while she spoke.

"Then she's nothing to sleep in tonight."

After a minute, during which Jahnet moved nearer to the fire, still holding up her pajamas and staring at her grandmother, Jahn said, "She—" He glanced at Sue's small figure. "I used to have some old nightshirts somewhere." He looked at Jahnet and smiled faintly, almost with mischief. "She made them before we married."

Rachel said, formally: "Please don't bother. I can sleep in anything . . . in my shift," she added, seriously, with a proper folding of her lips, and turned her eyes away from Jahn's face.

A smothered and hysterical laughter began suddenly in Sue. She felt herself shaking with it, her lips sputtering, and glancing up, seeing Jahn's suddenly red face, she sank upon the bed and hid her face in her hands. Jahnet smiled uncertainly, looking from one face to the other. "What's a shift?" she said. A high, rounded burst of laughter broke through her mother's hands and stopped abruptly. She rose and looked at Jahn. She said, very seriously, "I'll find her something."

"Don't bother," Rachel said again, her eyes vague and wandering. "I wish I had my trunk, though. All my checks from—from—" she stumbled confusedly, "from a friend were in the tray." She put her hand up to her mouth and let it fall back slackly. "They steal my mcney."

Jahn and Sue glanced at each other significantly. "Don't worry," Jahn said. He put his hand out to touch her mother. "You won't need any money now." She drew back from his outstretched hand and turned her face away, frowning. Her glance fell on the crib beside her. She bent forward at once and lifted the comforter back from the sides, so that she could see. Her grandson lay asleep, his small, dark features turned phlegmatically up to the ceiling. She pointed at him awkwardly with her thumb.

"This child," she said, "what's his name?"

"Lars, Mamma. Larson, for Papa."

"Larson?" She started, looked slowly upward toward Jahn's face, and remained gazing at his eyes. "Oh." she said. She glanced down again and bent over the crib. Her eyes were strange and trance-like. "Well," she said, and rose briskly, turning herself around to the fire. "Lars, is it? Larson was your father's name? I can't say I know any Larsons. But I knew a woman once that married a man of that name. It was his first name." She shook her head. "I haven't seen her in years."

She turned herself about again, holding her skirt out to the drying blaze while they stared at her. Watching them, the child felt a cold wind move down her spine, lightly and unmeaningly.

IV

Fanny Forrest lay dying that spring. "I'll bring my woman up to the house afore long!" James said, laughing in Chanson's face when she remarked that Fanny should have a nurse to attend her. James had by this time grown spiritually fat on evil, as Henric had grown serene. They had forgotten the fever of James' desire to murder and the anguished fascination with which Henric had replied to it. They had begun to trust each other, they were more alike. . . . In that fact, Chanson thought, as she returned one afternoon to Choctaw from a visit to Fanny, lay her own destiny, whatever it was to be.

She was extremely tired. Her hands moved nervously, yet with an ache of lassitude in the knuckles on the steering-wheel. She leaned back and drove more slowly, making her eyes watch the young underbrush pushing up along the sides of the road. Fanny, she thought, might die within the week or she might last the summer out. Fanny's waiting was like her own stretched and listening dread before the imminence of some word from the state capital where dispassionate and honest judges read the briefs and arguments of Ibsell versus Ibsell. She sat up straight again. Whether she watched the underbrush or not did not matter. Fanny's thin, gasping cough sounded in her mind.

The car slid down the hill toward the bridge over Two Mile Creek. She pressed her foot on the brakes. Around the curve of the hill beyond the bridge, another car was coming on slowly, half-stopping to see if she would take the narrow bridge first or wait for its passage. She turned the wheel a little to the right and waited. Kate stuck her head out the window to watch how her tires came on the raised planks, glanced up, and saw her. They waved at each other. Kate's car rolled across the bridge, turned to the right, and parked in the shade behind Chanson's. Chanson got out and walked back. She put her narrow, brown-shod foot up on the running-board.

"So you are going to see Mother Ibsell? I have just left Fanny."

Her tone moved out strongly and warmly. Kate put her head on one side as if to listen critically. "How is Fanny?" she asked.

Chanson shrugged and turned sidewise to watch the road. "She's alone there except for the children. They're all idiots."

Kate smiled briefly. "The Forrests run to idiocy."

"And how is Mother Ibsell?" Chanson asked, turning back to her.

"All right. She sits off by herself and still seems not to know Sue and Jahn. She's visiting them, she thinks."

Chanson shook her head slowly, with an expression of regret softening her dark features. "I would like to see her," she said.

Kate did not answer. Listening to her silence, Chanson

stared at the late afternoon shadow on the roadbed. Now and then the small leaves on the honeysuckle growing up out of the creek bank over the bridge, stirred and grew still again.

"And Jahn Ibsell?" she said. "Is he waiting, too?"

Kate looked at her swiftly. "Waiting—? He's set his Negroes to the spring plowing." She shut her mouth firmly.

Chanson nodded. Presently she smiled peculiarly, and seemed about to speak. But remaining silent a moment or two longer, her expression changed again. A wagon was coming around the curve of the hill. "I must go," she said. "Goodby." She got back into her car, hearing Kate drive off behind her. She sat still until the wagon crossed the bridge. She drove slowly on to Choctaw.

When she reached her house just at dusk, a white envelope hung halfway out of the metal mail-box as if somebody had taken it out, seen that it was worthless, and had thrust it back out of the way. She plucked it from under the lid and entered the hall with it. She laid it on the console table against the wall while she took off her hat. Then she glanced down at it slowly, without much interest. Mr. Peebles' firm-name stared at her from the upper left-hand corner of the envelope. She took it up and ripped it open. A smile, cruel and sensuous, as if she savored an ironical pang, formed on her lips as she read.

At this same moment, Kate and Sue sat on the veranda of the house in Red Valley, discussing the substance of the letter Chanson had opened. The late afternoon sunshine flickered on the gently moving leaves of the wistaria vine at one end of the porch. Small clouds of dust rose now and then from the red-clay road in front of the house.

"No, it's not that," Sue said, wearily. "It's just that they think they can send him Peebles' bills and he'll pay them. They want to make him pay, not just worry him."

"I ought to be surprised at Henric," Kate observed, acidly. "He's an Ibsell, after all." Her thin, mobile lips curled.

"It's been awful," Sue said, "all the time. But now it seems worse. Maybe we're just worn out, waiting again after the first defeat. It's been going on so long." She gazed at Jahnet, who was lying in the green-and-red-striped hammock under the elms on the lawn. "And having her here too. . . . Half the time I don't know whether I'm sane myself or not. It's just one thing after another. As soon as we think we can rest from it a little, they think up something else. It goes on and on."

Kate nodded and began to fan herself, though it was not hot. "Jahn's showing the strain lately."

"He's in town now, seeing about a lunacy commission they wanted to form so they could appoint a guardian for her. They want one of themselves appointed, of course . . . to control the land while it's still under litigation."

"Yes, and they're looking ahead, too," Kate said, briskly. "They want that settled before the Supreme Court hands down its decision. Then they can go right ahead and dispose of everything, they think."

Sue pressed the nails of one hand against the thumb of the other, and nodded restlessly. "Well, he called up just before you came and said he'd got it set aside for this time. . . . Some way," she said, vaguely, "but anyhow, they can't appoint a guardian for her because he refused to have an alienist examine her."

Jahnet turned over in the hammock and gazed at the side of the house where her grandmother sat with Black Fanny beside the crib, watching young Lars.

"He has to pay for everything," Sue said. "The court costs for the first suit and all those stenographers and Lipscomb. And all the time checks to his mother." She turned her head and looked at Kate. "Did you know," she said, bitterly, "that they sent her back here without a rag? Martha went to Zack's for her trunk, went along when she sent the dray, and there Paula was, with everything out of the trunk. She was cutting a jacket for herself out of Mother Ibsell's fur shawl. She said she thought she had a right to do it; nobody thought Mother Ibsell would need the things again." Sue's voice mimicked indignantly. "Martha was so mad she could have died. She got the things all packed back, but the clothes were in an awful fix, some ripped up, and we couldn't find a one of Mother Ibsell's papers, not even her bankbook."

Kate pressed her lips together, nodding her head slowly. "Small gnats sting worse than big hornets," she observed meaningfully.

"They seem worse to bear than the big things . . . and now this!" she burst out with sudden anger. "Sending him Peebles' bills with a note saying he's responsible for his mother's debts. They've done it three times and they know they can make him think he's got to do it. They know how he is! Of all the—" She broke off and sat bent forward in the chair, pressing her fingers against her thumb.

Kate looked at her from under the corner of her lashes. The girl's cheeks were white and frail-looking. She said, dully, as if to herself, "The bill was filed in her name and I suppose they may not be legally liable to Peebles."

Kate drew in her breath shortly. "And how is Rachel going to pay it if her money's gone?"

"Oh, Jahn can pay it!" Sue cried, recklessly. "He can pay everything, for all of them! He's paid now till he hasn't a cent left till next fall when the cotton's sold."

"Cotton's down again," Kate said, almost tonelessly.

"They'll keep saying he's responsible for her debts because he promised to support her. It's just the sort of thing they'd think up!"

Kate was smoothing the skirt of her gray linen dress. "Small gnats," she remarked again.

"Living with an honest man—!" Sue exclaimed and broke off. "He'll pay it. It's his mother's debt. He'll think he's morally responsible. Her good name . . . and everything. He'll pay—and not think of what it'll cost me!"

With the letter in her hand, Chanson returned to the veranda and sat down. That peculiar, savoring smile remained on her lips. Presently Henric came up the street from his office and turned into the yard. She stood up and looked at the envelope, waiting.

"Why have you not hidden this from me like the others?" she said.

He sat down in the swing, crossed his legs neatly, and looked at her, his head tilted upward.

"My dear Chanson . . . what is it?"

Her cat-like eyes turned suddenly in their sockets and glared at him. An expression of complacent satisfaction lay over his features. She looked swiftly away.

"This bill from that common fool, Peebles. He tells you here, it is the fourth he has sent to you."

His flat, black eyes gazed opaquely at her.

"Of course, Chanson. The other three I have sent on to Jahn. He, most certainly, is responsible for Mother's debts."

She smiled faintly. After a minute she threw the envelope onto his knees and turned away. "Do you know that your mother still recognizes no one?"

Behind her, she heard him taking the sheet of paper out and unfolding it to read. She gazed at the honeysuckle vine on the trellis clinging to the porch, feeling a certain sentimental affection for it. His swift, brittle chuckle burst out almost snickeringly, like James' laughter. "'Understanding you are to be appointed guardian for your mother . . . I must earnestly beg you . . .'" he read with a dry, still irony. He slapped the paper against his wrist. "Jahn defeats himself when he defeats us. . . . The poor fool, he's certainly gone to pains to prove his responsibility. . . ."

Chanson turned slowly around. "But, my Henric," she said, "he does not wish his mother to go to Marston's, that is all!" She walked the length of the veranda and turned back. "I think I would like to go home for a little while."

When, stealthily, she looked at him, his lips were drawn tight against his teeth. She met his eyes suddenly.

[254]

"You'll stay here," he said under his breath, without threat or bluster, but as a statement of inexorable fact.

She veiled her eyes. "Yes. . . ." She bowed her head suavely, with a mock humility. "My very dear lord!" she said.

v

When the hot days of early summer began, Rachel Ibsell sat by the window in the middle room, and watched the wagons go past to the fields, piled high with the implements of work or with the great, rubberized bags of nitrate of soda that is spread over the furrows when young corn is knee-high. The shape of the fields and their color lay in her mind. She dreamed on them a little, with old, half-formed memories starting up vaguely in her heart, but she held still to that separation of life from self which she had begun on that night at Zack's when she had torn up her wedding certificates and strewn her wedding flowers on the floor. To her left, in the lane, Negroes came and went from the shop with hoes over their shoulders, and now and then she heard the slow shuffling of the bellows in the shop and the sharp clang of a hammer on the steel points of plows.

"It's going to be a good year for cotton," she remarked. "Rain on the stalks, hot dry sun on the opening bolls, and few weevil." After she spoke, she remained silent a long time, staring at the fields with an expression as if even the earth, the monster and master of all her young years, had become alien to her. She stirred a little in her rocker and looked up over her shoulder at Jahn, who sat behind her in the room, working on his account books. She said, "This is all familiar to me, somehow. I seem to remember I used to visit my friend Rachel on her farm."

He glanced up. "Of course," he said, gently. "You have a farm, Mamma. This farm."

"I own a farm?" She turned completely around, staring at

[255]

him, and presently she frowned. "I wish you wouldn't call me Mamma. I'm not that old, to be called Mamma by strange young men."

"But you are my mother."

She moved her head slightly, dissenting with impatience. "It would be strange," she said, "if I was your mother. I never married, much less had children." She gazed at the floor, turning away from him, with strange, tranced eyes. "No . . . it was my friend Rachel who had children," she murmured slowly to herself.

"Mamma—you're Rachel. Your name is Rachel."

The words fell through her mind like sand sifting between dry roots of grass. She looked up at him again. "My name?" she said, vaguely, and remained staring at his great shoulders and wrists. A look of fear came into her eyes as if once, somewhere, she had seen the imminence of danger leap from his great size across her. She said, "You don't remember my name!" and smiled suddenly, cunningly, almost with evil, turning and hiding her face.

Behind her, she heard his silence, and was afraid. Then he moved and she waited. But he did not approach her; he went past her chair, and she heard him in the next room saying to the girl who was his wife: "She knows! Sue, I know she knows . . . !" She glanced sidewise to the door between the rooms, puzzled by the despair in his low voice. "What does it matter to him?" she murmured, strangely.

Slowly, without reason, she began to tremble. The shaking of her knees announced it to her first, and then she felt her whole body jerking in the chair. She looked at her hands, trying to hold them up to stop their nerveless vibration. "Why am I trembling? Why am I trembling?" she said to herself, and the soundless voice moved in her mind like an outside whisper coming from a long distance. She put her hands down and forced herself to look resolutely out the window. The lane was empty now, with nothing in it for her to see. She began to listen again to the talk in the next room. Sue's voice came softly, without words, a gentle, lilting run of changing tones. She frowned faintly, disliking the voice; and then she heard the front door open and shut. "He's gone out," she thought, and immediately felt her body grow still and steady again. The house, emptied now of that vast, hard statue of bone and impregnable muscle, changed around her as if the air in it grew clearer and safer. She almost smiled as she bent again to watch from the window.

She had, for the remainder of the day, no feeling of the divisions of time. Tireless, not knowing how hours could lengthen and drag like harsh rope over the tender skin of impatience and anxiety, she sat by the window. Her mind was dark and calm, circling ceaselessly and whisperingly on the memories it would not admit to the sharp, forming substance of its upper self. Like a photograph hidden in the dark room, forgotten there, and never dipped in the acid that forms shapes and figures from its pale blur, her mind lay in the darkness of her skull. Yet, close to that pale blur the acid crept and the light, coming near and then trickling sidewise, blocked by minutiæ of dust and paper, rags of events that held the present from the light of the past. And as the acid crept and turned sidewise, and she remained unknowing of herself or of the beings she had created, she existed in a timeless, unspaced void, alone with that lost and forgotten Rachel who had sinned darkly. She wandered with her, she stumbled and fell and bruised herself again, all unwittingly. From this diversion of unconscious memory, she rose to eat and to stare politely at the strangers around the dinner table, and came back again to the window. "Who is that child?" she said to herself, and then she felt the question, with the wonder behind it, drop away into the soundless depths of her bosom.

Bard Lipscomb came at night, when the supper table was cleared and she was sitting formally in the living-room, allowing, as was seemly, these strangers to make conversation with her. She stood up to shake hands with him. His tall, vivid figure seemed familiar to her for one instant. Her lips trembled faintly. "I'm glad to know you, sir," she said, and sat down again.

Across from her, on the divan, Jahnet sat with her legs hanging down against the brown plush upholstering. She frowned a little, immediately averting her eyes from the child and looking at Sue and Jahn. "A friend of your family, I suppose?" she inquired, and inclined her head toward Lipscomb.

Jahn nodded, glancing at her once with troubled, intent eyes, and then looking away. His fingers beat a short, fumbling tattoo against the arm of his chair and stopped. Sue said, "This is Bard Lipscomb, Mother Ibsell," and watched her to see if the name aroused in her any response.

She gazed at Sue, noticing suddenly the low neck of the girl's pale-green dress, and thinking it singularly inappropriate to the dignity of a matron with children. "But then they don't dress now as they used to," she murmured aloud. Her voice astonished her. She glanced quickly away from Sue toward the tall, dark man standing above her.

"Ah, Rachel!" he said, and sighed. His mad black eyes stared at her sadly. He added, presently, "I think you know me, darling, don't you?"

Jahn said, slowly, "Leave her alone." His voice had a smothered sound.

The lawyer shook his head, remained looking at her for an instant longer while she gazed from him to Jahn and back again, and then he turned abruptly to the writing-desk on which he had laid some packages when he came in.

"Presents, little Jahnie," he said. "What do you want—candy?" He held the package on a level with his chest. "Heavy, heavy, hangs over your head. . . ." He sat down on the divan beside her. "What do I get for this, Jahnie?"

She stared at him with her lips pursed tight to hold in her excited breath, and shook her head.

"All right," Lipscomb said. "Where's the little boy? Where's Lars?" He glanced all around the room as if he did not know that the baby lay in his crib asleep in Sue's room. "All right, Miss Sue, bring out Jahnie's brother. We'll feed him the candy."

Jahnet said, swiftly, "What do you want me to give you?"

He pretended to think, his head on one side, and his black eyes twinkling rapidly at Rachel. "Well, now, let me see. . . . Jahnie," he turned to her, looking grave and making his voice low and solemn—"Jahnie, they tell me you've got a sweetheart—" He paused to watch her shining eyes.

"In my youth," Rachel remarked, suddenly, "we were not allowed to talk about sweethearts until we had one." She gazed at Bard Lipscomb, thinking him senile and improper. "Self-respect," she said, "was always considered above everything else then. Especially with children."

There was an instant of silence, during which they all stared at her and then away. Jahn bent over and picked up the brass tongs from the hearth. He swung them back and forth in his hands without seeming to know what he was doing.

"Rachel," Bard Lipscomb said, abruptly, "don't you remember me?"

"I'm sorry. I don't think I've met you before." She folded her lips almost primly and slid her arms along the rests of the chair. Her cuffs, she noticed with pleasure, looked as neat and as fresh with starch as they had this morning when she fastened them to the sleeves of her dark voile dress.

Jahn looked up briefly and lowered his head again. He swung the tongs backward and forward, an expression of protest on his face, but he remained silent. Sue stirred in the chair beside him, reached out and touched the tongs. After a second, he put them back against the rock sides of the fireplace. His arm brushed over the fire screen with a little rustling noise that all of them could hear.

Jahnet said, "That's my Grandma, but she never has spoke to me."

Rachel turned her head from the child, turning it slowly and almost carefully.

Bard Lipscomb got up suddenly, reached for the other package on the writing-desk, and sat down again. He unwrapped it slowly. The rustling of the paper sounded loudly in the room. Beside him, Jahnet bit with bared, white teeth into the chocolate squares from her box. Without looking at her, Sue said, "Pass your candy around, Jahnet," and held out her hand for the box. Her eyes remained on the package in Lipscomb's lap, and dilated a little with pleasure in the sight when the lid came off on a shawl of soft, lavender wool. "This is for Rachel," Lipscomb said. He turned to Jahnet. "Little Jahnie, take it to your grandmother. . . ."

Rachel Ibsell said, "For Rachel, did you say?" Her voice was half-sharp, half-strangled.

Jahn's hand reached sidewise for the tongs again, picked them up, and swung them back and forth. Sue's soft, whispering voice murmured: "How lovely! Jahnet, take it to her."

"But I don't know where Rachel is." The voice drew back from them, sharper and weaker. "I can't find her." Her hands moved outward in a short, faint gesture.

In the new silence the child got up, holding the lavender shawl folded on her outstretched arms, and walked up to her grandmother. Her short, white skirt hung stiffly, crumpled a little where she had sat on it. She stood without speaking, looking up into that yellowed, averted face. After a moment, she turned around questioningly to her mother; but instantly she looked back and laid the shawl across the old woman's lap. She straightened slowly, with the sense of gentle, dramatic ease which children possess, and walked back to the divan. When she was sitting down again with her knees drawn up under her chin, Rachel's hands had touched the shawl, lightly and wonderingly. The fingers began to stroke the soft, curled wool.

"Rachel," Lipscomb said. "Rachel?"

She glanced at him, startled, and quickly lowered her head again.

"Rachel?"

She did not look up now, but continued to move her hands over the shawl, caressing it.

Jahn stirred heavily. Yet, again, he kept silent as if he listened for some word that, once spoken, would release her forever from the bondage in which she lived to a self that he remembered and loved.

"Rachel, don't you remember old Gansaret community, and the winter nights there, before you ever saw James Forrest, when we went to frolics over the creek? . . . Don't you remember, Rachel?"

She looked up blindly, thrusting her head forward. "Do you know where Rachel is?" The words came out like frozen points of pain, swift and bent, turning back on themselves before they were said.

"Do you know where Rachel is?" The voice was heavier now, less sharp and more fluent, as if something in her had eased a little. The child looked up, startled by it, and sat holding her candy, watching. Bard Lipscomb's head turned a little, away from Rachel, and then he was still, staring speculatively at Jahn where he leaned over with his elbows on his knees, turning the tongs abstractedly in his hands.

Sue frowned at Jahnet and got up and took the candy-box from her, setting it on the mantelpiece out of reach. "Do you see anything of Paula and Zack?" she asked, conversationally.

"Nothing. They say he walks the streets at night as he's done since the beginning, leaving Paula alone in the house, and that she calls Miss Chancie up at one and two in the morning, crying and saying she's dying. . . ." He shook his white head. "Zack goes to the office, but that's all."

"Zack?" Rachel Ibsell said. "Zack?" The name whispered out of her, cold and quivering on the air. Her face did not move, only her hands grew still on the shawl and trembled suddenly. Out of her yellowed features, her eyes glowed, tranced and mesmeric, and seeming sightless. She said, slowly, "Nobody has talked to me about Zack," and burst into tears. Her mouth screwed up like a child's, puckering with grief, and the tears slid slowly down her sightless eyes. "Nobody—nobody—!" she cried, and rocked herself back and forth.

The tongs slipped from Jahn's hand onto the stone hearth, ringing across the tilted hollow of their silence, and he stood up slowly, with a gesture of horror. Beside him, Sue was motionless, her face whitening as if the wind blew on it, drawing the skin with cold.

"Rachel—" Bard Lipscomb bent toward her, rising in the same movement, and touched her trembling shoulders. "My dear! . . . Oh, my dear! don't cry! Zack's all right! He's well and fine. . . . You can go to him!" he added suddenly, with a leap of pity for her. "You can go to Zack, darling!"

She whispered: "Oh, I want to go! I must go to him, my poor child!" She began to rise, pushing herself up, trembling, holding to his shoulders. "I must hurry. Where are my things? I must start right now. . . ."

Jahn stood without speaking. He felt suddenly on his knees the touch of Jahnet's arm. He stooped and pulled her up against him.

"What is it, Daddy? What does she want to go to my uncle Zack for?"

He shook his head, telling her to be silent. "You can't go tonight, Mamma," he said, gently.

She stared at him, seeing his huge limbs outlined against the light and hearing in his voice a hard, impregnable resistance to her pleas, a fierce cunning that sought to console her for the night so that she would forget in the morning.

"I must go! I must go!" she cried, and began again to weep. "Bard . . . you must take me. . . ."

Lipscomb, feeling a shiver of cold thrill in his muscles at her use of his name, moved back from her and looked at Jahn. "Maybe this will bring her mind back," he said. "Zack was always the one she felt needed her most." His glance held with Jahn's while Sue said, "She can't start tonight, you know that, Mr. Lipscomb." He gazed at her face and looked back at Rachel, nodding slowly. "That's common sense," he said.

"Come, Rachel," he turned to her. "You can go as soon as you're ready. You have to get ready. Look" . . . he stooped and picked the shawl from the floor . . . "you've dirtied your shawl; it'll have to be cleaned before you can go. And your other clothes, they've not come in from the laundry yet. You musn't go with your clothes half-ready; you don't want to make Zack ashamed of you."

"No . . . not ashamed," she repeated, watching him with her still, brilliant eyes. "But I must go soon," she said. "I must hurry and go. I'll go soon, as soon as . . . so he won't be ashamed," she repeated again, turning to leave the room.

Suddenly, as if she had remembered her manners, she turned back and bowed to Jahn. "I want to thank you for taking me in when you didn't know me. You've been very kind." She walked slowly from the room.

Jahn moved brusquely and stood against the fireplace, hiding his face from them.

VI

"That woman is late," Rachel Ibsell said, "that woman that was coming to take me to Zack's." She sat with Sue on the front veranda, and fanned herself with trembling, brown-veined hands. The heat waves rose in white, gaseous shimmers from the empty road.

Sue looked at her. "Kate? But it's hardly time for her to be here yet. You dressed too early; you wouldn't wait." She stopped and looked at the sun waves. "I wish you'd eat something," she said then. "You wouldn't eat breakfast."

Rachel nodded and kept her eyes on the road, straining forward for a sight of Kate's car. "That man, your husband, he's unmannerly," she said. "He wouldn't stay to say good-by to me, but ran off to Black River to get new pine. He needn't think," she said, strangely, "that I don't know he doesn't need pine for the fences now."

Sue said, slowly, "Don't you know Jahn couldn't say good-by to you? You're leaving him to go to Zack." She stopped herself, and said again, "I wish you'd come inside and eat something, or let me have Black Fanny bring you a plate out here."

Rachel got up and began to walk to and fro across the porch. "That woman—why don't she come?" she cried. "I couldn't go yesterday, and now I have to wait. . . ." She paused, stared hard at the road, and said with a slow, almost furious grief, "She's not coming!"

Sue preserved a dull silence, sitting sidewise in her chair and listening to the sounds from within the house. She gazed at the sweat beads breaking on Rachel's forehead.

"Did that man, your husband, call Zack today and say I was coming?"

"Martha called him, Mother Ibsell. Today and yesterday, too."

"Yesterday!" she exclaimed, opening her mouth with horror. "Yesterday!" She began to go down the steps. "Then he's been waiting all this time; he—I'm going!" she muttered. "I'm going if I have to walk!" She went swiftly across the yard toward the gate, a curious, bent figure walking hurriedly and mumbling to itself with angry, absorbed determination.

Behind her, Sue called out once, and then stood up and went after her. "Mother Ibsell—" She put her hand on the old woman's shoulder. "Mother Ibsell, you must wait for Kate; it's too hot. . . ." she said. "You can't walk!"

Rachel wrenched away from her, striking at her hands. "Leave me alone, you! Hussy, that's what you are with your low-necked dresses!" She fumbled at the gate.

Black Joe was coming down the lane toward them with a basket over his shoulder. Sue called to him suddenly, keeping her fingers around Rachel Ibsell's arm to hold her. "Bring my car," she said, "and take her. She won't wait. . . ."

The car crossed the bridge above Sand Caves, going toward

Choctaw. Rachel glanced to the left at the leaning rows of dwarf sourwood standing pale in the intense heat. "There's a woman up there, dying," she said to Black Joe. "Her name's Fanny. That's the same as your wife's name, ain't it? She died yesterday and that kept me from going to Zack's until today." She stared at the brown running slope of the hill as it moved backward from the car.

"Yas'm," Black Joe said. He bent forward over the steering-wheel, not looking back over his shoulder at her in the back seat. "Miss Fanny they had her fun'ral yus'day."

Rachel said, musingly, "I didn't go, but they said my brother Zie preached a fine sermon. . . ." She picked up her purse, held it a second, and laid it on the empty seat beside her. "Did they say her husband had already brought another woman home?"

"Yas'm. . . . They say Miss Fanny she walk' last night."

"Walked?" She sat up with her hands grasping the seat on each side of her. "That must have been the woman the little girl saw."

"No'm. Little missy she jes' dream. Don't no chile see ghostes." He paused and gave attention to his driving. His head moved from side to side, watching the road-glare with a nervous attention. "She see you when you walkin' the floor, mos' likely," he said then, gently. "You been walkin' since you foun' out you want to go to Mis' Zack's."

She seemed not to hear him, but twisted her body sidewise on the seat and craned her neck around to look back where her trunk was fastened to the rear of the car. She nodded with satisfaction. Yes, it was still there; they hadn't lost it. She wiped her forehead with her white hemstitched handkerchief, and stared into the heat.

"Are we nearly there?"

"Jes' crossin' Two Mile, Ol' Miss. T'won't be but 'bout five minutes now."

Rachel touched her hat nervously and gathered up her purse, her fan, and her handkerchief. She leaned forward, staring across the Negro's bent shoulders through the windshield. "Did that man back there let Zack know I was coming?" she asked, suddenly.

"Yas'm. He call' Miss Martha an' she call Mis' Zack. He know, all right, Ol' Miss." He paused, and his smooth, thick voice came softly. "Mos' likely he out lookin' fo' you right now."

Rachel nodded, and asked immediately: "Why didn't that man come with me, Joe? And that girl, his wife? Why wasn't that man there to say good-by to me when I left? I should have liked to thank him for his kindness to me."

"Mos' likely he have his business to 'tend to, Ol' Miss. Mens that works they can't be takin' the day off any time."

She sat back with relief. "Of course he had his work to see to. His farm." She brooded an instant on the long furrows she had seen from the window of the room they had given her. "Right now's his busy time, I expect."

"Yas'm. The layin'-by, it all got to be done right now."

The streets moved back from them, vague triangles and planes of bleached asphalt to her eyes. The car turned suddenly, and then slowed, running along a street where green lawns encircled small white houses. She sat erect and grasped her purse and fan more tightly. The little bungalows slid by. The car stopped against the thick turf of the last lawn on the block. She saw the red dahlias beside the veranda. The green door was closed. "Want I should go up an' tell 'im you're heah?" Black Joe got out. "'Spect that be bes', Ol' Miss."

Rachel fumbled her purse on her knees and felt her forearms trembling slightly with anxious excitement. Her head shook uncertainly on her neck. "No, no. . . . I want to go in. . . ." She began to try to open the door, getting up before she put her hand on the steel handle. "I'm going in . . ." she said.

"Did the door open?" she asked, and felt herself mounting the steps, Black Joe's hand sweating under her elbow. She stopped with her fingers touching the fine meshes of the

[266]

screen, and stood watching while he pressed the bell button. The bell rang inside the house.

It rang on silence, a shrill, squalling jangle across the throbbing layers of stillness in the unseen rooms beyond. Suddenly the last peal of the bell stopped. Then, startlingly, it rang out again under the Negro's finger.

Behind Rachel Ibsell the town seemed to rise and fall, pulsing in its moving noises, to rise and fall and come nearer, and then, slowly, to fall backward and hum with heat and distance. In front of her, the bell rang once more and hushed. She stared at it, her head bent, knowing the facts of the town's noise, the pealing bell, silent now, and the closed door. She said, "He's gone away. . . ." Her head bent lower, leaning to that closed door as if degrees of frozen trance bent her there.

Black Joe moved away from her. She heard his feet going down the steps and around the house, through the grass of the lawn. She knew when he stopped at the small side porch. A single fall of speaking tones came to her out of her listening silence. Then she heard Black Joe walking on the grass again.

He did not speak when he reached her, but touched her arm slightly to turn her around. She understood, presently, that she was going down the walk toward the car. The sun beat on her shoulders. He said: "I seen Belf'y at the side doah. Miss Paula she sick in the hospital." He helped her into the car and she sat down. Her gaze moved vaguely onto his face and saw his eyes staring at her from the bald, whitish spots around them.

"I reckon us's bettah go on back home now, Ol' Miss?" He grinned at her faintly, with pity and understanding.

"Home?" she said. "Where's that?"

"Belf'y, he say Miss Paula say not let you come in there; so I 'spects us's bettah . . ."

She tossed her head from side to side in nervous exasperation at the heat and the sound of his voice. Yet the sense of his speaking entered her mind now. "Belfry? Then it wasn't Zack. He's gone away?"

Joe blinked at her. "Yas'm. He to the hospital."

Somebody was sick and he had gone away. He went to the hospital with that sick person who said, "Don't let her in here," and he had not told them she was to come in.

Rachel held her purse tightly, clutched against her knees. "Was it the heat made him sick?" she asked, vaguely.

"It 'bout noon, Ol' Miss. We bettah go back an' git us some lunch." After a minute he added, softly and placatingly, "Us's can go round to Miss Martha's till afternoon if you wants."

"Martha? . . . That's my daughter?" She looked at him slowly. She said: "Henric? We could go to Henric's. Miss Chancie is there. . . ."

"I 'spect us ought to go to Miss Martha's, Ol' Miss."

His reluctance puzzled her, so that she stared at him for a minute. Some furtiveness of memory woke in her mind then, allowing her to know during a single instant who she was and by what routes she had come here to these closed doors. She saw, far off, dwindling in the fields she had looked at that morning, the white figure of her son Jahn and knew why he had not been with her to bid her good-by. The noise of the abruptly-starting engine filled her ears. Far back in her mind, the memory and the knowledge sank, drowning now under the soft sound of the moving car. She held it a second longer, while her eyes watched the bleached asphalt rising in front of her to the steep escarpment of the hills around Choctaw. She looked, suddenly, at the white columns of Billy Nelson's house, and all that lay in her skull was white and still.

But when she had passed up the walk and her feet were on the veranda steps, she said, slowly, "My children don't want me." She glanced up at the white columns above her head, and then, looking down again, she saw through the open door a figure moving across the dim light in the living-room. She plucked at Black Joe's shirt sleeve. "Come away," she said. "My children don't want me, I must go off and not bother them any more."

Martha paused in the door with the screen half open. "Why, Mamma, what ———?"

"I'm going away," she said, hurriedly. "I know you don't want me."

Martha's dark brows twitched faintly; she turned her eyes away from her mother. "What's happened, Joe—?" She turned around to Billy Nelson, who appeared behind her, looking over her shoulder with his napkin in one hand.

"Mamma's here."

Billy's brown head came further forward. He pushed the screen open and stepped out onto the porch, smiling. "Why, Mother Ibsell, come in!" he said, heartily. His eyes, which formed half-moons when he smiled, twinkled at her shrewdly. "I'll bet you're hungry," he said. "Martha and I are just having lunch."

"What's the matter, Joe?" Martha said again. "I know she's been to Zack's. I knew she was going, but what ———?"

Black Joe shook his wool-matted head from side to side, and put his elbow up on the porch floor as he stood by the steps. "Bless' if I know. . . ."

While they gazed at him, thinking suddenly that Paula's pregnancy was but eight months old, Rachel cried: "Come on away! I worry my children. I must go back. . . ." She stopped, letting her voice trail, and said, softly, as if to herself, "Back where?" She turned around and went down the steps, out into the sunshine.

"Mamma, come in," Martha said, gently. "Black Joe's hungry."

Rachel turned around. "Do you know where my children are?"

Nelson stared at her, his dark blue eyes alert in his pleasant, brown face. "Ah, let her go back to Jahn," he said, easily and boyishly. "She wants to go back to Jahn. Don't you, Mother Ibsell?"

"Yes, yes, back to Jahn." She peered at him with dark eyes that glanced sidewise to Martha's astonished and displeased expression. "You go into the hall there and look at your mother lying stark in her bed!" she cried, suddenly, gesturing upward. Closing her mouth firmly upon the last word, she seemed to watch Nelson's startled, slight jump. "Go and look," she whispered. "Your mother knows how you want to send old women away. . . . Back to Jahn!" she ejaculated. "So you'll not be worried by the way they take up your wife's time and walk the floor at night." She half-turned, ready to go away, and paused to peer an instant at Martha. Her daughter glanced perplexedly from her to Nelson, seeming not to know with whom to be displeased. "Good-by, Martha," she said in an unconcerned and blunt tone, and started abruptly down the walk.

"Come back—!" Martha looked helplessly around. "Mamma, you can't go away like this! Billy, you might make her come back!"

"Oh, she's all right," Billy said, pleasantly, folding his napkin. "Joe'll take her back to Jahn."

The Negro looked at them shrewdly. "I don't know . . ." Martha's voice trailed as she watched her mother going rapidly down the walk. "She wanted to go to Zack's. . . ."

Black Joe said, soothingly, "I'll take care o' her, Miss Martha."

She started, glanced at him, and nodded with relief. "Take her home," she called after him.

"Yas'm." He hurried to catch up with Rachel.

Billy's full, self-satisfied voice said, "She'll forget she came down and couldn't find Zack. She'll be all right."

"Yes, yes," said Rachel in front of Black Joe. "Yes, I'll be all right!" Her tones lifted with a strange, hard fury. Black Joe put his hand lightly under her elbow. "Go to Jahn!" she said, and stumbled a little, walking hurriedly ahead.

"Yas'm. Us's 'ull be goin' back right now," he said, stopping to hold her elbow until she could catch herself upright again. "Yas'm. We's jes' a-goin' now. . . ."

She jerked her arm from him. "Fool!" she said. "The

world is full of fools!" She stopped and turned around twice, looking dazedly about, her eyes blind in the glare from the pavements.

Black Joe took her arm again. "Yas'm, the car's right heah. . . ."

She followed silently his guiding, and allowed herself to be helped into the back seat. She leaned out the window.

"Are they still on the porch?" she said. "Still watching?"

"No'm, they's gone in."

She leaned back with a sigh. "Come on away," she murmured. "My children don't want me."

He turned the car about and let it coast down the hill. From behind him her murmuring voice said, "Miss Chancie 'u'd know; she'd know where Zack's gone to." His muscles gathered uneasily. "Yes, I must just go around there and ask," she continued, her voice growing louder and almost precise, as if she were imitating somebody. "I must find out where Zack's gone to so I can write to him. Poor child, he'll get lonely without letters from his mother, and it must be months now since I lost his address and didn't write. . . ."

Her voice grew more and more finicking, false, and imitative.

He stopped the car beside the curb. She was sitting upright, with her mouth fixed in a pious line, like a child pretending to be a society lady.

"Look heah, Ol' Miss, I'se jes' a nigger. I got to do what you says so long it ain't ag'in what Mis' Jahn say. But us's ain't got no business round to Mis' Henric's." He laid his hand on the back of the seat with an emphatic pat. "That's gospel, us's ain't got no business round theah!"

She looked at him with anxious eyes, suddenly dropping her air of pretense. "I have to get Zack's address. Miss Chancie 'ull know; she always knows what's going on in the family."

"Mis' Zack he jes' to the hospital heah in town," Black

Joe said. "Us's ain't got to go to Mis' Henric's to fin' that out, Ol' Miss."

Her eyes turned away from him while she tried to compose her face. "I want to go," she whispered, her mouth twisting. She wept unashamed. "I must find out where my boy is. He was never right and I have to look after him. Something may have happened; people could take advantage of him. . . ."

"Yas'm. . . ." He looked away from her, sat a moment indecisively, and suddenly turned back to the steering-wheel. "Yas'm. Us'll go fin' where Mis' Zack is."

He threaded slowly through the hot streets, sparse with the noon traffic, past Joe Rosenbens' store on the corner, and turned east into Melchior Street. Chanson's shrubbery gleamed darkly against the brown curves and angles of the house and against the blinding glare from the whitish-gray cement on the sidewalks. There, in that noonday sun, it seemed to the Negro, the house lay still and waiting, with danger hidden in it. He stopped the car and got out. "Ol' Miss, you le' me go in an' find out fo' you. Ain't no need you gittin' out in the sun ag'in."

But she was already up, fumbling with the handle to the door and trying to get out. "I want to see Miss Chancie," she begged.

"No'm, Ol' Miss, you ——"

She pushed his arm back and went past him, almost running, through the iron-grilled gate, and up the walk. He followed her nervously, and waited in the yard beside the steps while she walked to the door. "Mis' Jahn gonna be mad with me 'bout this," he said above the pealing tinkle of the bell through the house. "You come back, Ol' Miss." He looked helplessly at her back and heard inside the hall Henric's steps coming forward. "Ol' Miss, you ——"

"Be quiet!" she told him, suddenly, and opened the door herself. She went in. He shuffled his feet on the grass, looked about, and then gazed steadily, with fear, at the closed door. The sweat on his black face turned cold.

VII

Sue was alone in the house with young Lars when the telephone rang at three o'clock. She laid him down on the bed, noticing momentarily how clean he smelled from his bath, and went into the hall. She put the receiver to her ear. Joe Rosenbens said, "Miss Sue . . . ? Jahn's nigger is here—" He broke off, as if waiting for her exclamation.

She turned half around and sat down in the chair by the table holding the telephone. A chill spot of fear mingled with a restless, unhappy anger burned suddenly in the pit of her stomach.

Rosenbens had to wait, to speak again. "Miss Sue?"

Her voice said, "What's happened?" She stared at the floor.

"It's his mother ——"

"I knew it was. She went to Zack's this morning."

"Yes . . . Well, Miss Paula is in the hospital; went this morning. Mrs. Ibsell wanted to go around to Henric's. I don't know—I can't get it clearly. The nigger is scared. She got him to carry her around there, and she went in. Henric— It seems, Miss Sue, that Henric came out and ordered the nigger off the lawn. He waited in the car then, and Henric ordered him away from there. He says he could hear her crying in the house and Miss Chanson talking angrily. . . . The nigger doesn't know what to do."

Her voice came little and cold and clear. "I don't know what to tell you, Mr. Rosenbens."

"Well . . . I happen to know that this business of a lunacy inquisition is coming up again. They've worked it quiet, but it's coming up ——"

She interrupted, "Jahn's not here. He went to Black River before breakfast with most of the Negroes after some new pine for the fencing." She stopped and said, "Where is Mr. Lipscomb?"

"Out of town. His secretary says he'll be back about dusk."

He waited again and said, "Shall I go around there, Miss Sue, and see what I can do?"

Her thoughts moved slowly. "No," she said. And then again, "No. Thank you, but there's nothing—Where is Martha?"

"Mrs. Ibsell went to Martha's and left. They couldn't keep her. Miss Martha's out at James Forrest's this afternoon. She went out right after lunch to see something about James' children."

"I see." She put down the receiver, setting it carefully on the table, and stared out the door at the hot sun on the pasture mounds. His voice poured faintly out at her. She picked up the receiver again.

"Can you find Zack anywhere? Is he at the hospital?"

"He's there, but his wife—the little baby, Miss Sue, and ——"

"Yes. All right." She waited a minute, and asked with sudden swiftness, "James Forrest, is he ——?"

"No. He's at home, so I understand from Mr. Thurston. He was just in."

"All right . . ." she said, and heard the foolish, mechanical repetition with something like shame. "I'll . . . we can't do anything till Jahn comes." She added, slowly, "He may not be back before late tonight."

The silence in the receiver flowed over her. Joe Rosenbens' voice said then, "Shall I send the nigger on home?"

"Yes . . . I suppose so. . . . Thank you, Mr. Rosenbens."

She put the receiver down suddenly, saw it gleaming on the table, and clicked it sharply into the steel brackets. Raising her head, she saw through the living-room windows to James Forrest's house on the western hills. Martha was there. She looked again at the telephone, useless now because James did not have one in his house. She sat in a kind of lethargy, without even thinking to herself that she could go to James Forrest's house to warn Martha.

[274]

VIII

The closing of the door behind her was, for a moment, like the soft slide of a shutter across a portion of Rachel's brain. She walked down the hall toward Henric with the manner of one who had been in the house for months. "Where's my Bible?" she said. "I haven't seen it in a long time."

He hid his surprise. "Why, Mother, I don't know." He turned around toward the dining-room and raised his voice. "Chanson, where's Mother's Bible?"

Chanson appeared on the threshold of the dining-room. "Good afternoon, Mother." Rachel gazed at her dark, lean grace with pleasure, and suddenly noticed that she was not smiling. Instead, Chanson gazed at her with grave lips and enigmatic eyes that slid, slowly and stealthily, from her face to Henric's, flicked across his countenance and seemed to start at what they saw there, and then slid back to Rachel. Rachel turned her head and looked at Henric.

He was standing beside her, tall and immaculate, his lips smiling even while they pressed together, his cheeks flushed with a sort of excitement. His head shook with a nodding motion on his long neck, keeping a strange, gloating rhythm with the soft, slick movements of his clasped hands. She stared at him with surprise and then with disgust. "Stop that foolish jittering, Henric!" she said. He started, stared at her, and then with a short laugh moved past Chanson into the dining-room.

Chanson said, "Who's waiting for you, Mother Ibsell?"

"Oh, nobody. Nobody at all!" Henric said from behind the door. "She's come for a little visit, haven't you, Mother?"

Chanson's body grew motionless, and her yellow eyes, in which the cat-like pupils gleamed so cruelly and fascinatingly, became blank, copper disks of watchfulness. "Somebody is waiting for you, Mother, I think," she said, softly.

Rachel stared at her, with something twisting in her mind, moving up from the dark depths of consciousness, sliding over and over again, and then, painfully, pressing upward once more. Without knowing what she meant to say, she murmured: "Go away! My children are tired of me." She tilted her head to one side, listening to what she had said; and presently, looking from Chanson to the door behind which Henric was hidden, she asked for her Bible again. "I feel like reading in it a little. I think it would settle my feelings. The story of Joseph. . . ." A sudden, sardonic mockery lit her eyes and she murmured, "'Their sheaves made obeisance to my sheaf. . . .'"

Henric called from the dining-room, "Come in and eat a little, Mother. We're just finishing lunch."

She walked to the door, with Chanson going past her to the opposite end of the hall. Peering in at the table, at the food, she shuddered faintly with a swift sickness pressing cold in her stomach, and turned away. "I don't feel like eating; I'm too hot." Chanson came back to her and took her arm.

"Black Joe's waiting for you in the yard."

She looked up at Chanson's face. "Well . . . yes, I must go. Give me my Bible. Rachel wandering in the wilderness. I must read that. Give me my Bible."

Henric came up behind them, thrusting his head between their faces. "Take Mother into the library, Chanson. Black Joe is just going off."

She felt Chanson's balked silence moving over her like a distant, foolish warning, and looked at Henric. His flat, black eyes regarded her steadily. "Go into the library and rest, Mother."

"Yes, rest. . . ." She turned aimlessly around, hunting for the purple draperies which hung before the library entrance. Henric had gone to the front door and opened it. "What does he want to keep me for? My children hate me?" she whispered suddenly to Chanson. When she heard the question and saw the Creole's still, impassive face, something light and cold ran the length of her spine. Chanson did not move. From the front door Henric's voice rose with abrupt anger.

"What are you hanging around here for? Go on back to Jahn Ibsell—at once. Do you understand, at once? I have no use for you in my yard!"

She sprang suddenly forward. "No, no. Leave Jahn alone! Let me out! Let me go! Jahn's waiting for me. Don't quarrel with Jahn, Henric. You break my heart with your quarreling ——!"

He thrust her clutching hands back and shut the door, turning around to her. "Why, Mother! It's nobody but Black Joe. He was trampling down the lawn. Of course I had to send him off."

Chanson moved slowly and came toward them, walking steadily, her hands clenched at her sides. Her face was cold and motionless with anger.

"So you will lie like that, Henric Ibsell! You will behave like a beast. I understand what is in your mind; perfectly I understand! Do you hear me, you shall not do it. No. For the young who can be cured, for the violent, that is all right; but for the old for whom there is no hope, no. Will you go on now, will you shame your blood and make me hate you forever?" She saw him opening his mouth to speak. "Ah, be still, fool!" she cried, and flung around from him. "Be still forever!" She stopped again, and stood over Rachel Ibsell. "Will you stay here and let him do what he likes with you, or will you go home now? Wake up, old woman, and remember what you know!"

Rachel gazed at her with still, tranced eyes. "Oh, love, oh, my son, oh, never again, never!" she murmured, strangely, and clasped her hands together with an abrupt, confused gesture. On the instant she began to walk up and down the hall, up and down. Watching her, Chanson saw that she stared at something they could not see. Wild, strained expressions of grief, of intense and watchful anxiety, of profound anguish, ran rapidly over her features. "Come out of the cave, come out before the merchants come!" she whispered. "See! The camels are there. . . . Come out, oh, come out, my son!" she cried. As she uttered these despairing words, she was near the library entrance. She stopped a second with the draperies touching her breast, and then, slowly and somnambulistically, she walked through them. From the library her voice rose again, cracked and eerie. "My son, my son, answer me! Come out before the merchants come!"

Chanson sank suddenly onto the wall sofa, and sat staring at the polished floor around her feet.

"Don't you see!" Henric whispered, urgently. "With the lunacy inquisition coming up again! We can get Dr. Stanhope here again. . . . It's evident now, evident. . . ." The full, gloating whisper moved darkly on the air. Chanson shook her shoulders and turned aside from him.

"Be still!"

"Why should I be still? You're in it as much as I am. You started it."

She rose to her feet with a gesture of escape. "Not this. I did not start *this*," she said. She stood looking down at the floor. Suddenly she threw her head back. "Oh, perhaps I did! I wanted the land, the money from the land for you, to prove . . . I was willing to fool her a little; it amused me to fool her, she was so certain and so domineering! And I wanted money. . . . But I never meant this, not this, Henric!" She looked at him almost pleadingly. His eyes stared at her without expression until suddenly a white flame of anger ran under the dark skin of his face, pinching all his features together in a mask of despairing rage.

"No!" he burst out. "No, you meant to prove to Jahn he couldn't marry! You dogged him and sneered at him from the first minute I brought you home, trying to fasten his eyes on you, and then when he married Sue you had to pay him out, revenge yourself! You think I didn't see it? You think I was blind? Everybody saw it; James, Martha, they all saw it and laughed about it. And I was willing enough to make him lick dust before me, I was willing enough." He stopped himself, and forced a strained, histrionic laugh. "Now you can't stand it, can you? your love is getting hurt too badly!"

Her mouth opened. A shudder of interior laughter began in her diaphragm, and stopped weakly, as if the immeasurably ridiculous required no amusement. She sat down again and stared at his white flaming face.

"But, Henric," she said, presently, "it was you I loved. You . . . understand that now?"

"Love!" he screamed suddenly. "Don't rave to me like a lying, cheating cull about love! I know your love, I know your eyes when they looked at him!" He turned around crazily and ran to the door, flinging it back and shouting at Black Joe.

She listened a moment, not to his words, but to his tones, hearing beneath them the soft, helpless shuffle of Rachel Ibsell's old-woman shoes on the library floor. She got up and went into her own room and closed the door.

Sitting on her bed, she heard him come back down the hall and go into the library. In a few minutes, a car started outside, and she knew that Black Joe was leaving. Henric's voice murmured suavely in the library, its full, neat tones interspersed now and then by the ragged, sick cries of Rachel Ibsell's agony. All at once there was silence. Chanson looked at the clock on her dressing-table, staring at it sightlessly, without feeling or thought and with no knowledge in her except the instinct of the afternoon's swift passage. When she knew that a long time had gone by, she heard the sound of a car. She got up swiftly, thinking wildly and hopefully that it might be Jahn Ibsell coming; and then, from the hall rose James' loud, blustering voice. She walked to her door and locked it.

"Well, I got here!" James declaimed in the hall. "I got here! Who you got in the library?"

Henric said frozenly, "Mother."

Chanson heard them go into the library. She returned to her bed, stood beside it indecisively, and then sat down again. She wondered dully if Henric knew how she had gone to Jahn

Ibsell at Sand Caves. . . . But it did not matter, she thought, it did not matter at all. She gazed out the window in front of her. Where her marigolds had bloomed last autumn, a row of violets glanced greenly against the sunlight now, the leaves rank and luxuriant, with no blossoms among them. The hot summer wind blew for a moment strongly out of the west, and then slowly the leaves of the violets and the white, glancing shadows on the fence above them grew still.

She heard footsteps in the hall, James' and Henric's, and the sound of that old woman's shoes moving reluctantly and draggingly between them, as if they had her by the arms and pulled her on. Henric's voice said: "Be good now, Mother. We're taking you to Zack as fast as we can." With all her body still, Chanson listened, and counted the steps as they went toward the door and reached it. There was an interval of silence. The door slammed.

Chanson got up and went to the clothes-closet over against the head of her bed. She took down her overnight bag and filled it, moving slowly and with abstraction. When she had snapped the lock and put the key inside her purse, she stood before the dressing-table mirror and put on her hat. Slowly, beside her face, formed the large, subtle lineaments of Jahn Ibsell's countenance. His blue eyes gleamed white, with a film of blindness over them. She turned away, picked up her bag, and went out into the silent hall.

She heard without surprise or feeling the gentle trill of the telephone bell beginning. Thrusting her overnight bag beneath one arm, she picked up the cradle and leaned against the wall. "Hello?"

Mr. Peebles said, "Er.— How are you, Mrs. Ibsell? Could I speak to Mr. Ibsell for a moment?"

A slow, wary interest ran under the cold tightness of her abstraction. "He's not here." She added, immediately, "Out of town, Mr. Peebles. I will take the message."

She heard him hesitating. "Well . . . it's just that—" He broke off. "You know of course," he said then in his formal, legal voice, "that the Supreme Court notifies me, as Mr. Ibsell's attorney, of the outcome of the case? The decision has just arrived, and I am sending it on to Mr. Ibsell by the first mail . . . unless he wishes to come up for it? I might tell you"—he hesitated, and grew more formal—"that the Supreme Court has reversed Chancery's decision in Mrs. Rachel Ibsell's favor and has rendered a decree denying her relief and dismissing the bill of complaint."

Her diaphragm heaved again, like a subtle and sensible continuation of that incompleted laughter over Henric's jealousy. She set the telephone softly down and leaned against the wall, shaking with a wild, hilarious glee that pained her with its stubborn soundlessness. Suddenly her mouth straightened. She stood up from the wall, looked once again at the now persistently ringing telephone, and walked out of the house.

On the street in front of Garner's furniture store Bob Garner spoke to her. "Good afternoon," she said, and was about to pass on when his voice behind her said: "It's sad about the little baby, huh, Mrs. Ibsell? I was sorry to hear it."

She turned back, feeling the still heat of the day gathering in her ears. "What is it? I don't understand you!" she said, sharply.

"Why"—he stammered a little—"Zack's little baby. He drew three breaths and then died—like that." He turned his fat fingers outward. "Well . . . in the midst of life . . ." he said, vaguely, and looked away from her.

"So!" she answered him, suddenly. "So! For two deaths, Fanny Forrest's and this child's, Mother Ibsell is lost."

She walked swiftly away from him. At the corner she hailed a taxi and was driven rapidly to the railway station. "So . . . for Fanny and for that dead baby," she said, while she sat inside. And suddenly she thought that the born-dead and the dead-with-old-age these were fortune's lucky children. "And I have yet my life to live!" she said. She got out of the taxi and went inside the station waiting-room. Far up the tracks, coming nearer and going south, a train turned with immense and seeking sibilance on its great flanged wheels.

IX

From the narrow barred windows high on the third story pale distorted faces looked downward upon the great stone circle where the driveway ended. The late afternoon sun cast glimmers of shadow and light over the English turrets and over the secret, dark stone of the walls. The front door stood open. The corridor was vast, vaulted, stretching to the wide oak staircase, with frets of white marble railing the domed glass in the center of the ceiling. Through it the sunlight glanced downward in bars and circles of opalescent and milky luminance, and lay across the door into the waiting-room.

"Where is Zack?" Rachel said. "Is Zack here?"

A silly-faced young woman in a starched white dress and with a blatant cap cocked sidewise on top of her brown hair stood in front of her, holding a pad of paper and a pencil. "Is it a self-committal case?" she said. Her eyes passed professionally over Rachel's face. "Or are you bringing her in?" She looked at Henric and James with indifferent eyes.

"Self-committal," Henric said, and coughed delicately, lifting his white hand to hide his mouth.

"That's right!" James nodded and winked at the girl. "Her father died here; she kept wantin' to come."

The young woman looked from one to the other of them. "Dr. Stanhope will see you in a few minutes," she said, and turned away. "Just have a seat here." She vanished around the edge of the door with a flick of her skirts against the white stone walls.

"Is Zack here? Is this the hospital?" Rachel said.

Two men in gray coveralls swabbed the floor at one end of the room, rubbing the dingy mops slowly and methodically up and down. They neither lifted their faces nor turned their

[282]

eyes aside from the streaks of wet darkening in front of them on the brown tiles.

"Patients," James said, pointing. He snickered senselessly.

The swishing noise of the mops whispered in Rachel's ears like a voice trying to tell her who and what she was. She sat meekly in the chair Henric had pointed out to her and watched the two men, her hands folded on her lap, her eyes tranced and brilliant. Her head appeared to shake slightly, as if in mockery of Henric, on her thin, corded neck. The pit of her stomach was cold and empty from hunger and weariness. The two men moved slowly across the room. Their mops touched the wall above the divan on which James sat, slithering along the floor, and their bodies came up against the wall. They stood motionless, with stiffened limbs. The silly-faced nurse came in, turned them around, putting the mops back into their hands, and shoved them forward. They moved slowly across the floor, mopping with even, exact strokes.

"We'll take your mother now," the nurse said.

Henric and James rose, one going to each side of her, and raised her from the chair. She swayed dizzily. The nurse took her hand and led her forward out of the waiting-room, down the long, vaulted corridor, and through a door behind the stairs. She saw other young women there in starched dresses and white caps. On the grayish, cement floor, smelling of creosote and disinfectant, stood a pair of white scales, a dressing-table, and a square, painted box like a clothes-chest. A blue apron hung from one of the hooks along the wall. The nurse's hands touched her on the shoulders, gently pushing her down upon the white chair. One of them knelt and began to take off her shoes. In front of her, the silly-faced young woman stood with pads of paper and pieces of cardboard on which words were printed in neat lines. Another nurse came forward and unbuttoned her dress.

"No, no!" she said. She stirred with terror, putting her hands over her chest, and looking up at them. "No . . . don't.

I was never in my life undressed before people. . . . No, I ——"

In the doorway a man stood with a white apron covering his chest and legs and rubber gauntlets on his hands. He spoke in a loud, cheerful voice. She sprang up and tried to hold her falling garments. The nurses smiled at her and gently drew her dress back from her shrunken shoulders. She shrank away from them into the chair, sick with shame and weakness. "I was never undressed before," she said. "There's a man here. . . ." She began to cry.

The man came toward her and put a stethoscope over her naked breast. The silly-faced young woman watched, a pencil ready between her fingers. The man spoke, and she made rapid marks on the pieces of cardboard. "Stand up, please," one of the nurses said, and took the rest of her clothes from her.

In the waiting-room Henric had looked around for a telephone, crossed one leg, jerked it down, and crossed the other. James sat upon the divan, curling his mustache and watching with a cold, sly amusement. Henric flushed, and sat still. The long minutes crawled by, inching their way through the wet, hushed whisper of the mops on the floor. Once they heard their mother cry out, weakly and incoherently. The mops swished again. Suddenly there was silence, and turning his head, Henric saw the two men in gray coveralls standing frozen against the walls. He glanced toward the door; the nurse was not in sight.

"Hey?" James said, slyly, under his breath. "They let the bugs out here, don't they?"

Staring at the men, Henric became unpleasantly aware of their formless corpulence. He had not before noticed that they were fat; now, their white, bloated bodies seemed to swell under the shapeless bag of the coveralls. A strange nurse, not the one he had seen before, came in and turned the two men around. The mops swished on the floor again.

Henric got up hastily, jerking his tie into place. "Ah . . .

where is the telephone, please?" His voice moved urgently; a certain relief appeared on his face.

He walked behind the nurse, almost stumbling in his hurry, and felt on his neck James' breath. "Damned nurses got the big head. Nothing but sluts, anyway!" He jerked around, stared at James angrily, and pushed through the door into the closed booth at the front of the hall. He picked up the telephone with one hand, slamming the door shut on James' spying face with the other.

His tongue pronounced automatically the number of his own telephone. The frightened impatience in him welled up over his listening so that the hoarse buzzing on the line seemed to come from a long way off. He snapped the receiver down into the cradle, picked it up again, and heard the operator's "Number, please." He spoke rapidly, and grew suddenly still, waiting. An instant or so later he pushed out of the booth, white-faced and shaking. "Chanson ——"

"Dr. Stanhope will see you now." The voice cut swiftly and indifferently across his frightened anxiety. He stared at James' face, scarcely seeing it, and composed himself. As he followed the nurse down the hall, with James at his heels, he became aware of the darkening of the sunlight on the domed glass in the ceiling. It was late, dusk almost. He straightened his tie above his jerking neck, and entered Dr. Stanhope's office.

"Tell me," his mother's voice was saying, "is Zack here? I came to find him. . . . Am I Rachel Ibsell or is she my friend? Why did they undress me? I remember waiting for Zack to come home and hearing him say something about the dwarf, and then I don't remember anything until I got here and couldn't find him. I know he's in trouble. . . . Why did they undress me and make me ashamed? If I'm not Rachel Ibsell, why do I have sons? I've never been married. Is that why they made me ashamed? . . . It was raining that night and now it's hot. Did I catch a cold coming here?"

The doctor looked up, past her where she stood in front of

his desk with the nurse holding her arm, and met Henric's eyes. He nodded distantly, with his gaze passing over James Forrest and going back to Rachel.

"Yes, you are rather weak, Mrs. Ibsell. We'll keep you here for a few days and let you rest and get well."

She nodded weakly. "Are you Jahn? One of my boys is lost, the one they call Jahn. You remind me of him. And Zack is sick; he's in the hospital. Yes," she said suddenly, in a different voice, "I'll be glad to rest. I'm tired. But I must get home in time to 'tend to my cows. One of them is freshening tonight, I think. Jahn said he put down some extra hay for her to lie on." Her head turned and her eyes wandered over her sons' faces. "Go away!" she murmured. "I hurt my children; they have no father, and they made me ashamed. . . ."

The doctor glanced significantly at the nurse, and she took Rachel's hand. After a second the old woman followed her slowly, bent forward from the waist and stumbling as she went. They heard her voice a moment in the hall, and then the click of an elevator came to their ears. They glanced at each other, and Dr. Stanhope was watching them.

His fingers moved over the desk and took up a pile of cards. "Now," he said, "we have here a record of this case as self-committal." His pencil marked on the card and then wrote swiftly. "I am changing that. The case is obviously committal by relatives." He glanced up. "We try to have no falsity on our records."

Henric cleared his throat, saw James' mouth opening, and did not speak. After a minute he heard James' silence.

Dr. Stanhope said, "According to our examination, your mother is suffering from a form of senile amnesia. This amnesia was, quite probably, subconsciously deliberate in the beginning. She had reached a point where a division from self was necessary in order to go on living at all. The subconscious takes care of that; it is a defensive mechanism at times. Now, apparently, she is recovering her awareness of herself as Rachel Ibsell, but her amnesia is no less pronounced."

He tapped his pencil on the desk and stared at them out of cold, gray eyes. "You understand that all terms are uncertain and relative in a discussion of this sort. When I say that her amnesia is senile, I do not mean that it follows all the usual lines of senile amnesia. All manifestations are necessarily individual. Authorities often differ on the type of insanity. And when I call her present amnesia no less pronounced than it was in its former manifestations, I mean that her new and wavering identification with her former self is simply that: new, wavering, unreal. At moments she is herself, at other moments she identifies herself with a Biblical character. No manifestation is lasting or unchanging. You will understand me when I say, more simply, that she is old and that she is trying to sustain life under the burden of a great grief. Neither her mental nor her physical strength is equal to it. . . ."

He tapped the desk again with his pencil and stared at their dark, closed faces. "Whether she will ever know where she is or not, I cannot predict; there is a chance that she will. I advise you, then, to withdraw your application for her committal and take her home."

They stood without moving, looking back at him. James snickered suddenly. "I think not," he said. "Ain't this place supported by taxpayers for her kind? I should pay taxes for this and then be bothered with her at home!"

"She will be better here, I'm sure, Doctor," Henric said, suavely.

Dr. Stanhope looked down at the pile of cards again. "I see. You understand that we accept patients only on the condition that they remain in our care until they are cured? That is our new rule."

"Yes, of course, Doctor. . . . Anything we can do to co-operate," Henric said, nodding precisely.

The doctor smiled slightly, and glanced up at him, opening his mouth for a further question.

From upstairs, falling down from the third story in a great, fluttering rush of sound, came the concerted screams of women, rushing, rising, dying. Henric licked his lips and stared frozenly at the doctor, stiff with fear. "God!" James said. He stepped backward from the open door of the office.

The slight smile remained on Dr. Stanhope's lips. "Just the chorus of our nymphomaniacs," he said. "We usually manage to keep them quiet until later. The real orchestra starts about nine o'clock. . . ." He rose suddenly, and picked up the cards. "Good night, then."

They walked side by side down the long, dusky corridor and out onto the stone steps leading down to the great circle. "God!" James said. "That screaming, did you hear?" Henric wiped his forehead, and got into the car. "I thought he'd ask us if we were her legal guardians. I think he was going to when that screaming . . ."

The engine started under his foot, he leaned forward and drove swiftly down the oak-lined avenue. James' arm brushed his elbow. "That's right, he could a put a crimp in us with that, couldn't he?" The car swerved onto the main highway, running now with the rush of Henric's nerves, controlled too long in Dr. Stanhope's office, past the university and across town into Melchior Street.

A long way ahead, he saw the dark windows of the house and felt its still emptiness smothering on the lively dusk. He lifted his foot from the brakes, the car slid with a screeching noise on the asphalt, and then straightened and stopped. James looked at him with fury swelling the purple veins on his forehead. "What in hell— Listen, if you ———"

Henric was on the veranda, jerking the door open and rushing through the silent rooms. As he ran, staring and listening, a faint, fine dust seemed to rise from the stillness and to sift over his nostrils, choking him. He came again into the hall, and stopped, seeing a shapeless figure outlined against the faint twilight coming in through the open door. After a second James' voice spoke to him. He sank onto the divan against the wall.

James turned on the lights and came toward him. "What in

[288]

hell ails you? . . . Chanson gone?" he demanded suddenly, looking about, and grinned.

Henric looked sidewise at James, through his spread fingers. "I knew it . . . I knew it all afternoon," he muttered, and heard the words, pitiable, revealing. James sat down beside him, touching him with his knee. He drew back. His white face, hidden still by his hands, stared with a set, accusing fear.

A step sounded on the veranda, beyond the open door. Bard Lipscomb's tall figure came into the light and stood looking at them. They rose together, slowly, and stared at him as if he might be a ghost, their heads turning when he came nearer and stopped in front of them. James jerked suddenly. "Why—hello, Lipscomb? What are you doing here?"

"I'm hunting Rachel." His head turned toward the library where the purple draperies hung over darkness, and then toward the door beyond the stairs where her room had used to be. "I just got in from a trip. . . ." His high, orator's voice paused; he looked quickly at Henric, and said, "I saw Miss Chancie in the station." His face changed, smiling faintly. "Her train's gone now." He looked again at the closed door beyond the stairs. "Where's Rachel?"

James stepped back, moving slightly, and Henric's eyes turned and watched him, staring at the wen on his neck with a sudden fascinated loathing.

"Miss Sue was calling. Jahn's not at home. She said Rachel was here. Where is she?"

James snickered softly and slyly, and so abruptly that Henric, staring at him, started. "In Marston's."

The lawyer stood motionless. Suddenly, he cried, "My God! you had no right to do that!" He stopped, breathing heavily with anger, and said: "Well, you've played it out, you fools. And you're too late. The land's Jahn's tonight." He lifted his clenched hands and let them drop, and stared at their frozen faces. "You fools, you— Did you think anything you could do would change the Supreme Court? You've been trying, worrying, ever since the thing began, and now . . . you're too late, but Rachel is in Marston's!" he cried, incoherently.

"Jahn's!" they said under their breaths. Their eyes locked.

"You're lying, by God!" James shouted, and started forward. "You're lying, damn you!" Bard Lipscomb's motionless figure stopped him; he fell back and said, dully: "You're lying. You've not heard from the Supreme Court."

"Marston's!" the old man burst out, suddenly. "Your mother in Marston's, put there to die!" His shoulders seemed to cave in and his whole body to grow flaccid. Across him, the brothers watched each other with an abrupt, strange wariness of doubt and suspicion. He moved slowly from between them, along the hall, and out the door. They seemed to wait, to listen for his footsteps to depart.

"Call Peebles!" James cried, suddenly. "Call Peebles!" He leaped toward the telephone and suddenly stopped, looking at Henric.

From the library the soft, silver chimes of a clock rang out. Their mouths closed, their muscles grew tight, listening. "Nine," Henric said. "Nine. . . ."

He heard James move and clear his throat, and looked away from him, counting intently in his mind. ". . . two . . . three . . ." James' black animal stare gazed at him, like his own eyes watching him in a mirror . . . ". . . four . . . five . . . six. . . ." He bit his lip and closed his eyes. ". . . seven . . . eight . . . nine. . . ."

A cold wash of terror sprayed his flesh, out from his nerves. "Nine," he said again. "Nine." The empty house spread out about him, the dust of its silence sifting thickly over his nostrils while he seemed to hear clearly from north of town the massed, falling scream of women rushing down through the floors onto a vast, stone corridor where the moonlight fell in convolutions of still horror.

X

The starlight fell coldly over the massed wagons and over the tethered animals. If any prescience had lived in it to speak to men of their changes and their fortunes, it might have said to Jahn Ibsell that he was always held by the necessities of labor or by the obstructions of human sentiment from that place where he was most needed. As it was, the starlight remaining incommunicative, he accepted without impatience the slow dragging of his Negroes at their work until it was too late to return along the rock cliffs overhanging Black River. He lay awake, pillowed on his saddle midway between the pine forest and the river, and thought sadly of his mother in Zack's house tonight. Perhaps, he thought, she was better there; maybe Lipscomb had been right: she would come back to herself in Zack's house, as strong people are always strongest where there is weakness for them to guard. His thoughts paused, and she came before his mind's eye like a strange, sad picture colored with love and regret. . . . Staring at it, he slept. The cold starlight moved and shone in his face, and moved again, and became with the passage of time less starlight than gray dawn. He dreamed of his wife, feeling her image move across the dark surface of his sleeping worries like a sudden, swift circling of light upon which he struggled to open his eyes. The sun was coming up redly behind the pines. The starlight was still on the river. He got swiftly up, called to his Negroes, and rode ahead of them toward Red Valley.

The long white envelope on the tin flap of the mail-box was like a shape he had seen there before. He took it in his hands and it felt cold to him. Behind him in the country road the wagons paused and turned out around him, rumbling past his motionless figure on the sorrel stallion and in between the red clay banks that led to Sand Caves and the white farmhouse. The morning breeze blew along his forehead and belled slightly the back of his blue shirt. He read slowly, with that unused clumsiness characteristic of men whose intelligence runs ahead of their acquaintance with words, balks them, and turns them back to start over again.

Jahn Ibsell, et als
vs
Mrs. Rachel Ibsell
Appeal from Choctaw Chancery Court

The break in the black lines stopped him. "'Et als.'!" he said to himself. His lips curled in scorn of the vagaries of law which lumped together all heirs of whatever interest, formal or real, virtuous or evil. He looked up and turned the envelope over and saw that it had been mailed at ten o'clock last night from Lipscomb's office. The mules' stretched necks as they turned in the road flashed an instant before his eyes, and then he looked down at the thin legal paper again. Suddenly his hands shook, he fumbled the leaves over, searching for the decision past all the citations of precedent. He came upon it on the last page. ". . . hereby reverses the decision of Chancery . . . and renders a decree denying her relief and setting aside the bill of complaint. . . ." His lips stopped moving, he looked up, and after a minute remembered to breath again.

The start of joy moved in his chest like an intoxication finding its way there, and suddenly stopped. "I have beaten my mother," he thought; and started, as if somebody else had spoken to him. Out in front of the horse, a leaf fell spiraling to the ground. His eyes followed it, and slowly with some compulsion beyond the ordinary bending him, he leaned heavily forward, clasping his hands over the pommel of the saddle and stared at the stallion's roached mane. He became aware of the Negroes' eyes watching him from the turn in the road. He sat up and folded the sheets of paper. His glance fell on one of the Negroes, who was just then edging his team into the Red Valley road. He spoke, scarcely knowing what he was saying.

"Here, take this to Miss Sue and say I've gone to town."

The Negro looked at him curiously and half-fearfully. "Tain't no bad news 'bout Ol' Miss, is it?"

He turned the stallion and moved out through the wagons. "Yes," he said, strangely.

The sides of the red clay road, furzed thickly with small underbrush, rushed past him. Words from the paper leapt in his mind. "It is impossible to conclude that Jahn Ibsell conceived or inspired the idea of a conveyance to him by complainant. . . ." Once again that strong, fitful joy for his vindicated honor moved in his breast; and once again fell downward, dragged by the slow, sucking tides of the guilt that had endured, furtively and palely, in him since the night when he stood in his mother's door and announced his approaching marriage. Peebles' bills, sent on to him and marked in Henric's small, precise handwriting, came into his mind. And then, across them, visible as if they lay before his eyes, swept the brown, far-hidden reaches of his furrows, rising richly against the colorless horizon. He shook his head as if to clear it of mists.

The stallion's hooves clicked evenly and rapidly on the dry roadbed. Puffs of dust rose behind him. "I have beaten my mother," he thought again. "Behold, a whirlwind of the Lord is gone forth in fury, even a grievous whirlwind. . . ." He remembered the words; he heard them. It seemed to him that he had lived only for this, to hear forever in his ears her words and to see her, a strong and sour woman, crouching, beaten by her son's hands, her son's self-hidden treacheries. "I had no right, no right . . ." he said to himself. "The land is not mine, I took it with lying, I promised her." He saw her in the pasture, walking softly over the wet grass, saying, "Promise you'll never leave me. . . ." He thought: "I left her. Now I have beaten her."

The stallion's hooves splashed through Two Mile Creek, rang in the valley, and struck gravel from the last hill. The roadbed leapt smoothly beneath him. Suddenly, Choctaw lay below, huddled in gray mist, the spires of the university suspended above the town with the solid turrets of Marston's breaking through moated sunshine behind them. He stopped the horse and gazed ahead.

Once, when he was seventeen or thereabout, he had stopped on this hill, holding the mules taut with the wagonload of farm produce piled high on the bed behind him. That, he thought, slowly, was a long time ago, before he learned to lie and not lie. He heard dimly within himself the lapping of blood against the walls of his veins, and knew how they all, his mother and his brothers and himself, lay under the rising sunlight like figures of pasteboard set there to the domination of a little time before they grew pale and shrank in their own minds and the winds that had blown through their quarreling and their hatred should lift them like fragments of withered paper and blow them away. The still pain of his thought gathered in him. He saw again his furrows stretching limitless and dark, the level plain rising to the curve of the sky.

"I did not pay for it," he said to himself. "No man could pay for that, or buy it." It seemed to him suddenly that the earth was the daughter and the wife of God . . . and for man a granary and a charnel-house. No man could own her or call her his own. No man had ever paid for her except in the delusion of his sweat and in the urge to feed his children with pride. He thought that he could have chosen between the earth and Sue and that, lying, he had taken both. No man could own a woman and the earth, the flower of God's loins and the temple of his worship. He shook his head slowly, staring at the town below him; and smiled. . . . A man, he thought, was like a pig caught between the boards of a fence; he must go squealing all his life between the laws of God and the temptation of God's beauty . . . but a man could loose himself, he could pull the fence over on himself.

He was still smiling, peculiarly, with a cold, eerie knowledge marking his features, when he got down before Rosenbens' store.

As he crossed the sidewalk there, Zack came against him, running out from the door and clasping him round the shoulders. He stumbled backward an instant, dazed by surprise and seeing but dimly who held him and the gathering faces in the doorway, Peebles and Rosenbens and Garner and faces he did not know. He looked slowly down at Zack's white, upturned countenance, raising his arms at the same time to loosen Zack's clasp. Rosenbens' voice said, clearly, "Jahn . . . go easy now!" He looked up again in astonishment, and then downward, seeing with a dull uncomprehending wonder the seeping of thin, bluish tears from Zack's closed eyes. After a minute, when he realized that his brother lay heavily and slackly against him, like a child relaxing against the strength it clung to, he put his hand on Zack's shoulder and shook him slightly.

"Zack! Zack! Stand up. . . ."

The gentleness of his own voice sounded in his ears. He stopped and listened to it, and said again, "Zack! Stand up!"

When after a moment that relaxed and leaning body did not move, his cheeks flushed half-angrily. "Zack, you're a man! Stand up! You can't act like this!" He was muttering, keeping his voice low, away from the listening ears in the doorway. He saw Joe Rosenbens start toward him and then, looking down again, he saw Zack's eyes staring wide and childishly. The pale, small mouth moved.

"It was dead . . . Jahn, it was dead. . . ."

Jahn looked around at Rosenbens questioningly, while he tried to lift Zack away from himself.

"At the hospital. . . ." Rosenbens began to explain in a low matter-of-fact voice. He leaned over and took Zack's arm. "Get him on the other side; take him in my office."

They plucked his clinging arms away, held him up, and began to walk with him through the door, past the faces there. Peebles' voice came loudly in an aside to Garner: . . . "owes me money, won't pay it. . . . Never expect any honor from those Ibsells again. . . ." Jahn looked around and could not find Peebles' face. He turned again and lifted Zack across the threshold of the office and into the chair beside Rosenbens' desk. The pale, vague eyes stared at him hopefully and sadly.

"They buried it that night." He leaned forward and whispered. "They buried it in a shoe-box. Why are they ashamed of dead babies?"

"Yes, Zack. Don't talk about it." He sat down in the chair across from him, stared at Zack's lifted, working face, and then turned his head toward Rosenbens. The two men looked at each other over Zack's shoulders.

"He seemed all right," Rosenbens said. "Except that he was here, waiting for you. He stood about, sat in here for a while, and then went outside. He didn't bother anybody. No outcry, nothing. But I did notice that he seemed like a whipped child. And then when you showed up, out he went. . . ." He shook his head, curving his long, amber fingers over his chin. "I never saw anything like it, but I suppose you've always expected something, eh?"

"Paula's at the hospital. Where's Mamma?" Jahn said, suddenly. He started up from his chair, stopped, and went up close to Zack. "Zack! Where is Mamma?"

The weak eyes wandered over his face and grew warm and luminous. "You'll look after me, Jahn, won't you . . . when the dwarf comes . . .?" He turned his eyes aside, swiftly, to the corners of the room, and whispered, "The dwarf came last night . . ." His fingers plucked at the desk in front of him.

Jahn Ibsell sat down and wiped his forehead with his shirt sleeve. "I'll look after you," he said, hoarsely.

Rosenbens stared at him and then up at the door, seeing Bard Lipscomb there. His fingers curved over his chin. "Come in, Bard," he said.

Jahn turned around in his chair. After a moment, Lipscomb came up to him and put one hand on the top rung of the chair back. "Well . . . we won, Jahn," he said, gently, in a light, soft voice. He gazed at Zack.

Jahn looked up at him, listening still to the echoes of his voice and finding a warning, a hint, in the slow, inscrutable tones. "What is it?" he said, suddenly.

Bard Lipscomb walked away from him and leaned out the window with his back to the room. The red brick walls of the alleyway along which transport trucks were driven loomed in front of him. "They've got Rachel in Marston's," he said, presently, without looking around. Behind him, there was silence. "They took her last night about dusk, before they knew about the decision." He turned around, looked at Jahn, and then looked away.

Jahn Ibsell had not moved. He sat in the chair like a man whose blood has turned to stone. Nothing lived in his face except the blue eyes which blared dark with comprehension and horror.

Lipscomb swallowed suddenly and loudly, and was not able to speak. The silence went on, dragging, heavy.

Slowly and strangely, in that white immutability of countenance, came the slow pouching of black circles under Jahn Ibsell's eyelids. He put his head down on his arm and held it there.

Joe Rosenbens cleared his throat. "Don't take it so hard, Jahn. She doesn't know where she is yet, and you can get her out. Henric and James had no right to take her there."

Lipscomb shook his head slowly. "No. . . . Anybody can take in a patient. Anybody. They would have taken her if Black Joe had carried her in. And they don't let them out. But I've started proceedings for a court hearing on it. Maybe we can—manage . . ."

Zack's strange, childish voice said: "Let's go fox-huntin' tonight, Jahn. You promised me. Don't let Paula come, don't let her come. She screams at me. . . ."

Lipscomb stared. "My God!" he said.

Jahn looked up at him and then at Zack and saw the scant tears running down his face again, turning the features to a sodden white mass like rain-soaked paper. "They buried it last night," Zack said. "I killed it. I thought it was the dwarf. . . ."

Jahn got up suddenly. "All right, Zack. Let's go home." His strong, clear voice paused and fluted roughly, with an immense and burning mockery. "Come on, Zack. I can't have two of you in Marston's."

Rosenbens said, mildly, "There's no need for you to do that, Jahn."

Jahn looked at him. "What else can I do?" he said, suddenly angry. "Leave him here and let them get their claws on him?" He glanced at Zack again, and said, slowly, "He was never bad; he was weak."

Bard Lipscomb moved across the room, touched his shoulder, and held out his hand. "I'm glad you won. . . . Don't have any regrets now, or worry about—" He closed his lips tightly and almost tremulously so that he should not say, "your mother," and gazed away from Jahn's face.

Zack walked softly up to Jahn and stood timidly before him. "Let's go fox-huntin', Jahn."

Jahn turned abruptly and went to the door. Zack followed him, walking with the soft, pad-pad steps of a child. Bard Lipscomb closed his eyes for a moment and leaned against the wall. "It's too much on the boy at one time," he said. "But I reckon he's been expecting it, it's been coming a long time. . . ." Suddenly, feeling Jahn before him again, he looked up. "Yes, Jahn?" he said.

"Sell it," Jahn said. "Sell it all except the two hundred acres that came from my father. Let all that was hers go back to her now." He stopped and then repeated gently. "Sell it, and pay her debt to Peebles with it. Pay Henric and James the money I promised them in the deed."

"No, no!" Rosenbens cried, almost with anguish. "No, Jahn, there's no need, no sense, you—you sacrifice your-self ——!"

Jahn looked at him slowly, and then back at Lipscomb. He walked out of the office without speaking. For an instant they heard his steps, with Zack's pattering behind, before they were swallowed up in the noise of the aisles.

XI

Now and then during the morning, Jahnet came out to the front veranda and stood watching the progress of the auction; then she went back into the house. Long Jim Chambers pointed her out to Mose Thurston. "Thar she is; thet's the little girl." Mose turned around and faced toward the house windows. "Mis Sue en Zack, they hain't showed this day, hev they?" he said. "Well, I do know they're a miserable people now!"

"Wonder Henric ain't here," Long Jim remarked. "I heered as how he was expected, the place bein' open to public auction en all."

"Him!" said Mose, scornfully. "He's shut up in his house, a shakin' thet head of his on his neck en mourning fer Miss Chancie. They say as how Elder Gurney went down to 'im en he put him out'n the house."

"Ought to. No preacher's got a right mixin' hisself up in sech as Elder Gurney's mixed hisself," Long Jim said.

He stared gravely at the auctioneer standing upright on the third and last mound of the pasture. "Brought that auctioneer from Milletson, I expect?" he said. The auctioneer's voice came faintly, yet clearly, over the moving heads of the intervening crowd. Below the mound and a little to the west of it, a deep pit had been dug the afternoon before; now from its depths rose slow curls of smoke edged at intervals with a streak of flame and the savoury smell of barbecued beef.

On the other side of the mound, along the road, cars and trucks stretched back the distance between long Jim's and Mose's position near the yard fence to the woodland at the first curve of the road. A few Negroes, knowing that this event foretold their removal from Red Valley to other lands and new masters, mingled with the crowd or stood about, idly staring. Others of their relatives and friends could be seen rushing from the hog pasture with droves of pigs and fat sows or driving down from the barn cows and calves to the newly built pen below the auctioneer's mound.

One or two little Negro boys circulated among the men with watermelons and cantaloups. For this private trade, organized on the spur of the moment by the pickaninnies themselves, there were not many customers. There was a local superstition that whisky and melon do not mix. Each man, if he were at all convivial, had brought with him his pint or two of corn liquor. As the morning wore on, cries of tipsy mockery began to rise from the drinkers against the auctioneer's shouts. Joe Rosenbens went among the crowds, cautioning good manners and quiet. "Remember the family's in the house back there," he said.

"Might say noise worries Zack," Long Jim commented as Rosenbens neared him and Mose. "Zack he'd think hit was Miss Paula screamin' at him ag'in." He glanced backward toward the house, as if to see there from one of the windows Zack's turgid white face.

"I don't see Jahn nowhere," Mose said. "Must be up to the barn helpin' git out the mules." He gazed down the road where a group of men were loading calves and pigs into a truck. "Pore Jahn, he's a losin' today all him en his mammy got together in a score of years. Life hit do go so sometimes."

Long Jim spoke to Joe Rosenbens, who had come round to them in his circuit of the crowd. "He gittin' his prices, Mr. Rosenbens? Me en Mose we kain't hear so good from here."

Mose jingled a few coins in his pocket. "Didn't come to bid, jest to look on." He glanced up. "I see Bard Lipscomb up there behind the auctioneer, a-talkin' to him."

"Well, you've got a good place for looking on," said Rosenbens, glancing about at the fence corner in which they stood. He folded his arms and lifted his hand to rub the fingers back and forth over his chin. "He's getting fair prices. But only fair . . . only fair. . . ."

"Be the land sold yit, Mr. Rosenbens? Jim en me we heered it had, but not who to."

Rosenbens looked cautiously around. "It was bought up by secret bid. I don't know myself who got it. I understand, though, that he's to keep it until his crops are gathered this fall. That's all I know, they didn't buy the crops."

Mose regarded him frowningly. "Don't reckon Henric got it, do you? That'd be too much!" Rosenbens shook his head. "Warn't the price right to pay his mother's debts and pay them brothers o' his what he signed fer in the deed thet he's hevin' this sale now?" He stopped abruptly. "Pay *her* debts! Pay *their* debts!" Mose burst out. "I'd a seen them en Peebles roastin' in hell afore I'd a paid one red cent!"

"Ah, but thet ain't Jahn!" Long Jim said. "He's got honor, Mose, en he believes in his honor."

Rosenbens said, calmly, "I understand the price was all right. But for farming two hundred acres. . . ." He shrugged and gestured toward the near corn fields. "A man doesn't need all this stock and tools. There's to be a sale of farm implements this afternoon."

Jahn Ibsell appeared in the lane, walking behind three Negroes who were driving before them a herd of mules all linked together with knotted bridles. The young man's face wore an expression of especial clearness and openness. As he came through the gate behind the mules and passed the three men, turning his head to speak, the strange vibrance of his being radiated itself over them. They followed him with their eyes.

"Well," said Long Jim, presently, "hit's a quair world en none of us kin do airy thing about hit's turns en changes. . . . Know how Mis' Ibsell is, Mr. Rosenbens? She's been in thet place no more'n a week yit, has she?"

Joe Rosenbens shook his head. "I hear rumors, that's all. I believe there has been a demand for a court hearing to take her out, but she hasn't risen from her bed since they carried her upstairs that afternoon."

"Ah, en she'll never rise no more!" Mose said, moodily.

Joe Rosenbens left them and walked back through the crowds. They could hear his silencing voice. "Remember the family now," he urged. "Aye, en you'd not think any of us could forgit 'em!" Long Jim muttered under his breath.

He turned his head toward Mose. "Must be they're passin' out the barbecue now."

He and Mose walked toward the pit, glancing up at the sun to see whether or not it was yet noon. A little later, they returned with paper plates of barbecue and stood alone by the fence corner again.

"Thar's the little Jahnet come out ag'in," Long Jim said, pointing with his knife on the point of which quivered a morsel of meat. "She stands jest like Mis' Ibsell, don't she, hands behind her back. Made like her fer thet, I do believe."
He swallowed.

Three wagons piled with farm machinery passed down the lane and through the gate and drove toward the auctioneer. "Must be the mules is gone already," Mose said. "Lord! . . . Lord! . . ." He shook his head sorrowfully, relishing the gesture.

"But who could a bought the land?" Long Jim wondered, gazing out at the fields. "All this near he keeps hit, the near fields en the house site en the pasture, all his father's land. But the woodlands en the far fields, them that was Mis' Ibsell's they're gone."

Lipscomb approached them, carrying a paper plate. He backed up against the fence and stood silent for a moment. "The machinery's going," he observed, suddenly. "It'll soon be over." He stopped eating, and wiped his forehead. "I remember the day Rachel bought that hay-rake they're hoisting up there. Bought it herself one day when she was in town . . . long before the trouble came up. I remember she came up to my office and asked me to come down to Garner's with her and look it over. She said Jahn had been talking about a hay-rake, but she wasn't sure whether this was the kind he wanted or not. . . . That was all bosh. She knew as much about hay-rakes as any man, more than I did, but she . . ." His voice trailed.

Mose Thurston fidgited a moment and then said, "Know who bought the land, Mr. Lipscomb?"

The old man started, and looked at the barbecue on his plate. "Marston's," he said and turned around to set his plate on the gatepost. "Yes, Marston's. . . ."

"Marston's What's an insane asylum want with land?"

"To raise fodder fer the crazy folk, ye nit-wit!" Long Jim said. He stood silent, looking at the old lawyer. "How is Mis' Ibsell?" he asked, presently.

Lipscomb's eyes dimmed. "She's not been out of her bed since she—" He stopped, and exclaimed in a suppressed, harsh voice, "Red tape! Dam' doctors think everybody's crazy; won't let her out; got to have a court hearing to prove Henric and James had no right to put her there—!" He walked away suddenly.

"I expect he thinks there's not time," Mose said in a hushed voice.

Long Jim cleared his throat. "Mose, I reckon maybe him en Mis' Ibsell was always good friends. He laughed at her a lot, en sometimes he was downright mad at her, but I don't reckon there was ever any selfishness in his feelin' for her."

He turned again to watch the auctioneer's violent gestures and to listen to his hoarse, strained voice. "The afternoon's a-goin'," he said, sadly, "en the farm stuff . . ."

A few hours later at sunset, when he and Mose had reached the curve in the road and turned back, the pasture was deserted. A single cow bawled disconsolately on the mounds for her calf. From the blackened grass around the barbecue pit faint streamers of smoke rose slowly upon the still evening air.

"Well," said Long Jim, "Rachel Ibsell's debts is paid now en her name is clear."

XII

The massed electric light from the shaded bulbs along the walls bent under the domed glass in the ceiling as the calyx of a flower bends upward, and curled in four distinct petals of misted radiance around the dark center of the shadow hanging from the transparent globe. On the floor the light was crepuscular and shifting, seeming to rise and fall over the soft echo of the nurse's steps as she came toward them, and to float in particles of mist around the sweep of her skirts. She spoke in a hushed voice: "You may go up now. The others are all there. You won't disturb her; she talks continuously and recognizes nobody." She paused. "Her strength is going rapidly. . . ."

They remained standing in front of her, at the foot of the wide staircase. Presently, Sue whispered, "Let's go up." She put her hand on Zack's arm and turned her face around toward Jahn. He said to the nurse, "How much longer?"

"Perhaps an hour, perhaps two or three . . . whenever her strength gives out."

Turned half around on the bottom step of the stairs, with Zack above her and her arm through his, Sue waited, looking at Jahn. The misted lights appeared to flow like liquid, coagulating around his face with the white, hard gleam of porcelain. His eyes were shadows, dark and still, with strange upwellings of an almost imperceptible glow from them. He drew slowly back from the stairs, and turned his head away, hiding his features.

"Go on up. I'll wait down here. . . ."

Before they could speak, he went back toward the waiting-room and disappeared through the door there.

"Has he gone?" Zack said. "Where has he gone?"

[304]

"Hush!" Sue whispered. "We'll send for him. . . . Let's go on up."

The nurse walked before them up the stairs, leading the way without speaking. Muted silence hung on the landings and in the corridors. Their steps echoed hollowly on the copper rims of the wooden stairs and their shadows weaved darkly on the walls beside them. The nurse stopped before a closed door and whispered to them. Through it, rustlings of sound came as if from far away. "Go on in," the nurse whispered. They stepped across the threshold, and stood still, staring at the white bed in the center of the room and growing slowly aware of the figures standing in the half-darkness around the walls.

On the floor under the window there were faint streaks of light and dark, like patterns of the bars behind the lowered shades. The small, dim lamp on the table threw circles of yellow and white over the cream-colored counterpane on the bed; and there Rachel Ibsell lay, her wasted body hardly showing under the covers, her yellowed face sunk deep into the pillow, her eyes staring up at the ceiling. They gazed at her, and looked quickly away, up at the standing shadows.

Martha rustled up close to Sue. The two women glanced at each other, whispered, and Martha stood back. Sue looked at Kate Ibsell, seeing her slowly fanning herself, with her face lifted and her eyes fixed on the blank space of wall above the bed. Martha whispered to Zack and grasped his arm. Billy Nelson moved near to them and stood a little behind Zack.

"I thought she kept talking," Sue whispered. Nobody answered her, and presently Zack said, loudly, "Poor Mamma!"

The nurse cautioned them, "Please be quiet."

Sue saw James and Henric in the darkness on the other side of the bed. But Bard Lipscomb was not there. Slowly and creepingly, Sue grew aware that Rachel was regarding them with steady, glazed eyes. She spoke suddenly.

[305]

"I'm going to sleep now. It's late. Have Zack bank the kitchen fire, Martha. Jahn won't be in till late." She lay still a moment, lowering her lids and turning her eyes away from James and Henric. "It'll be cold in the morning," she remarked, drowsily.

"Cold!" James exclaimed, loudly. He made a gesture toward the opposite wall, including all of them in his speech. "She talks about cold all the time. Why don't Stanhope come in to see about her, that's what I ask? I believe she's been cold ever since she come here; she ain't been 'tended to. I don't see," he grumbled over the nurse's caution, "why in the world we wasn't let know about her condition before now. They've let her lie here and git worse and worse and said nothing to any of us!"

Martha moved out from the wall. "Shut up, James! You brought her here!" She burst into sudden, choking sobs.

"There, there, it's all right, honey," Nelson said.

The nurse stood up. "I'll have to ask you all to leave the room if you're not quieter." She turned the sheet back over Rachel's hands and sat down again.

James said, "We'll go when we're ready, and not before. She's our mother, not yores!"

A swift horror went around the room. Sue averted her face and looked down at the floor. Zie Gurney came in abruptly, walking heavily, and advanced at once to the bed before the nurse could stop him. "Well, Rachel?" he said. He turned away from her immediately as if he had no interest in her, and looked around the room. "I had a time gettin' here. Looks like you could a waited for me, James, and let me come in in yore car!" he said, bitterly. "I had to hire a way down; cost me four dollars."

The nurse said sibilantly, "Please be quiet!"

He turned around and glared at her, and then backed against the wall beside James. "Why don't she go out," he said, "and leave the family alone here with her?"

"Leave us here!" Henric exclaimed, suddenly, in a loud,

strained voice. "It's indecent enough as it is, positively indecent all of us standing around here!"

"If you think that," Kate said, coldly, "leave, yourself. Some of us here that she quarreled with think more of her than you do."

The horror that was in the room, lurking behind their bitter and complaining voices, grew thick. Sue put her hand up to her mouth and leaned against the wall, holding Zack's arm tightly. Martha's sobs continued, but she was standing out from Billy now, a little in advance of Sue and Kate, looking at her mother. "It's as if I kept feeling she couldn't die," she said, mournfully. "She's not been sick long enough . . . she was all right when she stopped at my house that day."

The nurse's voice came icily, "Please be quiet."

"She didn't eat that day," Kate said, imperturbably, as if the nurse had not spoken. "She wouldn't eat breakfast and no one gave her any lunch. She was old. She couldn't stand the strain of all that was done to her that day." She stared at Henric with hard eyes as if she could kill him, not for what he had done to Rachel, but because, being an Ibsell, he had done it. "No woman I know was ever treated so. . . ."

Over her voice, flattening it from existence, fell suddenly the twisting screams of the nymphomaniacs abovestairs; and under them, orchestrating their wild desire, came the thick answer of the caged men who stood with hot eyes, grasping the bars of the windows and staring out upon the moonlight.

"Good God!" Henric cried. "Stop it! Oh ———!"

Suddenly, low and clear in the silent space of the room, rose Rachel Ibsell's voice. "Jahn! Jahn!" Once, twice, she cried the name, sending her breath out into the cataleptic stillness beneath those aching cries from above. Against them, moving underneath all that monody of longing madness, came a walking on the stairs, a slow, measured lifting and setting down of feet . . . in the hall, on the dark oiled floorboards. The door opened, letting in a surge of sound, and closed.

Jahn Ibsell stood in front of it, like a man who has answered a call his ears have not heard. His face was still, lifted, listening, so that Sue's heart recorded without recognizing the poetry and the submission of his look.

The screams fell away, softly to wails, above which the heavy roar of the great beasts died; and then the silence beat in on the room and stretched out in a soft circle of relief. Henric tore at his collar. Looking away from Jahn for an instant, Sue saw Zack weeping beside her. The tears seeped in bluish, heavy drops from under his closed eyelids. Martha turned in white-faced horror and took him in her arms.

"Kate?" said Rachel. "Kate?" Her head struggled to lift from the pillow. "Martha . . . has Jahn come yet?"

Jahn fell on his knees beside the bed and put out his hand to touch her. She stared away from him, her eyes glazed and blind. "Martha, leave the fire alight. I think I'll set up and wait for him; he's gone to that girl." She turned her head. "Listen! Is that him out there at the well, talking to the horses?"

"Mamma," Jahn said—"Mamma, I'm here."

She turned her face away from him. "Kate?"

Zie Gurney went up to his sister and took her hand. "Rachel, don't you know me?" he said. "Rachel, sister, trust in the Lord now, He'll point the road clear for ye!" She struggled faintly with her fingers in his, trying to draw back. The nurse said, "Please move away, Mr. Gurney." He looked at her angrily, his eyes misting sentimentally. "Move away! Talk to us and ye let that screamin' and hollerin' go on here. No doubt it's what killed her!" He held Rachel's wrist tightly and stared defiantly at the nurse.

"'Eh?" Rachel said. Her strange, tranced eyes wandered blindly, humid with a bluish vapor. She laughed suddenly. "You're getting old, Kate. You've got wrinkled. . . ." She jerked her hand feebly, and then lay still with closed eyes. She began to sing in a high, cracked voice.

"Such wondrous love is this,
O my soul, O my soul!"

"Rachel, don't you know yore own brother?" Zie demanded, tremulously.

"Leave her alone, Uncle Zie! Leave her alone, for God's sake!" Martha cried, suddenly. "You're to blame for this, you're more to blame than anybody; you told her she was crazy—you put the notion in her head and drove her here!" She burst into sobs again. "If ever anybody was betrayed by the ones they trusted ——!"

"Be still!" Zie Gurney said. He stepped out into the room. "You, an ignorant, lying female and a heretic to the true Church, you ——!"

"We can't even let her die in peace!" Martha screamed. "You get out of here. If you think you're going to preach her funeral—!" Her voice mingled with the nurse's threat to call in Dr. Stanhope to put them all out. "Call him in then!" James shouted. Martha drew in her breath, gasped and stared.

Jahn stood up by the bed, turning his face toward Martha. She gulped and turned blindly to Nelson. "There . . . there," he said and patted her shoulder softly.

"Call him!" James went on. "This is his place. Why ain't he here lookin' after her? Call him in!"

"Be quiet!" Jahn commanded. James looked at him and shut his mouth.

Sue moved vaguely. "Hadn't we better go . . . hadn't we better go out so things will be quiet . . . ?" she said. They stared at her, and she gazed at the silent, icy nurse sitting beside the bed, and then at Jahn. He stood up straight in the middle of the floor, his hands clasped in front of him, his head bent down in misery.

"Disrespect, disrespect frum everybody!" Zie Gurney burst out again. "The younger generation is lost, fools stumbling on their way to hell!"

"Oh, for God's sake, shut up, you doddering old fool!" Henric screamed, suddenly.

Rachel's slow mumbling cut across his scream, silencing him. Her lips moved, stumbling without sound, and then her eyes opened and gazed straight ahead of her. Her lips moved again, and murmured, faintly at first and then loudly, the sound growing and becoming a slow, insistent wail. The nurse stood up and turned her head on the pillow and sat down again. The voice stopped an instant and then, swiftly, harsh and cracked with fear, it rang through the room. At first there were no words to it, nothing but a high, eerie sing-song that washed coldly against their tense ear drums, and then came words, isolated, weeping in a furious, sick mono-tone:

"Cursed . . . cursed . . . the land and the children . . . cursed, cursed . . . the blood and the land. . . . The light's out. There's your mother, there . . . cursed, cursed . . . lost and unforgotten . . . cursed. . . ."

The slow, shrill rise of her voice cut their hearts chillily and fell back. From the corners of their eyes they looked at one another and then at Kate. She was motionless, bent for-ward, her face white and her blue eyes strangely compas-sionate and self-accusatory. Abruptly, when that cracked old voice had ceased to mumble, she raised her head and looked at them appealingly.

"No!" she said. "No, not like this—!" She stopped and was still, and suddenly ran swiftly to the door. "No, no!" she said under her breath. "I never meant this. Not this—!" She slammed the door behind her and they heard her stumbling down the steps.

"Well, it's good enough for her," Martha said, harshly. "If she'd never made Mamma believe in that silly supersti-tion—" She stopped, feeling Nelson's warning hand tighten on her arm, and looked at him.

Jahn shifted his feet and then stood still again, looking over the bed at Henric and James. In the pale light their bodies were half hidden, with nothing of them except their eyes and the shapes of their heads clear to him. He thought that he saw, behind the dark glass of their eyeballs, the flitting of thoughts. It seemed strange to him to realize that their heads, in which the thoughts moved and creaked guiltily and unremorsefully, had emerged from the same womb as his.

The nurse stood up again and moved back from the bed, going behind him. He glanced down at his mother. Her head was turned to one side, toward the door, and she was listening. A change like a flash of soft lightning went over her eyes so that, slowly, he knew what footsteps she was hearing on the stairs outside. He bent over her, took her hands, and sank gradually to his knees.

"Look at 'im!" James whispered. "Got to be the big ike now same as always!"

Rachel smiled, hearing footsteps, thinking she heard Jahn's steps ringing down the vaulted corridors and echoing on the stairs. Her eyes grew murky and dim and unfocused, and she turned once, struggling in the bed. Her head moved from side to side, her mouth open, gasping. Behind him, Jahn heard the terrible, impinging rustle of garments moving nearer, bending curiously to see her die. He put his arms around her body, as if to shut out the eyes behind him. Suddenly, looking up, he saw Henric and James staring at her face. A violent, sudden, and helpless hatred stabbed his heart. There was no way he could cover her from their sight.

Her hands moved slowly, coming together on her bosom as if she wished to pray. "God—?" She spoke softly, whispering. "God—?" Her body bent, twisting upward and sidewise above her struggling, clasped hands. "God, God, tell me where he is, tell me!" The cry rang softly in the room; she fell back, and murmured under her breath, "O come out before the merchants come. . . ."

Once more her face changed and she lay like a child asleep. She breathed in and out slowly, her breath light in her nostrils. Around her they moved, hovering nearer and looking down in a silence through which the cold, gorgeous hum of finality might be heard, sifting, rising, and falling under the dim electric bulb. She smiled and sat up in bed, moving before they could stop her, and bent forward, listening, searching the darkness over her eyes.

"Hush!" she whispered. "Hush! . . . Is that him out there . . . is that his face in the door . . .?" She looked up, her eyes transfigured with light. "Jahn?" Her hands groped. She saw him and knew him. "My son!" she cried, "My son!" and leaned to him, falling against his shoulder. "My son, stay with me; promise you'll not leave me!" Her eyes smiled and her mouth fell open. Her head slid slowly down his arms and onto the pillow.

"Is she dead?" James said, harshly. His voice echoed over the professional movements of the nurse, straightening the sheets.

Martha said, slowly, with wonder, "She's sleeping. . . ."

"Hush, for just a little, please, all of you," Jahn said. He looked at his mother.

Now, for her, he thought, there were no lights, no colors, no forms. Rachel slept, breathing sparsely of this final air, her mind light and alive, poised like the high breast of a young girl who looks for her lover. And in her sleep, permeated by a light and airy patience, marked by the smile on her face, nothing floated, nothing gave voice. Her fine, small nostrils flared wonderfully to the impalpable thing that sang —O clear and its voice perfumed!—in the waiting silence. Bending above her, shielding her face from the gaze of his brothers, Jahn's eyes grew darkly beautiful with the details of her form, the eyes closed and the hands clasped on the breast and the legs stretching long under the white coverlet. He kissed her forehead, swiftly, as once she had kissed him.

A thin, sleek rattle rustled in her throat. She drew over to the left, nearer to him, and smiled again. Then, as if a hand had passed over her face, bewildering her, the light left it and it settled slowly to the carved silence of a mask. The eyes opened stealthily, halfway, and were still.

After a moment the nurse said, "She has passed on now. . . ."

[312]

They moved, they exclaimed, and grew silent. They stood around in small knots, whispering, looking sidewise at the bed. Presently, one by one and two by two, they went out. After they had gone, Jahn Ibsell rose. He leaned over and pressed softly with his fingers her eyelids, closing her dark and watchful eyes. From the hall outside he heard Martha's quiet, helpless sobbing and Sue's whispered comfort. He went out and left his mother, knowing that she was alone now, alone with the roots of her being, alone and free with nothing to hear or see or wait for. . . .

EPILOGUE

IN THE MORNING, WHILE THE FEELING OF SUNSHINE WAS STILL cool in the dawn, Jahn Ibsell appeared alone on one of the mounds in the Ibsell pasture. He faced the east where, beyond the meager fields still belonging to him, lay the acres that had been his mother's and were now Marston's. Soon carpenters and surveyors would come there; and hammers, he thought, bitterly, would ring their futile and banal noise over the land that Rachel Ibsell had bought with grim heartaches and body aches. On her land the barracks of the insane would loom, blotting with shadow the furrows she had given to the plow and to the harvest. He closed his eyes, shutting the lids together with a motion sharp and involuntary, a gasp of relinquishment. When he looked up again, his sight whirled dizzily.

At a point midway between the pasture lands and the fields the morning mist was slowly rising, streaming upward in long, almost funnel-shaped sluices of white cloud. Under it, the faint shimmer of dew untouched by the sun could be seen glowing now and then as if the earth shook itself gently. Around this peculiar and almost indistinguishable movement, under it, and informing it with meaning, lay an immense darkness, the sensation, rather than the color, of the land. While he looked, Jahn Ibsell saw the shaken furrows grow still, and their darkness wait, as if to announce to him where he had seen another darkness like theirs.

Slowly, out of the rolling film of his brain, poised the picture: the domed lights, the death-filled bed, and the shadows in the corners of the room. The dark earth color, the sensation of death to him now, seemed to rise before his eyelids and to flow over the staring blue of his sight with a limitless and unceasing flow. He felt his body leaning toward it, the hardness and the pain in himself dissolving under the sweet, soft lean of desire. The furrows steadied again. He saw them with the gaze of a sick man whose starved nerves yearn toward home, so far, so ordered, so familiar, so dear. He stood saying to himself, "If I go there . . .?" and knowing how his muscles would flow out and rest in the brown loam. But his bone was still and stubborn. He leaned to the sensation of death, yet stood back and watched his desire going and could not go himself. His bone endured, recalcitrant to softness. Suddenly he wrenched himself forward, headlong down the mound, as if to plunge into that dark quiet, and brought up sharp, stumbling and staring all around him.

His dazed eyes saw without noticing how the mist, rising higher, swept to westward, encircling his figure for an instant, and then moved on above him.

The screen door on the front veranda banged loudly. He started and stared toward the house with a peculiar and mindless concentration so intense that, knowing Jahnet was there, he yet did not see her until she was attempting to climb the gate fence. "Help me, Daddy!" she shouted. "I can't get down!" He stood without speaking or moving toward her. The pale blue color of her dress impressed itself insistently on his mind. She jumped down from the gate, sprawled an instant in the road, and then was up and running toward him. She called something, the sense of it going over his head in a windy sweetness. She ran with exaggerated, long steps, throwing her body from side to side in the effort. His lips parted.

[315]

"Don't be doing that," he heard himself saying. "It looks tomboyish."

She stopped and stood still, gazing at him. "Why don't you want me to be like a boy? Black Fanny says my grandma was jes' like a man."

He felt a strange, cool stillness gathering in him from the force of her earnest gaze. From eyes so blue, a look so tart, so sturdy. . . . The thought formed words in his mind, speaking to him there like a quiet ejaculation of wonder and pleasure. He kept repeating to himself, and saying, "That I should find my mother in my daughter . . .!" He smiled faintly, and heard his quiet, parental reply to her question:

"Your grandmother was not a very happy woman."

He gazed at her yellow hair on the collar of her blue dress. Suddenly he bent down and picked her up so that she was against his chest, her face above his, and her hands resting on his shoulders. He said, "Do you know you're getting to be such a big girl now that you can go to school next year?"

Her eyes grew secretive and frightened. "I don't want to go. I want to stay with you. Lars can go."

"No, no, darling. . . . You mustn't be like your grandmother. . . ." He shook his head above hers, smiling with a queer, drawn mixture of pleasure and sorrow. "No, darling. . . ." He put her down abruptly, and stared at the fields, seeing there in his mind the symbol of Rachel Ibsell's covetous love in the already prefigured shapes that would rise uglily and cheaply over the land that was Marston's.

She touched his hand. "Daddy?"

"Yes?" He looked at her.

"I forgot to tell you. . . . Mamma's coming, and Lars. We're all going to walk with you, Daddy." She reached up and put her hand in his.

The screen door opened again. "Hadn't we better go to meet your mother and your little brother, then?" he said to her.

She nodded. She stepped down from the mound before him.

"Yes," she said, and marched ahead of him. "We have to be polite. . . . When you want to be by yourself with anybody an' there's somebody else wants to be there, too, you have to be polite," she explained, solemnly and philosophically. She walked forward with her hands crossed behind her back, as Rachel Ibsell had walked.

Following behind her, he looked up and met his wife's gaze across Lars' small black head. She smiled at him, almost timidly, with a shadow of wondering pain and fear for him behind the golden iris of her eyes. He took the little boy from her, holding him high against one shoulder, and put his other arm around her. "Well, darling . . .?" he said, gently. A sudden, swift glow seemed to expand all her body with joy; her cheeks flushed, her lips parted, little tendrils of her dark red hair blew softly about her forehead. He pressed her shoulders yet more gently, and looked off from her.

Above the furrows left to him the sun showed faintly, coming like a slow, revolving disk through the white, clouded dawn above Marston's land. He looked back at his wife, and drew in his breath. His lungs felt unpressed, unburdened, open to the clean air of living.